Bootleggers, Lobstermen & Lumberjacks

"The Wild American West be damned! Matthew P. Mayo's *Bootleggers, Lobstermen & Lumberjacks* is a fascinating—and often absolutely blood-curdling—narrative of New England's darkest and grittiest historical incidents and characters. A consummate storyteller with a lively, entertaining voice, Mayo has brought to life New England's most evil pirates, scalpers, witch-hunters, and ax-murderers, along with a few equally chilling accounts of accidents and natural catastrophes. For good measure, there are even a couple of raids on New England by Nazi and Confederate soldiers. *Bootleggers, Lobstermen & Lumberjacks* is American history at its most violent and authentic. Edgar Allan Poe would have loved every story in it."

—Howard Frank Mosher, award-winning author of *A Stranger in the Kingdom, Where the Rivers Flow North,* and *Walking to Gatlinburg*

Bootleggers, Lobstermen & Lumberjacks

*Fifty of the Grittiest Moments in the History
of Hardscrabble New England*

MATTHEW P. MAYO

Guilford, Connecticut

To buy books in quantity for corporate use
or incentives, call **(800) 962-0973**
or e-mail **premiums@GlobePequot.com**.

Project editor: Gregory Hyman
Text design: Sheryl P. Kober

Library of Congress Cataloging-in-Publication Data

Mayo, Matthew P.
  Bootleggers, lobstermen & lumberjacks : fifty of the grittiest moments in the history of hardscrabble New England / Matthew P. Mayo.
    p. cm.
  Includes bibliographical references and index.
  ISBN 978-0-7627-5968-2
  1. New England—History—Anecdotes. 2. Frontier and pioneer life—New England—Anecdotes. 3. New England—Biography—Anecdotes. I. Title.
  F4.M16 2010
  974—dc22

                                                          2010030113

Printed in the United States of America

10 9 8 7 6 5

For Gayla, Bill, and Jeffrey Mayo, hardy New Englanders

For Rose Mary and David Smith, who chose New England

For Jennifer, who chose me

For Guinness and Nessie, who aren't choosy at all

∽

Contents

ACKNOWLEDGMENTS xv

INTRODUCTION xvii

1. PILGRIMS' PROGRESS 1
   A rough Atlantic crossing is followed by frigid temperatures, scurvy, starvation, and death. . . . Welcome to the New World. (1620)

2. DUNGEON ROCK 7
   In a cave near Lynn, Massachusetts, pirate Thomas Veal guards his treasure— until the Great Earthquake of 1658 buries him alive. (1658)

3. THE GREAT SWAMP FIGHT 13
   The Narragansetts are attacked deep in Rhode Island's Great Swamp by a force of 1,200. Hundreds of children, women, and old people are shot, bludgeoned, and burned to death. (1675)

4. THE CANDLEMAS MASSACRE 18
   Two hundred Abenakis raid York, Maine, killing, kidnapping, and burning. Jeremiah Moulton sees his parents scalped. He doesn't forget . . . or forgive. (1692)

5. A CRUSHING END 23
   During the Salem witch trials, more than 150 people are imprisoned on charges of witchcraft, twenty-nine are convicted, nineteen are hanged, and five die in prison. Giles Corey is not so lucky. (1692)

6. A MOTHER'S ANGER 29
   Hannah Duston of Boscawen, New Hampshire, kills and scalps her sleeping captors . . . to avenge their brutal murder of her baby. (1697)

7. BOON ISLAND'S CURSE 34
   A midwinter wreck strands fourteen sailors on this barren rock six miles off the coast of York, Maine. Only ten survive for twenty-four days, without fire, by eating what meat is available. (1710)

Contents

8. PIRATE TREASURE 40
    "Black Sam" Bellamy captures the treasure-laden Whydah. *But as the crew nears its home port of Cape Cod, a tempest strikes, and the ship's timbers begin to crack. (1717)*

9. THE BRUTALITY OF NED LOW 44
    Vicious pirate Ned Low captures a Boston whaler, tortures the crew, steals their food, and sets them adrift to starve. But he's still not satisfied. (1723)

10. THE MEETINGHOUSE TRAGEDY 50
    The frame of the new Wilton, New Hampshire, meetinghouse collapses, dropping fifty-three workers three stories to the ground—followed by tons of trusses and tools. (1773)

11. ANN STORY'S CAVE 54
    A falling tree kills her husband, and Indians burn her cabin, but Ann Story stays on her hard-won Vermont land, living in a riverbank cave and helping capture Tories. (1775)

12. BUNKER HOLE 60
    Mainer Jack Bunker hijacks a British ship full of food stolen from colonists. The British give chase, so he runs it into a hidden cove, cuts the masts, and waits. (1775)

13. THE KNOX CANNON TRAIN 66
    Colonel Henry Knox leads eighty yoke of oxen, dragging fifty-nine cannons, three hundred miles in fifty-six days over mountains, lakes, and swamps . . . in winter. The British siege is soon broken. (1775)

14. A MANLY SHOWING 73
    During Connecticut's battle of Ridgefield, Colonel Benedict Arnold's horse, shot nine times, falls on him. A charging redcoat demands surrender, but Arnold refuses. (1777)

15. REVOLUTIONARY WOMAN 79
    Dressed as a man, Deborah Samson is wounded fighting for the Continental Army. She pries a musket ball from her leg with a knife, but a second ball is lodged too deep. (1782)

Contents

16. SHE-PIRATE! 85
Rachel Wall lures innocent rescuers to their deaths at the hands of her concealed crew. But the game wears thin . . . and piracy in Massachusetts is a hanging offense. (1782)

17. TOUGH TIMES, TOUGH PEOPLE 90
In February, Seth Hubbell and his family trek one hundred miles on foot to the raw wilderness of northern Vermont. His livestock and crops die. Then life grows difficult. (1789)

18. THE WILD EAST 95
Mrs. Graves of Brookfield, Vermont, spends all night lunging with a pitchfork at a bear intent on savaging her swine. But as she grows wearier, the bear grows angrier. (1800)

19. THE BLACK SNAKE AFFAIR 102
A century before Prohibition, an illicit load of potash instigates animosity, mayhem, and murder between smugglers and the federal militia on Vermont's Winooski River. (1808)

20. THE LEGEND OF SKINNER'S CAVE 107
Smuggler Uriah Skinner is trapped on his secret Lake Memphremagog island by federal officers who take his boat—and leave him no way off the island. (1808)

21. RUNAWAY POND 111
A Glover, Vermont, man's plan for more water works too well: Trees, boulders, buildings, bridges, and livestock are ripped free and carried for miles. (1810)

22. "1800-AND-FROZE-TO-DEATH" 116
Killing frosts in each month of the year across New England result in crop failures, starvation, disease, and mass exodus—all the makings of a famine. (1816)

23. THE WORST MISTAKE EVER MADE 122
Threat of a crushing landslide forces Samuel Willey, his wife, their five children, and two hired men from their home in the heart of Crawford Notch. Big, big mistake. (1826)

24. MASSACHUSETTS BAY MAN-EATER 128

Angler Joseph Blaney attracts the attention of two great white sharks in the middle of Massachusetts Bay. They are considerably larger than his dinghy. (1830)

25. VORTEX OF DOOM 133

As their mother watches from shore, two brothers in a schooner are sucked into the gaping maw of the Old Sow Whirlpool, off Eastport, Maine. They aren't the first . . . or the last. (1835)

26. REBELS . . . IN VERMONT! 137

A Rebel raider and his gang attack a town on the Vermont-Canadian border, robbing banks, setting fires, and forcing hostages to swear allegiance to the Confederacy. (1864)

27. AROOSTOOK LYNCH LAW 142

When he steals a pair of boots, Big Jim Cullen never dreams he'll be the star of New England's only lynching. (1873)

28. THE HARTFORD DISASTER 148

The engineer of the night express from White River Junction works to make up time, though winter track conditions are dicey, especially on bridges over frozen rivers. (1887)

29. NORTH WOODS FREEZE-UP 153

In northern New England, weeks of 40-below temperatures force loggers to kill their horses, cut off their own frostbitten digits, and fight like caged rats. (1887)

30. THE GREAT WHITE HURRICANE 159

In March, a nor'easter wallops the Northeast coast, dumping fifty inches of snow, whipping up fifty-foot drifts, and grounding or wrecking two hundred ships. It takes weeks to tally the dead. (1888)

31. THE LAST VAMPIRE 166

To ward off vampiric spirits of the recently deceased, a young Rhode Island girl's corpse is exhumed, her organs are burned, and the smoke is inhaled by family members. (1892)

Contents

32. . . . And with an Axe 171
In Fall River, Massachusetts, thirty-two-year-old Sunday school teacher Lizzie Borden opens her parents' heads with a hatchet—and is never convicted of the crime. (1892)

33. Lobstermen Fisticuffs! 177
In December 1894, tensions cause Cape Porpoise lobstermen to sink boats, threaten lives, and brawl in the streets. The arrests instigate conservation practices still in use today. (1894)

34. North Woods Ice-Out 183
A spongy lake, a load of logs, two horses, one teamster, and an unscrupulous clerk are a recipe for disaster in Vermont's northern forest. (1895)

35. The Portland Gale 189
A nor'easter drags the steamship Portland*'s 192 passengers and crew out to sea. The waves increase, the boilers grow cold, and the vessel weakens. (1898)*

36. King of the River Hogs 194
A New Hampshire line-house full of drunken rivermen, a big bouncer with arms like tree trunks, and a wiry little drive boss named Jigger Johnson. Guess who wins. . . . (1905)

37. The Human Shingle 201
A Vermont farmer takes advantage of a fair winter day to fix his barn roof. But his aging joints stiffen, the day grows cold, and he freezes to the roof. (1907)

38. Malaga Island 206
The mixed-race residents of Maine's Malaga Island are evicted, and all traces of them are removed. Even the bodies in the cemetery are exhumed. (1912)

39. Logjam from Hell 211
The last great log drive on the Connecticut jams 65 million board feet of logs, flooding homes, barns, bridges, streets, and railroad tracks in North Stratford, Vermont. (1915)

40. ROCKET RIDE 217
Two young men climb aboard illegal slideboards to descend Mount Washington's Cog Railway tracks in mere minutes. But without brakes, their trip is quick—and painful. (1919)

41. THE BOSTON MOLASSES DISASTER 222
A massive storage tank bursts, and 2 million gallons of molasses pulse outward in a forty-foot-high wave. It's lunchtime, and people are out enjoying a warm winter day. (1919)

42. RUM-RUNNING LOBSTERMEN 226
One Maine island lobsterman doesn't like strangers nosing in his traps—which happen to hold bottles of illicit booze—but a shotgun blast solves all sorts of problems. (1924)

43. QUEEN OF THE BORDER RUMRUNNERS 232
She's the brains of a border-hopping band of bootleggers, and one night, with five hundred clanking bottles aboard, Hilda Stone is tailed by agents . . . and her smokescreen fails. (1925)

44. KINGDOM DEATH RIDE. 238
Winston Titus needs to make a bootlegging run from Canada through Vermont's Northeast Kingdom. But the smiling teen doesn't count on two border agents—or their guns. (1927)

45. BLACK DUCK'S BIG NIGHT. 243
Loaded with alcohol on Narragansett Bay, the Black Duck *is raked with machine-gun fire from a Coast Guard cutter. Soon, the deck is covered with blood, booze, and glass. (1929)*

46. THE SEA FOX. 248
It's Cape Cod Captain Zora's biggest haul of hooch—and the Coast Guard is closing in. Losing the boat will wipe him out, but it beats prison. Zora reaches for the gasoline. (1932)

Contents

47. Brady Gang Slain! 253

A lust for more firepower brings the infamous Brady Gang to a Bangor, Maine, sports store, but it's their request for a tommy gun that draws the FBI. (1937)

48. Hurricane of the Century 259

The storm savages Rhode Island without mercy: A manned lighthouse disappears, an entire beach community is obliterated, and a full school bus is claimed by the sea. (1938)

49. Downeast Nazis 265

A German U-boat creeps twelve miles up Frenchman's Bay to sleepy Bar Harbor, Maine. Two Nazi spies slip ashore, lugging suitcases—Operation Magpie begins. (1944)

50. Maine Coast Trap Wars 270

Island lobstermen squabble over territory. Trap lines are cut, threats are hurled, gas tanks are filled with rotted fish—and then the shooting begins. (1949)

Art and Photo Credits 277

Bibliography 279

Index 288

About the Author 298

ACKNOWLEDGMENTS

My thanks to many, including Charlie Campo, chief librarian at *Bangor Daily News*, Bangor, Maine; Ann Zuccardy at National Life Insurance Company, Montpelier, Vermont; U.S. Coast Guard; Library of Congress; National Archives; National Oceanic and Atmospheric Administration/Department of Commerce; Belfast Free Library; Portland Public Library; University of Maine's Fogler Library; Historic New England; Maine Historical Society; and New England Historic Genealogical Society.

Thanks to Melissa Falcon for the sweet molasses tip; to Dale Kuhnert and Barney, a most dynamic duo; to the Pezzanis, a salty salute from *HMS Bucket*; to Guy, Ace of Adventure; and to my editor, Erin Turner, for admitting that New England has grit, too. . . .

My humble thanks to the people of New England, past, present, and future—special people in a special place.

And last, though first in every way, my deepest thanks go to my dear wife, Jennifer Smith-Mayo, for all of her invaluable effort, help, and support. How 'bout some chowdah?

—M.P.M.

INTRODUCTION

I was raised in New England, born into families with deep roots here. My parents are both hearty and hale, complex and straightforward, much like the climate in which they were raised, and in which they raised me. They grew up on the ocean in Rhode Island to hardworking families and worked hard themselves, quahogging in their own skiffs and generally messing about in boats. That they ended up dairy farming in the lush hills of Vermont's Northeast Kingdom isn't so ironic, considering their rural New England heritage.

Before our move to the Green Mountains, I spent my first decade in Little Rhody. I recall hearing from my folks all about its global significance, despite its diminutive size. And I remember reading a sign explaining something called "The Great Swamp Fight"—never has a phrase been so evocative to me. It continues to intrigue me, even after all these years.

The New England of my childhood is remarkably the same as that of my adulthood—it is still largely a rural place of rolling fields, close-cropped in summer; of cows in pastures; of hot-sand beaches and rolling surf; of old stone walls and historic markers; of the clank of rigging on masts in small fishing harbors; of rows of dinghies jostled by a lobster boat's slow wake; of the spiced scent of oak and maple leaves, all colors, drying in the autumn sun; of the late-fall crunch of acorns underfoot; of shoveling paths in the snow, to the barn from the house, well before sunrise.

New England is a place of watching the Red Sox with Grandma, while Yaz rounded third and headed for home; of taking long Sunday rides with my parents and little brother (I won't mention the lollipops he worked into my hair as I dozed in the backseat) while my father said, "I know just where we are. . . ." Much of the time he did, but the times he didn't were richer, for not only did he take the ribbing well, but we all surveyed the undiscovered countryside of those Sunday rides, each of us finding some new detail to mull over as we headed back home to feed and milk the cows.

But not before we happened upon a new ice-cream stand, each one somehow better than the previous week's discovery. And that brings me to another New England truth—it's home to the best ice cream you'll find anywhere. And chowder. And lobster, johnnycakes, maple syrup, pies, beef stew with dumplings—maybe not gritty, but darn tasty. Perhaps I'm biased. . . .

And what's more, New England is known and loved the world over. Just mention the phrase "New England" or "Maine lobster" or "Rhode Island clamcakes" or "Vermont's Northeast Kingdom" in a room full of folks from the Midwest or the Deep South or the West Coast or Australia, for that matter, and you'll have the attention of everyone in the room—and you'll see wistful looks and hear yearning in their voices. That's because in addition to a long and fascinating history that in one way or another touches everyone in the United States, New England also offers the promise of a simpler, humbler time.

Here in rural New England, houses still wear white clapboards, general stores still get the bulk of your shopping business, backyard gardens are the rule and not the exception, and county fairs still hold livestock in higher esteem than midway attractions.

New England also represents the country's first frontier. Long before settlers dared venture west, they traveled north from their coastal settlements to the rugged terrain of northern New England—Vermont's Green Mountains, New Hampshire's Whites, the Longfellow Mountains in Maine. It is from these intrepid, hardy folk that the well-known Yankee traits of frugality, resourcefulness, and, yes, even suspicion of strangers arise.

I now find myself on the coast in New England, having somewhat reversed the northern journey of my youth, but I count myself beyond fortunate to have grown up in a place where I was the one who fetched the cows from the pasture, who searched for the one overdue old girl, only to find she had calved by herself in the same stand of pines they all seemed to use for that noble purpose, close by that bend in the river where I fished with my brother.

And this rich experience I would have been denied had that irrepressible frontier spirit, that Yankee urge to go it alone and build a better life not been passed to my parents, and so, on to me, distilled down through the centuries from those early intrepid New England settlers.

❧

For the neophyte, New England is a region made up of the six most northeastern states in the United States, among them the smallest in the nation: Rhode Island, Connecticut, Massachusetts, Vermont, New Hampshire, and Maine. Geographically, it represents the United States in microcosm, with its broad rolling farmland, raw rugged peaks, lush river valleys, thick old forests, and a varied, bold coastline.

Superlatives abound here: New Hampshire's Mount Washington, the highest point in New England, boasts the world's highest recorded wind speed (231 miles per hour) and is the official home of the world's worst weather; Maine's Acadia is the most visited national park in the United States (with north of 2 million visitors each year); Vermont produces more maple syrup than anywhere else in the United States (a million gallons per annum); and Yankee lobstermen supply more of the tasty crustacean to the world than any other seafaring set (nearly 100 million pounds per year).

New England came by its name from Captain Smith's 1614 expedition to the New World, where he spent several months exploring the coast. On his return to England, he worked up a map on which he labeled this region as New Albion, or New England. The name stuck.

The term "Yankee" is a little more difficult to pin down. Most frequently, though, in each of its many derivations and definitions, it refers to someone from New England. During the French and Indian War, a British general used the term, with a sneer, in reference to native New Englanders. The name stuck and is worn with pride (although it has been usurped by a certain ball club in hopes of gaining extra credit through geographic proximity— sorry, chums, it's the Red Sox or none). Anyone descended of Yankee stock knows they carry within them a little something special worth crowing about.

New England is also home to a variety of Native American tribes, among them the Abenaki, Narragansett, Mohegan, Passamaquoddy, Wampanoag, and Penobscot tribes, whose greatest gifts to the early settlers, ironically, would also ultimately prove to be the tribes' undoing. Despite being given ample reasons to behave otherwise, the Indians, largely trusting and noble, were also selflessly generous with their knowledge, food, tools, and land. Without their assistance, the Pilgrims would have surely starved, and their fragile grip on the rocky shores of the New World would have failed. And so, we stand on the shoulders of giants.

⚮

In this book, I have covered the years from roughly 1620 to 1950. Selecting these gritty historic moments, while a pleasure, was no easy task, solely because there were hundreds, if not thousands, from which to choose. And the reason for that is simple: New England is the cradle of the United States of America, the first region of this vast nation to be permanently occupied by European settlers. It has been here a long, long time, and some of these stories will be familiar to readers (even if they are "from away" or "flatlanders," as old swamp Yankees like to say).

Though there's a hearty helping of gritty tales about each of the evocative occupations mentioned in the title—bootleggers, lobstermen, and lumberjacks—this book also offers a diverse selection of historic moments that, collectively, I hope will illustrate for the reader the varied hardships the early settlers met with courage and overcame with humility. I hope the reader will also gain a better understanding of the impressive place that is New England, and of the impressive people who choose to live here.

This is a work of nonfiction, though I have added dialogue and supporting characters when resource materials were less than fulfilling. In many instances, firsthand information and eyewitness accounts vanished when those involved died. The facts—locations, dates, times, and more—are correct to the best of an amateur historian's research abilities. Maintaining the inherent integrity of the events has been my foremost task, and careful research has gone into grounding each chapter in the solid New England bedrock of fact. The temptation to push and pull each story was slight, as these tales are full of themselves and needed little enhancement.

Indeed, the history of New England brims with true tales of desperate days when Indians and settlers battled for dominion over this rocky but fertile region; where, on hardscrabble hill farms, folks turned their hands to anything that might yield a profit and help put food on the table, from tending beasts to logging to high-stakes cross-border runs smuggling illicit alcohol, livestock, and other goods—and always, it seems, with musket fire whizzing by and the law in high dudgeon.

At one time the great forests of northern New England were filled with tough men engaged in dangerous work for low wages. They faced long hours and stretches of isolation that often resulted in tragedy: In winter, lake ice would give way, and men and horses dragging log-laden sledges would plunge into hundreds of feet of cold, black water, never to be seen again. And come spring, massive log drives sometimes resulted in jams that flooded towns and ripped out roads, bridges, and railroad tracks.

And lest we forget, the rocky New England coastline hosted numerous pirates through the centuries, among them Captains Kidd and Blackbeard. But it's the day-to-day seafarers who deserve our awe: They had more to fear from the sea itself than from burgling buccaneers. These hard-weathered people risked life and limb to face the Sisyphean task of dragging a living from a danger-filled sea that delivered freak storms, roiling surf, jagged, hidden obstacles, and dense, weeklong fog banks. And they did this as they plied the waters of what has been called the most unforgiving stretch of coastline in the world, with untold numbers of shipwrecks serving as a constant reminder of the dangers that awaited them.

Colonial patriots fought starvation and disease and crossed mountains and swamps to oust the British from their brave, new country. Brutal nor'easters hammered coastal villages and cities, claiming hundreds of lives and sinking scores of ships in a single night. Witch trials killed dozens of innocents by imprisonment, hanging, and crushing. And Prohibition's coastal and border rumrunners risked all they had—and then some—for fun and profit while machine-gun fire stippled the night in the heat of high-speed boat rides and hot-pursuit car chases.

So, if you define gritty in part as showing courage, resolve, and pluck in one's daily life, of being tough and uncompromising in the face of adversity, of showing humility as a matter of course rather than choice, then yes, most definitely, you'll find there's grit to spare when mining the rocky hills of New England's past. Let's get digging. . . .

—*Matthew P. Mayo*
Coastal Maine
Winter 2010

1

PILGRIMS' PROGRESS
(1620)

After two months at sea, the overcrowded ship Mayflower *arrives in the New World late in November 1620. The crossing is fraught with storms, births, a death, a cracked beam, and one passenger being washed overboard in a gale (though he grabs a rope and is saved). The winter brings more disease—scurvy, pneumonia, tuberculosis—and ample hardship. Before the Pilgrims' first winter is over, more than half of the 102 souls will be dead. Welcome to the New World.*

⁓

The wooden shovel snapped again, right at the base of the oft-repaired shaft, and with it, Isaac Allerton snapped and sank to his knees in the muddied snow. Two men rushed to his side and tried to lift him by the elbows, but he lashed out, slapping and waving his arms, pushing them away and shouting, "Where is our God? Why does He allow this?"

The men looked away from him and shook their heads. Only when Allerton fell to the sullied earth did he allow himself to be dragged from the burial ground atop the rock-solid slope the weary settlers had chosen.

And it was here that he would bury his dear wife, Mary, who had given birth to a stillborn son just the day before, on February 25, 1621. He was now the sole parent to their two surviving children, Bartholomew and Remember. Their servant boy, young John Hooke, for whom he had felt a fatherly responsibility, had also died earlier in the year.

"Come, Isaac. If we are to prevent this from happening, we must attend to the needs of the others. There are so few of us who are capable now. . . ." John Carver's voice trailed away on the stiff wind off the Atlantic.

These people had elected him as their governor, but that had been in November, when they had landed, and that seemed a lifetime ago. He, too, wished this had turned out differently. He was so tired. Never in all his days in England—before he left for the Netherlands with the others, bad as the persecution might have been—had he thought that he could feel so unaffected by death.

Carver looked down at the shroud covering the dead woman and her dead newborn son. Theirs were the fifteenth and sixteenth deaths this month alone. In December there had been six; in January, eight. Each month the death tolls had risen. What would March bring? At this rate, few of them would be alive by the time the trees put forth their spring leaves.

Allerton's rage was understandable, thought Carver, facing the gaunt faces of the men gathered to help with the burial. But surely they should not question their fealty to Him. As if in response to his thoughts, Allerton rose from the ground, filthy with snow, with mud caked to his rag-wrapped legs. He spoke in a voice strong with anger and defiance: "Is it God's will that all of these good people die? Is that what our God teaches us?"

Carver sighed and closed his eyes. "You are a man in the grip of deep grief," he said. "We understand if you don't feel the fullness of devotion. But neither do we expect to hear blasphemy."

"I tell you, we have not seen the last of the deaths!" Allerton's face shook with anger. "Women, children, babies, men—it does not matter. The scurvy, pneumonia, and abominable conditions in which we live have rendered life here a fruitless endeavor."

"That is enough, Brother Allerton. The people gathered here do not need to hear such hopeless talk." John Carver stared at the thin man with eyes of flint and a tight-set jaw. He saw in that stretched face the depth of his grief and knew that any spark of hope the man might have had for his future had been extinguished with the passing of his wife and child.

"Go now," he said, "And rest. We will dig this grave and summon you when it is time."

But Isaac Allerton did not move, except to shake his head slowly back and forth, the hopelessness of the situation rendering him and those around him more heartsick with each passing second. The wind on that day in late February sliced like knives of the coldest steel as it penetrated to the hearts and bones of the religious pilgrims. So many deaths, they thought. When will it end . . . when we are all dead?

☙

Susanna White dreaded going back into the low, dank common house designated for care of the sick. She dreaded it, and yet she knew it was her duty to help those afflicted with scurvy and worse. Bad as it might be, though,

Mayflower *approaching land*. After a late start, the overcrowded *Mayflower*'s two months at sea were fraught with storms, sickness, births, a death, a cracked beam, and one passenger being washed overboard (though he grabbed a rope at the last second and was saved). The ship arrived in the New World in late November 1620—and then the Pilgrims' hardships really began. *Courtesy Library of Congress*

it was much better than the hold of the *Mayflower*. They had spent two cramped months in the belly of the boat, with no privacy, no protection from death and disease, and no respite from the unending rise and crash of the ocean swells. They had crossed the Atlantic in pursuit of a better life, but it had not been a better life—at least not yet. In February she had lost her husband, William White, father of her two sons, five-year-old Resolved and little Peregrine, who was born in the harbor at Provincetown—the first babe born in the new land.

Now it was June, and she was married to Edward Winslow, whose own wife had died in March, nearly a month to the day after William's passing. Susanna's marriage to Edward was the first in the New World. He was a good man, kindly in his ways, a leader of men, which was apparent from the counsel others begged of him. And of utmost importance to her, he was fond of her boys.

Of the more than fifty people in their group, nearly half were too ill to do much more than cough and moan. Including herself, eight people were tending the sick, while those men who could muster the strength were ashore, cutting down trees and dragging them without the benefit of beasts of burden. She saw the men dragging logs half a mile to the beach, where they would be cut into lumber. Each log represented more payment on the loan the pilgrims undertook in order to make the journey. Their contract had promised lumber, dried fish, and furs for a period of seven years.

Susanna did not see how they could meet those terms, for they were made when there were more than a hundred people committed to the plan. Now, however, less than half that number were left alive. She drew in another gulp of fresh air and, ducking down, pushed aside the heavy layers of fabric that served as the wattle-and-daub structure's door.

The air inside stifled her. The stink of open sores that would not heal, of human waste, of the same breath passing from one to another and back again was outdone only by the sounds that rattled inside the sick space. Ragged, hacking coughs and moans met her.

"Another died today," said young Priscilla Mullins in a low, solemn whisper. Susanna paused and nodded, her hand on the young woman's shoulder. She had given up asking who the dead were, for she knew them all and it was never made easier.

During an arduous two-month journey across the frigid Atlantic in late autumn, many of the 102 passengers became afflicted with scurvy, pneumonia, and tuberculosis. Conditions were cramped, and the Mayflower's scant foodstores had become rotten and moldy in the ship's hold. As it was, the provisions were barely adequate for the planned number of passengers, let alone the dozens of extra passengers it carried.

The Pilgrims (a term not widely used in reference to these settlers until 1820) made their first landfall in the New World on November 20, 1620, at Cape Cod, in what is now Provincetown Harbor. They ventured ashore and discovered an empty Indian village, where they unearthed stores of corn buried in mounds. The settlers proceeded to steal the corn (for eating and for planting the next year) and looted the wigwams of various useful implements and items. And in searching for more corn, they destroyed burial mounds and then looted the graves. They claimed the providence of God as justification for their actions and vowed that they would repay all in good time. The Indians were not impressed.

A month later, on December 21, 1620, the first of several landing parties set foot at what became known as Plymouth Plantation, but what the local Indians, the Wampanoags, called Patuxet, a village abandoned three years before, following a smallpox epidemic brought on by European traders. Several of the residences still contained unburied corpses.

That first winter was a brutal time for the Mayflower passengers. Various illnesses beset them. The unexpected severe winter weather caused them further woe and hampered efforts to fell trees and build shelters, and the men spent their working days soaked and freezing. By the following November, the date of the first "Thanksgiving," just 53 of the initial 102 people who made the journey from England were left alive. Of them, only four were adult women.

Susanna Winslow's second child, Peregrine White, was the first English child born to this group of settlers, and the first white child born in what came to be known as New England. Priscilla Mullins lost her parents and brother on the journey to the New World, and in the spring of 1621, she wed fellow Pilgrim John Alden. Theirs was the third marriage in the New World. Isaac Allerton became forefather to two U.S. presidents: Zachary Taylor and Franklin D. Roosevelt. Allerton's daughter, Mary, outlived all the original Mayflower passengers, dying in 1699 in Plymouth, Massachusetts, at the age of eighty-three.

The local Indian tribes, though harshly treated by earlier expeditions from Europe, were nonetheless responsible for the survival of the settlers of Plymouth Plantation. Their strongest native ally, Tisquantum, better known as Squanto, had been captured in 1605 with others of his tribe and brought to Europe for sale as a slave. Squanto learned English and became an indispensable friend to the Pilgrims, settling with them at Plymouth. The colony probably would not have survived without his assistance. Squanto helped the colonists negotiate peace with local native tribes and taught them how to catch fish and plant crops, the results of which enabled the settlers to survive that vicious first winter.

Within a few years, however, subsequent European settlers demanded more land and resources from the Indians for little or no remuneration. In time, the Indians' trust was repaid with hard treatment as outcasts and second-class citizens in their native land.

2

DUNGEON ROCK
(1658)

Pirate Thomas Veal outfoxes British officers by hiding in a cave near Lynn, Massachusetts, where he lives for years, guarding his treasure—until the Great Earthquake of 1658 buries him alive. People will search for his treasure for centuries.

❧

T he two young lads, Lucas Harlow and Jory Whetherby, walked side by side on the dark lane along the Saugus River, heading out of town and home toward their families' neighboring farms. Over their shoulders they each swung a burlap sack full of early apples, their laughter interrupted only by their crunching of the crisp fruit.

"You eat another one, Jory, and you'll turn into a horse."

Jory whinnied and laughed through a mouthful of apple, spraying the mash at his friend, but Lucas had stopped short in the worn lane. He put a hand on Jory's chest, lowered his sack of apples to the ground, and held up a quieting finger to his mouth. Jory looked to where his friend pointed. There, in a band of shifting moonlight across the mouth of the Saugus River, sat a bold dark ship at anchor.

They looked at each other and then crouched down. Creeping close to the riverbank, they hid behind a boulder. The ship seemed blacker than the lining of Parson Schenkler's frock coat, darker than the bottom of the rock-lined wolf pits at midnight, just up the road from the harbor—but not black enough to disguise the soft smack of the rigging and the creaking of the ship as it rode the tidal swells rolling in. The ship flew no flags atop its masts.

"Pirates?" said Jory.

Lucas didn't answer, for it seemed impossible that Lynn, Massachusetts, would be overrun by pirates on that stiflingly still August evening of 1658. But it was.

Though it was not yet fully dark, the boys watched with growing dread as a longboat from the ship's rail was lowered into the water, followed by a stout-looking wood-and-steel chest that caused the men on the ropes to

Dungeon Rock, Lynn, Massachusetts. Pirate Thomas Veal lived for a time in the network of caves in the forest at Lynn, Massachusetts, guarding an alleged treasure—until the Great Earthquake of 1658 buried him alive. People have searched for his treasure ever since. *Courtesy Library of Congress*

strain and grunt. Then four men silently rowed the bobbing craft up the Saugus River until they reached the Iron Works.

Full dark soon descended over the harbor like a cloak, and the boys scooped up their sacks. Before bolting home, they ran to the nearest house to unburden themselves of this exciting but frightening news. Within hours, cottages in the little town were abuzz with fear and speculation. Men sat before their cold fireplaces, rifles laid across their laps.

They didn't have long to wait for answers. Early the following morning, workers at the Saugus Iron Works found a note pinned to the door. Its contents were plainly written and consisted of a request for shackles, hatchets, shovels, and other implements. Silver coins were promised as compensation. More out of curiosity than commerce, the workers fulfilled the requests, and the silver was left at the specified secret location. And to the satisfaction of all involved, pirates included, this procedure was repeated several times over the following months—until someone in town grew fearful and notified British soldiers garrisoned nearby.

The troops tracked down the pirates to a campsite in a glen near the river, and the chase was on. Despite the difficult terrain, the soldiers caught up with three of the men within days. But a fourth pirate evaded capture, leading the soldiers on a wild chase through the woods, where they lost all trace of him.

Luck smiled on the lone pirate, for he found safe refuge in the natural cave nearby in which he and his three fellows had hidden the laden chest just a short time earlier. The soldiers eventually gave up the chase, satisfied that the three they caught would suffice at a public hanging, and so they did.

It was in this cave that the escaped pirate, Thomas Veal, lived. In time, he also worked from here as a member of the community, mending shoes and trading with the locals. He was treated with caution and regarded as harmless, though odd. He was, after all, an outlaw pirate living in a cave full of untold wealth not far from their town.

✑

The first rumble rained hunks of jagged black rock down on Thomas Veal's head. He had been sitting in the dark on the edge of the crude bunk on which he slept, deep beneath daylight, in the damnable cave where he had been forced to hide so long ago, when he had thought that he would have the last laugh, for the treasure would be all his.

He recalled that he had searched in vain for the box of plunder. After a few days, he had been forced to admit the truth of what had happened: At least one of his three fellows must have absconded with the treasure before the soldiers came to the glen; otherwise, he would have found it long ago in this twisted, cramped network of dank cavities and dead ends.

Veal moaned as yet another chunk of rock dropped on his head. He had awakened to the mighty rumbling, suddenly aware that someone, maybe the entire population of Lynn, was using gunpowder to blast him out of his cave!

"Lord above, don't let them do this to me! I have nothing!" He repeated this last assertion loud enough, he hoped, to be heard by whoever was trying to roust him from his adopted home. Then he yelled at the top of his lungs, "There is no treasure!"

Many times he had snorted out loud in laughter at the thought of what he knew the townspeople believed—that he was sitting on the treasure deep in this cave. If that were the case, he wanted to ask them, why would I fix your footwear for a meager few coins? Why would I barter my labor for food and goods? Why, in the name of God, would I be living in a hole in the ground like a rat?

But it hardly seemed funny now. If indeed he had a fortune in pirate gold, didn't they think he would have been long gone from this dank hole in the ground? He pulled on his boots and made his way up the crude steps he had chipped into the hard rock. They led to the surface from the largest chamber in which he lived.

With his left arm he braced himself against the wall; with his right arm he thrust aside the mat of woven branches that formed his door. He was nearly to the top, shouting, "No! No! Stop, I tell you!" when his world shook with the force of a thousand cannon volleys. And that's when he knew this was not the work of mere gunpowder. At the same time, his right foot slipped off the outer edge of the top step, and he pitched back into the blackness below.

He came to his senses, groggy and shaking in the dark, and clawed at the ground beneath him. It was the dry, dusty dirt and spiked rock of the cave floor. With great effort Veal coaxed his small fire to life and from that lit his oil lamp. He raised the lamp and looked toward the only way he knew out of the cave. But it was no longer there.

⚬⁄⁄⚬

"The man was a scoundrel hunted by the law, His Majesty's forces."

"Yes, I know. But that does not mean we should leave him to die like a trapped rat, does it?" Jim Harlow shook his head and continued on, not concerned with how his neighbor felt about the outlaw-turned-shoe-mender who lived in a cave in the wilds of Lynn Forest.

The neighbor, farmer Jedediah Whetherby, muttered a few choice oaths, but plowed through the waist-high brush just behind Harlow. Within minutes they arrived at the slight clearing where Harlow knew the cave to be located. Or at least he thought it was the spot. Never before had he seen such a changed landscape. "Jed, surely this isn't the place. . . ."

Beside him, his neighbor stood looking at what the earthquake had wrought: the tumble of rocks, some half as big as an ox, strewn about as if for fun. And in the midst of it all was the massive, house-size crag that had marked the entrance to the hermit pirate's cave. Harlow scrambled over freshly scarred boulders, shouting, "Thomas Veal! Thomas Veal? Are you there?"

"He's dead, Jim."

"How can you be so sure?"

"Look around you, man! Surely he was crushed by that." Whetherby gestured at the massive, upended crag that had driven deep into the cave's mouth and said, "There is no way a man could live through this, Jim. No way at all." He let his arms drop to his sides.

⌘

Far below them, a small flame guttered and then collapsed in a wisp of smoke, and a broken, bleeding man leaned back against a rock and groaned in the dark.

⌘

For two hundred years following the Great Earthquake of 1658, the caves, and Veal's trapped remains, went undisturbed. Then in the 1830s, two attempts to breach the caves were made with gunpowder, to no avail. In 1852 Hiram Marble and his family bought the five acres surrounding the caves, which had come to be known as Dungeon Rock. As a spiritualist, Marble believed that the spirits of the dead can communicate with the living. According to Marble, he had received word from the deceased Thomas Veal that excavating the caves would result in Marble's guaranteed prosperity, with which he intended, at least in part, to help spiritualism gain a level of credibility it had thus far not achieved.

Marble built a two-story home and assorted outbuildings at the entrance to the cave, and for fifteen years he and his son, Edwin, blasted and dug, bucket by bucket, into the cave, the seemingly random directions of their tunnelings determined by conversations Marble had with spirits. In 1868 Hiram died, and Edwin continued digging, expanding the bizarre network of tunnels, until his own death in 1880. Edwin is buried under a large piece of pink granite beside the cellar hole of his family home.

Though various minor artifacts were found over the years, including a sword that the Marbles claimed belonged to the entombed pirate (refusing to believe townsfolk who admitted planting it there as a hoax), no treasure was ever unearthed.

But in the intervening years, the land has given pleasure to more people than a trunk of doubloons ever could, for it is now part of an extensive municipal parkland known as Lynn Woods. In addition to tours of the tunnels of Dungeon Rock, the park includes the Rose Garden, the Stone Tower, and the Wolf Pits, used by seventeenth-century residents to rid the region of a large, voracious population of the reviled creatures.

3

THE GREAT SWAMP FIGHT
(1675)

On a frigid December day in 1675, 1,200 colonial militia, Pequot, and Mohegan warriors attack the Narragansetts at their fort deep in the heart of Rhode Island's Great Swamp. More than three hundred women, children, and old people are shot, bludgeoned, and burned to death. The tribe regroups and vows to fight another day.

❧

You cannot expect us to join Metacomet in this war. It is a war of death—death to our people. And it is a war he will lose!" Canonchet, sachem of the Narragansett tribe, bellowed his words, his nostrils flaring in anger.

The woman to whom he spoke was the tall, black-haired Queen Wetamoo, at once proud and vain. So tall and daring was she that she seemed more like a warrior, unafraid of anything. She folded her arms and stared at him in defiance. The other women looked away, down at their babies, off toward the bark walls of the wigwams. Hers was embarrassing behavior for a woman of the tribe, though some secretly admired her open brazenness. But she was the wife of a sachem, of course, so that made all the difference. And her first husband, Wamsutta, had been chief of the Wampanoag tribe.

Canonchet gathered together his robes tightly about himself and with a growl turned his back on the impertinent woman. Her eyes narrowed, and she half-grinned at her small triumph as she surveyed the few young warriors, old ones, and young women. She pulled her long wool coat about her face and left the wigwam.

Outside, the wind had increased, and with it came the beginnings of another storm. Tiny pellets of snow, like frozen seeds, drove at her face. So, the bitter season had begun—to match our mood, she thought. She sighed and walked aimlessly toward the wall of upright logs, sharpened at the tops. The Narragansetts had hidden themselves deep within the Great Swamp on a five-acre hump of land surrounded by bare trees and thick undergrowth. Except during winter, when it was frozen, the swamp was a squelching mire that the English wouldn't dare enter.

Wetamoo stared into the snow. Why could they not see that joining with her brother-in-law, Metacomet, now sachem of the Wampanoags, was the only way to stop the English from stealing all of their land? Sitting here in the Narragansett fort in the middle of the Great Swamp was no way to pass the cold season, not with Metacomet in need of their help. She knew the ways of the Wampanoags better than anyone here. Pah, they did not see the forest for the trees.

A shout from one of the young boys peering through gaps in the logs pulled her from her reverie. Several men had already hurried to his side. He pointed, directing their attention out beyond the wall at something. A deer? Surely, she thought, he could figure out how to pursue it himself.

Still, something about the boy's cries drew her closer to the growing knot of warriors, a mass of men huddled in their blankets and wraps.

"I saw something move, I tell you the truth. Out there, beyond that largest oak." Most of the men pressed their faces to the logs. What could the boy mean? Surely it was an animal.

"Hunt it up, boy," said Tamano, an older warrior who Wetamoo knew to be a gruff, uncouth man, but also one of the tribe's best hunters. His remark brought laughter from the retreating men. When he turned and saw Wetamoo, the smile slid from his face. Another boy shouted, but his warnings were not of deer but of men.

"The English! The English! They are coming to attack!" He retreated from the log wall as if it had bitten him. The men all rushed back to the wall and looked out through the spaces between logs. And their sudden shouts and dashes toward the village and up to the guard posts were all that Wetamoo needed to see. She, too, ran toward the wigwams, shouting warnings and thinking two steps ahead of herself. Lives would be lost this day, and she had to make sure they were not children's lives.

☙

The first shot heard in the enclosure caught Tamano in the eye. He stiffened for a moment before wavering and dropping to his knees. After exhaling his last breath, he fell sideways to the frozen ground. The screams of children being dragged from wigwams rose from the enclosure and were quickly drowned out by volley after volley of rifle shots cracking the crisp December air. Wetamoo watched as those of her tribe were cut down—the old, the young, it didn't matter to the English.

She gritted her teeth. The Narragansetts only wanted to be left alone—their only crime had been to give shelter to Metacomet's young and old. Very few of their warriors had joined the fight. But she knew, even as she tried to usher her people out into the swamp, that it didn't matter to the whites. The Europeans wanted all Indians dead or driven away. She realized then that they would never stop, never be satisfied with the land they had already taken. They wanted more, always more. When would there ever be enough to satisfy them? She knew that this day would crush the tribe's spirit forever—unless she could do something about it. But what?

The battle seemed to continue for hours. There were moments when the warriors had the upper hand, but then the English would advance. She was close enough at times to see the fear on the faces of the soldiers, some of them just boys. She did not care; if given the opportunity, she would draw their blood.

As she ran at an English militiaman, her club held high, she saw her people fleeing, stumbling through tangles of dense trees. What would be out there for them in the swamp? Canonchet had chosen this spot well as a place of safety for all Narragansett tribe members to spend the hard winter. The knob on which they built was the only high, dry spot in the whole of the vast swamp. It was surrounded by downed trees, two of which they used as bridges to reach the fort. But they had not finished building it and would never do so now.

Wetamoo lunged at the nearest soldier, driving him to the ground with a shout and a grunt. She grabbed for her knife, but it was hidden in the folds of her thick coat. The soldier swung an arm free from under him and pushed himself up, lifting her off his shoulder. The free arm arched upward, and the knuckles caught her full on the face. It burned, though she had felt worse from her husbands.

As if to goad her into a deeper frenzy, a woman's scream rose from a flaming wigwam but then ceased with a gunshot as abrupt as a slap. Beneath Wetamoo, the soldier shouted at her, punched her, kicked, bit, tried to buck her off, but she clung to him long enough to swing a length of branch as thick around as her forearm. She drove it straight down at his head. He tried to block the blow, but it was too late. She swung again and again, until only one unmoving eye stared up at her from a mask of gore, his body dead to the world.

She pushed herself off him as other English soldiers ran by, some fleeing and some in pursuit of the Narragansett warriors. At that instant, the screams all about her seemed to increase, and flames rose high from hundreds of wigwams, scorching the few low, bare trees still left in the enclosure.

To her right, a wigwam made of bark and branches began to smoke from a thrown torch. Wetamoo heard whimpering from within and dashed inside. In the dim interior, she found two children and an old woman, their grandmother. They were huddled in a far corner and partially hidden beneath a blanket and firewood she had dragged onto them.

"Get up, old woman! You will die in here. They're setting fire to the entire village!" But the old thing shook her head and bent even lower, pulling the two children tighter.

Wetamoo growled and dragged the three of them to their feet. The smoke belched forth as the walls blossomed in blazing flames higher than their heads, spreading across the walls and ceiling with the speed of a gunshot. She hoisted the two children under her arms, snatched the old woman's wrist, and dragged her through the flame-wreathed portal of the wigwam's door.

Black smoke rising from other burning shelters helped hide Wetamoo and her charges, but the screams of those trapped inside made her groan with heartsick compassion. She wanted to get these three away from the village and then go back for others trapped in the flaming wigwams. The old lady stumbled and tried to pull free of Wetamoo's grip, but the young woman was strong and dragged the old crone, screeching, through the thick undergrowth.

Ahead, she saw others of the tribe, running deep into the swamp, stumbling through the snow and frozen mounds of swamp grass. A near-naked child howled and groped his way back toward the flaming fort. Behind her the screams had lessened, but those that rose into the sky were the animal sounds of agony. She heard fewer shouts from the warriors now and knew that the militia soldiers would soon hunt down the rest of them, for it was clear to her they had no mercy, such was their hatred and fear of the Narragansett tribe.

With what strength she had left, Wetamoo scooped up the screaming lone child and, with the others, hurried away from the horrid place and deep into the swamp, the bloom of anger and revenge rooting deep within her.

During the infamous King Philip's War (Metacomet was also known as King Philip), on Sunday, December 19, 1675, 1,200 colonial militia, plus allied Pequot and Mohegan warriors, joined forces to confront the bay-dwelling Narragansetts at their swamp-surrounded fort near what is now South Kingstown, Rhode Island. The tribe was attacked from all sides, and more than six hundred wigwams were burned, many with their residents still inside. More than three hundred Narragansetts died that day, including women, children, and old people.

Wetamoo survived the attack and rallied three hundred warriors. With her brother-in-law, Metacomet, she continued raiding English settlements, beheading prisoners and burning settlers' homes, in part as retribution for the loss of life that day in the swamp. She fought a losing war, and in August 1676 she was down to twenty-six warriors when they were ambushed. She tried to escape by swimming across the Taunton River, but she was swept away and drowned. Wetamoo's naked body was found by the English, who hacked it apart and mutilated it further. They then cut off her head and perched it atop a pole in the town of Taunton.

The Narragansetts, who wanted little more than to remain as neutral as possible in Metacomet's war with the English, had retreated to the swamp and built up a defensive compound, where they hoped to ride out the war without having to commit to either side. But the colonists considered them to be potential allies of the Wampanoags. And so in a carefully planned preemptive attack, the colonial militia descended on the Narragansetts, ultimately goading them into a war in which they desired no part.

Metacomet, too, met his end in August 1676, in Miery Swamp in southern Rhode Island. He was shot in the heart by John Alderman, an Indian working with the English. The chief's body was quartered and draped in the trees. As payment for the deed, Alderman was awarded the chief's head and one hand. He sold the head for 30 shillings, and it was displayed on a pike in Plymouth, Rhode Island, for twenty-five years. He charged people a fee to peek at the dead warrior chief's withered hand.

The Great Swamp Fight, or Great Swamp Massacre, was the largest and most notorious fight in King Philip's War, which was largely a reaction by the native tribes of the region against increasingly oppressive English dominance and seizure of their land.

Beginning in June 1675 and petering out in Maine in 1677, King Philip's War took a mighty toll on both sides: While six hundred to eight hundred colonists died in battle during the war, 3,000 native lives were lost, and several hundred more Indians were sold into slavery in Bermuda, among them Metacomet's wife and young son.

In 1676 Joshua Tefft, an Englishman, was accused of assisting the Narragansetts and fighting alongside them in the Great Swamp Fight. As punishment he was hanged, drawn, and quartered (a particularly brutal form of punishment involving disembowelment, then dismemberment)—and may well be the only person in U.S. history to be treated in this fashion.

Although we now know that New England's native tribes had inhabited the region for 30,000 years, this mattered little to the invading Europeans, who arrived in greater numbers and in greater frequency by the shipload, requiring land of their own, to carve new lives for themselves in the New World.

4

THE CANDLEMAS MASSACRE
(1692)

On a late January morning in 1692, two hundred Abenaki Indians raid York, Maine; kill one hundred colonists; take eighty captives; and then torch the town. Four-year-old Jeremiah Moulton watches as his parents are scalped. He survives but doesn't forget . . . or forgive.

∽

The last of the two hundred Abenaki warriors trudged up to the edges of the assembled group. All fell silent and stared up at their leader, Madockawando, a lone Penobscot who promised them action and no more talk in the face of yet more unacceptable behavior by the vile English.

"Fellow warriors," he said, from atop a boulder. Madockawando spoke in a bold but subdued voice, for on a cold, clear early morning such as this, voices carried far, and the Abenakis did not wish to lose the advantage of surprise. "We are nearly to the town. Show no mercy, for the English have shown none toward us. If this Massachusetts governor John Leverett has his way, no member of any tribe will be allowed firearms, and if that happens, we will be as harmless as toothless old women. We must strike back, and we must do it now!" Despite their desire for a quiet entry to the still-dozing town, a rousing cheer, equal parts pride and bloodlust, boiled up from the gathered warriors.

They had traveled through dense forest much of the night from their previous day's encampment, and now, rested and ready to show the colonists that they were a proud race and not mere children to be ordered about, the warriors unstrapped their snowshoes, piling them at the base of the rock, and readied their knives, tomahawks, and rifles. Some of them shucked outer layers of clothes—they had no desire to be hampered in the coming task. None of them uttered a sound, save for the occasional grunt of satisfaction to signify they were ready. With a few deft arm motions, Madockawando led the mass of men south along the river to the still-sleeping town of York.

∽

Jason Macomber pulled in a deep breath of fresh air and almost smiled. It had been a long winter so far, but the game had been plentiful, and his rifle shots had found their marks. He hadn't needed to head out this morning looking for deer, but he liked being up before others, liked the stillness, the cold, and the gray dawn making him feel as if he were alone in the world.

Ahead of him sat the big rock marking Chase's Pond Road. He followed the road for a time, giving his legs a chance to recover from the hard work of stepping tall in the deep snow, even though his snowshoes helped keep him somewhat on top of it. As he drew closer, he slowed his pace and squinted, for it appeared that the snow had been freshly trampled as if by a herd of deer—or men. There had been a dusting of snow the night before, so these tracks were fresh. But what would anyone, let alone a crowd, be doing this far out of York, and so early?

Macomber was almost to the rock when he saw the great mass of snowshoes, some wedged in the snow, most heaped in a pile on the backside of the rock. There must be hundreds, he thought. He stepped closer, and then he recognized them for what they were—Indian snowshoes.

His heart hammered in his chest. He crouched low and looked all about him, but no one was there—just woods and snow. His breath billowed in great frosty gouts, and he knew with the speed of a gunshot that a raid on York was under way. He ran toward home, his breath coming in stuttering gasps, praying he wouldn't come upon any Abenakis—and praying he wasn't too late.

✑

The hatchet caught Jeremiah Moulton's mother on the side of the head. She fell to her chest and grunted, her fingers and legs twitching; then she lay still. But her open eyes were fixed on her boy, four-year-old Jeremiah, who watched from beneath the bed. He had no time to scream as the dirt-crusted hand of an Indian groped for him. The snarled shouts of his father pulled the Indian away. He watched the running legs of countless other Indians scissor past his hiding place. His father's voice reached him again, and he yelled in response, but his father's screams drowned out his own efforts. There in front of him, between himself and his mother's prone form, he recognized his father's boots and leggings.

Again, he nearly crawled out, for surely there could be no better protector than his father. Then the man's legs bent forward—he's coming to get

Take Care of Yourself *by Roy F. Heinrich, 1939.* On a late January morning in 1692, two hundred Abenakis raided York, Maine, killed one hundred colonists, took eighty captives, and then torched the town. As more European settlers moved in, Indians, tired of losing their land, stepped up their attacks, and the colonists were hard-pressed to defend themselves. *National Life Insurance Company*

me, thought the boy—and his father's body pitched forward, his head so close that young Jeremiah could reach out and touch it. But his head was nothing that could be touched. It was covered in slick, flowing blood like a bright red nightcap.

Beyond his father lay his mother, and another Indian was crouched over her, cutting off her hair. In no time her head looked like his father's, and Jeremiah wondered if she, too, was wearing a red nightcap.

Were it not for the screams of his parents and others, and the hoots and strange tongue of the Indians, young Jeremiah Moulton might have thought that this was all for fun. But something told him he must stay far in the corner, under the bed. He scooted even farther backward on the packed dirt floor and waited, trying to not cry, to not shout.

As the day's early sun lit the cottage, the sound of screaming and rifle shots lessened and gave way to a distant sobbing and the increasing crackle of fire.

And then he saw flames, as if they had jumped from the hearth and were looking for him, dancing around the room. Jeremiah stared at them, a cold feeling gripping him. What did this mean? But he had little time to think about it, for the smoke that came with the fire crawled even closer, choking him. He knew he must leave, must run, but he didn't want to leave his parents.

Finally, he did run from the little house and saw shapes in the smoke, men who were pointing and shouting. They would help him; they would know what to do. He ran toward them. As he drew closer, he stopped. These were not his father's friends. These were Indians. He saw their leggings, and he knew they were those of the man who did that . . . horrible thing to his mother. But there, too, was his father's friend, Mr. Macomber, swaying before the Indian. Then the Indian reached out, something in his hand flashed dull in the firelight, and Mr. Macomber fell forward, holding his belly.

Jeremiah turned to run, but a dirty hand gripped him by the arm and lifted him up high. He felt as if his arm might snap, or just pull away from his body. A small cry slipped from his mouth but died in his throat as he stared into the blazing, angry eyes of an Indian.

❧

Late in the day, the smoke hung thick and low over the defeated little town. Those who were left alive were gathered by the Indians and tied with hemp and leather thongs, and the ragged line was led for weeks on a forced march to Canada.

The screams of Jeremiah Moulton's parents, and the memory of their dead eyes staring at him, would haunt him for the rest of his life—even after he exacted his revenge some three decades later.

❧

At the end of the seventeenth century, the native tribes of the New England region were increasingly oppressed by the growing presence of English settlers, as they had been for more than a century. A boiling point was reached when John Leverett, the governor of the Commonwealth of Massachusetts, ordered local Indian tribes to give up their firearms. Despite strong opposition by his military advisers as well as citizens of many towns, including York, Leverett did not rescind his decree.

The Indians who made up the Wabenaki Confederacy, a gathering of Abenaki, Maliseet, Passamaquoddy, Mi'kmaq, and Penobscot tribes, regarded the decree as a death sentence. Already forced off their land and severely afflicted with disease brought by the English settlers, they reasoned that without firearms they could not hunt, and so would starve. The governor's refusal to rescind his decision was the last blow to an already reeling native people. They struck back as effectively as they knew how, staging a series of raids such as the one on York. The French, who were battling the English for control of the region, employed the situation to their advantage by encouraging and in some cases participating in such raids.

Eighty survivors of the Candlemas Massacre were taken captive and forced to march to Canada before being ransomed by Captain John Alden, son of two original Plymouth Plantation settlers. (Just a few years later, Alden would become one of the accused in the Salem witch trials.)

Ironically, it was the Abenakis' raid on York, as well as similar raids, that would have a lasting and devastating effect on the tribes in years to come as scores of their captives from those raids, once ransomed and returned home, would later take up arms and become unrepentant hunters of Indians. Thirty-two years later, Jeremiah Moulton, fueled by vivid memories of the Indians' raid on York, led a number of brutal retaliatory raids, including one on the Norridgewock tribe at their village in present-day Madison, Maine.

That raid, on August 23, 1724, was effectively a slaughter that wiped out most of the village and was in part a response to that tribe's continued raids. These had been instigated and led, some say, by Jesuit priest Father Fasles, who lived among the tribe, converting them to Christianity. Depending on one's historical perspective, Fasles either attempted to quell the tribe's warring instincts or perpetuated anti-English sentiment by instigating further raids on English settlements.

A half century later, in 1774, that same tribe provided crucial and much-needed assistance to Benedict Arnold's raiding party as they journeyed up the Kennebec River to attack the British stronghold in Quebec City. The Norridgewock considered it a form of repayment for what the British had done to their tribe fifty years before.

5

A CRUSHING END
(1692)

During the Salem witch trials, more than 150 people in Massachusetts are imprisoned on suspicion of witchcraft. Twenty-nine are convicted by the courts, nineteen are hanged, and five die in prison. Giles Corey, however, is not so fortunate.

◈

"It is God's will, Giles Corey," said Sheriff George Corwin.

"God's will that I am damned if I do plead and damned if I do not?" The old man turned away lest he say anything more that might further endanger his wife, though he knew there was little more he could do on her behalf. The woman will be hanged, he thought. My third wife and so, my last. And I, too, will be put to death. How, I do not yet know. But I have heard rumor of the vicious ways people who do not plead, people such as myself, are treated. He gritted his teeth, closed his eyes, and uttered silent prayers to the God who, he knew, would not abandon him. But he doubted it was the God to which these men were paying attention.

"So you still refuse to stand trial to face the charges of witchcraft?"

Corey, a respected, eighty-year-old farmer, spun back around and faced the haughty magistrate, staring at him through the barred wooden door. "What would be the point in such an exercise?" He shook his head, not taking his eyes from the man. "Thus far nothing but convictions have resulted. No, you will get no such pleasure from me, young man."

The sheriff sighed. "There is no pleasure derived from rooting out the demon's evil seed. And yet it must be done." He flipped a corner of his cape over his left shoulder and walked away down the narrow hallway, his boot heels echoing off the stone flags.

Giles Corey felt a tight knot of anger deep in his gut. It was the same every week. And every week his anger at the foolishness of the situation grew. But this week was to be different; he had been told so.

◈

The five months he had been held in prison had passed slowly, and he thanked his God time and again that before his arrest he had the time and sense to sign over deeds and all ownership of his property to his two sons-in-law. If he had not, his holdings would become the property of the Crown. And he would indeed rather be damned than give them anything more than what he and Martha were going to give them—their lives.

He had no intention of confessing to being a witch. The very idea was preposterous. He had not reached eighty years by pandering to the whims and mass opinions of the public. The only thing he might be accused of—and had been a good many times over the years—was being hot tempered, for all the good it had done him.

Now, after all these years, he had begun to believe fully what he suspected most of his life—that people can convince themselves to believe almost anything. Those young girls accused him under oath of being a "dreadful wizard" and said that he had told them to write in the Devil's book, that a ghost had come to one of them, claiming it had been a person he had murdered. If this affair didn't spell the end of his days, he could almost find humor in it. Almost.

"Giles Corey . . . ," said the fat man in the jailer's suit.

"Ralph Brinkman, you know it's me. I've been in your cell for five months. And I've known you most of your born days."

The man stared past Corey, cleared his throat, and began again. "Giles Corey, by order of the court of the Commonwealth of Massachusetts, I am ordered to transport you to the churchyard adjoining this courthouse."

So, this was it. Even to the end it was a formal affair. He had prayed all night for a reprieve, knowing it would not be the case.

As two men escorted him out of the Salem courthouse, crowds of people, some of whom he recognized—two, in fact, were from a farm neighboring his—shouted vile accusations at him.

"Devil!"

"Satan's spawn!"

"Corey, you wizard!"

They reached the corner lot, surrounded by townsfolk, many of whom he had known their entire lives, and a few of whom were as old as he. Many others he did not know. And the reason that they gathered, he knew, was that the form of punishment he was about to endure was unheard of here in the colonies.

The Witch No. 2. Though public humiliation as a form of punishment was commonplace in colonial New England, the Salem witch trials, which began in 1692, brought about a new level of public frenzy. More than 150 people in Massachusetts were imprisoned on suspicion of witchcraft, twenty-nine were convicted, nineteen hanged, five died in prison, and one was pressed to death with stones. *Courtesy Library of Congress*

The magistrate bade him strip off his shirt, by now a stringy garment ill-suited to the name, and ordered him to lay down on his back in a rough-dug pit twelve inches deep. The earth was cold on his bare skin. Even his anger would not keep him warm this day. He hoped that neither his dear Martha, from her cell, nor any of his children or theirs, could witness this dreadful spectacle. Even as it began, he could not believe it was happening to him.

The sheriff and gathered magistrates stood well back from him. The sheriff said, "Giles Corey, on this day of our Lord, Monday, September 19, 1692, it is the opinion of this court that since you refused to plead yourself guilty as a witch, you are to undergo *peine forte et dure*—that is, strong and hard punishment—until such time as you admit your guilt . . . or until you expire."

The sheriff nodded to the two men standing nearby with thick wooden planks. These they placed on Corey, leaving only his head, arms, and legs poking out from underneath. The men then placed heavy stones, one by one, on the boards, grunting as they did so, positioning them over his stomach and chest. Within seconds, something deep inside him popped, as if a carrot had snapped in two.

The immediate pressure pushed every last breath from him, and he prayed that the end would be swift. Already his face, fingertips, and feet felt as though they might burst with the slightest pressure.

For two days he was left with that initial weight pressing on him. Breaths came in shallow gulps and gasps, and the feeling in his limbs left him early on the first day. At the end of that first day, the jailer had tried to force bits of moldy bread between his lips, but Giles expelled them with his tongue. "Water, give me water," was all he said. The man, with a pained look, only shook his head and walked away. Corey periodically lost consciousness and was disappointed each time he revived that he had not yet died.

"It is the third day, Giles Corey. How do you plead?"

His mind was swimming with thoughts of moments from his life, of the pitiful proceedings of these past few months. I will be damned, he thought, if they take my farm, for the sake of the lies of hysterical children. His only satisfaction was knowing that these fools would one day get their own comeuppance.

"Giles Corey, I say again, how do you plead?"

"More weight . . . ," he said.

And the men did indeed add more weight. The crowd, smaller now, stood back, and the angry oaths that mere days before had echoed around the courtyard now subsided to low murmurs, spiked with random gasps from women who could not bear to see what was happening to Giles Corey.

As the weight was added, Corey neither cried out nor admitted to anything of which he was accused, though he had heard a series of snaps and pops, and he knew they were his bones. Soon now, he thought, I will just collapse.

The only thing he said was "More . . . weight . . . ," in hopes of hastening his death, for the pain was unendurable. His face felt like a swollen sack near bursting. Once again he lost consciousness.

Through a shimmering veil of light and shadow, shapes came into view, and for a moment Giles Corey clearly saw the jowled face of Sheriff George Corwin staring down at him from where he stood atop the rocks on Corey's chest. And then the sheriff reached toward him with the tip of his cane and pushed Corey's protruding blackening tongue back in his gasping mouth.

∽

From February 1692 through May 1693 throughout Massachusetts, more than 150 people were arrested and imprisoned on suspicion of witchcraft. Twenty-nine were convicted by the courts, and nineteen—fourteen women and five men—were hanged. Five others died in prison. To the end, Giles Corey refused to enter a plea and was crushed to death on September 19, 1692, three days before his wife was executed by hanging. No one was burned to death at the stake, a fictional notion associated with the Salem witch trials.

Though outlawed in England for two decades preceding the trials as an extreme and torturous form of punishment, peine forte et dure—*during which the victim was pressed to death by the weight of stones—nonetheless was settled on as sufficient punishment for Giles Corey.*

Although much of his extensive property, most notably valuable land, had been seized by the courts by the time Corey was arrested in April 1692, the eighty-year-old farmer did write a last will and testament while in prison. He pleaded not guilty to the charges of witchcraft, and since every trial thus far had ended in a conviction, he felt he would not give authorities the satisfaction of feeding their frenzy.

The history of the United States is peppered with instances of unchecked mass religious fervor, but it is the Salem witch trials that are synonymous with religious extremism. However, accusations of witchcraft in New England began long before 1692. As early as 1647, an execution on the grounds of witchcraft is said to have taken place in Connecticut, and three women were executed the following year for the same crime.

Eunice "Goody" Cole was accused of witchcraft at least three times in her life, the first time in 1656 in Boston, where she was flogged and imprisoned for four years, even though she was sixty-four at the time. She survived further periods of imprisonment, the last one for fifteen years, before being released to care for her ailing husband. When she arrived home, she found that he had already died. In 1680, when she died at age ninety, a pauper reliant on the charity of those who had accused her of witchcraft through the years, the villagers carted her body to a field, stabbed her through the heart with a stake, hung a horseshoe on it, and buried her in an unmarked grave. She remains New Hampshire's only convicted witch.

Giles Corey's gruesome public death did much to hasten the end of the Salem witch trials, though it would be May 1693 before the last court trial took place. Martha Corey and two others, hanged on May 22, 1692, were the last batch of prisoners to lose their lives to the accusation of witchcraft.

Sheriff George Corwin died a few years later, in 1696, of a heart attack at the age of thirty. At his death, Phillip English, who had been accused of witchcraft during the trials and whose property had been seized by Corwin, demanded payment, effectively placing a lien on Corwin's corpse, thus preventing the lawman's burial until English received appropriate monetary compensation.

Within days after Massachusetts governor William Phips's own wife was accused of witchcraft, the good governor ordered the immediate release of all prisoners still being held on charges of witchcraft.

6

A MOTHER'S ANGER

(1697)

While her Indian captors sleep, Hannah Duston of Boscawen, New Hampshire, mas-sacres and scalps them to avenge their savage murder of her baby. But because Duston is a woman, the £25-per-scalp bounty is given to her husband.

✑

Mary, what is that commotion outside?" Even as she spoke, Hannah Duston sat up in bed. Though still weak, having given birth but seven days earlier to her twelfth child, she had grown weary of her forced rest. Widow Mary Neff, her neighbor and friend, had been an invaluable help to Hannah in caring for the baby girl, Martha.

Mary rose from tending the fire and, carrying the sleeping baby, peeked out the front door as the shouting drew closer.

Hannah Duston recognized her husband's voice. "It's Thomas! Something's wrong, Mary. . . ." Her breath stopped, and her body felt as though it had turned to ice. Could she have heard him right? Were Indians attacking the settlement?

Mary Neff ducked back inside, slamming the door. One look at her shocked face convinced Hannah that it was true. And her thoughts turned to her seven surviving children. She prayed that Thomas would get them to the garrison in time.

"Mary, run to the garrison! I will try to stop them. Mary, do you hear me?"

The quivering woman held the screaming baby tight to her chest and slipped out the door, crouching in the squelching spring mud, and then dashed across the yard. A harsh shout burst at her from beyond the corner of the house, and a warrior bolted forward, grabbing her by the throat and dragging her back toward the cottage.

Hannah stood beside the bed, color rising in her pale cheeks. With no warning, the door burst open, and three Abenaki warriors ran into the room. In seconds an Indian was on her, and she noticed the greased skin of his face, the hot stink of his breath like rancid meat, the anger in his eyes.

He grabbed her by the arm and with his other hand rammed hard knuckles against her mouth. Her eyes teared, and still she fought him, kicking and shouting. But already there were too many of them. Where did they all come from?

She tried to bolt for the door, but a short warrior barked a command at her and pushed her toward the fireplace. Another threw a dress at her and indicated he wanted her to dress herself. She did as he bade her, her hands shaking. She still heard the baby crying just outside. So, she thought, Mary didn't get far. But at least the baby was still alive.

The rest of the Indians tore apart the house, ripping clothing, throwing utensils, upending furniture. They stole much, filling cloth sacks with anything that they thought had value. And all too soon they grabbed her by the arms and pushed her out the door. She lost a shoe in the fracas and didn't know until much later, so numbed had she become. The last thing she saw was an Indian hooting as he splashed lamp oil inside the little house. Another tossed a burning stick in the open door, and flames the colors of sunset flowered, crackling and consuming the once-happy home.

Once outside, she heard shouts and screams. From all over the settlement she saw houses, barns, and sheds aflame. People were running, being chased, with blood streaming down their faces. She saw bodies, too, of her friends and neighbors, flopped in the dirt. She couldn't tell who they were, but she didn't see any of the clothes her children had been dressed in.

Within a mile of leaving the village, Hannah was struck again for moving too slow, and as she fell to the mud, the Indian who had hit her grabbed little Martha, still screaming, from Mary Neff's hands. The woman shouted and punched at the Indian. With a quick clout, he knocked her to her knees.

Hannah shook her head to clear her thoughts, and an Indian gripped her hair in a tight fist. And then a scream rose from her throat that startled even the Indian who held her by the hair—but only for a moment. He looked to where the first Indian stood, but a few feet away, and his laugh pierced her like an arrow to the heart.

Hannah Duston watched as the warrior swung her one-week-old baby girl by the feet and dashed her head against the trunk of a gnarled apple tree. After a half dozen swings, he tossed the silent, lifeless body to the ground and rejoined his fellows in beating their gathered prisoners.

❧

"Are you in agreement with me, Mary Neff?"

The older woman didn't respond. Hannah squeezed her friend's arm and repeated her whispered question. Mary nodded. Hannah knew how she felt, for all thirteen of the captives had marched with no respite for days northward, and they were split into two groups days before. Their own smaller group was now encamped with their captors on an island in the middle of a wide river, at a spot where two rivers formed one. The ice and snow they were forced to plunge through had shredded and bloodied their feet. They were worn out, frozen from lack of clothing, sore from the chafing ropes about their wrists, aching from constant beatings, and heartsick at the savagery they had witnessed.

Now, Hannah and Mary Neff were alone, except for the only other captor, a fourteen-year-old boy named Samuel Lennardson. He had been a captive of this particular Indian family for eighteen months and was treated like a dog.

That evening, they were told that the next day they would be marched northward to Canada. Hannah knew what awaited them: a life of enslavement, or abuses beyond anything she could imagine. She longed to learn the fate of her seven children and her husband. She prayed with each step of the march that they were safe. And she nurtured an anger that only a mother who has been violently robbed of a child can feel.

"Mary, young Samuel is with us. That makes the three of us against the twelve. We can escape, but only when they've fallen asleep. They think that because we are women, we are weak, and they think he is only a boy. We will soon be home. Have faith, Mary."

Hannah said this as much for her own sake as for Mary's. The boy was fully willing to make his escape, as he held no love for his captors. Hannah lay still that night, her mood grim and decisive.

෴

The fire had burned low, with only a few scattered coals casting the slightest light on the faces of the Indians who lay close to its waning warmth. Even though Hannah knew they were outnumbered—there were twelve Indians, seven of them children—she also knew it was time to do whatever needed to be done if they were to escape. It was to be tonight . . . or never!

Hannah and the boy, Samuel, set to work with the vigor reserved for threshing season as they swung down the stolen tomahawks again and again onto the heads of their sleeping captors. Hannah gritted her teeth even as the gore flew at her, smearing her tattered, filthy dress. An Indian woman, though wounded, escaped from the clearing with a young boy and soon vanished in the night. Seconds later Hannah heard splashing from upriver.

"Samuel, don't let them escape!" The boy bolted from the firelight but returned a short time later. "It's no use. I can't even see where I'm going. They must be far from here now."

"No matter, Samuel. No matter. Mary, come to the canoe. Grab what foodstuff you can, and weapons, too. We must make haste and gain distance on the river while we have the advantage of night."

Samuel pushed two of the long Indian canoes into the river. Taking another canoe, the three escapees slid it into the water and paddled with the current, as fast as they dared on the nearly moonless night. Hannah silently cursed the thick cloud cover and pushed her sticky hair back out of her eyes. As she did so, she stopped paddling and uttered an oath of reproach. "How could I have been so foolish! Samuel, Mary, we must turn back. There is something I've forgotten to do."

Despite their protests, they helped her to turn around the canoe, battling the slow, strong current to make their way back to the island.

"Samuel, come with me. Mary, hold this canoe safe. We shan't be long."

The pair stole back to the grisly campsite. All was as they had left it minutes before. And with no more hesitation than the Indians had showed when they killed her friends and murdered her baby, Hannah snatched a knife from the belt of one of the dead warriors, grasped his greased hair, lifted his bloodied head, and sawed away the top of the Indian's scalp. Samuel did the same to three other adult Indians, as Hannah turned her attention to the six remaining dead, all children, sprawled where they were struck by the tomahawks.

For a brief moment, she stayed her bloodied hand, the knife blade dripping black in the night. Then she thought of all that had been taken from her own family, from her friends. Together, she and Samuel finished the fiendish task. When they were done, she wrapped the fresh scalps in a ragged hunk of cloth the Indians had ripped from her own loom when they looted her house.

They ran back to the canoe, and as Hannah climbed into the stern, Mary peered behind her, looking close at the sopping bundle. "What is that? Oh, Hannah, no, you didn't. . . ."

Hannah grunted. "Our story will carry more weight now. Besides, they may fetch a price and would have been wasted otherwise. It may make them think twice about attacking us in the future."

"You don't know them as I do," said Samuel. Then they all grew silent as they leaned into the hard task of putting distance between themselves and the gory scene.

⁂

It took the trio nearly a week to reach Haverhill, where they had a joyous reunion with their families. They learned that in the raid twenty-seven people had been killed and thirteen taken captive.

The three former Indian captives received overwhelming fanfare and accolades. Thomas Duston appealed to the government in Boston for compensation for losses suffered and for a revival of the government bounties paid for Indian scalps.

Mary Neff and Samuel Lennardson were each awarded 12 pounds, 10 shillings. Thomas Duston was awarded 25 pounds, on his wife's behalf. The story suitably impressed people throughout the colonies, and it so impressed the governor of Maryland that he sent Hannah an inscribed silver tankard. Samuel Lennardson was eventually reunited with his father in Connecticut and settled there, marrying and raising a family.

Not only is Hannah Duston the first woman in the United States to have a statue erected in her honor, but there are actually two statues of her. One is on the island in Boscawen, New Hampshire, where the scalpings took place. In one hand she holds a tomahawk, while the other hand clutches a number of scalps. The other statue, in Haverhill, Massachusetts, shows her holding a tomahawk while reaching, grim-faced, toward an unseen captor.

Apparently, abiding love of one's children is not necessarily a trait that ran in Hannah Duston's family. Her father was widely known as an abusive parent and was called before the court on more than one occasion for excessive violence toward his children. And her sister, Elizabeth Emerson, murdered her own illegitimate twin infants. She was convicted of the crime and was hanged.

7

BOON ISLAND'S CURSE

(1710)

On December 11, 1710, the Nottingham Galley *wrecks on this barren rock six miles off the coast of York, Maine. Fourteen crewmen survive, but two die of injuries and two others drown. The remaining ten cling to life for twenty-four days in midwinter, without fire, by eating what meat is available.*

❧

"S wede . . . Swede!" George White shook his friend's shoulder hard. The man stirred, slowly opened his eyes, and within seconds he grimaced in terror. The cold sliced through him. He had hoped this wasn't happening, but he knew now this was no dream. "God, Georgie, why didn't you let me die?" Swede flopped back to the bare rock, his head bouncing.

"That is no way to think, man. We're alive! And unhurt . . . most of us."

After a few moments, the prone man licked his lips and said, "How many of us made it?"

White leaned in close. "All of us."

"All fourteen?" The man raised himself up on his elbows.

"Aye. But the carpenter is not well. He has a head injury, a snapped leg, and he can't seem to move at all, only his eyes. And when he tries to speak, he sounds as if he's gagging." He shifted and dragged himself closer to his companion. "There's nothing left of the *Nottingham*. She's broken up, and this island is naught but rock—with nothing but a bit of sailcloth for shelter."

"We must be near the mainland."

"We are, man. See for yourself."

With much effort, Swede sat up and shielded his eyes. He stared for some time and then nodded. "We can make that." He turned to his friend. "What's more, we have to. Look at this!" He motioned about them, at the gray sky, the chopping surf, the barren rock, the flopped bodies of their shipmates. "We'll die within days. And I don't know about you, Georgie, but I have no desire to starve or freeze to death here on this filthy rock."

With his rag-wrapped hand, filthy and crusted with blood from cuts and scrapes sustained from the wreck, he slammed the unyielding gray mass beneath him.

"Count on me, Swede. We can make a raft from what's left of the wreck."

∞

"Oh, sweet Lord." The speaker raised a hand to his scabbed lips. "The raft has swamped." Ten living men were arrayed, standing and seated, along the thin western end of the island. None of them needed their fellow to point out what had happened, for they all saw it. Each of them had been sorely tempted to join the men on the raft. They envied the two bold souls who struck out on their own, even if the raft was a ramshackle affair, barely big enough to accommodate them, and with only a splintered length of planking to help steer.

Some of the men on the shore wept openly, not even shrouding their eyes as they scanned the vicious December chop of the Atlantic. The cloudy edge of the mainland was teasingly within reach, but the never-ceasing waves made the six-mile stretch before them seem like an impossible journey.

"Maybe they'll make it back," said the captain's mate, Christopher Langman. He staggered to his feet and ran forward, ignoring the slopping water wetting his frostbitten feet. "Swim! Swim back!" He waved his arms above his head, but he soon dropped them to his sides in exhaustion. He turned back to the cluster of nine men. "I don't see them." He turned back to the water. "Do any of you see them?"

They watched the man, their haggard, bearded faces showing the desperation he voiced. But they also knew that their friends were already dead in the numbing December water.

Captain John Deane, a tall, hunched fellow who had never been too close to any of them—he was from Suffolk; that was all most of them knew—limped forward and put a hand on the man's shoulder. "They're gone, Langman, and will not be back. God bless 'em."

"No! No, no. . . ."

The men turned from the sea and trudged back up the jagged slope of rock to the highest point, barely the height of two or three men above sea level. No one spoke.

Boon Island Light Tower. Diminutive though it may be, at four hundred square yards in size and a mere fourteen feet above sea level, and with no soil or vegetation, Maine's Boon Island nonetheless has sported a signal beacon in one form or another since 1799. Through the centuries, keepers and their families withstood severe weather while living there, including seventy-foot waves in 1932. During the Great Blizzard of 1978, the storm was so intense that the keeper and his family retreated up the 133-foot tower—the tallest in New England—and were airlifted off the island the next day. The light has been automated since then. *Courtesy Library of Congress*

At the far, eastern end of the island, the men tried to avert their eyes from the stiff bodies of their two comrades, both of whom had succumbed to their injuries within days of the *Nottingham*'s wreck.

∽

"What do you think we'll do, Langman?" Captain Deane said. "I don't see that you've caught all that many fish, have you?" The captain looked more like a stick than a man, and despite his unusual height, he stood stooped and measured his words as if he had just run a great distance. The other men looked no better. Their clothes hung in tatters, and their feet and hands were wrapped in filthy rags. They all shivered and twitched from the cold. Huddling in groups, they hugged each other in hopes of finding some warmth.

"We've all tried," Langman said in a softer tone. "But the fish and the few birds are too fast for us. And every day we grow weaker."

The captain shook his head, bent down again over the dead carpenter, and continued peeling strips of frozen meat from the shriveled, snapped leg before him. His hands shook as much from horror as from the unceasing cold and desperate hunger. Tears brimmed in his eyes and rolled down his long, scabbed nose.

"Come around, men," the captain said in a cracked, raised voice. "And take this meat. It is nothing more than a way to sustain yourselves, for it is our duty to keep ourselves alive as long as we may. Someone is bound to rescue us."

Deane knew that unless he maintained the helm, his men would not follow, perhaps not until it was too late to do any good. He stood, still clutching the broken-bladed knife, and ran his sleeve across his nose and mouth. The men's eyes were on him, he knew, but he didn't meet their gaze. Instead he stuffed a hunk of frozen meat into his mouth and squeezed his eyes shut. He chewed forcefully, knowing that the men were judging him on this very act.

He straightened his back and stood as tall as he could. And though the meat was just a frozen bit of something to chew and held nearly no flavor, he fought with all his drained strength the urge to gag and spit out the life-giving meat. He swallowed, nodded his head as if in agreement with someone, and opened his eyes.

Slowly, more slowly than their physical condition demanded, the men filed over to the two frozen bodies. The captain bent again to the task at hand.

❧

"This might not be so bad if . . . if we had some way of making a fire. That's all we need . . . a little heat and this would have a fair taste, I dare say. . . ."

"Langman." The captain rested his long, thin hand on the young man's shoulder. He leaned in close, his voice gravelly and hard. "Do not forget what it is you are doing. Do not speak of this task so lightly."

The young man nodded and kept his mouth pinched tight, sudden shame flowering on his face. "Yes, sir."

❧

The small fishing schooner had ventured out farther from shore than it needed to, but it was a fine, clear day in early January with calm seas. Late-morning sun glinted off the low, blue-black swells, and the skipper felt he had let her run a bit. Off in the distance he could just make out the rock.

"Boon Island, they call it." He nodded toward it.

"Why Boon?" said his brother.

"Oh, 'bout thirty years ago, in 1682, I believe it was, a coastal trader, the *Increase,* wrecked there. Four men spent a long summer month on that unforgiving rock."

"What's there now?"

"Nothing. And more of the same."

"Take her in closer, eh?"

"Why not?"

A few minutes passed as the small ship cut through the water. The skipper's brother held the brass spyglass to his eye and squinted through it. "I thought you said there was nothing out there."

"There isn't. It's a barren place, rock and nothing more. Birds in summer."

"I swear I see something moving out there."

"Seals or birds."

"No, bigger, taller than that."

"Let me see." The skipper took the spyglass and scrunched his red, weathered cheeks. "Dear God. I think I see . . . people? But it cannot be!"

The closer they drew, the more agitated the figures became. Finally, the little fishing schooner was well within sight, and the skipper saw that indeed there were men on that little spit of rock, ragged men like spirits, waving their arms and slowly moving back and forth. Some of the men were prone, raising arms and nothing more. Some of them were bent, kneeling, their hands clasped together as if praying.

⁓

While Boon Island's most famous wreck is that of the Nottingham Galley, *the 300-by-700-foot mass of raw granite rock, which has an elevation of fourteen feet above sea level, has hosted numerous other wrecks. The first recorded shipwreck was that of the* Increase, *a coastal trader, in the summer of 1682. Four men lived there for a month, subsisting on birds' eggs and fish. Smoke from their fire was seen from the mainland, and as they considered their rescue a "boon from God," the island was thus christened. For years after the* Nottingham Galley's *survivors were rescued, local fishermen left barrels of provisions on Boon—in anticipation of future wrecks.*

The island has been home to a series of beacons, lighthouses, buildings, and keepers and their families. The first two lighthouses on Boon, dating from 1799, were destroyed in storms. The current tower, built in 1855, is the tallest in New England, at 133 feet.

One nineteenth-century keeper died during a storm, and his wife kept the light in operation, only to lose her mind through grief and loneliness. She was found weeks later wandering the little island. She died shortly thereafter. Another Boon Island lightkeeper, William Williams, liked the quiet life there so much that he spent twenty-seven years as its keeper. During World War II, the families of two Coast Guard keepers watched from atop the tower as a German submarine surrendered to the U.S. Coast Guard.

The blizzard of 1978 hit the island hard, bringing the raging surf up and over it. The keeper's house, built in 1899, and other outbuildings were destroyed, and the light-house was battered hard enough that hunks of it were ripped away. The keepers retreated up the tower and were rescued the next day by helicopter. Since then, the light has been automated and now runs on solar power.

In February 1944, the 438-foot British freighter Empire Knight *ran hard aground on Boon Island and broke in two. The stern section, containing the cargo hold, settled on the bottom, at 260 feet, a mile and a half from the island. In 1990 records indicated that the* Empire Knight *had been transporting mercury on its fatal trip forty-six years before. It was then determined that the barrels containing the mercury had long since deteriorated, releasing the toxic cargo. Official word is that the mercury, all 16,000 pounds of it, has settled in the bottom of the hold.*

8

PIRATE TREASURE
(1717)

Captain "Black Sam" Bellamy and his buccaneers capture the treasure-laden, three-masted Whydah. *Months later, on April 27, 1717, as the crew nears its home port of Cape Cod, a tempest strikes with seventy-mile-per-hour gales and forty-foot waves. The ship's timbers begin to crack.*

◦◦◦

It has been a long year, thought Samuel Bellamy as he looked about him, still awed by his situation. Never has a man done so well in such a short amount of time, of that he was convinced. As if to confirm this for himself, in his mind he recounted the capture of a lifetime—this very ship, the *Whydah*, a three-hundred-ton, triple-masted English slaver barely a year old. The *Whydah*'s captain had just sold a load of slaves, and the ship was brimming to the gunwales with gold, jewels, and countless valuables when they ran it down. It had taken them three days to do so, and then Bellamy had seized the massive beauty for himself. That had been in February, just two months ago. He smiled at the memory.

He had immediately fitted the ship out with an additional ten guns to bolster its already stout collection of eighteen cannons. The *Whydah* was truly an impressive raiding vessel. Now its hold was loaded with an additional thirty cannons, plus the plunder of nearly fifty ships, and followed by the *Mary Anne*, captained by his best friend, the able Paul Williams. Yes, life was good. He smiled as he thought of the one thing that would make his life perfect—he would soon see her, his lovely Maria Hallett. Then he would show her parents that he was worthy of her hand!

"Captain Sam."

Bellamy roused from his reverie and looked to the speaker, the powerful, half-blooded Mosquito Islands Indian, the equal of whom he had not yet come across. So impressive and quick in his learning was John Julian that Bellamy had made him pilot of the *Whydah*, his latest, best, and, he hoped, last conquest. "Yes, John?"

40

"I don't like the look of that fog." The pirate king followed the man's pointing hand toward a black, roiling mass far in the distance. "And this wind, the chop it's raising is not a good sign."

"We'll take the necessary precautions, but these are things we cannot change, John."

The big pilot nodded his head and said, "We're headed dead for it. My guess is by midnight."

Bellamy laughed. "John, this ship is 105 feet long and loaded with the weight of our plunder, her own twenty-eight guns, and thirty more stored belowdecks. She will plow a furrow through any storm the seas can dish out." He turned to go below. "Besides," he said over his shoulder, "I am on my way back to see the good Maria Hallett, and nothing will stop Black Sam Bellamy from appearing on her doorstep ere another day has passed!" With a satisfied laugh he disappeared below.

John Julian said nothing but stared straight ahead into the descending dark, the approaching fog, and the stiffening wind portending a coming storm.

∽

John Julian knew it was near midnight, though there was no moon. And tonight, the blackest hour proved to be a vicious thing, indeed. "It's a nor'easter, captain!"

Bellamy nodded. The wind battered them both and carried with it slicing rain and pelting sleet, mounding up at their feet and causing the bustling crew of 144 to lose their footing on the slick deck.

"We are drifting, captain, and I can't do a thing about it. We've pulled down our cloth, but it's done no good. . . ."

The captain nodded as he wrestled with the ship's wheel, knowing the weather would have its way with them. They had drifted close to shore, though he couldn't tell how far they were from the unforgiving shoals off the Cape.

His answer came in seconds, as the *Whydah*'s port side slammed hard, as if driven from starboard by a mighty hand, pitching the ship toward shore. The yawing bulk of the *Whydah* groaned, and men hollered all about him, the fear in their voices rising above any bravado they still had. Sand! They had grounded on a shoal—damnable sand!

They were not far from shore, nor in water any deeper than their keel—surely less than twenty feet. For even through the slashing rains and driving winds, Bellamy thought he could see the weak, wavering points of light from what must have been homes, or perhaps swinging lanterns from townsfolk, but a few hundred feet away.

And even as the growling power of the nor'easter worked its unstoppable will over the groaning ship, even as he barked orders and pushed the men to do their utmost in the face of terror and hopelessness, Bellamy thought of little else but his dear Maria.

He sensed the tremors under his feet, running through the vast slabs of decking like shivers from a deathbed even before he heard the moans that ran from her keel straight up the masts. And that's when Black Sam Bellamy knew that all was lost, that his beloved new raider, the *Whydah*, would be no more, for her masts would soon be gone.

Wind like none he had ever experienced whistled from down the coast at them, forcing each man to turn away from it lest it pluck the eyes from his face. The waves, cresting up the height of the masts, curled over the ship like great hands, clawing down on them from forty feet on high. And in the brief lull between waves, the men saw fewer of their fellows on deck in the shrieking gloom.

After the moans came a cracking like a thousand trees swept aside under a giant's hand. The mainmast, with its ragged rigging and furled canvas, trembled one last time and then snapped. It was as if the *Whydah* had waited for this moment. She groaned and slowly, surrendering to a decision not her own, listed and slid seaward, another wave driving straight at the rising deck.

In the last moments before the ship was dragged below, through sheets of wind-driven surf and keening wind, Bellamy heard the screams of his trapped, crushed men. Gripping the rising port rail, Captain Black Sam Bellamy howled raw rage into the teeth of the mighty gale, howled for Maria and a life unlived, even as he rode the great vibrating hulk of the *Whydah* down into the fierce, roiling torment of the sea.

⚬⟋◦

In its last moments, what had begun as a slow roll became a violent slam seaward as the mass of tons of pillaged goods and almost sixty cannons, more than half of them stored in the Whydah's *hold, shifted as the ship capsized. The decks burst apart, and within seconds the gutted ship collapsed and sank, leaving a trail of wreckage strewn along the ocean floor for four miles.*

The day following the storm, the shoreline along *Eastham* was littered with the corpses of 102 pirates. And though the coastline was also strewn with enough washed-up goods to keep wreckers busy for days to come, none of the Whydah's real treasure was recovered at that time.

According to testimony given by the two surviving members of the 144-man crew of the Whydah, it had been carrying, in addition to other valuables such as ivory and sugar, between four and five tons of gold, silver, jewels, and jewelry, all divided among 180 fifty-pound sacks stored belowdecks in chests.

Most of this loot went unrecovered until the ship's discovery in 1984 by ocean explorer Barry Clifford, who in the coming decades would continue to recover artifacts—200,000 of them to date—and treasure from the wreck. He has since founded the Whydah Pirate Museum in Provincetown, Massachusetts, so that the public may learn more about life at sea—and the lives of pirates—in seventeenth- and eighteenth-century New England. The wreck of the Whydah is the only significant pirate treasure ever recovered.

Doubling the tragedy of the Whydah's sinking is the fact that another ship in Bellamy's fleet also sank in the storm that night, seven miles south. Seven men survived that wreck. Of the nine survivors of the two wrecks, six were tried in Boston and hanged for piracy, though King Charles had already signed an order some weeks prior, pardoning all pirates.

One man, Thomas Davis, who had been pressed into service under Bellamy and had become carpenter aboard the Whydah, was pardoned. John Julian, thought to be no older than sixteen at the time of the wreck, was imprisoned and, because of his race, sold into slavery. Julian was of mixed race—part black, part Mosquito Islands Indian—and was the first recorded black man to operate as a pirate in the New World. He was bought by John Quincy, grandfather of future U.S. president and abolitionist John Quincy Adams. Known thereafter as "Julian, the Indian," the Whydah's former pilot was executed in 1733 for murdering a bounty hunter sent to retrieve him after one of his many escape attempts. Julian's body was given to medical students for dissection.

Black Sam Bellamy, so named because he eschewed the fashionable powdered wigs of the time and instead wore his long black hair uncovered and pulled back in a ponytail, was often called the Prince of Pirates and the Robin Hood of the High Seas. He had an endearing habit of sparing crews of the ships he captured and offering them work as hands in his own employ. A good many took him up on this offer.

It is said that Samuel Bellamy's lover, Maria "Goody" Hallett, witnessed the wreck that night from high atop the cliffs. For years afterward, she roamed the coastline, searching for her beloved pirate. Eventually she was condemned as a witch and killed. Hallett's spirit is said to still walk the cliffs of Wellfleet, near the wreck site, looking out to sea toward her lover's watery grave.

9

THE BRUTALITY OF NED LOW

(1723)

Angry after a narrow defeat in which he lost most of his crew, his flagship, and a fortune aboard her, pirate Captain Ned Low captures a Boston whaler eighty miles offshore, tortures the crew, steals their food, and sets them adrift to starve. And still he's not satisfied.

✍

Y ou will, you scab! You will!" Captain Ned Low's rage bulged his eyes, purpled his neck and forehead, and distended his nostrils. He clapped the cowering man before him with another hearty blow to the ear. The man's legs buckled, but his hands were tied and his arms were gripped firmly by sailors with unsure smiles on their grimy faces.

"I won't. . . . I can't." The imprisoned man sagged and wept, his sweaty features a soft mask of sorrow, the side of his head a welted knot from the near-constant beating he had been receiving for the past five minutes.

The abusing pirate stood back, his eyebrows arched high, his mouth an exaggerated frown. "He 'won't,' he says. He 'can't,' he says." Low looked about him at the ragged men who were his crew. "He will not do it. Will not tell me where the ship's gold is kept."

"There is no gold. I tell you there is no gold!" The man wept on, sobs pulsing from his bloodied face. "We're a fishing vessel, that's all. A whaler. No money on board."

"Then that's all the worse for you. For you told me something I cannot abide. The words 'can't' and 'won't.'"

All was quiet, and the stricken man finally looked up, curious about the lull in the proceedings. What he saw made his tear-streaked face blanch.

Ned Low held up a blade, longer than a knife, though not quite a sword. But it carried a sharp edge, of that he was sure.

"What are you going to do? What are—"

The captain's free hand lashed upward and clamped the man's lips tight together as if he were squeezing a bee to death. He shook his head no. "I'll make a deal with you. If you tell me you can't or won't do something once more, I will run you through." He paused, waiting for the man to

A Buccaneer *by Alfred Rudolph Waud.* Since 1623, when Dixie Bull became New England's first official pirate, New England's coastline has teemed with piratical activity, as the Northeast had so many ports of trade. Blackbeard buried a great stash of silver bars on an island off Portsmouth, New Hampshire, but to date it has not been found—unlike the wreck of the *Whydah,* off Massachusetts, the largest verified pirate wreck and treasure ever recovered. But no pirate who sailed New England waters was so brutal—and so mad—as Nasty Ned Low, who once sliced off a sailor's ears and forced the man to eat them . . . before killing him. *Courtesy Library of Congress*

respond. The man breathed hard through his nose, snot pooling on Low's fingertips. Low yanked up and down on the man's lips, nodding the man's head for him.

"I am pleased to see you agree with me. Good. Now, if you never again utter the word 'won't' in my presence, you will live. Is that understood?"

Again, he worked the man's head up and down as if he were working a child's toy.

He let go of the man's lips, frowned at the goo running from his fingertips, and wiped them on his breeches. "Salt, please? Someone bring me salt." He looked up at his men, who stared back at him as if he had asked for someone to make the ship fly instead of sail.

He sighed, and quick as a slap, his relaxed features contorted and purpled again. He screamed, spittle spraying the faces of those nearest him, "Salt! Bring me salt! I daresay you'll find it in the galley!"

Salt was retrieved in short order. Low received it with a half-smile and a slight bow. "Now then, my guest. It has occurred to me that perhaps you are not yourself just now. I can't help but wonder if a meal might help you to relax. Hmm?"

The man merely stared and trembled, his pinched lips now bunched and puckered from the twisting and pinching they had received.

The speed with which Captain Low's hand and blade flashed upward was impressive. Before the captive or his minders grasped what was happening, Low had slipped the blade straight down in one clean swipe and held up a glistening nut-brown ear. The man screamed. The gathered crew was silent. Captain Ned Low gasped as if in sheer shock at what had happened.

Then he made to repeat the process with the other ear, but the man jerked his head away, screaming the entire time, his ragged cries hoarser than ever.

"Someone cover his mouth. Someone else grip him tight by the hair." Ned Low wagged the glistening blade at two men in instruction. "Now, where was I? Oh, yes." He began slicing off the other ear but stopped halfway and said, "Did you hear something?" Then he tossed back his head and howled like a hermit in a seaside cave.

"There now," said Low as he studied the two bloodied ears on his palm. "I always like to use a pinch of salt on my food. It does so enhance the flavor, don't you agree?"

But the man to whom he spoke was too busy pushing out ragged screams and half-formed words that no one could make out.

Low's face became stony once again. He drove a hand into the salt cellar and smeared the gray stuff into the bloodied flesh of the severed ears. "Now, a question: Will you join me for a snack?"

The horror on the prisoner's face held at bay every other emotion roiling inside him.

Low barked a laugh. "Oh, that's good. I do so hate to eat alone." He held up one of the ears, a salt-crusted knob of blood and rubbery flesh. "Will you snack with me?" He held it closer to the man's mouth.

The prisoner shook his head, his eyes wide. He tried to back away, but strong arms held him firm. Without knowing they were doing so, the assembled pirates held their hands over their mouths. No one said a thing, but no one looked away.

"No! No, no, no, no! I won't do it, I won't, I won't—" Sudden realization stopped the man's raving. The entire deck was silent.

Low tilted his head to one side. "I thought we discussed this little matter, sir? I can see you are not a man of your word. Well, if there is one thing that can be said about Captain Ned Low, scourge of the world's seas, it's that I do keep my word."

He jammed the ears into the prisoner's mouth, clapped a hand over the mouth, and yelled, "His nose! Pinch the bugger's nose!" A wide, grimy hand reached in and did as the captain bid.

In less than a minute, the man swallowed the mouthful of ears, his own ears.

Low stood back, wiping his hands on his leggings, and said, "There now, was that so difficult?"

He strutted the deck for a moment. Then he spun on the man and said, "Now, remember when I said I am a man of my word? Yes? Well, good. Because you made me a promise, and I promised that if you broke that promise, I would kill you. Well, sir, by my recollection, you are a breaker of sacred oaths. And so. . . ."

He flicked the thin blade outward and rammed it to the hilt in the man's naked gut, pulled it out halfway, and sliced across. The man stared down as his guts pushed out, hung for a moment as if hesitating, and then spilled downward, slapping to the deck. He swayed a moment, a gurgling sound rising in his throat, his eyes wide. Low stared back at him, his own eyes wide in mockery. Even as he did this, he pulled his pistol, cocked it, held it to the man's forehead, and smiled as he pulled the trigger. The percussive echo rolled across the becalmed sea, eighty miles from shore.

"Search the ship. Then burn it." Low stalked off down the deck and then stopped. As he spun around, his men froze, not daring to look at him. "On second thought, my boys, take everything of value, and most importantly, everything that is edible, slash the rigging, cripple the mast, and throw the sails overboard. Then set the crew adrift. Yes, that will do nicely."

As he stalked away, he muttered, "Serves them right for having nothing of value for Captain Ned Low when he comes calling."

❧

On July 19, 1723, twenty-six of Ned Low's pirate gang were hanged by the law near Newport, Rhode Island's Long Wharf. They were then buried on Goat Island, outside Newport Harbor, between high- and low-tide lines. Low's anger was intense at having lost his flagship, Ranger, and with it his right-hand man, plus a good many crew members and most of his fortune, to the HMS Greyhound, a ship sent forth with the sole purpose of capturing Low and his gang.

After he set adrift the Boston whaler, Low attacked three fishing boats off the coast of Rhode Island. He decapitated the captain of the first, sent the crew ashore, and burned the boat. His inconsolable rage fed his urge to torture. By the time he captured two more fishing boats, he had become so violent that his crew refused to partake in the tortures he ordered, and he was forced to move on.

The New England coast fairly teemed with privateers, pirates, and piratical activity during the seventeenth and eighteenth centuries, the period that has most influenced our current perceptions of pirates. However, self-styled Captain Edward "Ned" Low is still considered the most brutal and bloodthirsty of the pirates operating during this era.

When in northern waters, Low was known to haunt the New England coast, particularly from the Isle of Shoals off the coast of New Hampshire northward to Nova Scotia, looting and then burning ships. These wrecks still attract treasure seekers today.

In June 1722, while sailing northeast waters, Low confronted the crews of thirteen New England fishing vessels. He told them that unless they surrendered, no quarter would be accorded them—and they surrendered. He kept the largest for his new flagship. Then he pillaged and burned the rest, forcing the sailors to join him or die.

One of the sailors pressed into service that day, Philip Ashton, a native of Marblehead, Massachusetts, escaped from Low in March 1723 while in Honduras and made it to uninhabited Roatan Island. There he lived as a real-life Robinson Crusoe for sixteen months.

He had refused to sign Low's ship's articles, binding him to the life of a pirate. For this he was beaten, whipped, chained in the hold, and repeatedly threatened with death.

That he lived through this, and then escaped, only to live as a castaway before being picked up by a ship from his native state, says much about the hardiness of this New England man. Ashton later wrote an account of his ordeal, but it seemed so fantastic that many readers considered it fiction.

Though he operated as a pirate for just three years, Ned Low packed in enough swashbuckling piracy for five lives. During that short length of time, he captured approximately a hundred ships, most of which he burned. It seems that his brutality knew no bounds—and often went unchecked, so afraid were his crew.

Among his incidents of torture: A Portuguese ship's captain dropped a bag full of gold into the sea rather than see it fall into Low's clutches. For this Low cut off the man's lips with his cutlass, broiled them, and fed them to the gagging captain—before murdering the man's crew. Another time he burned alive a French cook because he felt the man was "greasy and would fry well." It is also recorded that when he captured the Spanish galleon Montcova, he personally slaughtered fifty-three of its crew (most of them officers), but not before forcing one to eat the heart of another before killing him.

Though his demise is the subject of debate, the version most accepted is that his own crew finally set him adrift in an open boat without provisions. Two days later a French ship rescued him, but upon discovering who he was, the French gave him a short trial and hanged him in 1724 in Martinique.

10

THE MEETINGHOUSE TRAGEDY
(1773)

On a fine September 7, in 1773, the people of Wilton, New Hampshire, gather to raise a new meetinghouse. But the dream becomes a nightmare when a huge center roofbeam gives way, dropping fifty-three workers three stories to the ground and collapsing tons of trusswork, joists, and tools on them.

⸎

The rich, spiced scent of fresh-baked, Dutch apple pie curled its way over to George Lancey's nostrils. He smiled, knowing it was his Elizabeth's pie that he smelled, of all the others laid out on the tables off to the side of the building lot. Had to be—hers was the best he had ever tasted. He drew the adze back for one last swing at the beam he had been shaping on the ground between his feet. Thick, curling wood chips were ankle deep, and the tamarack and hemlock he worked gave off rich, tangy wood smells.

He paused a moment and turned his head toward where he had last seen Liz, who was soon to give birth to their fourth child. He secretly worried about her, going into the cold months with a young one; what's more, he had only spotty opportunities for work just now.

But today there was little of that worry on his mind. He peered upward at the mass of trusswork above him that was taking shape—for what seemed hundreds of feet above and in all directions, men swung along massive rough-hewn beams, stopping here and there to pound in oak pegs, fit together corner trussing, and step from one beam to another. They were sure-footed and strong, to a man. Good company, indeed.

And there was his Liz. God, but she was a pretty one. And with warm sun and fine friends all around . . . and soon, good food. He saw the light blue of Liz's calico dress, the smooth rise of her cheek, downy like a young apple peeking from beneath her sunbonnet, and her hands resting on the swell of her belly. He hoped it was another boy; but if it was a girl, he hoped it would be like her. She laughed at something one of the two women standing with her said. Then two things happened at once.

As Liz turned, her eyes met his, and though it was a warm, cloudless September afternoon, the seventh day of the month, a sound like a lightning strike filled the air above. Before he had time to raise his head, he saw the smile slip from his wife's face, her brown eyes widening in horror.

∽

Straddling the mighty ridgepole, nearly thirty feet up in the air, Abe Winkler had to admit that there were few finer ways to spend such a glorious day. He took a deep breath and surveyed the burgeoning town. He had been here since 1761—the year before the town got its name—twelve years next month. With his wife, Prudence, and their three children, they had staked claim to a fifty-acre parcel north of town and had arrived so late in the fall that he was sure they would either starve or freeze. But neither had happened. And as he and his wife and children had prospered, so it seemed had the town.

But the years since hadn't been as good to them as he had hoped. Within a few years, Samuel, his only boy, had died of an infection from a wound he had gotten when he fell off Old Stout, their draft horse. Then six years ago cholera had taken his Prue.

But his two girls, bless them, were both married now, and here he was, working on this new meetinghouse with his sons-in-law. Far below were his girls, and their young ones, too—his grandchildren. Life was indeed rich again. He was proud to know that this new meetinghouse would have special meaning to these young people and that he was here to help make it so.

He recalled the last meeting they had had a month before at which they had finally voted on whether to build the new meetinghouse. Unlike so many meetings that ended up in sour looks and arguments that never seemed to end, this one had been a happy affair, with the men nodding in agreement.

Prue would have loved this day, thought Abe Winkler as he looked about from where he sat on top of the world, waiting for the Schmidt brothers to peg their end of the ridgepole. And it occurred to him, as everyone else was hunched over, that if he sat up straight, he would be the highest person in the town, and perhaps beyond. Even if only for just that moment.

He stretched his back, feeling a slight chill as his sweat dried, and heard the jeers and good-natured shouts of the men. Far below, he saw children romping on the grassy lawn surrounding the old meetinghouse. Nearby, the women of the town had just laid out what looked like scores of pies and tarts. And he spied crocks of cider and baskets of apples. The year's crop was already bountiful. Everyone looked so happy—there didn't seem to be a frowning face among them.

His eyes trailed from the lawn over into the raw-wood framework of the structure taking shape below him. It would be a fine meetinghouse, the best in the region, if he had any say in the matter. Just under him, he saw the massive pole that two-score men had labored to raise into position to hold aloft the very ridgepole upon which he sat. But now, that mammoth trunk, still with bark on, was moving away from the spot it was wedged. Falling, it looked like. But that couldn't be the case. . . .

Abe didn't understand. Was someone beneath it, playing a game? The next instant, the ridgepole on which he and a half dozen others straddled seemed to settle. A sudden loud crack resounded, the like of which he had never heard, not even when felling a huge white pine. This was starker and more biting.

Any words Abe thought to utter never came, for the ridgepole collapsed under them. He saw more than fifty men all about him with the same look of shock on their faces as the great wood frame, like a web all about them, caved in the middle, from the ridgepole downward, dragging with it all the men he knew. He knew they must be bellowing as much as he, but there was no sound save for the almighty snapping and tearing of beams as they drove down into one another.

As Abe dropped, he heard his own voice push from him, sounding like an echo in a cave, and it was soon drowned out by loud, crashing, ripping sounds that didn't make any sense.

❧

Within seconds it was over. For the length of time it takes to draw in a breath, nothing could be heard but one small beam as it shifted and clunked onto its side. Then the air filled with screams of agony from men crushed and pinned beneath weighty hemlock beams and with screams of terror from wives and children and more than half of the men who had been working at various tasks away from the center of the building. A goodly portion of the structure had caved in on itself because the center support pole, in this case a stout tree, had kicked out of its footing. And then all was lost.

The men working on the ground and in the framework in the midst of the structure fared the worst, as massive, twelve-inch-square timbers dropped down on them. People watching the progress saw that once the supporting pole let go, the center beam, with nothing to support it, snapped. And suddenly, down fell the sweat-soaked men who straddled it, along with their hammers, hatchets, adzes, and axes. Without the support of the central beam, the walls had nothing to hold them upright, and they too toppled under the slamming weight of the timbers from above.

When Abe came to, he throbbed with more pain than he had ever known. He saw a face lean close over his, and then the center of that face grew smaller until it disappeared. The roar in his ears was nothing more than the sound of the ocean swelling and receding, over and over again. And that was the last he knew.

⌘

Of the 120 men working on the structure, 53 workers plunged three stories to the ground, and tons of trusswork, planks, joists, and metal tools collapsed down on them. Five died, and all the others were injured, many seriously.

A letter depicts one eyewitness account: "[The horror] cannot be described; and could only be equaled by the blood and brains, shrieks and groans of the dead and wounded. . . . Of the fifty-three that fell, not one escaped without broken bones, terrible bruises or wounds from the axes."

Wilton resident George Lancey was one of the five men killed, leaving behind his wife, Elizabeth, who was six months pregnant with their fourth child. Another of his fellow builders that day was Simeon Wright, whose ankle was crushed by timbers. It healed poorly, and thirteen years later he accidentally reopened the old wound with an axe and bled to death.

Accidents in eighteenth-century New England were more likely to result in death or permanent disfigurement than are similar unfortunate events today. Common hazards included felled trees that bounced back and crushed or maimed the woodcutter, hydrophobia (rabies), bone breaks, frostbite, slipped axe heads, and much more.

There are numerous accounts of old people and toddlers in New England pioneer families pitching forward into the great fireplaces that dominated homes in the old days, usually with disastrous results. One Scottish immigrant wrote to his parents: "My little boy which has Been very unwill [sic] these two months he fell in the fire and Burnt one part of his Head."

Unfortunately for accident victims, medical treatment was often not available, as doctors were few and far between. And if a doctor could be tracked down, his remedies included such popular treatments as copious bleedings; doses of ground blister beetles; forced garglings with molasses, butter, and vinegar; and stockings hung round the neck and filled with salt pork, onions, and cow dung.

11

ANN STORY'S CAVE

(1775)

A falling tree kills her husband, Indians burn her cabin and crops—and yet Ann Story and her children continue to work their hard-won land. They sleep in a riverbank cave—until they are found by Tories. Her only hope lies with the far-off Green Mountain Boys.

✍

Amos Story felt a small glow of pride when he looked at what he and his eldest child, thirteen-year-old Solomon, had accomplished in a few short months. They had chosen the site well. And the cabin was a solid log affair with plenty of room for the entire family of five children, Ann, and himself. Plus, the clearing near the creek, ideal for planting, had plenty of daylight filtering down through the surrounding trees.

Amos intended to take down another six trees. Then he and his son could head back to Connecticut to retrieve the rest of the family and their goods, and he could relocate his brood to this rugged wilderness outpost that was to be their home.

Amos made a show of spitting on his hands and then winked at the boy. A few more bites with his trusted axe and he would have this surly old maple down. "Solomon! Be aware of the tree now."

"Yes, Father. I'm well away."

The forest echoed with the thick sound of Amos's axe sinking deep into the unforgiving rock maple. The hurried whacks of the blade were drowned out by what sounded to Solomon like the beginnings of a long, deep sigh. As he watched, envious that his father was the one to finish off the final strokes of each of the thick, mighty trees they felled, the tree seemed to stiffen as if it were a man shot in the back. Then it slowly pitched, dragging its branches against other trees as it dropped.

Amos scuttled backward and lost his balance just as the tree crashed against the stump-pocked clearing. The trunk bounced, then slammed down onto the thin man, and lay across his chest, pinning him to the earth. His head bounced as if it were a green apple dropped on a rock. Solomon screamed and bolted to his father's side. The man's chest was a squashed mess, like something that had burst, and his arms and legs were bent at odd angles.

Solomon knelt and laid his own face close to the man's mouth. "Father! Father, can you hear me?" Solomon wavered between screaming and grabbing his father and shaking him. The only thing he heard was the last of a faint breath pushing out of his father's bloodied mouth, and then he was alone in the big woods.

⌒∽

Ann Story saw Solomon glance toward the cave's entrance, then back to the coughing baby, Emma, the daughter of Esther Hamlin, a young pregnant woman and former Indian captive they had found lost in the woods not far from their cabin.

"That cough doesn't sound good, Mother. The Tories—"

She widened her eyes and shifted them quickly toward the four other children, sitting on upturned log chunks, playing at cat's cradle with Esther.

"Eat your supper, Solomon. There's little we can do until morning, except rest for the day ahead and give thanks that we're all still here and still safe."

He nodded, and for a moment as he stood, his hands pushing against his knees, she saw her Amos there in him, almost as if it were the briefest of visits. And over her washed measures of grief, exhaustion, and happiness at seeing him again, even if it was through their son. All still here, she repeated to herself. All except one.

She shifted little Emma in her arms and recalled Solomon's lone arrival back home in Connecticut, sooner than they had expected, and looking ragged. Even as she had looked beyond him into the yard, she knew she would never see her dear Amos again.

It must be the cave, with its damp rock and earthy smell, that made little Emma so croupy. But Ann had little choice. Should the Indians or Tories decide to fire the cabin again, they would have an escape route—her babies would not be trapped.

In the bankside brush they heard the heavy crunching of someone not taking care to disguise his footfalls. Certainly it was no Indian. Ann and the children froze, all except little Emma. Her loose coughs and discomfited crying were more than Ann could conceal.

Do Women Need Life Insurance? *by Roy F. Heinrich, 1942.* In 1775, despite severe hardships—a falling tree killed her husband, her cabin and crops were burned by Indians, and Tories constantly harassed her—Ann Story raised five children, continued to work her land, and supplied Ethan Allen's Green Mountain Boys with vital information that resulted in the capture of numerous Tories, earning her the title "Mother of the Green Mountain Boys." *National Life Insurance Company*

"What is this? Who's in there?" Someone slashed through the dense undergrowth close to the mouth of the cave they had carved in the riverbank of Otter Creek.

Her eyes met Solomon's.

"It's Ezekial Jenny, that foul Tory sympathizer!" he mouthed, fear and hatred colliding on his young features.

She nodded, even as the vile voice cracked their peace again. "I demand you show yourselves, in the name of the Crown!"

Two of the children whimpered. Their mother held up a hand, pointing one stern, work-calloused finger in warning, and they quieted themselves.

She motioned to Solomon to douse the light and then tend to the children. She looked to Esther, who nodded in assent to Ann's unspoken request. Then Ann Story crept to the low cave's entrance.

"Mother, no!" Solomon whispered, but he knew she would not be dissuaded.

He heard her push at the rough wooden door they had fashioned, then at the mass of brush and limbs they had piled there at the entrance. "It's only me, Mr. Jenny," she said, sounding thin and worried. A ruse, Solomon knew. And in her arms, little Emma cried and coughed.

It bothered Solomon to hear his mother chatting with this Loyalist swine. He felt his face flush and wished sorely he could take matters into his own hands—then they would have the man's weapon, and the world would be safer with one less Tory-lover in it.

From the rustling and snapping of twigs, it sounded as if the man were trying to push past her. "Where are these rebels you think you so cleverly hide? These Green Mountain Boys . . . I demand to know!"

Ann Story leaned as if burdened by a great weight. "Hush, child, hush," she said to the baby. "This man will not harm us."

Solomon heard a grunt from the Loyalist, but his demands continued. "I demand to know where the Green Mountain Boys are hiding! Tell me now, so help me, or I will shoot you!" The man raised his rifle to the woman's face.

From inside the cave, Solomon heard the hammer of the man's rifle click back into the deadliest position of all. Esther made a small sound, worried for her baby, and held the children tighter. Solomon shook his head and held a finger to his lips. Esther said nothing.

Despite the rage and fear warring within him, Solomon knew to trust his mother, and that he must keep the others quiet. Fortunately they seemed to know the importance of the situation and kept still.

"Ezekial Jenny, I have no fear of being shot by so consummate a coward as you. Now off with you and leave me alone!"

The man's ranting had lost its edge. He stomped and mumbled and eventually stalked off. Ann watched him for a long time and eventually scuttled back through the brush. As the day dawned, she led the children up through their subterranean passage and into the cabin.

Esther made breakfast while Ann summoned Solomon to her side. She ripped out a page from the Bible and scratched a note.

"Mother, the Bible!"

"Hush now, Solomon. I dare say we'll be forgiven. We've no time to waste. Now take this note to the Boys. Tell them we've learned a great deal. They will know what to do."

"But what did we learn?"

Ann smiled and leaned close to him. "Didn't you wonder where I went after he left us? Why it took me so long to return to the cave? I watched and followed that fool, Ezekial Jenny. I know what direction to send them after him. And he'll have a camp full of his kind, no doubt."

Solomon adjusted his belt and sheath knife. She pressed two biscuits into his hands and hugged him. "Be safe, my boy. But you must succeed. For I fear this is only the beginning. If we can best them early in the game, much will be gained by the feeling of success it will foster among the men in the militia."

Solomon stared at his mother for a few seconds. "You honestly surprise me, Mother, though I should not be. You're so wise. . . ."

She smiled. "If there's any wisdom in this, it is born of desperation. Now hurry, there's no time to waste. But be cautious, son." She kissed him on the forehead. He smiled and shook his head.

With a last look at his mother and the rest of the family, Solomon slipped with practiced ease into the cold of the early morning.

"He's so quiet, he could be an Indian," said Esther, standing beside Ann.

Ann Story watched him for as long as she was able, worrying over the fate of her family's freedom and the fate of her bold eldest child.

❦

The woman known to us as Ann Story began life as Hannah Ann Reynolds in Preston, Connecticut, on September 17, 1755. She married the first of her three husbands, Amos Story, when she was fourteen years old. They had five children together, and by the time she reached her early twenties, she was a widow. Undeterred by her spouse's untimely death, Ann stuck to their previous plans and moved to their homestead parcel of nearly unimproved land in Salisbury, New Hampshire Land Grants (later Vermont). The next year, in the spring of 1776, local Indians, who were British sympathizers, burned down the cabin her husband and son had built the previous year.

Scrappy as ever, Ann and her children rebuilt—but this time with escape for her family in mind. By this time Ann's household had expanded to include a wayward pregnant girl who had been an Indian captive on a forced march to Canada. The girl had fallen far behind, so the Indians left her to starve to death. Ann rescued her and helped her birth the baby.

As a much-valued aide to the renegade independent militia known as the Green Mountain Boys, Ann Story helped provide shelter and food and was an unsuspected liaison for message exchanges. When offering her services early during the Revolution, she said, "I cannot live to see my children murdered before my eyes. Give me a place among you and see if I am the first to desert my post."

It is this straightforward, no-nonsense demeanor and dedication to the colonists' cause that helped earn Ann Story the nickname of "Mother of the Green Mountain Boys," though a good number of them were her age or older.

The Green Mountain Boys were formed in the 1760s by Ethan Allen; his brother, Ira; and their two cousins, Seth Warner and Remember Baker, as a direct reaction to the worsening state of affairs between settlers in the New Hampshire Land Grant region—from the Connecticut River west to the New York border (now Vermont)—and the Crown-backed governments of New York and New Hampshire.

The Revolutionary War brought increased responsibilities for the Green Mountain Boys. Despite paltry troop numbers, in a single week in May 1775 they managed to capture three fortifications, including Fort Ticonderoga, Fort Crown Point, and Fort Saint-Jean. And what's more, the capture of Fort Ticonderoga occurred without a single shot fired.

12

BUNKER HOLE
(1775)

In a brazen move worthy of Robin Hood, Maine's Captain Jack Bunker hijacks a British ship full of food stolen from colonists. The British give hard chase, so Bunker runs the ship into a secret cove, cuts the masts, and waits for the worst.

❦

There she is." Jack Bunker's voice was nearly inaudible over the slap of the waves against the rocky shore to their right a dozen yards away. Indeed, his companion in the canoe, Rufus Twitchell, almost missed the comment altogether, as he was in the stern with his head down, digging hard with his paddle with each fresh gust from across the Sheepscot River. But he had heard his good friend, Cap'n Jack, who had rested his dripping paddle across the gunwales, his head tilted up and looking at something.

As they bobbed a few feet farther, into view came a British vessel, its Union Jack snapping in the fresh breeze. Broad of beam, the ship sat in the water like a big duck, tethered to the bottom less than a hundred yards offshore. And Rufus knew just what Bunker had in mind.

"Jack, please tell me plainly that you are not contemplating what I think you are. . . ."

"Rufus," said Bunker. "All up and down this coast, folks are starving. Our very families and friends at Somes Sound are starving. Why, your own children, the dearest little ones I've ever seen—save for my very own, of course—are like mewling kits denied the teat."

Rufus felt his face heat. "Friend or no, Jack, I'll not—"

Bunker held up a hand and smiled. "I did not say that to raise your hackles. I said it to persuade you to help me do what we came here to do." He resumed paddling. "If you still have the stomach for it." He said this last over a broad shoulder, already digging deep with his paddle.

Rufus scowled a moment more and had almost decided to crack his paddle over Bunker's head for good measure, when the man winked at him. "Won't it be fun?" Rufus knew there was no turning back. He had known it from the moment Jack burst in on him and Mary and the children eating their meager breakfast of boiled mush a few days back.

Despite the possibility of food that rightfully belonged to colonists and not as confiscated goods in the hold of a British ship, his Mary had tried to keep her husband from attempting the foolhardy errand with Bunker. Now that they had found their quarry, Rufus knew that nothing short of a British musket ball would stop Captain Jack Bunker, a militiaman and his closest friend since childhood, from stealing the British ship bobbing at anchor at the mouth of the Sheepscot River off Wiscasset.

∽

Rufus knew that their short trip, from the nub of a point, out of conceal-ment, then on to the lee side of the ship would be the most dangerous time in their escapade thus far, but there was no other option for them. Both men leaned into their work and didn't bother glancing shoreward.

In their little canoe, Bunker knew they were sitting ducks. And yet no sentries seemed to notice their approach. He had a creeping suspicion that this very ship, so laden with stolen food, was either unmanned or peopled with sleeping Tories. Either way it was bound to be exciting work. He glanced at Rufus, but the man's face, as usual in times of bold action, was unreadable.

Soon, their canoe clunked against the far side of the ship and Jack stood gingerly, bracing himself shipside, his fingertips securing a tenuous grip between the ship's caulked planking. He guided the canoe aft a few feet to a pair of thick ropes, above which smaller lengths dangled from the rail a dozen feet above their heads.

"I'll climb aboard first and inspect. Make haste in tying off the canoe. If she's truly empty, we'll hoist it aboard when we can. But join me as soon as you're able." Jack reached up with one brawny arm and, hand over hand, hoisted himself up a few feet. Hanging there, he looked down at his friend. "And Rufus? Good luck to you." He winked and continued on up the rope. Within seconds he had disappeared onto the deck without a sound.

Rufus himself was halfway up the rope when Bunker's face appeared above him. It gave him such a start that he thought he might drop down-ward, straight through the birchbark canoe.

"It's all ours, Rufus! All ours!" His whispered glee was contagious, and soon Rufus was crouched on deck beside him, discussing their escape.

"The good news is that we'll have a mighty head start on the red-jacketed rogues." Bunker's face settled into its usual grim smirk.

A full minute passed while Rufus tied off a sheet from his position portside before he relented. "So, Jack, what's the bad news?"

Bunker smiled. "You may have noticed that we aren't the only ship in the harbor."

As if on cue, a shout from shore made them both look up. The lone, raging voice was soon joined by others, and unjacketed men in various stages of dress, all of them shouting, pushed a longboat into the surf. Two missed their opportunity to jump into the already half-filled transport. In their rage they slapped at the surf before dragging themselves back to land.

Despite the impending danger of the situation, Jack and Rufus chuckled at each other even as they ran back and forth, busy with all the tasks a crew of a dozen or more usually performed. Fortunately both of them had grown up on the coast, spent their lives in boats, and knew the Maine shore as well as any men.

A crack sounded, then another, followed by a rapid volley of a dozen more, like rocks smacking other rocks. Whistling sounds hissed in the air all about them, and some of the balls thudded into the thick wood of the ship. "I don't think they appreciate what it is we are trying to do, Mr. Twitchell." Jack was half-crouched, pulling a sail with one hand and, by stretching far behind himself, correcting course with the ship's wheel.

"And just what is it, exactly, we are going to do with her, Mr. Bunker?" Rufus finished securing the anchor rope and scurried aft to help Jack.

"I haven't thought that part out quite yet. But when I do, you'll be the first to know!" Bunker laughed out loud now, seeing they had caught wind. "The wind is with us, Rufus. We'll make good time yet."

"And so will they!" Rufus's shout brought Jack's head around. Even before he looked, he knew what his friend meant. Sure enough, already there were several British ships bristling with men, shouting angrily as the longboats' oars dipped and flashed. They were headed down the coast to the larger ship anchored in the distance.

◦⁂◦

"This fog has been a boon to us, Jack, but we're just a few hours ahead of them. I hope you have a plan once we reach the cove."

As he walked the deck, Jack peered through the wispy trails of sea smoke curling about the deck, his hand resting on the battered hilt of a cutlass he had taken off a dead Loyalist some months before during a skirmish in Machias. Since then, the blade had proven useful a number of times.

Jack smiled and raised his eyebrows. "A plan, is it? Well, Mr. Twitchell, a plan is what you'll get."

But he said no more for a time. Then, with his usual suddenness, he seemed to have come to a decision, and strode manfully to the helm. "We're almost there, Rufus. Best let me guide her in. I know the particular harbor better than you do, and it would indeed be a shame to lose her out here among the rocks, stuck up like a sore thumb for all the British navy to see."

Within minutes Rufus knew what his friend had in mind, and he gripped the rail hard. "Jack, isn't this Little Spruce Island?"

"Just east of it." Bunker smiled as he steered the ship straight toward a cove not much wider than the little ship. The wind was with them, and the ship sailed like a horse galloping into a stall after a hard ride.

Jack looked at his friend's squinting face and smiled. "Relax, Rufus. It's sandy here."

"There's not a sandy spot in the whole of the downeast coast, and well you know it, Jack."

The captain threw his head back and howled with laughter. "That's what I like about you, Rufus. You're always so optimistic!" And with that the ship grounded not twenty yards from shore. Rufus heard nothing of the scraping, groaning timber sound he expected.

"She's a grounded thing now," said Jack, rubbing his hands together as if he were trying to kindle flame. "And it will take a mighty moon tide to free her. We scraped a few rocks coming in, but all in all, it was remarkably free of incident. I can't imagine they'll see her in here. After all, we're pretty well hidden among these little islands. Good thing the tide was with us, though. Could have been a hairy trip. . . ."

Rufus stared at him, his arms folded across his burly chest.

"Right you are, Rufus. You asked for a plan, and a plan you shall have. Ahhh . . . let's see." Bunker rasped a hand across his stubbled chin. "Well, as wooded as this harbor is, we still must disguise her as best we can. Aft starboard and the transom will take the most effort. You'll need this." Jack handed the battered but honed cutlass to his friend. "And hack all manner of tree and branch from that thick shoreside growth there and there."

Rufus nodded and moved to unlash the canoe from the deck.

"I'll work at the two masts, then yell to you when I need help," Jack continued. "We must drop them tonight, for if I know our enemy well, before dawn has reached us, the reprobates will attempt a patrol all through these islands, and they would see her masts before anything else. But if they're down, they shouldn't have any reason to come nosing among these rocky little knobs. I can't imagine they will. Unless they're intent on killing themselves. We have the advantage of knowing the region, and they do not."

"Good show, Jack." Rufus smiled, saluted Bunker, and swung over the side.

"If we pull this off," said Jack to himself, "we'll have made a good many enemies and filled a good many colonists' bellies."

⚮

Commander Timms sent a young ensign up the mast to act as lookout and another to the end of the bowsprit searching for a sign of the thieves and the stolen ship. They saw nothing but damnable islands covered in firs, and fog, rocks, fog, rocks, and more fog and rocks. Considering the rocky shoreline, he knew by sore experience that there was little he could do if they did find them, other than rain cannon fire down on them. And that would risk losing their ship and the much-needed provisions on board.

"Sir, I am afraid that—"

"I do not want to hear of your fears, lieutenant." Timms strode aft, coming to an abrupt stop in front of his second in command, Lieutenant Bean. "I will have those rogues!" He barked this last command so close to the younger man's face that Bean had to pull back or risk losing the tip of his nose when the commander ground his jaws shut. Commander Timms turned away then whipped back and said, "And when we do find them, no quarter will be given. They will be hanged—for a start."

⚮

The Gulf of Maine, including the stretch of coastline called "downeast"—a nautical reference to the direction sailing vessels traveled from Boston to Maine, since they had to travel downwind to head east on prevailing westerly winds—is riddled with islands, 4,500 of them, ranging in size from rocky nubs to great, broad landmasses.

As a native boy of the downeast coast, Jack Bunker knew the myriad inlets, cuts, harbors, and holes into which a well-sailed craft, at just the right time of the tide, might be maneuvered. And if luck, tide, fog, and time were right, the vessel might go long enough to unload and distribute much-needed provisions for the suppressed and starving coastal residents from whom the food was stolen in the first place—which is just what he did when the British ship chasing him failed to find his hiding place.

The downeast section of Maine had long been alluring to the British navy. In June 1775 the seaport town of Machias was ordered to supply lumber for British army barracks. The town's citizens declined, and the British warship Margaretta *cruised into the bay. Undaunted, the Machias citizens, armed with pitchforks, muskets, swords, and axes, attacked the ship with their own lumber-hauling vessels. They defeated the British in this, the first naval battle of the Revolutionary War, taking the* Margaretta *as a spoil of war—five days before the battle at Bunker Hill.*

The colonists, however, were not always so fortunate when it came to defending New England's waters. In July 1779 an entire American fleet was lost trying to recapture the coastal town of Castine, Maine, from the British. The Penobscot Expedition was the largest American naval expedition of the Revolutionary War, consisting of nineteen armed ships, twenty-four transports, and a thousand men, compared with Great Britain's ten warships and six hundred men.

So brutal was the American loss—474 militiamen were killed, wounded, or captured, and all ships were lost (only thirteen British regulars were killed or wounded)—that the commanding officer was court-martialed. The battle was the United States' worst naval defeat until the attack on Pearl Harbor, 162 years later.

13

THE KNOX CANNON TRAIN
(1775)

Colonel Henry Knox leads eighty yoke of oxen, dragging fifty-nine cannons, three hundred miles in fifty-six days, from Fort Ticonderoga to Cambridge . . . in the dead of winter. But harsh weather, exhausted men and oxen, thin ice, and sinking boats prove nearly too much to overcome.

⸎

I am confident, sir, that should the plan work, we will no more be plagued by the British army occupying the fair city of Boston."

His hat held behind his back, the young man who stood before George Washington betrayed his nervousness by swallowing audibly. His mouth was dry, and understandably so. The commander in chief of the Continental Army stood before him, unsmiling and seemingly ready to send him packing—for impudence and sheer brazenness, no doubt.

Oh, life had been easier and quieter in his Boston bookstore, but nowhere near as exciting, and the time for helping the fledgling nation was now. Henry Knox knew he could not live with himself unless he had done his all. Besides, the plan should work, thought the young man. And he had been asked to offer his thoughts on the matter.

Washington narrowed his eyes but kept them trained on those of the young man. Continuing to regard him, the general finally spoke. "Gentlemen, if we do nothing but continue as we have been, the outcome will likely be less than favorable to us. I am not sure how much longer we can maintain our stalemate with the British forces. If, on the other hand, we elect to support Mr. Knox's bold mission, a mission I would expect he would undertake and oversee . . ." Washington inclined his head toward the pudgy young man.

Knox swallowed, nodded twice, and said, "Yes, sir."

"Then at the very least we will have made an effort toward action. And that, gentlemen, in my experience, is never effort wasted." His stern face, with brows drawn, regarded the very air above the table of silent men. Then he looked at them in turn until each man nodded. Finally, Washington said in a firm voice, "What will you need?"

Hauling guns by ox teams from Fort Ticonderoga for the siege of Boston, 1775. In an attempt to dislodge the British from their long-held occupation of Boston, in 1775–1776, Colonel Henry Knox of the Continental Army led eighty yoke of oxen, dragging fifty-nine cannons weighing sixty tons, three hundred miles across rivers, mountains, forests, swamps, and lakes in fifty-six days . . . in the dead of winter. The arrival of this new firepower convinced the British to evacuate the city. *National Archives*

"Sir?"

"The operation, to get the artillery here from Fort Ticonderoga."

Knox didn't hesitate: "Men, sir. Men and oxen."

"Good, then you shall have them. I needn't remind you that the Continental Army and indeed the outcome of the war is counting on the success of your expedition, Mr. Knox."

⁓

"Sir, we've been hard at it for a week now since your arrival, and I have to say I'm pleased. All forty-three cannons, six cohorns, eight mortars, and two howitzers from Fort Ticonderoga have arrived, towed from the fort on sleds by a yoke of oxen each."

Henry Knox nodded to Reilly, one of his assistants, and said, "I'm afraid we've had it easy. Until now, that is." Knox, in his newly minted rank as colonel, looked down the length of Lake George and watched the black mass of approaching winter weather barrel toward them. A gust of sharp wind tugged at his longcoat and pushed hard at his face. It stung like an unexpected slap.

He watched his men making fast the last of the fifty-nine guns on the flat-bottom gundalow, and though he rarely doubted his own judgments, some doubts now crept into his mind. Sixty tons of artillery, he thought. *And I am the man responsible for getting it to Boston safe and sound, and with all speed possible.*

Knox drew in a lungful of icy air and said, "To Fort George, then, at the southern end of the lake. And pray we don't get iced in." To himself he added, "But pray for enough snow once we arrive." He looked at his brother, John, whom he had charged as captain of the massive craft, and forced a smile. "Once we get these guns to Boston, it will have been well worth all the effort."

∾

The sound of the great craft grounding on a rock just below the surface stopped everyone cold. How would they free it? The weight of the load was such that it might have to be unloaded. But how could they do that on water? Who would be the one to tell Colonel Knox? The men had been at it hard for two weeks, and their journey had barely begun. A sense of bleak foreboding settled on them like a heavy cloud. But still they pried and levered, and the ship eventually floated free. Their cheering echoed down the long length of the lake.

The next day, Colonel Knox, who had sailed ahead in a smaller ship, paced the southern shore of the lake, staring into the descending dark. Where was his precious load? He had already dispatched a rider to find out. And within minutes, the man galloped up, his wind-reddened face set in a grimace.

"Well?" said Knox, unable to contain his desperation.

"The gundalow sank, sir."

"Sank? What?"

"Sir, the men, under your brother's charge, are working feverishly on refloating it."

Knox felt his throat fill with bile, and despair overwhelmed him. The utter hopelessness of the undertaking seemed impossible to overcome.

And yet two days later, as if by a miracle, and with the mighty efforts of all the men, the laden craft was floated once again, and it made its way to the southern end of the lake.

Knox surveyed his men's efforts as they built the forty-two bulky transport sledges in anticipation of the arrival of the eighty yoke of oxen that would drag them.

Now we need snow, he thought, or it would have been just as well to lose the entire load in the murky depths of Lake George. We must make up our lost time; we must make it to Boston. But other than to maintain constant supervision to ensure that his directives were carried out as quickly as possible, Knox said nothing of his concerns to the men, nor did he express anything but confidence in his letters to Washington. But to his diary, he trusted his doubts and fears.

✍

Knox awakened to hearty shouts from the men. He was used to such sounds, particularly in winter, when living under campaign canvas became especially rough, but these were barks of . . . joy? What could it mean? Nothing of consequence, he thought, and he wished they would show a bit more consideration so that he could roll over for a few more minutes of sleep. But though it was still dark, he knew it was time to rise and get on with the day's events. If only we had enough snow to proceed with our heavy burden on to Boston, he thought. Then his eyes snapped open. It was Christmas Day! How he wished he was with his dear Lucy.

He rubbed his eyes and swung his legs around to the edge of the cot. As he rubbed his knees, a sudden jolt wagged the tent canvas above him and brought him to his feet. He threw open the flap, and wonder of wonders: There was more than a foot of snow on the ground—heavy, dense snow. He smiled and nodded toward the men who had obviously hit his tent with a snowball. They were feeling the same elation that he was feeling.

"What a gift," was all he could think of to say.

"Yes, sir. Though I fear it may be too much of a fine gift."

"Too much?" said Knox. "Oh yes," he kicked at the snow with his boot. "I see what you mean. No matter." He entered his tent and held the flap open. "Now we can proceed."

"Today, sir?"

"Yes, today. Nearly a week has passed since I wrote to General Washington. He is no doubt expecting us."

◦◦◦

Mile after mile the men trudged in snow that at times reached their knees. Their feet were numb and wet, and the oxen fared even worse, charged with dragging tons of iron on ill-equipped and overloaded sleds through the same deep snow, up and down steep inclines and ravines. A half dozen men strode ahead, searching with poles and their own legs for hidden holes, stumps, boulders, and other impediments buried in the heavy snow.

"If we make four miles today, sir, I think we'll have done all we can," said Reilly. "The men and the beasts have put in a good show, but dark is coming, too early for my liking. The men need rest, and the oxen aren't responding to our switches—they're just too tired to care. Whipping them isn't doing a bit of good."

Knox nodded, feeling guilty once again for riding his horse alongside or behind the column, well above the seeping cold of the snow.

Less than an hour later, the camp was set up, and the animals were tended. The mess crew had a treat of stew on the boil, using hunks of venison from the buck one of the men had shot the day before. A hot meal will do us all a world of good, thought Knox, as he surveyed the cannons, testing the ropes lashing the formidable weapons to the sledges. All seemed to be in order, save for two, which he requested be retied.

And so it goes, he thought, as he watched men lean back against the cannons and doze off in mid-conversation with one another. One poor fellow didn't bother with hacking pine boughs for a bed and had merely kicked a hollow in the snow for himself and laid down like a beaten dog, even skipping his meal. They weren't yet halfway to Cambridge, but if he were counting on sheer strength of will and determination, these men had plenty of pluck. Unfortunately, they also had to rely on the animals, and they seemed all done in.

◦◦◦

"The Hudson River is proving to be our bane." Knox barked an oath. Then winced as he watched a second test cannon crack through the ice and disappear into the roiling river below.

"This is no good, man! We simply cannot lose another cannon. We cannot!" He stalked off upriver by himself, while the men returned to camp to wait until the ice thickened.

Three days later, on January 8, the ice proved strong enough to support the heavy loads of oxen and cannons, and in a single day, twenty-three of the forty-two sleds crossed. And, wonder of wonders, we just might make it, thought Knox, as the last of the two lost cannons were retrieved from the water with help from the locals.

The great expedition, which Knox referred to in his diary as the "noble train of artillery," entered Massachusetts and found renewed vigor with eighty yoke of fresh oxen. By January 24 they reached Cambridge, having averaged more than five miles per day during fifty-six days of travel. Word was sent to General Washington, and the troops in the besieged city of Boston were both hopeful and relieved.

∽

The barrage of gun- and artillery fire had begun a half hour before. Colonel Knox looked down below him, toward the harbor, where Washington's gun batteries let fly volley after volley of covering fire in hopes of distracting General Howe's forces away from the goings-on at Dorchester Heights.

In front of him, behind him, and all around him, soldiers, volunteers, and militiamen, all hopeful Americans, were putting their shoulders to the wheel—in many cases quite literally—in order to maneuver the fifty-nine guns to the top of Dorchester Heights.

"I'm about done in, but I can't be the only one."

"Keep your mouth quiet, soldier."

Knox didn't know who uttered the harsh rebuke, but he couldn't disagree. This was no time for chatter. Any effort at all was to be spent in getting the artillery into position atop Dorchester Heights, and they had only one night to do so. Six weeks had passed since Knox's gun train had arrived, and the plan had been set in stone, with no room for failure. And tonight was the time when it all had to happen. Every last bit of it.

∽

The next morning, on March 5, 1776, British General Howe stared up in awe at Dorchester Heights. He is noted to have said, "The rebels did more in one night than my whole army could have done in one month."

For on the preceding night, hundreds of Americans, under cover of darkness and with the protective, distracting fire of Washington's gun batteries hammering at the British defenses, dragged all of Henry Knox's guns to the top of Dorchester Heights, even while other Americans hastened to build emplacements. To visually reinforce the threat, a great many logs were painted to resemble cannons. The partial ruse worked, though the fifty-nine guns Knox and his men dragged for three hundred miles in fifty-six days were indeed in full working order.

❧

While the Americans certainly deserved much applause for their extraordinary efforts that night, they owed a large debt to Colonel Henry Knox, a humble, twenty-five-year-old bookseller and brilliant military tactician, because the transportation and setup of his "gun train" proved the final blow that by March 17, 1776, began to drive the last British troops and Tory sympathizers from Boston, ending a yearlong, deadlocked siege of that pivotal ground in the American Revolution. Many Loyalists departed Boston for Halifax or headed back across the Atlantic. Among them were Mr. and Mrs. Flucker, staunch Loyalists and Colonel Henry Knox's in-laws. Neither Henry Knox nor his wife, Lucy Flucker Knox, ever saw her parents again.

14

A MANLY SHOWING

(1777)

On April 26, 1777, during Connecticut's battle of Ridgefield, Colonel Benedict Arnold's horse, shot nine times, falls on him, his troops scatter, and, at saber point, a charging redcoat demands surrender. Arnold refuses. Close by, General Wooster rallies his men one last time.

✑

The day appears ours, men. We have routed the enemy at their own game." Cautious cheers rose into the air, along with a few grimy hats. But the speaker, Colonel Benedict Arnold, calmed the men with his raised hands. "The day is young, and there is still much to do." The men nodded. "And let us not forget that we are outnumbered five to one. Our advantage lies in the defense of these barricades and breastworks we have constructed."

A few hours later, after the third British charge, Colonel Benedict Arnold recalled that brief, rousing speech. How quickly the tide of a battle can shift, he thought as he watched his troops, outnumbered five to one, break and scatter.

He knew it might happen; he had half-expected it all day, in fact. His scant forces, the ragtag crew of fierce, devoted men, were exhausted and stretched too thin, and their line softened. Through the blue haze of choking powder smoke, Arnold saw first one man buckle and bolt, limping and dragging his musket with a wounded arm. Then another, and another. Still others seemed confused and stared about themselves, almost as if they had just given up.

He spurred on his mount, yanking the reins and turning the mighty beast hard to the left, and jumped over a low barricade of splintered oak kegs, and the fallen forms of two men, one of whom it pained him to see, as he knew him well. And with a savage yell, he raised his sword high, waving it and shouting in an effort to press his ragged men forward. They were weakening but still battling, all the while trying to rebuild a fleeing rear guard. But before he looked back toward the line of skirmish, his trusted mount staggered. He knew the beast had been hit. Then he felt the jolting

Colonel Benedict Arnold. Benedict Arnold distinguished himself in battle numerous times fighting for America's Continental Army. He suffered multiple wounds, had his horse shot out from under him, and marched his men 350 miles through Maine's raw wilderness to lead an ill-fated assault on Quebec City. But after being passed over repeatedly for promotions and seeing others claim credit for his tactical decisions, Arnold could take no more, and in 1780 he switched his allegiance to Great Britain.
Courtesy Library of Congress

impact as several more musket balls slammed into the rippling silver hide of his fine horse, and he knew he would lose him.

"Here is a pretty sight," he growled even as the Americans' front line broke. He saw that some of his men had bolted and now fled, saving those they could as they made their escape. Still others continued to fight. He shouted to them to run. It was pointless to stand and fight when they were routed. Men would die in vain, and they would be needed again soon. The American forces had been overrun. Some would be taken, he hoped for their sakes, as prisoners. Others, he didn't doubt, would be shot in the back.

Arnold looked about him and found himself alone, facing the advancing horde of redcoats less than thirty yards away. The firing British troops advanced, and he felt more musket balls slam his horse, even as it sank, slumped, and then dropped, heaving, on its side, pinning his leg under its thrashing body. Piteous moans and squeals rose from its trembling, bubble-and-blood-flecked jaws. Arnold pushed with his free leg against the beast's quivering back. A voice, close by, forced him to look up.

"You are my prisoner! Surrender! Surrender!"

Arnold saw the British soldier running at him and slipped his hand on the curved butt of the pistol holstered on his saddle. As he did, the redcoat aimed his musket at the pinned man's chest. Another few yards and the bayonet would do its worst.

Again came the demand: "Surrender!"

"Gaah! Not yet!" Arnold freed the pistol, aimed it, and fired, all in one smooth lift of his hand. The ball took the redcoat just below the throat, felling him. Arnold wasted no time. Still clutching his pistol, he rammed it hard on the horse's flank. The action produced a last desperate flail from the dying beast, and Arnold slid free his pinned leg. Bent low, he limped toward a wood, nearly losing his footing twice on the raw spring ground slicked with mud and the blood of his fellows. The smoke-thick air about him filled with shouts, groans, and the whistle of musket fire. Arnold vowed he would gain as much ground as he could before he was cut down. His men, he had seen when pinned beneath his horse, were mostly gone, scattered or wounded, with many still writhing in the mud.

He ran as fast as he could on his injured limb. The shots followed him, whizzing into the trees, cutting through the bare branches and the undergrowth, which thickened the deeper he ventured into the swamp. The crack of musket fire lessened and eventually stopped. Still he kept on, making what he hoped was a wide arc back toward safety.

Earlier in the day, General David Wooster had split his troops, sending the bulk of them ahead to engage the British and prevent them from digging in and entrenching themselves in Ridgefield. Wooster took two hundred men and pursued the smaller contingent of British forces, who were also ultimately headed to Ridgefield.

"They succeeded, sir." The panting young private stood before Wooster, trying to control his heaving chest.

"Who succeeded at what, young man?"

"I'm sorry, sir. The citizen soldiers, sir. They went ahead of the enemy, as you requested, and fired the bridge. It's impassable, sir."

"Good work. Tell them that, private." Wooster turned to his second in command. "That won't stop General Tryon, but it will delay him. And that's what we're trying to do. At least until reinforcements arrive to give Colonel Arnold the fighting chance he needs."

"What now, sir?"

"Now?" The tall, thin man—who, at sixty-seven, was older than the two hundred men before him by many years—raised his arms and said, "Now that we have the element of surprise, we engage the enemy." A hushed murmur of approval rippled through the assembled troops. Another scout returned with news that Tryon's rear guard was stopped just a few miles north of Ridgefield to fortify themselves with a brief breakfast.

"We have them, gentlemen. Take what prisoners we may, and advance."

An hour later, Wooster and his men had regrouped, surrounding forty captured British soldiers, but they were disappointed that they had killed only two of the enemy.

"We go again in an hour. We must cripple them before they get the opportunity to strike fully. Arnold's forces would never withstand it."

As they marched as quietly as they could, they came upon three pieces of artillery that belched death at them—Tryon had become wise to them. The enemy opened fire, and the ragtag band of men under Wooster scattered.

General Wooster ran forward, waving his saber and shouting, "Come on, my boys! Never mind such random shots!" The sight of this bold man advancing alone on the enemy bolstered the ragged mass of militiamen.

And then one of those random shots pierced the general's chest, driving him to his knees. The British closed in, and the hand-to-hand combat grew fierce.

General Wooster's cries of pain were masked by the redoubled efforts of his men as they fought like the cornered creatures they were. Finally, a panting British officer stood tall before Wooster, his sword drawn, and lunged forward to deal a death blow. He was driven back, and Wooster's men carried their fallen leader to safety.

∽

General David Wooster's efforts at slowing General William Tryon's advance on Ridgefield bought Arnold and General Gold S. Silliman's troops time to dig in at Ridgefield. Alas, it was not enough to rally General Wooster, who succumbed to his wounds five days after the battle. He died at the house belonging to Nehemia Dibble, the same house that General Tryon had used as a personal headquarters days before when the British had marched through Danbury.

Though crushed by the loss, Wooster was also proud of his troops' actions and of the men who gave their all for the cause. His last words were: "I am dying, but with a strong hope and persuasion that my country will find her independence."

∽

On their march from their landing place at Westport to Weston, more than 2,000 British troops looted, pillaged, burned, and murdered their way across Connecticut. In addition to taking prisoners during the battle of Ridgefield and other local skirmishes, British troops burned an Episcopal church and scores of other structures, including homes, stores, shops, meetinghouses, gristmills, sawmills, and barns.

Scores of farm animals were slaughtered, stolen, or driven off, and the British army, feeling boisterous after that day's victory, plundered the townsfolk of their provisions, clothing, and valuables, leaving many with little or no food.

Despite such horrible occurrences, a plaque marking the gravesites of some of the day's dead introduces a measure of humanity: "Eight patriots who were laid in these grounds companioned by 16 British soldiers, living their enemies, dying their guests."

In Ridgefield, Connecticut, markers indicate the sites at which General Wooster was wounded and at which Colonel Arnold was nearly bayoneted. And a British cannonball is still lodged in a corner post of the Keeler Tavern.

∽

Benedict Arnold distinguished himself a number of times during his years of military service; despite his best efforts, however, some episodes during his military career ended poorly. Chief among them was the valiant but tragedy-laden, ill-fated expedition that he led through the wilds of Maine to invade British-held Quebec.

After traveling 350 miles—twice the distance he had calculated—in two months through unforgiving terrain, he arrived at the St. Lawrence River with six hundred starving men out of his initial force of one thousand. They continued with their planned siege of Quebec City, and though they were joined by another force invading from Lake Champlain, led by Richard Montgomery, they were soundly beaten. Arnold was wounded, Montgomery was killed, and more than 350 men were taken prisoner. The remaining forces retreated to Fort Ticonderoga.

Despite the many heroic efforts Benedict Arnold made on behalf of his country's struggling cause, he will forever be best known as "turncoat" and "traitor" for switching allegiances and fighting for the British cause. Never was that more apparent than when he led British forces to victory over the Americans in the same region of Connecticut three years later.

Arnold justified his switch of allegiance by pointing to the poor treatment he received at the hands of the Continental Congress. He was, he claimed, wrongfully passed over for promotion on a number of occasions. It is obvious that during several military engagements, including the battle of Ridgefield, he more than earned advancement. Other officers took credit for his tactical and battlefield accomplishments. Moreover, his left leg was repeatedly injured in battle. He had it set, but so poorly that it ended up two inches shorter than his right leg and pained him greatly for the rest of his life.

This treatment, coupled with his strong opposition to America's alliance with France, caused Arnold to shift his allegiance. In August 1780, in command of West Point, he worked toward weakening it and turning it over to the British. His efforts were discovered, and he was forced to escape down the Hudson River, skipping out on a scheduled dinner date with General Washington.

After the war, in 1782, Arnold settled in London, England, with his second wife. There he was well received by King George III and the Tories, though not so well by the Whigs. He helped set up his two sons in a mercantile business in St. Johns, New Brunswick, but he returned to London, where he died in 1801, at the age of sixty, sickly from various ailments. He was buried in St. Mary's Church in Battersea, London, without military honors. When the church underwent renovations a century later, his remains were placed in an unmarked mass grave.

15

REVOLUTIONARY WOMAN
(1782)

Uxbridge, Massachusetts, native Deborah Samson fights for the Continental Army—dressed as a man. She allows doctors to treat her head wound, but she slips away soon after to protect her secret and to pry a musket ball from her leg with a knife. But a second ball is lodged too deep. . . .

∽

Though she had already taken two musket balls to the left thigh, it was the slash to the head from that vicious, greasy-haired British officer that hurt the most. It had come from nowhere, and though she had been knocked to her knees from the bullet wounds, his slice, followed by a thump with the butt of his saber, drove her to the ground. She lay there, desperate to rise, tasting the ooze of the field's mire of dirt, horse manure, grass, and what must have been her own blood.

She concentrated on blinking, on forcing her eyes wide, on hearing. The sounds of battle seemed to fade in, then out, as if someone were shouting in her ears and then turning away. She saw the dank gray haze of powder smoke drifting above her head.

"Is he dead?"

Something prodded her in the gut and the arm and lifted her face from the mud. "Head looks stoved in. I'd say he's a goner. We best get to the moaners whilst we still can."

With the most effort she had ever put into anything in all her twenty-two years, Deborah Samson, known to her fellow soldiers as Robert Shurtleff, pushed out a long, low moan. She was sure no one heard it. . . . But yes, there was breath—reeking of tobacco and rotten teeth and whiskey—wafting in her face. "You alive? Hey, that you who made that whimper?"

They lifted her from the mud and laid her on her back on a filthy stretcher. All around her, the battle sounds had diminished, the smells were not quite so rank as before, and the sky above was breaking blue through the parting haze of powder smoke.

⁓

"Now we will see about that thin soldier there," said the French doctor. The fighting that day had been long and fraught with all manner of brutal wounds, and he offered what relief he could to the brave soldiers of the Fourth Massachusetts Regiment. He wiped his hands on a smock so blood-smeared that it was black. His hands did not come clean, but he seemed not to notice.

He walked to the tall soldier's side, peeled off the sopping, stained muslin pad from the soldier's head, and with a firm hand turned the thin face to the left and right.

"This is a nasty saber cut you have here. We will treat it as best we can." He looked down at the length of the soldier's body. "Is your leg wounded?"

"No, sir. It's only mud."

"Good, good. That cut is enough to worry about."

But "Robert Shurtleff" noted with relief that the doctor had already turned to other wounded soldiers. Just as well, she thought, for I am near to fainting dead away from these wounds.

After her head was cleansed and bandaged, she grabbed her musket and hat and made haste to leave the stifling confines of the medical tent, limping and grimacing against the waves of pain that coursed upward with each step. It took some doing, but the young soldier found a secluded spot in a tangle of fallen logs and bramble thatch away from the wretched sounds of the field hospital.

The young soldier slipped out a penknife and flipped back the flap of her long coat to reveal two blackened holes in the pants' thigh. "Can't let them know. . . . Can't let them know. . . . They'll kill me if they find out . . . shoot me."

She gritted her teeth, breathing harder now, and slipped the knife's long blade under the trouser fabric. She slit the wound hole in both directions and peeled back the matted fabric. She drizzled water into the wound and then took great care to wipe dirt and blood from the puckered rim.

She fished out a thick sewing needle, pulled in a deep breath, doubled over the leather strapping of the musket ball pouch, and bit down hard on the leather. With trembling hands she probed the wound with the needle and knife blade to fish out the lead ball. Twice she lost consciousness for seconds at a time. Sweat dripped steadily off her forehead, down her long nose, and puddled on her lap.

Three times she felt sure she had the ball tweezed and tried to lift it out of the ragged, bloody hole, only to have it slip back out of sight. The buzzing in her ears caused her hands to shake worse than ever, and her head wagged as if she were palsied. Then she passed out again, still holding the knife in the hole in her thigh. As her hand slipped down, the blade sliced sideways into the wound, and she came awake with a scream.

Only vaguely aware that she was probably still within earshot of her fellows, she choked off the scream by biting down harder than ever on the leather strap.

She pulled in deep breaths through her nose, forcing them in and out, in and out, snot and spittle and sweat pooling and running down her chin, but her head felt clearer. She set to work again, and within seconds, almost as if she were being assisted by a divine, experienced hand, she lifted out the misshapen offender—she guessed it had hit her leg bone. It glistened with blood, her blood, and she felt the blackness of unconsciousness seeping in and enveloping her. Her body felt cold.

Her customary strength seemed to be failing her. She had relied on this strength first as the only girl among the ten boys of the family in which she was raised as an indentured servant, then in her days as a schoolteacher and weaver, and most recently as a hard-fighting, long-traveling soldier who never complained and rarely spoke.

She kept to herself, of course, for always there was the fear of being found out. And if she was found out, she knew with certainty that she would be stripped bare and shot before her fellow soldiers. The very thought made her shudder. Worse than death, that fate would be. Worse than death.

As much as she fought that creeping feeling of blackness, she felt herself failing in the fight. This must be how it is to die, she thought, unable to do anything, to muster any amount of strength to help herself. At least I tried. At least I haven't left behind children who would grow up not knowing me. . . .

When she again came to, the day had worn down to late afternoon. It would be dark within a few hours, and she still had to pull the other ball from her leg, several inches farther down. This she attempted until the waning daylight left her squinting, barely able to see her hands as they probed the second puckered hole in her leg.

∽

"While you are healing from your wounds, soldier, you can still walk, though with a limp, so you will be assigned to General John Patterson. He's in need of an assistant, someone to bring him his meals, tend to his clothing, that sort of thing. With your thin stature, and your ability to read and write, no offense intended, we felt that you could be more useful than others of the company."

"I understand. And it will be an honor to help the general in any way I might be useful."

"Good, good. Glad you feel that way, Shurtleff."

All this she recalled from the confines of the clean, quiet room in which she had awakened. If only I could have stayed that way, helping the general. No one would have ever known. But my wounds caused further sickness, and now here I am, bedridden and no doubt found out for the fraud I am. They will surely shoot me now. . . .

Deborah reached down and lifted the quilt that covered her. Her breasts were unbound, as she knew they would be. She was clothed in nothing but a thin nightgown. Her throat tightened, and she felt the hot sting of tears. She hadn't allowed herself to cry in self-pity in years, if ever. She found it a sign of weakness and mopped her eyes with the quilt.

The glass doorknob squeaked and clicked as it turned, and the door slowly opened. Deborah ran the back of a hand across her face and sat up straighter against the clean pillows.

"Hello?" The face of a man appeared. He smiled when he saw her and stepped into the room, closing the door quietly behind himself.

Deborah nodded but said nothing.

He stood by the bed and looked down at her. "You fainted while attending General Patterson. It's your wounds, they're still causing you trouble. I fear you are more ill than you realize." He took her wrist in one hand and held his watch in the other. Then he smiled at her again and said, "I . . . know."

"Will they shoot me for it?" Her voice was the low, steady sound she had affected when she first stepped up to the table at the tavern in Middleboro, Massachusetts, to volunteer for the Continental Army.

"Shoot you?" He looked genuinely surprised at her question. "Why, I shouldn't think so. You are a wounded soldier."

"Then you haven't told anyone?" She heard her voice soften. I almost sound like a woman, she thought, discarding the thought as quickly as it came to her.

"Aside from my wife, no one knows your secret."

"Please don't say a word."

"That I cannot do. General Patterson will have to be told. But it will not go hard on you."

She looked down, her eyes trailing along the raised lump of her body under the quilt. Such a little difference. Such a pity.

"Why did you do it?"

She looked up at the doctor. "Do what?"

"Join the regiment."

She looked at him as if he had asked her to fly. "It seemed little enough to do for my country."

He regarded her a moment and then said, "I have met many men who had more compelling reasons, but who did far less." He smiled. "Don't worry. You are safe. You should rest now." He walked softly to the door and then turned with a hand on the knob. "May I ask . . . your name?"

She felt both relief and fear, though the relief felt stronger to her. "Samson. Deborah Samson, sir."

"Sleep well, Miss Samson. We'll talk later."

❧

Deborah Samson was born into a poor family of seven children whose father had run off, and she became an indentured servant to a farm family with ten sons. The rugged, outdoor life suited her. When her formal servitude ended at age eighteen, instead of marrying as was the custom then for young women, Deborah, at five feet seven inches tall, physically strong, and literate, went on to support herself by teaching school, working in carpentry, weaving, and taking in sewing.

In 1778 her patriotism was stirred to such a degree that she disguised herself as a man and signed the muster book as "Robert Shurtleff." She strongly suspected, however, that she had somehow aroused suspicions, so to avoid being found out, she didn't report for service the following day. But she couldn't forget how close she had come to serving in the Continental Army. On May 20, 1782, she gave it another try, and using the same name, she signed up and showed up.

After being wounded in a skirmish in Tarrytown, New York, she recovered somewhat, was promoted, and served as assistant to General John Patterson. During the summer of 1783, she contracted a fever, and Dr. Barnabas Phinney discovered her disguised gender. He kept her secret but did inform the general, who tactfully gave her an honorable discharge.

Deborah went on to marry Benjamin Gannett, a farmer from Sharon, Massachusetts. They had three children together and adopted a fourth. But financial woes dogged them. For a time, Deborah, her secret now well known, gave lectures about her time in the military. But the money was not enough to cover her debts, and she borrowed money, several times, from her good friend Paul Revere.

At a time when soldiers from the Continental Army had received pensions from Congress for service to their country, Deborah Samson did not, because of her gender. Eventually, in 1816, after petitioning Congress and through the assistance of Revere and Governor John Hancock, she was awarded the first-ever military pension given to a woman, $76.80 per annum. It allowed the Gannetts to repay loans and pay down debts.

Deborah Samson died in 1827, at sixty-six, of yellow fever, and her headstone bears the names of both of her identities. She is memorialized in Sharon, Massachusetts, in numerous ways, among them a statue in front of the library.

After her death, her husband applied to Congress for, and was granted, a widower's pension—another first. But it is her devotion to cause and country and her contributions to dismantling gender bias that are her most enduring legacies.

16

SHE-PIRATE!
(1782)

Feigning helplessness during storms at sea, Rachel Wall lures innocent rescuers to their deaths at the hands of her concealed crew. But the game soon wears thin . . . and piracy in Massachusetts is a hanging offense.

༄

He kissed her long and hard, just as he always did when he was excited and primed for adventure. And it didn't get more exciting than this, thought young Rachel, as she wound her arm through the rigging and grinned into the tossing, spitting storm, waiting for the unsuspecting ship to draw ever closer. Never had she imagined just a year ago on her parents' pitiful little Pennsylvania rock farm that she, Rachel, would be in the midst of a gale off the coast of New Hampshire, in the Isle of Shoals, about to commit thievery, treachery, wickedness . . . and worse!

Never did she imagine as a housemaid during their first few months of marriage in Boston, while her husband worked for less than a living wage aboard local fishing ships, that they would end up rich and leading lives others only dream of.

A wide smile spread across her face. From just behind the lashed barrels and netting piled high beside her, her husband, George, big, brawny man that he was, smiled up at her, winked, and said, "Now, girl. Give it all you've got. Scream for me!"

And scream she did. So long and so loud that for a time she even scared herself. She knew that the closer the ship drew, the more she must act, for the crew would have a spyglass directed on her. She had torn her dress and unfastened her hair. The pelting rain and driving wind did the rest, at least to her features. From all appearances, she was a lone survivor on a ship adrift in the storm.

Her husband and the rest of the crew of their fishing ship had dragged apart enough of the rigging and hoisted one edge of the tattered sail they kept just for such occasions. The stage was set, and her siren screams drifted across the chop of the Isle of Shoals toward the latest trading vessel to have the misfortune of meeting up with Rachel Wall.

"Are you hurt?" The voice came from a man at the stern of the ship, the *Bissunda,* so it read on the bow. He was the captain, by the looks of him. Rachel resisted the urge to laugh and instead tried to appear as if she were about to give up on life itself.

"I am alone and adrift! Oh God, please save me. Please help me!"

"We are here now!" he shouted. "Have no fear, dear lady. All will be well."

The sailors, a dozen in all, worked frantically to make ready their ship to pull alongside. The captain spoke something, but the whipping wind and snapping of the shredded sails drowned out his words. She had cleverly torn her dress top to expose more of her chest than even a familiar barmaid would show, and the crew of the approaching ship nearly tripped over one another to position themselves for a quick jump on board, each of them eager to be the man she would remember as her one true savior.

That honor, she decided, would go to George Wall, her pirate husband, crouched behind her, dripping wet, primed for blood sport, and ready to defend her. As the storm lessened, the sailors had made fast their ship to hers, and most had already swarmed aboard and were running toward her. She did not betray the hiding places of her fellows, but within seconds she saw the shock, then the terror on the faces of her saviors, and she knew that her own shipmates had once again gained the upper hand.

She was amazed that George's plan had worked in the first place. That it had worked every time since then was equally stunning to her. People did not ever grow any smarter, she decided. Just then, her husband sank his long knife upward into her first savior's gut. He never let her down, always using the same technique, and she knew that it would gain them the upper hand. "Surprise," he had said months before. "Surprise will gain us all. Dithering will lose us all."

It was over in less than half an hour. They had killed the entire crew, including the captain, and began loading the haul from the captured vessel to their hold—taking care to keep only goods that could not be traced and that they could sell with ease when they returned to Boston. When they had sufficiently looted the bobbing *Bissunda,* the murdered sailors were dragged into the hold of the now silent ship, and it was soon scuttled.

"So sad," said George, a huge, manly grin on his face. "Another ship lost during a powerful storm just off the Isle of Shoals." He shook his head and looked at her.

"How very tragic," she said, smiling. A roar of triumph rose about them as the handful of their fellows celebrated—by drinking the dead captain's allotment of fine rum and watching the last of the scuttled hull succumb to the squalling seas.

❧

"Why you down here, girlie? Aren't you Georgie's woman?" The rank, stale stink of old sweat and urine and whiskey rose off the skinny man as he bent his head low and peered at her. From what Rachel could tell, there were no others sailors about. She had hoped none would be aboard—that made pilfering easier—but with just the one, maybe she would be able to make a little extra money in the process. Only she hoped he wasn't too rough—she didn't like them rough. George was the only one who could treat her that way.

She had been plagued with bad dreams and night sweats for months, ever since George and the rest of the crew had been swept overboard in that gale, just like in a bad dream. They had all been drinking, and when the storm picked up, they went topside to lash down loose ends, but they never came back. She had managed to keep from being pitched off herself only by wrapping her arms in a rope, just as she did during storms when other ships were about and they had a job to do.

It was as if they had all played their parts too well. Rachel's screams for her husband, for the others of the crew, all fell on the uncaring lash of the storm. It seemed as if weeks had passed, though in reality it was little more than a few days, since her husband and most of the rest of the crew had been lost at sea. Only one injured crewman, Dicky Garnette, had survived the vicious squall. Every time she saw Dicky, lying there moaning, she wished he had been the one to die and not George.

She had yelled for hours, scanning the gray water with the spyglass, but to no avail. They were truly lost. Dicky was next to useless, injured as he was and flopping in his bunk with each swell and trough they ploughed through. By the time the fishing vessel found her, days after the squall, Rachel had lost much of the spunk she had had during their raiding days.

Since then she had been in a numb haze, disowned by her family. She hoped to resume what work she could get as a housemaid, but it proved difficult to find. She took to sleeping with sailors for a fee, usually in their bunks when the ships were in dock.

"Here," he said again. "What you want down here, eh, girlie?"

Rachel forced a smile and said, "What I want is something I bet you'd give me . . . if I ask plain enough."

The drunken sailor lunged at her, a whiskey laugh burbling up his throat.

⟡

"You are hereby found guilty of the crimes of multiple thefts of personal property and murder of the sailor Cluffy Tib—"

"I am no murderer! I am a pirate, and I demand to be treated as one!"

"Silence her!" shouted the judge. "I will not stand for insolence in my court! Silence that foul, murderous woman while I pronounce sentence."

The two court guards pressed her so close that they nearly broke her ribs. One clamped a large, foul hand over her mouth, leaving her nostrils working hard while the judge continued, red-faced and loud: "Pirate indeed. You're a woman and a thief and a murderer, and not necessarily in that order. And therefore, on October 8, in the Year of Our Lord 1789, you will hang from the neck until dead, Rachel Wall. That is my pronouncement. And may God in his infinite wisdom have mercy on your black soul. For no one else will."

⟡

To her jerking end, Rachel Wall swore that she was innocent of the murder of the luckless sailor she had been seen with in the hold of the docked ship, though she did admit to pilfering from various vessels and harbor homes. Her last heist proved her downfall. She attacked young Margaret Bender—who was wearing a bonnet Rachel found fetching—in the street. Rachel snatched the bonnet and then with her grimy hands tried to rip out the young woman's tongue in an effort to silence the victim's screams for help.

Rachel Wall, no shrinking violet and certainly no innocent, was the last woman hanged in Massachusetts. Historians also suspect that she was the first American-born woman to become a pirate. But she was not the only woman with connections to the pirates who plied New England's coastline.

Though no pirate herself, a three-day-old baby—born on July 26, 1720, on an emigrant ship from Londonderry, Ireland, bound for Boston—won over the black-hearted pirate Captain Pedro. He and his crew had boarded the ship, threatening to loot the vessel and then sink it with all on board. But when he saw the newborn, he offered a deal to her mother: *If she agreed to name the baby after his own dear, departed mother, he would free the lot of them. She promptly named the baby Mary. He also gave the mother a bolt of cloth for the baby's wedding gown. Mary later married James Wallace and wore a dress made of the green brocade kindly supplied by Captain Pedro. Throughout her life she was known as Ocean Born Mary.*

New England's largest mass hanging of pirates took place on July 19, 1723, when twenty-six buccaneers were convicted and hanged near Long Wharf in Newport, Rhode Island. This event brought about the capture of one Mary Butterworth, Rhode Island's most successful counterfeiter. Caught up in the after-hanging celebrations, one of her associates passed off a note that seemed suspicious to a clever barmaid, who alerted authorities. But so clever was Butterworth in her methods that no counterfeiting materials were found in her home, save for muslin, paper, ink, and a flatiron—items that could be found in most Rhode Island homes. Mary Butterworth, whose criminal career was ended because of the pirates' executions, was set free.

In the mid-eighteenth century, near Fall River, Massachusetts, an old crone lived in a hut on the Quequechan River. Superstitious locals, suspecting her of witchery, dragged her outside and killed her. They rummaged in the hut and found a love letter from years earlier indicating that she had been the mistress of the infamous Captain Kidd. The enraged locals then burned the hut.

17

Tough Times, Tough People
(1789)

In February, Seth Hubbell and his family trek one hundred miles on foot from Connecticut to the raw wilderness of northern Vermont, where his livestock and crops die and his wife and children sicken. Then life grows difficult.

❧

It seemed to Seth Hubbell that his suffering truly began one hundred miles from his destination, Wolcott, Vermont, a raw, thickly treed wilderness close by the Canada border. He switched that cursed little ox again and again, his arm growing sore with the effort and the beast's back welting with each successive lashing, and yet the thin creature would not move another step. By this time Seth's pity was buried so deep that it would take years to find. All he had in the world was here with him—his five daughters, the eldest of whom was but nine, his wife, an aged horse, and the brace of ox pulling the two-wheel wagon that rattled with a few goods, among them one much-used axe and a hoe.

He turned back to the wagon on which rode his daughters. His wife, Hallie, stood in the mud-churned snow beside the great wood wheel, watching him.

"That ox will fail us as sure as I am a man and you are a woman."

"Seth," she said. "Whipping the poor beast will do no one any good, least of all the ox. It is sickly, don't you see that?"

He looked at the exhausted beast, its head lowered and its tongue distended straight out of its muzzle like a blue stick. Rasping sounds came from the quivering beast's mouth. Even from the wagon it sounded like an imminent death rattle to Seth. He was not impressed.

"We could stop early today," said Hallie. "Give the animal a chance to rest. Tomorrow a fresh start will do us all a world of good."

Seth drew in a deep breath of icy air and nodded. He never expected he would be in the midst of the wilderness on this late February day of 1789. He breathed hard on his hands to warm his cold, work-knotted fingers, now almost frozen into the shape of claws from gripping the reins and the sapling he'd used to whip the beasts forward.

As he made a cookfire for his wife, who was busy herself with their five daughters, ranging in age from three to nine years, he reflected on the past few years. It seemed that his lot would always be one of privation and yearning: from Valley Forge with General Washington to the birth of five girls—alas, no sons yet—and then by himself the previous year, alone much of the time in the unforgiving wilderness. He had gone ahead, had selected the plot on which they would build, and had made a grand start at clearing the lot and even the beginnings of their future home.

It had been lonely, back-breaking work. He had made the lengthy journey with little more than an axe, a worn hoe, and the clothes he wore. He had longed for a yoke of oxen or a plow horse. The only food he had been able to procure all that time had been fresh fish from the creek, cooked on a branch over a small campfire. He had grown to hate the taste of fish.

He watched his wife, slicing what he guessed was their last onion into the stewpot. She was still pretty, though the girls and the hard work of their daily lives had aged her. Lord knows he felt older, too. But among all the difficulties, there had been blessings: Hallie, the girls—fine young things who would grow to help her soon—and being present at the surrender of Cornwallis at Yorktown. Indeed, blessings all.

⌒

Days later, the ox grew so weak that at midday each day of the rest of their journey, Seth had been forced to take the yoke of the faltering ox himself, not only pushing the sickly ox forward but also dragging the entire load with the one good ox working to compensate. Exhausting as this was, it worked—until fourteen miles from their new home, the ox refused to stagger another step farther. He could hardly blame the beast—the snow was four feet deep and nearly impossible to travel in.

Seth Hubbell was beside himself with anger, frustration, and worry. If they didn't have a team of oxen to clear the land and plant and raise crops for food and money, there was no way they could purchase another. And if he had just one ox, he would get only half as much done. He had been forced to leave the ox with a farmer in Johnson whose homestead was nearby, with the understanding that he would establish his family in Wolcott and then come back for the beast. The farmer was a nice enough fellow, but like most others, he had no provisions for the ox.

By then it was March 20, and hay was a rare, precious thing, indeed. For weeks Seth's team had to browse on twigs and brush for sustenance. He finally bargained for a bit of rare hay from a man in Cambridge, Vermont, using almost all of the last of their saved money. He carried bundles of hay on his back, five miles a day for ten days, from Cambridge to Johnson. Then the ox died.

∽

Months later, wind whipped and whistled about his head as Seth Hubbell crouched deeper into the hole he had carved for himself in the snow. He prayed for help, any help, pushing out the stuttering words between chattering teeth. How had it come to this? He was in the dark, barely clothed, with a bushel of corn beside him in the snow, the kernels unmilled and hard as pebbles, and he was still only halfway home. Fifteen miles lay between him and his wife and daughters, all thin as rails and the youngest two with the dreaded fever.

He had tried until well after dark to conjure flame from his flint, but the fuel was green, and his hands were so cold that he could barely hold the little stone. He realized that he had been striking the scrap of steel against his finger, and not the flint. He had not felt a thing. The mitts he had were old socks with more holes than yarn holding them together. He closed his eyes and curled tighter in the snow, and unbidden, the last conversation he had with his wife, several days ago, came to him.

His wife had said in a tired, cracked voice, "Seth, we are nearly out of meal again."

"I'll leave in the morning. I'll trade for corn." He rubbed the greased cloth on the steel of the old axe head, not looking at her.

"But we have nothing to offer. . . ."

He was quiet a moment. Then he said, "We have the moose hide."

"Seth, no. How will we keep the girls warm?"

"We'll make do."

The next morning, with the moose hide tied tight in a bundle and slung over his back, Seth had bidden his gaunt family farewell, offering a smile and telling them he would be back soon.

✑

Years later, the youngest girl, not yet married off, stared at him. She had been doing so for many minutes, before her father finally spoke. "Your mother . . . has gone to be with God now." She nodded. He stopped and turned his back to her. He had just buried Hallie and little Hortense, and his feelings were still raw. Without his wife, how could he be a father to this girl? How could he bear to live here without Hallie?

They had been there just sixteen years. During those early days, they had known the hardest of privations: walking fifty miles with the skin of one sable, just to trade it for meal for their little bird mouths; hauling a bushel of grain twelve miles to the mill, twelve miles back, one day a week for three years.

Then they had lost two milk cows and a brace of oxen to disease. Without draft animals for plowing, Seth had to toe in his seed for three years. And how many nights did his wife not take her meager portion so that her children might sleep without being plagued by pangs of hunger?

All these things, he thought, did Hallie endure. She was the partner of my darkest days, and bore her share of our misfortunes with becoming fortitude, only to be laid low by this roving sickness, now when hardships were fewer and food was not so scarce. Oh, if only I had succumbed instead of her, he thought, his work-gnarled hands pressed tight to the log wall before him. For then she could have taken the girls and fled back southward to her family, instead of enduring this never-ending saga of woe I have put them all through.

Seth Hubbell leaned his forehead against the wall, his eyes closed. He was so tired.

"Papa. . . ."

He turned again to face her and saw the girl still standing, watching him, her eyes red, but dry.

He half-smiled and gathered her to him. "We shall endure here," he said, stroking her hair. "For the sake of your mother and your sister. We shall endure."

✑

As with so many soldiers returning home from the battlefields of the Revolution, Seth Hub-bell was faced with little or no savings, the promise of a pension from a nearly bankrupt

Continental Congress, a malnourished wife and children, and few prospects for producing their own food. The chance for free (or nearly so) land, albeit raw wilderness, where wild game roamed and a family could live unencumbered by the scrutiny of neighbors, must have represented a heaven of possibility, especially for a poor man such as Seth Hubbell.

Published in 1829, the narrative of Seth Hubbell is a modest twenty-four-page tract (the veracity of which is attested to by no fewer than four justices of the peace). He wrote it himself in his dotage, at age sixty-five, some thirty-five years after he first ventured north to help settle Wolcott, in Vermont's hinterlands. Although the narrative is intended, as its introductory lines note, "for the private use and gratification of the sufferer," it is nonetheless a rare first-person account of the life of an impoverished pioneer as well as a highly readable catalog of the seemingly endless sufferings of Hubbell and his family. By today's standards, their struggles are extreme, but their story highlights the privation and hardship that faced the hardy souls who were redefining the edge of New England's raw frontier.

Despite seemingly unendurable hardships, history proved that Hubbell and his line not only survived but thrived. By his own count, when tallying his offspring, he had "seventeen by his two wives, thirteen of them daughters; have had fifty-one grand-children, and six great grand-children, making my posterity seventy-four souls"—and doubtless his descendants are still thriving today.

The information gleaned from between the lines in such accounts reveals a sad truth: Frontier women fared the worse for the wear than did their husbands. Since northern winters were long, New Englanders found distractions where they could. In an account from 1773, we know that a man named Pike, homesteading as one of the first settlers of Whitingham, Vermont, had twenty-eight children—ten by his first wife and eighteen by two subsequent wives. We are also told that most of his children lived to maturity, and we can also safely assume that his first two wives barely did.

If ever a monument testified to the rigors and ravages of life on New England's early frontier, it is the double headstone in Grafton, Vermont, dated 1803, that crowns the grave of Thomas Park's wife, Rebecca, age forty; her young son, Thomas Jr.; and her thirteen infants, all interred in the same grave, one at a time, as the barren years rolled by.

It was a grim but accepted practice that if someone took ill in the fall of the year, a grave would be dug, just in case the stricken person died. Otherwise, the frozen ground would prevent any digging until spring thaw. Another Vermont pioneer lost his wife in midwinter, and, lacking lumber for a coffin, he put her in a hollow log with stones stoppering the ends to prevent wolves and bears from savaging her corpse until he could bury her properly come spring.

18

THE WILD EAST
(1800)

Mrs. Esther Graves of Brookfield, Vermont, spends all night lunging with a pitchfork at a bear intent on savaging her swine. But as she grows wearier, the bear grows angrier.

✑

The screams stopped them all cold: Spoons hovered in midair before the open mouths of most of Esther Graves's eight children, and the youngest, an infant girl draped over Esther's right shoulder, stopped crying long enough for them all to tremble as they heard the shrieks again.

"It's the pigs! That bear's worrying the pigs again, I'm sure of it." Even as she said it, Esther passed the crying baby to her eldest, Emma, a solid girl of thirteen.

"I told your father to track it and shoot it before he left to help Uncle Ephraim. Now he won't be back for a week."

But the children heard no more from her, for she had hurried outside into the dark of the early November evening, only her shawl lifted over her head. The children scarcely had time to rush to the one shuttered window when the cabin door again swung open. They gasped as their mother's face poked back in the doorway. "And keep away from that window. Stay in the house and drop the bolt once I'm out."

Emma nodded. "Yes, Mama." But the door had already slammed shut behind the little woman.

Once outside, Esther Graves hugged the cabin wall, stepping with caution lest she distract the visitor. The pigpen, positioned to the west of the barn, lay silent as she edged closer to the squat bulk of the barn. She swallowed and pulled in a deep breath of icy air. She didn't feel nearly as brave as she tried to appear for the children. Her breath trailed out slowly as she walked, one hand pressed tight to the rough-sawn lumber of the barn wall.

She thought of her husband, Clarence. Of how this could have been avoided. Honestly, she sometimes wondered if he didn't have the mental wherewithal God gave a hen. Nor did she, come to think of it, since she had agreed to marry him too many years ago. "Curse you, Clarence. The one time I need you here for more than making babies and filling your plate and you're gone, off helping a blood relative that could care less about his nephews and nieces." No sooner had she whispered this than she heard the renewed screams of the three hysterical pigs.

Esther doubled her pace, not caring now that her feet made loud shuffling sounds in the fall leaves, and slipped open the small door that led to the manger in front of the barn animals—one dairy cow, her bull calf, an old plow horse, and two oxen. She snatched up the two-tine steel pitchfork, closed the barn door, and dashed the thirty feet to the rear wall of the pigpen. Half of the pigpen was covered with a sloped roof, and the remainder was open-faced.

She saw the backside of the pigpen well enough to toss the pitchfork onto the roof, grab a handful of skirts in one hand, and jam a toe between the unchinked logs of the pen. She launched her lean little body upward and grabbed for purchase at the loosely shingled roof.

It was nearly flat, and she scrambled atop and wasted no time in locating the dark, lumbering mass of the bear. It stood upright at the front edge of the pen and reached in as if it were a man swatting at bugs. She guessed that it had heard her, and probably could see her up there, too, but it appeared to take no notice of anything but the frenzied squeals of the pigs.

Esther listened to its chuffing and grunting, and for a moment she felt a bit worried and weak in the knees, though she prided herself on being a forthright woman of action and intent—one had to if one was married to someone as half-hearted as Clarence.

Several feet beneath her, the three pigs screeched and climbed on top of each other, slamming the logs and rocking the walls hard enough that she feared they might disrupt the enclosure and bring it—and her—down on them. And wouldn't that be a fine thing with a bear on the prowl.

The bear stepped, again like a man, around the corner of the pen. As it drew nearer, its raw animal stink reached her nostrils and raised tears in her wide eyes. No wonder the pigs were afraid, she thought. It's the smell of rancid meat and warmed-over death itself.

It also pulled her from her reverie of fear. That and the sound of her baby wailing from the cabin. Something had to be done about this intruder, and now.

She edged to the corner nearest the bear. By now the beast had worked itself upright and was using its rear feet to scramble up the wall of the pen. Without another thought, she thrust hard at the beast with the pitchfork.

Her first jab missed, but the second stuck into something that quivered and yanked away.

The savage growl of pain and rage pushed hot, rancid breath up at her. Less than an arm's length from the beast, she lost her footing and dropped seven feet, landing on her back in the churned, half-frozen muck of the pen. The great sow pig immediately spun and rammed Esther's ribs with her head. Next the sow would use her teeth. Esther swung the pitchfork's stout handle hard and caught the pig on the side of the head, the sow's squeals telling her she had scared more than enraged her. It gave Esther enough time to scramble to her feet.

She backed to the wall, felt the rough bark of the top log just behind her neck, and heard a growl. Hot breath curled about her neck and face. She screamed and bolted to the center of the pen, the pitchfork held at the ready. There was the bear, upright and swatting, just where she had been standing.

At its height it was taller than her husband and exuded, she knew, considerably more rank scent than did Clarence, despite the fact that he was not one for visiting the washtub on a regular basis. It roared, a ragged angry sound, and she heard her baby's wail, joined by the terrorized cries of the younger children from the house, not twenty yards from the pen. The sound attracted the attention of the bear, as well, for it stopped roaring and raised its head as will a dog sniffing the breeze for a scent.

"Not my babies!" she lunged at the bear, ramming with her considerable muscled might at the bear's head. It swung back to face her just as the pitchfork's tines jammed into its neck. Immediately the bear swung backward, whipping its head twice from side to side, and then dropped to the ground, the fork stuck fast. Just as the long handle was about to disappear over the side of the pen, she scrambled for it and yanked the pitchfork free of the bear's neck.

The pigs squealed behind her, and she felt something brush against her face as she stepped backward toward the center of the pen. She spun at it, swinging the fork high and quick, snagging something light-colored and floating before her face like a specter—she yelped and once again fell backward into the half-frozen muck. The flapping white thing was still there! She got up, taking care to keep the pitchfork held out before her, and poked at it. It winced with each poke but stayed put. She moved closer, looked at it—and laughed. It was her shawl, snagged on the edge of the roof from when she had fallen earlier.

She snatched it down, wrapped it tight about her shoulders, and at the edge of the pen peered into the dark. Sure enough, the black shape was shambling not ten feet away, mewling and grunting, barking and popping its teeth in pain and anger, making a commotion she thought would be enough noise for five animals.

✑

After the fifth attack, Esther Graves wondered how many more holes in its hide the bear could take, for she had landed solid stabs more often than not.

"Mama?"

It was her Emma shouting from the house, worried to death, and with all the children to tend. She had almost forgotten they would be waiting for her to return. "I'm fine, child. I'm safe, but I'll be here until daylight, for the bear keeps returning. Stay inside and blockade the door and window."

"But, Mama. . . ."

"Do as I say!"

"Yes, Mama."

She wanted to huddle with the calmed pigs for warmth, but that sow was not one to be trusted. She would rather shiver for a few hours more than have to doctor a limb torn and bloodied from a riled-up mother pig.

"You deserve to be eaten, pig. I should let that bear have you for the grief you've put me through."

As if in response, one of the younger pigs, the boar, grunted and broke wind.

"Just like a man," she said, convinced now, mostly from its indecisiveness and stink, that the bear, too, was a male. And then she realized that the morning light was growing. She could just make out the edges of the pigpen, the barn, the house, and, behind her, the sleeping pigs. She squished over to the front of the pen and, holding the pitchfork before her, peered over the wall. No bear in sight. She smiled and sighed.

✑

Though bear attacks in New England are largely a thing of the past—the last time a person was killed by a bear in New Hampshire was in 1784—black bears can still be found in all six New England states, most notably in the northern reaches of New England, America's frontier long before European settlers considered excursions of a westward nature.

Carving out lives in the mountains of Vermont, New Hampshire, and Maine, settlers often had to contend with bears, wolves, and mountain lions—also known as catamounts (cat-of-the-mountains) in New England.

During the Revolutionary War, a soldier left his young wife at their home in the woods of Warwick, Massachusetts. Knowing how vital their one pig would be to her survival, she brought it into the house. Unfortunately, a local bear got wind of the pig's new abode and tried to scramble through the open upper half of the door. The young wife met the feisty bruin with a metal shovel that had been heated red hot in the fireplace. She held it to the bear's face, whereupon it howled long and loud into the wilderness and was a nuisance no more.

An early settler of Marshfield, Vermont, Solomon Gilman sat in wait one night in a cornfield that had been repeatedly savaged by a bear. Soon the creature turned up and began dining on the succulent young ears. Gilman shot at the bear, but it leapt and landed on him. He managed to roll from under it but found that his entrails were dragging. He held them to his gut and ran for help. On close inspection, it was found that he had run clutching a handful of bear intestines. His neighbors were doubly grateful—for the killing of the bear and for the conversational fodder he had given them for years to come.

In 1634 a Maine-coast farmer, John Winter, suffered such severe losses to his herd of pigs—two hundred grunters in one season—that Maine's first court decreed statewide death bounties on the two marauders deemed responsible—wolves and Indians—if they were caught in the act of pilfering pigs.

Once a dominant predator with a huge range—from Alberta to Patagonia—the eastern subspecies of panther, or catamount, was by 1800 officially labeled extinct in Massachusetts. Some time before that, Dr. John Warner, brother of fellow Green Mountain Boy Seth Warner, one night lost a large calf to a bold catamount at his Vermont farm. The next morning, Dr. Warner, a noted rifleman, tracked the beast and found it, still feeding on the calf carcass. Warner shot and wounded the catamount. He reloaded and wounded it again, whereupon the cat climbed a tree. Warner shot it again, this time in the head. Still very much alive and angrier than ever, the catamount sprang at the good doctor. While his dog worried the frenzied animal from the rear, Warner clubbed the great cat to death, crushing its skull.

The carcass was stuffed and mounted on a pedestal outside a tavern in Bennington, where the Green Mountain Boys gathered. The tavern came to be known as the Catamount Tavern. That original cat and the tavern, which burned in 1871, have been replaced by a stone statue of a catamount. The statue, affordable and available at the time, was discovered to be of an African lion, a wholly different species than a catamount, though the only visible difference proved to be a tuft at the tip of its tail, which was lopped off to help ensure authenticity.

Alexander Crowell, Barnard, Vermont. Crowell shot this catamount on Thanksgiving Day, 1881, in Barnard, Vermont. Not only is it the largest mountain lion on Vermont's official record, weighing in at 182¹/₂ pounds and measuring seven feet from tail tip to nose tip, but it is also the last eastern panther confirmed killed in Vermont. Crowell had it stuffed and toured with it as an attraction. *Courtesy Library of Congress*

The very last eastern panther confirmed killed in the Green Mountain State was shot in central Vermont by Alexander Crowell, in Barnard, on Thanksgiving Day, 1881. It was also the largest on state record, weighing in at 182½ pounds and measuring seven feet from nose to tail tip. The big cat was stuffed, mounted, and for a time ferried about the region with signs that read: "Monster Panther—Don't Fail to See Him—An Object Lesson in Natural History." It is believed that catamounts are making a comeback in northern New England, with numerous sightings reported in Vermont, New Hampshire, and Maine since 1990.

Quadrupeds aren't the only curious creatures to roam Yankee hills. There are still several hundred rare eastern timber rattlesnakes in Vermont's western Rutland County. Although they now are a protected species, up until 1971 there was a bounty on them.

19

THE *BLACK SNAKE* AFFAIR
(1808)

On August 3, 1808, more than a century before Prohibition, an illicit load of potash instigates animosity, mayhem, and murder between smugglers and the federal militia on Vermont's Winooski River.

⟿

They may be an uncouth bunch up here in the wilds of the border-lands, thought Lieutenant Daniel Farrington, but they are also a crafty bunch, I'll give them that. A grim smile pulled at his mouth. But I haven't finished with them yet, he thought. He had encountered all manner of smuggling, from goods to livestock, in the year since he had been tasked with patrolling Lake Champlain Valley, and the Winooski River in particular, to look for anyone violating President Thomas Jefferson's Embargo Act of the previous year, 1807.

Farrington regarded the thirteen Vermont militiamen crewing the cutter *Fly*. "Make haste, men," he said. "There's a smuggler to catch, and this cutter can move faster, that much I know."

"Aye, the *Fly* can move, and plenty fast, too, sir," said Ellis Drake, his helmsman, "but I'm not so sure we'll need to." This last he said in a hushed tone, as he nodded starboard to the river's edge. There, beached and partially hidden, lay his quarry, *Black Snake,* a smuggling vessel laden with an illicit cargo of potash destined for sale in Canada.

"Row in, you men," Farrington directed in a hoarse whisper. And with a flurry of hand gestures, he divided the group, half to stay with him aboard the *Fly,* half to board *Black Snake* and accompany them back downstream with it. "We'll provide cover for the men on retrieval duty. But I bid you make haste, men. This is no time for idle chatter or dawdling."

The men nodded, and in short order they had accomplished what they thought would be impossible—an easy apprehension of a known smuggling vessel.

"Would that we could have caught them all as fine as this, nice and neatly bound—and as a bonus, the rogues all waiting for us aboard her like good little schoolchildren," said Farrington aloud, feeling more confident and less apprehensive with each dip and stroke of the soundless oars. The *Black Snake* followed somewhat to port and closely astern.

Mere minutes had passed, but his growing sense of relieved victory was short-lived as a violent chorus of oaths and shouts erupted from the swirling Winooski's ragged edge.

"Look lively, men! The smugglers are giving chase along the eastern bank!" Farrington scarcely had time to utter his words when a rifle shot cracked the midday air and Ellis Drake pitched forward, slumped over the tiller and gagging on the blood that filled his throat.

"By God, this will not do! Men, ashore! Take the *Fly* ashore—there! We'll play this game!" They dropped their sails, and his dozen remaining men scrambled out of the two boats, bloodlust raising their hackles, for Drake had been a man well liked among them. But even as they crashed through the undergrowth and gained a riverside path, more gunshots erupted all about them from the dense alders, followed by a resounding boom that carried with it sure death.

The Vermont militiamen immediately knew the sound as a wall-piece, an immense weapon with an eight-foot barrel that belched sixteen-ounce balls and buckshot. Farrington's right shoulder throbbed as if it had been punched. Then his left arm felt as though it had been shot off, so intense and immediate was the pain. But he soon forgot his pain when he heard his friend and fellow soldier, Asa Marsh, mere steps away, groan as if he had breathed his last—and indeed he had—for then the man whipped upright, stiffened, and crashed backward in a heap. Then a ball slammed young Lieutenant Farrington in the head, and he lost consciousness.

Within minutes the men retreated to the boats, lugging the limp forms of Marsh and Lieutenant Farrington. Then one of them swore in disgust as he noted that the smugglers also shot Jonathan Ormsby, an innocent farmer who had been working his field nearby and, on hearing the commotion, had run over to investigate.

The smugglers had done this for money and little else, thought the seething militiamen as they clambered back aboard the *Fly* and *Black Snake*. The soldiers gritted their teeth and vowed to hunt down the men who had done this.

∽

And within the week, they did indeed round up the sniping smugglers. Four of them were found guilty of manslaughter. Of the four, Cyrus B. Dean seemed to never shut his mouth about how he had a right to make a living trading with Canada, just as he had done for years, and no law that skunk Jefferson made was going to stop him. His fellow smugglers in custody did their best to distance themselves from him.

"Dean, shut your mouth, man." One of his fellows looked at the short, thin Cyrus and saw little trace of the man he thought he knew, the fun fellow he had accompanied on smuggling runs for months. "Don't you know they're about ready to hang us all as quick as look at us anyway? Surely even you can see that it would be wiser for you to keep quiet."

"That's easy for you to tell me, as you'll be let out of here soon." Dean sounded as if he knew something the rest of them didn't.

"How do you know that, Dean?" asked his fellow smuggler.

But Dean turned away from him and resumed his shouting.

Two days later, in September, before the judge, the lawyers, and the jurymen in the courtroom, Dean continually interrupted the proceedings, hampering the judge's attempts to keep order.

And so, within weeks of the incident, it came as little surprise to the other three men that they were pardoned and that Cyrus Dean was to be hanged. He had been painted as the ringleader, and he had indeed been the one to man the big gun, the one that did the most damage.

&

On November 11, 1808, Cyrus B. Dean was led to a specially constructed gallows in Burlington. And as he had the pulpit once again, he raged at the throng who had gathered to witness his execution. "How dare you let Jefferson's Democratic Republicans make a mockery of justice like this? And you call yourself Federalists? I damn you! Damn you all to hell and eternity for what you are about to do—for what you are allowing to happen!"

And then they did it—and Cyrus B. Dean swung by the neck until dead before a crowd of thousands.

&

As with Prohibition a little more than a century later, a federal law seemingly sound in theory proved to be disastrous in practice, especially at the local level for people eking out meager livings. Largely regarded as a bit of unfortunate legislation, Thomas Jefferson's Embargo Act of 1807 was a reaction to continued British aggression toward the United States and was intended, in part, to hinder British trade. Unfortunately, the law, as written, failed to prevent British imports from entering the United States.

The legislation was later rewritten, but from the start it proved fraught with prohibitive glitches and consistently brought more harm than good to citizens, especially in rural communities along the Canadian border in Vermont, New Hampshire, and Maine, where meager subsistence incomes were regularly supplemented with sales of hard-won potash, timber, livestock, and other goods.

Though this wasn't necessarily the case with the crew of the Black Snake, enforcement of the embargo made criminals out of otherwise law-abiding citizens, who broke the law doing what months before had been acceptable, encouraged trade with their neighbors. British Canada was Vermont's primary trading partner in the early days of the nineteenth century, but President Thomas Jefferson's Embargo Act of 1807, which prohibited trade with an increasingly hostile Great Britain, effectively hamstrung border residents who depended on free, open trade with their northern neighbors.

For years, Vermonters, already living hardscrabble lives, cautiously ignored the Embargo Act and continued to smuggle goods and livestock using what in later years came to be known as Smuggler's Notch, a winding, cave-riddled, narrow mountain pass in the Green Mountains running north to south. The Notch's brisk trade of smuggled goods, most notably livestock—simple to move because they are self-propelled—proved profitable for smugglers and vexing for federal revenue agents.

During the Civil War, fugitive slaves used the route to escape north to freedom in Canada. And during Prohibition, its convenient caves and twisting terrain became a favored route for rumrunners to smuggle illegal alcoholic beverages in the other direction, south from Canada to the thirsty masses below the border.

✍

In those dry years from 1920 to 1933, Lake Champlain was also a major artery for illicit booze ferried south in souped-up speedboats from Canada. For years U.S. Customs officials patrolled the vast lake, successfully nabbing all manner of alcohol-laden watercraft. Sometimes the bootleggers gave up without a fight, but more often than not the chase was on, shots were fired, and frequently men died.

Just below the international border at Rouse's Point, the lake conveniently narrows to a channel only a few hundred yards wide. It made an ideal spot for Customs officers to trap rumrunners. Of course, the smugglers didn't want to be caught, as was the case at 3:00 a.m. on August 12, 1932, when Customs Officers Armand Lavigne and Lawrence

Izard gave chase to a speedboat after it bogged down on a rope they had stretched across the channel, under the water's surface, for just such a purpose. Thinking capture was imminent, one of the two smugglers tossed sacks of illegal liquor into the water as the officers closed in with their patrol boat.

The officers rammed the rum-running craft, which was attempting to turn back to Canada, and Izard tried to leap aboard the smugglers' boat, but he was struck with a blow from a boat hook. Lavigne fired warning shots with his .45 across their bow, and Izard's next attempt at a jump was more successful. He scrambled aboard the boat, shouting, "U.S. Customs! Stop this boat!" But the rumrunners were having none of it.

They set on him with a club and dumped him overboard. Lavigne continued pursuit of the rumrunners, but his patrol boat was no match for their customized craft. He circled back and found Izard floating unconscious in the water. His life jacket kept him from drowning. The smugglers' boat was found several days later, abandoned in Vergennes, but the smugglers were never found.

20

THE LEGEND OF SKINNER'S CAVE
(1808)

Vermont smuggler Uriah Skinner is tracked to his secret island on Lake Memphremagog by federal officers who take his boat, stranding him in a cave with his smuggled goods and no way off the island. A century later, the cave is discovered . . . with someone inside.

✒

Captain Charlton leaned into the wind and urged his handful of men to row faster. "If there is one thing I will not stand for, it is once again losing that smuggling hermit on this bloody lake!" A low chorus of murmurs rose from his straining crew, even as Charlton kept talking. "Now that we know about that filthy hermit's island, there's nothing stopping us from nabbing him tonight." Charlton's thoughts turned to the tangled mess of vegetation that the locals called "Skinner's Island."

Far ahead in the pitch-black night, Uriah Skinner's dense and bushy beard hid a bold half-grin. The big man—a head taller than any local fellow—was far from a bumbling hermit. He leaned into his rowing, and the long craft gained another length. As with dozens of trips before, his boat was piled with crates and parcels. Few were stacked higher than the gunwales, but not so low as to deny him a tidy profit.

He had nothing against President Thomas Jefferson or his Embargo Act. If anything, he felt he should thank the man. After all, this piece of legislation was the reason he was in business. And a good business it was, too—better than getting a cow's muck-soaked tail across the face while trying to milk the beast.

Yes, sir, it was the best occupation he had ever tried. Except for the pesky federal soldiers dogging him each of the last three trips. Skinner felt sure someone down Newport way had tipped off the revenue men about his irregular runs to and from Canada.

No matter, he thought, as he put more shoulder into his task and mumbled aloud: "There's not an officer worth his salt what can find me once I've hid away among the islands on ol' Memphremagog." He nearly laughed but thought better of it. He had a decent lead on this latest batch of revenue hounds and felt good about his chances of disappearing into the undergrowth on his island.

With no source of light, save for the bobbing, wavering lantern of the far-off pursuing craft, Skinner tracked a straight course to the little island. By now, he fancied he could find it in his sleep.

Within minutes he felt the presence of the craggy, tree-lined isle just to his right. He slowed and guided the boat soundlessly into a narrow cleft between small rocks and green clumps of shrubbery. He tied the boat off and then parted thick, tangled growth at the water's edge that covered a seeming abyss—the expected rock wall was instead a deep cave, wide enough for five men laid end to end, tall enough for two or more, and deep enough that even in full daylight, the rear of the cave would barely be visible from the entrance. Skinner unloaded his smuggled cargo and secreted it at the rear of the vast cave. So far as he knew, no one else was aware of its existence. He had found old broken odds and ends that told him Indians might have used it, but that would have been a long time ago.

Skinner had barely enough time to return to the safety of the cave after stowing the boat away when sounds close by caused him to freeze, his heart hammering hard and his mouth dry. He had taken all possible care. Had he been found? But it couldn't be!

"I cannot imagine where he's disappeared to, sir. There's no trace."

"Bah. This time, men, we'll not give up so easily. For rest assured he is a man and not a specter, and he could not have disappeared without a trace."

"Skinner could have."

"Who said that?" The captain rounded on his men, a sneer spread wide on his face. "For that snide comment, we will stay out all night, or until we capture the smuggling rogue. No one can be allowed to flout the very laws of this burgeoning nation and get away with it—not just once, but time and again. No one. Now row on."

They put in at a low, rocky spit, and the captain ordered the men out and on alert. "Keep the lanterns lit, but low. We're looking for any sign at all of the man. We've all caught glimpses of him here and there. Plus, given the testimony of our spies, we can safely assume that the man, big as he is, will cause no end of trouble for us. Do not drop your guard for a moment."

The patrol scoured the thickly treed island for hours. Half the men returned to the boat and ferried the captain around to the other side of the island, where they were to meet the last of the patrol. And waiting for them was a handful of grinning men, standing at the shore. One of them held the mooring rope of a long skiff, the smuggler's craft.

The captain jumped out of the boat and into the water. "Excellent work, men. By Jove, we've got him now. He has to be here, has to be on the island, for he is too ugly to be a fish."

Though the men spent another few hours trammeling the island, they found no sign of Skinner.

"By God, I know he's here, but I'll be damned if we can find him." The captain gave the island one last rueful look and then said, "Very well, tie his boat behind ours, and we'll leave him here to think about his fate. If he likes this damnable island so much, then he can stay here and starve to death, for all I care. And there's an end to it."

From between long, hanging vines that concealed the front of his cave like hair covering the face of a pretty girl, Uriah Skinner watched the fat captain steal his beloved boat, *Lola*, and heard his boasts and oaths. He took all this in from his hiding spot deep in the cave. He longed to bellow, "Oh no you don't!" but he gritted his teeth and resisted the powerful urge, knowing it would result in nothing less than a long prison term, if not a hanging.

It mattered not to the patrol that the island was technically in Canadian territory, for he knew they would drag him back to the United States and try him there, as sure as the morning sun was slowly showing its face.

The towering brute Skinner sat in his cave all day surrounded by boxes of goods he had bartered and traded for in Canada, just over the border line. He grew hungry toward evening and ripped open box after box, even though he knew that this trip held little more than lace goods, hard goods, and a few bottles of brandy—but nothing to eat. The brandy would do him for now, but he longed for a tankard of ale, a loaf of crusty bread, and a wedge of farmer's cheese. He shook his head. Wishing never got anybody anything, he thought. He sighed, pulled out his pipe, and smoked until well into the night.

∽

Some years after Uriah Skinner's one-man smuggling operation was brought to an end and local folks who expected certain trade goods had long given up on the big, brooding trader as an absconding bad seed, the international border bisecting Lake Memphremagog became a resort region with grand hotels and all manner of distractions for vacationers to enjoy.

In the mid-nineteenth century, a guest at the prestigious Owl's Head Mountain House was out rowing and fishing the lake when a storm whipped the usually serene surface into a froth. He sought refuge on the nearest bit of land, Skinner's Island, and as he approached, he spied an overgrown grotto. The weeds and vines were thick, but he managed to make his way inside. And far back in the damp of the deep cave, under quavering lamplight, he found a human skeleton, somewhat large of frame.

Long before whites discovered the region's natural wonders, Abenakis feared the cave. They considered it the haunt of a dreaded water beast, which many now believe to be Memphre, the lake's oft-seen Loch Ness Monster–like denizen. The cave is guessed to be human-made and quite old, as evidence of human habitation of the region has been found dating to the Archaic Period, roughly 6,000 years ago.

Some years ago, a dam on the Magog River in Canada raised the level of the lake by more than six feet, and today the entrance to Skinner's Cave is no longer fully visible. The lake still sees significant boat traffic, both legal and otherwise, though it never saw as much smuggling action as it did during Prohibition.

Newport, Vermont, in particular, was known to be home to a variety of speakeasy taverns that sold booze ferried down Lake Memphremagog by enterprising locals. Many of the smugglers regarded the proceeds gained from the odd quick trip to Canada and back as a practical way to keep their families fed and their farms in operation during the otherwise hard years of the Great Depression.

21

RUNAWAY POND
(1810)

On the morning of June 6, 1810, a group of men gather to widen the outflow of Long Pond, high above the inhabited river valley below. The plan works too well: Mammoth trees, boulders, buildings, bridges, and livestock are swept up and carried for miles. In less than an hour, an entire valley is brutally altered forever.

❧

"If it weren't for these blamed trees, we'd be able to see the entire Barton River Valley below us there," said Bill Henry.

The other men stopped working, resting chins on shovel handles as they stood on the riverbank. They nodded in agreement as they passed the water crock from man to man. "Soon enough it will be a place that people will have heard about. Mark my words," said Bill. "This valley will fill with settlers, and they'll need trees to build with." The speaker took another swig of water. "And your mills will have all they can do to keep up with the demand, Wilson!"

A chorus of laughs sounded as the men returned to their tasks. After a few hours' work, with so many hands making the task move much quicker than he could have imagined, Wilson figured he could take all the ribbing they doled out.

"We'll have to carefully pick away at that three-foot berm we left to hold back the water as we worked." Bill looked to Wilson, who nodded agreement, and said, "Ready, then?"

"Ready. Give it a go and see what you get. Don't be too disappointed if the streambed to Mud Pond doesn't quite fill. You know how these things can be."

Wilson and Horace Felton picked at the three-foot-thick berm of hard-packed soil and clay. "Here she goes, boys!" The water sluiced over the last of the berm, and for the first few seconds it looked as though they might have to rethink their plan, so unimpressive were the results. Then, with no warning, the rest of the earthen dam burst, and a rush of water as tall as two cows pushed out at them. The two men who had picked at the last of the berm fell backward and were dragged up the newly formed bank by their fellows.

A round of cheers rose up as the men saw the burbling wash of water begin to course along the route they had worked with their shovels and picks. But as they watched, as quickly as the water burst forth, it sank out of sight beneath the new streambed they had dug. For a long moment the entire group stood still, mouths open and eyes staring. The water had just disappeared.

It soon became apparent to them that they had unwittingly dislodged a firm bottom layer of clay that for ages had held the water on the surface and flowing downhill.

"Oh God, what have we done?" But that was all Wilson had time to say, for at that moment the water rose again, away from the streambed they had shaped for it. A great surge of water pushed upward, then downhill, straight down the raw, wide ravine toward the valley floor.

The very world before them shifted and changed as the weakened north-end bank of Long Pond disappeared under a wall of brown water ten times wider than anything they had intended and higher than they thought possible. The men scarcely had time to shout as they helped each other scrabble for higher ground. As they watched, the pressure of the water bearing sharply downhill toward Mud Pond was too much for anyone to withstand.

"Run, Spencer!" shouted Pa Chamberlain. "You've got to outrace the water! Run down to the mill, then keep on going to the valley! Warn everybody you see!"

The tall young man, Spencer Chamberlain, nearly fell from the push his father gave his shoulder blades, but he regained his footing and, like a spring colt, dashed downward through the trees, glancing to his side the entire time, racing the roiling mass of water. He turned and ran higher upslope, and higher still as the mud and water and the ever-deafening roar pushed closer.

Wilson screamed, "My wife! The children!" and pitched his tools to the ground as he scrabbled up the slope. Just behind him the water lapped at his boots and swallowed his shovel and pick. As he passed Mud Pond at a dead run, he saw the great wall of water slow, almost as if it were gathering its forces for a renewed attack.

A minute later he reached their home at the mill, knowing but not caring that his hands and face were lacerated from branches and rocks as he fell scrambling down the steep drop to the mill. He kicked in the door.

"There you are—get out now!"

"Why . . . whatever is the—"

"No time. Water's coming, we'll all be drowned!" He snatched up his two children, a boy and a girl, one under each arm, and shouted at his wife again, "For the Lord's sake, get out now! Head for high ground." His children screamed and struggled in his arms. He gripped them tighter and lunged after his wife.

She ran to the door and said, "What's that noise?" Then she screamed as the biggest moving force she had ever seen bore down on them from above.

⁂

Though he had heard odd rumbling sounds from south in the valley, Coventry farmer Joseph Day had no time to investigate. The day was a fine one, and he hated to waste a minute of it. After a few more minutes stacking wood, he straightened and stretched his aching back. He still hadn't had his midday meal, and already it was late afternoon. He would soon be late for milking.

"A few more minutes won't make a difference one way or t'other." And he walked slowly up the hill toward his house and barn. He heard a noise behind him and turned to see his wife, with an empty pail in her hand, trudging up the worn path behind him. "Why are you sneaking up behind me, wife?"

"Now wouldn't you like to know." She smiled at him and held up the bucket. "Scraps for the hogs. Should be a good year for them."

"Aye," he said, turning with her to face the southern end of their little river valley. "Do you hear that?"

"Indeed I do." They both stood, watching, squinting, waiting. And within seconds, as the sound swelled from a dull thudding to a harsh roar, they saw a living thing, like a rolling storm cloud come to life on the land, only it was following the river, and devouring it at the same time, advancing on them with unchecked hunger.

"The river . . . it's alive!" Joseph Day looked at his wife. "To the house!"

They ran uphill to their home and stood before it, watching the advancing wall of water as it approached. "My bridge. . . ."

Even as he said it, the brown mass rolled over the stout log structure that had taken him weeks of effort to build the autumn before.

"Joseph, the sty!"

They both watched as the water washed right over the stout structure housing what represented much of their annual income. Mrs. Day dropped the wooden bucket and held her hands to her face, stifling her shocked sobs as she watched the piggery disappear. The bucket rolled down the slope and was sucked into the passing flood.

For a few seconds following the deluge, they heard what must have been the screams of their pigs as they were carried away, battered and thrashed in the torrent.

Within minutes, the churning water was replaced with a slower, calmer version of itself, though still swollen twice as high as the spring floods that engorged the Barton River each year. But it was no snow runoff that did this. And when the waters receded fully, within an hour, there was nothing left of their bridge, their pigsty, nor any trees, rocks, or logs for as far as they could see in either direction.

It was a long time before either of them spoke. But they were both thankful that they had built their house and barn well above the river flat.

✐

A handful of people, settlers of the long valley, gathered on the hill overlooking Barton Village. No one seemed unaccounted for. The few people stood quietly, hands to their mouths, as they watched the great wall of brown water thunder down the ravine, carving hunks of earth and undermining entire hillsides as it pounded downward toward the flooded valley below.

They watched as massive hardwoods several feet in girth were pushed over, snapped in half, and carried aloft on the churning waters. Indeed, so many massive trees were uprooted along its path that they periodically formed natural dams, the massive trunks interlocking in a ragged weave until the pressure of the water behind them built up and then burst free, sending full-grown maples pinwheeling into the current as the seventy-foot-high wall of water renewed its strength and boiled up again in a roiling mass.

The waters of Long Pond, Mud Pond, and all of the tributaries that fed the flood along the way managed to swell the Barton River enough that its force raised the level of Lake Memphremagog, twenty-seven miles north, by more than a foot. The next day, when the flood's path was retraced by curious locals who had heard the strange sounds and wondered what could have caused them, not a tree in the wide, sopping path was found to be standing.

Within seconds of being breached, Long Pond's waters ripped a chasm in places 120 feet deep and hundreds of feet wide, releasing the contents of the pond. Within minutes, nothing but mud issued forth from the wound. And even that thick sludge burbled downslope for hours. The entire catastrophe had taken six hours.

For miles around, people heard the mighty sounds of the crashing water, the snapping tree trunks, the slamming boulders—one 100-ton boulder was moved more than half a mile by the raw force of the water. Fish were found lodged in treetops forty feet up.

It is said that Lake Memphremagog's aquatic species were so startled that thousands of fish headed for the perceived safety of feeder streams and rivers, among them the Black River. And Coventry Falls was reported to have, in the days following the flood, a glut of 5,000 pounds of fish retrieved by savvy seiners.

✺

The day proved to be a cruel lesson in exercising caution in what you wish for, especially true for mill owner Wilson, whose family barely escaped with their lives. His grist- and sawmills did not fare so well. The only trace of his mills ever found was one little steel wheel, some miles downstream.

Vermont's Northeast Kingdom is one of the rare regions in the Northern Hemisphere where a number of water sources actually flow north. And Long Pond was no exception, because it lay higher than the north-lying Lake Memphremagog, which straddles the U.S.-Canadian border.

Though there were a good many close calls, remarkably no human lives were lost that day when Long Pond burst its banks, mostly owing to the sparse population of the region. But lives were also spared because Spencer Chamberlain was so successful at outrunning the savage wall of water and warning everyone of the impending flood.

To commemorate his mad dash, each August, on Glover Day, a footrace leads runners on the course the water took on that June day two hundred years ago. The route, now a primary artery for travel through the region, runs straight through the former pond's bed . . . and is called Dry Pond Road.

22

"1800-AND-FROZE-TO-DEATH"
(1816)

Mount Tambora's massive volcanic eruption in the East Indies in April 1815 instigates killing frosts in each month of the year across New England, resulting in crop failures, starvation for people and livestock, epidemic diseases, and mass exodus—all the makings of a famine.

❧

His corn crop was nothing more than a sickly patch of blackened nubs, his sheep and cattle were gaunt and constantly begging, and his youngest child had run into the kitchen, weeping and holding a songbird, one of the first robins of the season that they had seen. But it was dead, frozen. In June.

Since then he had found scores more birds, scattered beneath trees like leaves, and some waterfowl along the river and in the pond, stiff in death. Whether they died from a struggle against the unexpected ice or from the numbing cold, he did not know.

"It is the wrath of God, I tell you. Nothing else will account for such a vicious freeze and days of killing frost before the midpoint of June," said Josiah Redfield.

"Just because it hasn't happened in your memory doesn't mean there is no precedent," said his son-in-law, Norbert Quillins. "There has to be a reason, a tangible reason."

"You are wrong and tread dangerously close to uttering blasphemy. Norbert Quillins, I will not tolerate blasphemy in my home."

Norbert looked at his father-in-law and nodded. It would do no good to incur the man's wrath. While he loved Redfield's daughter, he merely tolerated her parents. He almost understood why the old man clung to the silly notion that God had something to do with this. But to Norbert it was nature's will, nothing more than the waxing and waning of the seasons. And he knew it would not last.

And as he expected, on June 5, the temperature rocketed upward again, and he eagerly replanted his corn. But that very night, something woke him and would not let him return to sleep. And then he knew what it was. He was cold.

"Louise, Louise! Wake up!" Norbert shook his wife awake from a deep sleep as she snuggled under layers of thick quilts.

"What's the matter, Norbert?"

"Make haste. The crops will die if we don't act soon. It's always coldest at dawn!"

"What are you talking about?" His wife stood, shivering. "It's June, Norbert." She shivered despite herself and said, "I thought it was a little cold when we went to bed."

"Yes, yes," he said, beckoning her with frantic hand gestures. "There may well be a killing frost, and we can't afford to lose the crop."

"But what can we do?"

He turned in the doorway and said, "Build bonfires to keep the fields warm. I've heard of others doing so. It may not work, but I'll be damned if I'm going to sit in here and do nothing." He bolted out the door, a high moon shining down on a still, clear night that reminded him more of a late October evening than an early summer night. "And bring the children!" he shouted from the darkness. "We'll need their help, too!"

Norbert dragged a ragged mess of dried brush from behind the barn and snatched up lamp oil from a cluttered workbench. This shouldn't happen in June, he thought. Not after the long, cold winter we've already had. Surely we deserve better than this. . . . But he knew also that if there ever was a place likely to have severe frost in June, it was Colebrook, New Hampshire, and especially here, in this low-lying valley farm. With fertile land often came early, bruising frosts. But not until autumn, surely!

Yesterday, he thought as he raced to his crops, just yesterday it had been near 80 degrees. Such a shift in weather did not bode well, not at all. He was beginning to think there might be something to his father-in-law's claim about God's wrath descending on them.

The next day brought lower temperatures, rarely climbing above 35 degrees. Frost covered everything in the morning, and the water trough bore an increasingly thicker skin of ice with each hour. Freshly budded and leafing trees succumbed to the freakish weather. The new growth had all blackened and withered, leaving bare trees looking as raw and bedraggled as Norbert felt. And then, late in the day on June 6, it began to snow.

His children ran outside, dressed as if it were December, and caught snowflakes on their tongues. Neither Norbert nor his wife smiled.

For the next two days, the family watched, stunned, as snow, sometimes mixing with pelting sleet, drove downward from a sky so thick with gray storm clouds that it looked to Norbert as if they would never leave. High winds cut in from the east, and by the morning of June 10, the snowpack measured twenty-two inches and continued to grow. It crusted over and had drifted in places to his waist.

"Another sheep froze to death today," he told his wife, hardly believing the words himself. "It is June, in the year 1816, Louise. By rights we should be working the crops in our shirtsleeves, not wondering where our next meal will come from."

Louise patted his sleeve, squeezed it once, and then turned back to the fireplace to stir the soup that seemed thinner with each meal.

The ice in their farm pond was now more than an inch thick. He shoveled a path to it and then chipped a hole for the livestock to drink from. Three times that day he went out to chip the ice free, but the animals were too cold to make the trek to the pond, too weak with hunger to move about. They should have been cropping green grass in the pasture.

No farmer he knew, himself included, had any feed saved from the unusually long winter. And all of them had already fed their families' corn to the livestock. If this mad weather stopped, there was still the chance of getting in short-season crops. But next winter would be a harsh thing. Already the children were exhausted, and he and his wife were gaunt.

⌒〜⌒

Mid-July saw a month's worth of healthy plant growth after early June's devastation. On the evening of July 12, Norbert and Louise sat quietly by the open cabin door looking out into the night, not speaking but enjoying a warm, caressing breeze. "A far cry from a month ago, eh, my dear?"

"Mm, yes. I was just thinking that myself."

"I will admit," said Norbert as he packed his pipe, "that I feel a little foolish in almost believing your father's silly notions of hellfire and damnation and the coming Judgment Day." He snorted a quick laugh and touched fire to the tobacco, puffing until it glowed.

"Don't be so quick to judge others, Mr. Quillins," she said. "It's only been a month since we've had a snowstorm."

He caught her eyeing him, a half-smile on her face, and they both laughed.

By the end of the month, unseasonably cold temperatures once again settled over the valley, and though no snow came with it, the chill air was enough to wither the delicate, month-old crops, especially in the low-lying farms.

All about him Norbert heard the laments from his neighbors, and his wife's parents were beside themselves with worry. "Surely this is the beginning of the end!" said the old man. Norbert said nothing. He wished he hadn't even gone to Sunday meeting, for there he found nothing but grief and woe and dire predictions for the end of the world. He knew for certain that the crops that had withered and died these past two weeks in July, of all months, had been his family's last chance for a long winter relatively free of gnawing hunger.

He was doing his best to keep the livestock sustained, but without proper food the hens were not laying eggs, the two milk cows had all but dried up, and the oxen were gaunt ghosts of themselves. The sheep, which he and their neighbors had shorn earlier in the season, were now too cold to survive in the exceedingly cold air and so were lying down and giving up.

He could not count the number of dead sheep, especially ewes and lambs, he had seen in the pastures as he returned from the meetinghouse. Nothing had come of the gathering, for there is not a man alive who can best nature. And no one had provisions enough to sustain their own families, let alone pool them for the greater good.

He looked out his open door at the small, blackened nubs of his third corn crop, the seeds for which took the last of their savings, and heard the woeful bleat of the starving sheep and the husky bellow of cows that had been so rationed in their fodder that they long had been gnawing the bark of trees in the pastures.

Not only were their fruit trees lacking any young fruit, but they had lost all their leaves and buds in June and had never recovered.

The last two weeks of August brought more widespread killing frosts, blackening any crops, even the hardiest—rye and wheat—that had survived to that point. By then Norbert had grown numb to the prospect of putting food by for his family. They butchered what animals they could, since the beasts were starving anyway, but it was not enough. When he hunted, he turned up only porcupines and two squirrels.

He had heard that people on the coast were faring much better, for they were exploiting the riches of the sea. Fish had never particularly appealed to him, but just the thought of it incited a growling in his stomach. He had resolved to bundle up the family and head that way, though it would have to be on foot as their horse was far too weak to make the journey.

He noted, with sadness, that his was one of the last families left in the valley. Fewer and fewer people showed up at Sunday meeting, and when he had asked, those who were friends of the missing said they had just up and left, walked away from their homes, their farms, and gone to look elsewhere.

"Better to starve to death trying to find a better life than to sit here and know that death is coming." After hearing that statement, he resolved to pursue a better life for his family.

But it would be another week before they would leave, mostly because his wife's family would not move a muscle. "The Good Lord put me on this patch of earth in this river valley to farm and to live or die by the bounty He provides, and I'll not go against His wishes." There was no reasoning with the old man. In the meantime, Norbert was forced to dig up the rotting seed potatoes he had planted months before, and it was these that his family ate in silence for most of the following week.

By September 11, temperatures again dropped to far below freezing. The next morning, in the frigid light of early dawn, Norbert Quillins bundled his weak wife and children into their warmest clothes and hefted a sack that contained their few most valuable possessions, and they departed at a slow walk for the coast. He had found no buyer for the farmstead they had carved from the wilderness, and he no longer cared.

&

The explosive volcanic eruption of Mount Tambora in Indonesia in April 1815, the largest eruption in recorded history, forced one hundred miles of ash, dust, and sulfuric acid into the stratosphere. The eruption and its aftermath killed, by modest estimates, more than 70,000 people and ensured that in New England, 1816 became known as the year of "1800-and-froze-to-death," "The Year There Was No Summer," and "The Poverty Year."

In New England, killing frosts in each month of the year caused widespread crop devastation, resulting in the near starvation of cattle, poultry, and other meat animals. Among people, these crop failures resulted in malnutrition, starvation, epidemics of disease, and increases in mortality—all the makings of a famine.

Frost killed more than 90 percent of New England's corn, one of the region's most versatile crops. Very little was harvested, and even less of that was usable. The ripple effects of this lack of crop growth were serious and far-reaching: Farmers were unable to meet their tax bills, and market prices for corn skyrocketed, jumping from 70 cents a bushel to more than $5 per bushel. Oddly enough, prices for beef and pork dropped, largely because of regional gluts on markets as farmers sold their weakening stock early, realizing they would not be able to sustain them through the coming harsh winter of 1816–1817 with little or no fodder.

People who lived on New England's coast began to turn to the sea as a more stable source of food. Weather events such as this one helped transform fishing from a means of sustenance to a means of income.

Families left New England in droves, beaten down by the abysmal stretch of hunger and crop failure—winters had been tough and crop yields poor since 1812—convinced that it would happen again. Towns such as Richford, Vermont, which before 1816 had sustained year-round, growing populations, dwindled to little more than ghost towns. Granby, Vermont, lost its articles of incorporation, so low had its population dropped. Still other New England towns sustained similar exoduses, were abandoned altogether, and ceased to exist.

Families gave up their hard-worked farms, and if they could not sell them, even at cut-rate prices, they simply walked away, leaving them for whoever might come along. And many people did come, particularly immigrants from Europe, another region that was laid low by the very same devastating atmospheric effects. In an odd way, the ill wind bore promising fruit as New Englanders headed west in droves in hopes of finding a better, more stable place to farm. New settlers from Europe took their places to ensure that New England, just a few decades later, would come to be considered the breadbasket of the nation.

23

THE WORST MISTAKE EVER MADE
(1826)

A violent thunderstorm in August 1826 forces Samuel Willey, his wife, their five children, and two hired men from their home in the heart of New Hampshire's rugged Crawford Notch, convinced it will be crushed in a landslide. They are wrong—but will never know how very wrong.

༄

The June rain hammered down all night, and by morning, though it still came down, the storm had lessened. It hadn't been a particularly wet spring, and for that Samuel Willey had been grateful. He and his two hired men, David Nickerson and David Allen, had made the most of it by adding rooms to the original house, expanding the stables, and making the property look its best. And it showed. But the rain was a welcome thing—even if the storm had seemed particularly savage.

The preceding night had been terrible, with the terrific crashing and rumbling of thunder, the brighter-than-daylight flashes of lightning illumining every nook and corner of their house. Samuel had given up on his nightly reading of the Bible and gone to bed.

He yawned and stretched his thick arms, grateful that the day began free of rain, though the day would be a long, gray one. Samuel peered out the front windows at the road, the roiling river below, and, lording above it, the face of Mount Webster, sheer and savage. No matter how often he saw it, for he saw it all day long—it was a feature impossible to avoid—its nearness and hulking presence still caught him by surprise.

Samuel walked out onto the front porch, where his wife, Polly, stood. "Samuel," she said, "this needs an edge before I can cut up the stew meat." She handed him the carving knife just as a sudden sound like nothing they had ever heard froze them to the spot on the front steps of their inn. In an instant, the entire cliff that faced them from across the river, and which moments before he had stared at, cut loose from somewhere beneath the cloud-wreathed heights.

Polly screamed and recoiled as if bitten. Samuel was too stunned to say anything. The two hired men paused in their work when they heard the rending sound of the great sheet of boulders, soil, and vegetation churn downward from the heights of the mountain.

They all felt the gust created by the great downward-rushing sheet of rock. A cloud of thick dust pushed toward them. They saw boulders larger than oxen tumble down the slope and come to rest in the river. Other massive rocks made their way across the river itself. Dust and raw rock debris still careened down the fresh slope.

∞

It had taken Samuel days to convince his wife that they were in no real danger of any such thing happening on their side of the river. She had run into the house screaming, herding the five children into the front room. By then they had all heard and seen what had happened, and the youngest three were weeping uncontrollably. Their mother's unmasked terror didn't help ease their minds. Even Samuel had considered flight as the prudent course of action.

But after a few days of consideration and talk with his wife and the two hired men, he decided that as a concession he would build a solid stone-walled shelter just downslope from the house to which they could all flee in the unlikely event that a rock slide should ever threaten their side of the valley.

The mountain directly behind them was no threat, he knew. But the summer had been a dangerously dry one. Such conditions made for weakened, thirsty soil, and on a slope even as seemingly stable as that one, with its ample trees and grasses, that might mean trouble, however unlikely.

Samuel sat at the kitchen table listening to the storm with the ever-present apprehension that gnawed at his innards. It had been a dry summer—the vicious storm in June had done little more than scare the wits out of them all, but since then there had been little in the way of rain.

Now he sat, his pipe clamped between his teeth, his tea grown cold, his index finger tapping the page of the Bible before him, on Psalm 18, which read in part: "The Lord also thundered in the heavens, and the Highest gave his voice, hail stones and coals of fire. Then the channels of water

Crawford Notch from Willey Station, White Mountains. Convinced that their home, in the heart of New Hampshire's rugged Crawford Notch, would be crushed in a landslide because of a violent thunderstorm in August 1826, Samuel Willey, his wife, their five children, and two hired men fled for safer ground. This would prove to be their biggest—and last—mistake. *Courtesy Library of Congress*

were seen, and the foundations of the world were discovered at thy rebuke, oh Lord, at the blast of thy nostrils."

And it was fast becoming a fiercer storm than the one they had seen in June. Samuel shifted his pipe to the other side of his mouth. A flash of lightning illumined the room, and behind him he heard his wife's soft step and a small whimper, too. It would be one of his five brood, he knew not which. But he knew they were expecting him to do something.

Samuel stood, set his pipe on the table by the Bible, and turned to his wife. "Well, my Polly, it appears as if it's feast or famine again this time with regard to the weather."

He knew they were all awaiting his decision. Unbidden, images came to him, flashes of June's storm, of a mass of raw soil and vegetation larger than a lake, sliding down the mountain opposite. He finally said, "Polly, get the children dressed. We will make haste and depart for our safety shelter."

She nodded and disappeared back into the dark hallway behind her. The woodshed door rattled with a banging fist, and before Samuel could respond, the door swung inward. It was the two hired men, both soaked to the skin.

"Men, what is it?"

"Why, Samuel, this is the worst storm yet! The river has burst its banks and even now is creeping ever closer to the road."

"What?" He did not doubt the men, and yet he felt compelled to rush to the window. At that moment, a lightning flash lit the scene. The sight of the great river—now so much wider and so much closer and lashing with violence—was as awesome as had been the slumping cliff face two months before.

He turned ashen-faced to them. "It will be upon us in another twenty minutes. We must leave, perhaps to our shelter."

But the men shook their heads, and Nickerson said, "I would not put my eggs in that basket, Samuel. If that river keeps rising, which seems likely now, the shelter is situated such that escape would be impossible. We would be trapped."

Samuel leaned against the table, almost lightheaded from the sudden danger they all faced. And the decisions would be on his shoulders alone.

"Then we should depart for higher ground."

The other men agreed, nodding rapidly.

Samuel turned and bellowed toward the darkened hall. "Polly! It is time to go!" But he needn't have yelled, for all six of them, Polly and the children—Eliza Ann, thirteen; Jeremiah, eleven; Martha, nine; Elbridge, seven; and Sally, five—filed into the room, the youngest two trembling, but there was not a wet eye among them. Samuel was proud of them.

He knelt before the youngest and said to all of them, "The men and I have decided that we will play a trick on this storm, just in case it has any tricks up its own sleeve." He winked at them and said, "Now, let us make haste, but all stay together. We must hold hands. He handed out what oil-cloths they had, taking none for himself, and donned his hat and work coat.

Scarcely had they stepped out the side door of the woodshed than the two lanterns they carried were blown out. David Allen clung to his, though it was now useless to them.

"Hold hands, everyone! Hold hands!" Samuel bellowed his command, even as the words whipped away in the lashing wind. He and his wife each carried a younger child and attempted to maintain contact with each other by gripping a coat and belt.

With no warning, thunder louder than that from the sky was accompanied with a crashing, pounding sound. They all froze and stared upslope at the source of the noise.

A prolonged slash of lightning ripped apart the veil of darkness that enshrouded them. And what they saw fixed them in place with a terror experienced only by people who know they are about to die—and die in a most cruel manner.

Samuel saw his greatest fear for months—a landslide of epic proportions. And it was the last thing that Samuel Willey Jr. or any of his family and hired men ever saw.

His last thoughts as the wall of stone and gravel rammed downslope and battered him were of his children and his wife, of the grandchildren he would never see. Even as his throat filled with gravel that choked him senseless, he felt an unfathomable black regret and longing for his children and wife. And with his last moment of cognizance, he wished they were somehow safe, that they would go on to lead long, long lives.

∾

Although landslides in mountainous regions are not uncommon, they are memorable when they result in deaths, particularly the tragic and entirely preventable deaths of so many people, many of them children. Between the crushing epic landslide above them and a roiling, swollen river below, the Willey family and their two hired men could not hope to win in such a predicament. And indeed they did not. All four adults—Samuel Willey Jr., thirty-eight; Polly L. Willey, thirty-five; and the two hired men, David Nickerson, twenty-one, and David Allen, thirty-seven—were killed, as were all five Willey children. Of the nine, only the bodies of the four adults and two children—the eldest child, Eliza Ann, and the youngest, Sally—were found. The bodies of Jeremiah, Martha, and Elbridge were never found. This is not surprising, given that the landslide measured thirty feet thick in some places.

The following day, worried friends and relations who lived outside the Notch hiked in to make sure the family could cope with the aftereffects of the flooded river.

The Willey home was found to be in perfect condition, so much so that nothing appeared amiss. Plates and cups lay on the table, and the Bible lay open and undisturbed. Neither the river nor the landslide had touched it. Because of a massive protective bench of rock directly upslope of the house, the landslide parted, diverting the flow of earth to either side of the abode. Had the Willey family stayed within their house, they would have lived through the hellish storm that changed the very landscape of Crawford Notch and the entire Saco River Valley.

During the same storm, a local family's log cabin rose from its foundation, with the family crouched on top, and floated along on the storm surge. The cowering people were certain they would be killed at any moment, but they all survived.

In August 1892 the third documented landslide in the recorded history of Mount Mansfield, the highest point in Vermont, peeled bare an entire flank of the mountain. A swath a mile long and half a mile wide lay stripped of vegetation and soil. Although no one was harmed in the slide, the storm did forge a wide, deep channel close by local farmer Oliver Papineau's house. While the abode remained standing, his pigpen was washed away. In the morning, Papineau trekked downstream half a mile and found the pen, and nearby, its sole occupant snuffled and rooted in the mud, seemingly content.

24

Massachusetts Bay Man-Eater
(1830)

During an afternoon of leisurely fishing from a dinghy in Massachusetts Bay, Joseph Blaney attracts the attention of two great white sharks considerably larger than his dinghy—and soon he's not the one who's fishing.

ↄ⸜⸝ↄ

Joseph Blaney clunked the oar blades into the dinghy and sighed, looking around him at the broad expanse of easy swells. "Peace at last," he said, smiling. It was a fine mid-July day to be out on the water. On the mainland, the air had been hot and stagnant, but out here on the ocean, five miles from Scituate, Massachusetts, the day offered cool breezes.

Comfortable swells carried the little craft up, then down again, though it never seemed to move any farther away from his son-in-law's schooner, the *Finback,* half a mile away. The outing was proving a fine distraction from work, and he was looking forward to catching a few fish, perhaps even a cod. He would show the men in the boat what an old man could do with a pole and a bit of bait fish!

Blaney rigged up the pole, spearing two ragged chunks of bluefish onto the hook. He tossed it a few yards out and waited. For more than an hour he worked the rod, sweat beading on his forehead, stinging his eyes. He lifted his straw hat and wiped his forehead with a kerchief and then dipped the line again in the tepid ocean water.

After he whipped the line out again, he cradled the rod in the crook of his right arm and dunked his left hand in the water to wash off the oily residue of the dead bluefish. He let his fingers waggle there, trailing in the green-black water, his cuffed sleeve drooping and wet.

Blaney watched his line with a contented gaze as it sagged into the gentle swells yards away. Something pushed and then yanked at his arm in the water. He jerked away and looked down at a ragged stump where his forearm had been. It now ended just below the elbow, squirting blood at the water inches below.

The wonderful fish, caught near Eastport, Maine, August 3, 1868. Though this is an artist's fanciful interpretation of the large basking shark that washed up dead on the shore of Eastport, Maine, in 1868, the creatures are capable of reaching lengths in excess of forty feet. While these summer visitors are often mistaken for great white sharks, the largest recorded catch of a great white in Maine waters was a twenty-six-footer caught off Eastport, Maine, in November 1932. *Courtesy Library of Congress*

He dropped the fishing pole and raised his mangled limb, staring at it as if it were something just discovered, a new type of animal, a disgusting animal. Blood geysered upward taller than a man. Blaney screamed. And even as he screamed—a piercing, ragged sound like a train whistle heard through a length of pipe—he wondered what had happened. What had caused this?

And then he saw something curve upward toward the surface three feet from the side of the little boat. He screamed louder and clawed at the air with his whole right arm. "Help me! For God's sake, help me! Help!" His voice carried across the water in all directions, rising up and out in the clear summer air.

From aboard the *Finback*, Captain Nathaniel Blanchard heard far-off shouts and squinted toward the sound. There, nearly half a mile away, was his father-in-law, in the dory, waving. And draped across the dinghy was a massive fish, thrashing and rocking the little boat.

"My word, that man's patience has paid off. He's outdone himself! We'd better get over there. It appears as if he's bitten off more than he can chew!" He and the other men laughed, even as the big twisting fish disappeared into the water.

At the same time, the crew of another fishing schooner that had been anchored closer to the screaming man saw the same scene, but they saw and heard it for what it was—a savage cry of distress. The captain lowered a dory with two stout crewmen, who rowed straight for the hellish scene.

⁓

The sleek shape appeared again in the water, just beyond Blaney's vision. Then it rose from the water and slammed down across the dinghy, its white belly stark and blinding against the dark water. The great thrashing creature seemed intent on sinking the little boat. The old man heard wood crack and felt the boat's ribs begin to collapse under the freakish beast's weight as it submerged the bow.

It thrashed as if on fire, its head whipping side to side. The eye seemed to fix on him, but it was the sight of the mouth that terrified him. It was a gaping thing with rows of jagged teeth set in raw, puckered flesh that looked as if it had been chewed and left to rot. Then as quickly as the fish slammed aboard, it was gone.

The little boat was filling with water, and Blaney's arm was bleeding worse now, even though he had tried to staunch the flow by jamming the ragged stump into his gut and bending over it. He heard himself for the first time and realized he was screaming, sobbing, and moaning all at once.

Blaney still sat in the boat, though it was nearly submerged. Feeling numb, he sobbed and shivered. It seemed like hours since the thing had ripped off his arm, but he knew it had been only minutes. Sweat clogged his eyes, stinging and blinding him from seeing more than a few feet in any direction.

The black water now swirled up to his waist. He tried to scream again, but his voice was blown out, and all he could manage were some wheezing, ragged bleats. The sun swam before him, its brightness piercing his eyes. He looked down and saw redness where his white shirt had been.

He looked up, still trying to keep his right arm waving, trying to keep the schooner in sight, for surely the crew must have heard him, must be close by now. . . . His sight surely played tricks on him, for suddenly, before him, blocking out all else, was a bigger mouth than the one he had just seen, opened wide and tall—he could have almost stood in it—and in there were rows of enormous teeth, set in puffy white flesh, seeping blood at the edges. Joseph Blaney felt himself rise up, and then that massive maw slammed down on him.

⌒

The men of the *Finback* had raised sail, the light breeze filling their canvas main, even as they kept an eye on Joseph Blaney. Their smiles faded as they watched. Seconds later, another fish, bigger than the first one, rose out of the water and crashed down onto the dinghy, upending the little craft and sending Blaney arcing upward. Then it snatched him out of the air before splashing down into the water, leaving nothing behind but a plume of spray and a roiling patch of foam.

⌒

By the time the men from the other schooner drew close, they heard the man's screams grow louder. Both looked over their shoulders while rowing and saw the massive fish—bigger than anything they had ever seen in lifetimes of fishing the New England coast. It rose up out of the water as if pushed from beneath, its impossible mouth open wide as it drove down on the man.

Unbidden screams rose from each of the rowing sailors. With some trepidation, they neared the spot. By then the dory, battered and listing, had risen back to the surface. And beside it floated a sopping, dented straw hat.

And that was all Captain Nathaniel Blanchard had to bring home to his wife, daughter of Joseph Blaney, sport fisherman.

⌒

Captain Blanchard, his crew, and his brother-in-law, son of the unfortunate Joseph Blaney, went out to the tragic spot in the Finback *the next day. They rigged up chum lines with hunks of mackerel on oversize hooks. Their efforts were shortly rewarded, as they* caught the first great white shark, which they managed to dispatch and then haul onto the boat. Shortly thereafter, they hooked a second shark, more massive than the first, at least sixteen feet long and with an estimated weight of 3,000 pounds. It proved too large to hoist aboard, so they killed it and cut it loose.

The shark they kept, the smaller of the two, was sold to a Boston-based sideshow, which charged 12½ cents for a peek. The Boston Gazette of 1830 told of the exhibition: "The shark now exhibited has two rows of sharp, serrated teeth in the lower jaw and one row in the upper jaw. Its mouth is large enough to take in a common-sized man—its skin dark and rough as a rasp."

In the early nineteenth century on the coast of New England, very little was known about sharks, and at the time all large sharks were called either "basking sharks" or "man-eaters."

Referring to a great white as a basking shark, however, is wholly incorrect. Basking sharks, though they can grow to be mammoth creatures of up to forty feet in length, are filter eaters and spend their time feeding on plankton near the water's surface. They are common in northeastern waters in the warmer months, and their corpses occasionally wash ashore along the New England coast. The largest basking shark ever recorded was landed in a herring net in 1851 in Canada's Bay of Fundy, north of New England. It measured 40.3 feet and weighed nineteen tons.

Though supporting information is limited, it is recorded that in November 1932 the largest shark ever taken in Maine waters was a twenty-six-foot great white, killed off the coast of Eastport, Maine. It is believed to have been the same shark that attacked a fishing boat some days prior.

On July 25, 1936, Joseph Troy Jr., sixteen years old, was swimming in ten feet of water at Hollywood Beach, in Buzzards Bay, Massachusetts, when he was attacked by a great white shark. Witnesses say that the shark measured ten to twelve feet in length. The boy was rushed to the hospital, where his mangled left leg was amputated. Unfortunately, the stress was too great, and the boy died just a few hours later. His was the last documented human death by shark attack in New England.

25
VORTEX OF DOOM
(1835)

As their mother watches from shore, two brothers in their schooner are pulled into the gaping maw of the Old Sow Whirlpool, off Eastport, Maine, and are never seen again. They aren't the first . . . or the last.

⌁

The Norwood brothers had just raised the jib on their two-masted schooner, the *Quickstep*, when Abner Norwood yelled to his brother, Robert. "That squall's coming in faster than I'd like. Help me get more cloth up—we need to get by the Old Sow, and quick!"

They watched a wall of rain sweep toward them, pummeling the ocean surface as it rolled in, pulling in a raft of black clouds with it. Far beyond, in outer Passamaquoddy Bay, a blue sky lorded over a serene scene. Of all the times for a squall to hit. . . .

The boat lurched to port, and Abner stumbled, smacking his knee against the wheel. "As long as we've been sailing together and you still don't know your left from right, nor tack from jibe!" Abner shook his head at his brother, though they both knew the sudden squall was the real reason they were drifting sideways toward that damned whirlpool, the Old Sow.

But even as they reefed the sail to avoid a knockdown from the squall, the *Quickstep* sliced toward the Old Sow faster than a runaway dray.

"Rock and a hard place, Ab!" Robert tried to smile and leaned into the wheel as their forward momentum slowed. Even as they worked, they both marveled at the odd sheet of water that surrounded them, ready to boil, but flattened as if a huge sheet of glass were held against it. The smooth surface was stippled with pockmarks that widened before their eyes; then it grew riddled with sudden holes a man could drop into.

Abner knew that behind them their mother watched from shore, as she always did—they were all she had left. They both knew it pained her no end whenever they went out, even though they were grown men. They had even argued with her about the purchase of the *Quickstep*.

Abner's hands gripped the mainsheet tight. Through the now-lashing sea spray, his younger brother's face was a blanched mask of terror. Abner, still facing forward, shouted, "Robert, what is it?" He almost hated to look behind him at what his brother saw, at the cause of their lack of forward momentum. But look he did—and he was immediately sorry.

At that instant, the two-masted schooner was yanked backward and began a slow spin around the rim of the massive Old Sow Whirlpool. As they watched, the very bottom of the ocean itself dropped away, and the gaping hole beneath them widened.

"We got no control, Abner!"

"Fight it as best you can, Robert! We'll make it through!"

Even Abner's mouth was closed, the seriousness of the situation not lost on him. He fought to keep the boat's starboard rail parallel with the rim of the whirlpool, and they rode it round and round, as if circling the downspout of a drainpipe. And the beastly hole widened and deepened by the second.

"We should jump, Ab! Swim for it!"

"Don't be foolish, Robert! We'd die without getting in a single stroke. Our only chance is to stick with the boat."

But it was no use. No matter what he did, there was no steering the boat. Abner looked aft, and any hope he had nurtured in the deepest part of him whipped away with the driving wind. The reason he couldn't steer the boat was because its hull, from amidships back, was out of the water.

The rudder hung in the air, flailing back and forth with his frantic attempts to right the schooner. And beneath the rudder, a near-black cauldron of seething water whipped and funneled deeper and wider with each passing second. Robert screamed as the boat tipped bowsprit up, and they slid stern first into the gaping hole in the water.

Abner lost his footing, and he gripped the spokes of the wheel, struggling to wrap one arm through its center. Far above, Robert hung from the rigging and howled Abner's name.

The bow still sliced into the circling waters, but soon the ship spun round and round, upright in a way no vessel was ever meant to sail. Soon the ship slipped below the rim of the vortex, and so, below the surface of the sea.

Something dropped by Abner and screamed his name, and he knew it was Robert, who had lost his hold on the rigging above as the ship spun faster and the crushing rush of waves roared all about them.

In his last moments Abner felt an odd calm there in the hole in the sea, gripping the wheel while all about him green-black water pulsed and swirled, not touching him, not much harming the *Quickstep.*

The very last thing he saw, far above, was the sky, once again clear and blue. The squall had finally passed—almost as if it were meant just for them.

If sounds from the shore had reached him, Abner would have heard his mother's long cries of anguish, of heartbreak, of denial that it was happening . . . again. She was losing her love to the sea, the cursed sea—to that vile Old Sow Whirlpool.

Then another sound rose out of the Old Sow's storming roar, and with the speed of an eyeblink the masts of the *Quickstep* pierced the funnel. The schooner whipped out of orbit, collapsed, shattered, and blew apart, taking Abner Norwood with it.

✍

One account of this tale relates that Robert was later found, unconscious but alive, floating in the bay, his arms tightly clutching an oar in a near-death grip. But in all accounts, no sign of Abner, nor a scrap of the Quickstep, *was ever found. Their mother watched the entire scene helplessly from the shore.*

The Old Sow Whirlpool is the largest in the Western Hemisphere and the second-largest whirlpool in the world. The U.S. Coast Guard has reported that, under the right conditions, the Old Sow can become a two-hundred-foot-wide hole in the sea. The Old Sow, which straddles the U.S.-Canadian boundary, is usually centered on the Canadian side of the borderline. Its intensity level, which fluctuates with the tides, reaches full power on a hefty incoming tide, which far downeast can exceed twenty-four feet.

With every incoming tide, 40 billion cubic feet of water floods into Passamaquoddy Bay, plowing through a trench 400 feet deep, and then hammers into both a 281-foot mountain and a southward-flowing countercurrent. All this underwater activity results in a roiling, confused stretch of bay that conjures unexpected troughs in the water, freakish bulges that look as if the bay is boiling, six-knot currents, and funnels like tornadoes ranging from less than a foot to twelve feet across. Add to this heavy winds from a squall and you have the makings of a Hollywood disaster-at-sea epic.

In the late nineteenth century, two men on a barge loaded with logs were pulled into the Old Sow's orbit and soon disappeared. No trace of the men, their barge, or their logs was ever found. Around 1912 Cecil Chaffee was out rowing in the bay and failed to work the oars hard enough to escape the pull of the whirlpool. In 1944 James Roland Mitchell

Sr., while sailing near the Old Sow, was knocked overboard by his boat's swinging boom. Both men drowned, unable to battle the strong currents.

In 1935 the Passamaquoddy Tidal Power Project was introduced to the bay in an attempt to harness the tremendous power of the extreme tides of the region—some of the most intense in the world. The project began, but only a series of dikes were built before funding was cut by Congress. Because of the presence of the dikes, now used by the railroad and Highway 190, the whirlpool lost some of its power and became more diffused and difficult to predict.

In addition, the advent of motorized vessels in the twentieth century helped sailors stand a better chance than ever of escaping the hungry maw of the Old Sow. But even so, each year people with engines, and many without, still fall victim to the brute or any one of its numerous smaller offspring, known as Piglets, swirling in the Old Sow's sty.

In 1995 a fifty-five-foot Deer Island fishing boat, the Fundy Star II, rolled over in the whirlpool when it became caught in a crosscurrent. A nearby boat rescued the three crew members. A few years later, another rescue was made when a pair of kayakers was drawn into the Old Sow. The husband made it to safety, but his wife was forced to spin until help arrived.

And as recently as December 2009, two recreational divers felt the Old Sow's mighty tug. One of them was pulled into the unpredictable current, where he spun while his partner went for help. By the time the Coast Guard arrived, the dizzy diver had managed to claw his way to shore.

26

REBELS . . . IN VERMONT!

(1864)

On October 19, 1864, a Rebel raider and his gang attack a town on the Vermont-Canadian border, robbing banks, setting fires, and forcing hostages to swear allegiance . . . to the Confederacy.

᪐

"Seem a little odd to you, Maynard, having all these young men around town?" The speaker, an old man not unlike his companion on the bench, save for the other man's walrus mustaches, paused in his whittling and looked at his friend from under bushy eyebrows. "When we were of age, with a war on, last place you'd find us was in a town, taking in daylight and growing soft."

Maynard Biggs finally nodded in agreement and said, "Could be they're Rebel raiders."

The first man, Elmer Rose, paused in his whittling long enough to send a ropy brown stream of chaw spittle into the dirt just beyond their feet at the bottom of the steps of Grissom's Store, where they sat most every day for several hours. "What in God's name made you say that, Maynard?"

"Not much, except their accents. Seem a little off, if you know what I mean."

"Yep, I do, now I come to think on it," said Biggs. He shrugged and went back to carving. "That's why I told Constable Smith." He looked up and said, "You think he'd do anything about it? Been eight, nine days now and a pile of 'em, must be near two dozen, come down from Canada. Said they was from St. Johns on a 'sporting expedition.'"

"Canadian cherry pickers is what I call 'em. There's a war on here, and they're siding with the Confederates in secret, reaping all the profits, and coming down here pretty as you please, knowing we can't refuse them." Maynard's voice had grown steadily louder, and his coloring matched it.

"Easy now, Maynard." Elmer half-smiled. "You'll get yourself in a tizzy, and where will we be? Only doctor around for miles is old Doc Royer, and unless you're a woman having a baby, you're sunk before you float." They were quiet a few moments, and then Elmer said, "Besides, when was the last time you heard of a grayback coming this far north? No, sir, that's a Southern war, make no mistake."

∽

On the afternoon of October 19, 1864, one of the first of two dozen young men who had drifted down into St. Albans, Vermont, from Canada more than a week before made quite a show of mounting the steps of the hotel across the street from the general store.

Elmer Rose and Maynard Biggs looked up from their whittling as the crowd of young men gathered, some of them stalking back and forth at the edge of the crowd, casting angry glances at whoever might walk by.

When the young man spoke, there was no mistaking the southern accent when he shouted, "I take possession of this town in the name of the Confederate States of America!"

A few gasps from the busy townsfolk who happened to be within earshot were drowned out by a good many more chuckles. But the sound of galloping horses and stray gunshots tipped the scales enough that people began to wonder about what the young man just said. But it couldn't be, they thought. How on earth could it? This was Vermont, as far north in the Union as you were likely to get.

Dust boiled up in great clouds along Main Street as armed horsemen drew near and circled the curious townsfolk. The man continued with his speech, and the horsemen herded the people onto the town common amid rising shouts of anger from the prodded locals. Above the din, someone shouted, "They're robbing the bank!"

One of the riders laughed and said, "No, we're robbing all three banks!" Then he fired a shot into the air. "Long live General Lee!"

A woman screamed, and a merchant in an apron lunged at one of the mounted men, trying to unseat him. He received a blow to the temple with the butt of a pistol. Though dazed, he kept pawing at the Rebel's leg. The horseman swung the pistol again, and a loud shot rang out. The dazed merchant grunted and sagged to the dusty street, his wife kneeling at his side, screaming, "No, Horace, no! I told you to leave them be!"

∽

"Why, you're nothing but a . . . a damn Yankee!"

The old man worked his chaw for a moment more, sent a rope of brown spit into the dust at Porkins's boots, and, shifting his chaw to his cheek, looked up at the man. "Yeh, and you can kiss my Yankee backside." He resumed working his cud and peeling on the half-whittled stick with his knife. It was taking shape, he thought. A fishing lure, perhaps.

"I am going to kill you for that, old man." Porkins eased the hammer back and raised his pistol. The sharp rush of gasps from a half dozen onlookers was the only sound on the dusty street, except for the rapid crunching of boots on gravel, followed by a voice: "See here, Porkins!"

Lieutenant Young strode manfully up to the hotheaded young Rebel and pushed down on the pistol with an open hand until it was aimed at the ground. Porkins eased off the hammer and holstered the sidearm.

Young leaned in and said, "As much as I'd like to see all these damnable Yankee swine swing, on general principles alone, I can't let you kill indiscriminately—especially an old man. Think of the outrage that would occur, think of the people who would descend on us from out of nowhere. Why, these Yankees would wipe us out in sheer numbers alone before we could succeed in our mission. Don't forget that we are on a mission and we must succeed."

Young stared at Porkins until the subordinate looked away and nodded. The lieutenant stopped in front of Maynard Biggs and watched him whittle for a moment. "Perhaps Porkins was right. . . ."

The old man spit again, this time close enough that it spattered on the speaker's boot. "To each his own, said the man as he kissed the cow."

Young's eyebrows rose, and then he strode away, shaking his head, trying not to smile.

◦౿◦

"Gentlemen, you will repeat after me, is that clear?"

The four bank employees just stared at the speaker and his two companions. What could he mean by this? That it was a bank robbery there was no doubt, but he just said something about swearing an oath . . . to the Confederacy?

"Gentlemen," said the speaker, as he cocked his pistol and stepped forward, striking it hard against the forehead of the nearest man, who happened to be the bank president. "I do so hate to repeat myself, but unless you are deaf and dumb, for the last time, repeat after me: I swear allegiance to Jeff Davis and the Confederate States of America."

The bank employees repeated it, and then the man said, "Good, now that you've seen the light, I'll ask you to lie down facing the floor. And no peeking. We shan't be long."

When the men complied, the speaker, Lieutenant Bennett Young, leader of the Confederate raiders, snatched up the large rucksack bulging with cash, bolted out the door, and hoisted his load, then himself, onto a waiting horse. His companions did the same. As the youthful leader looked back toward the bank, he saw the dome of a bald man's head rising up behind the low windowsill. Young fired a shot into the glass, and the large front window dropped away into hundreds of pieces, the gold lettering caving in on itself. Screams rose from inside the bank.

He laughed, and as he goaded his horse northward, he shouted instructions to the galloping gang about him: "Dash those bottles of Greek fire against the town's buildings, boys! Burn this burg to the ground in honor of all those fine Southerners who have been wronged! Burn this treacherous place in the name of the Confederacy that all may know our might is powerful and our reach is long! And cut down any man who dares to interfere!"

The raiders rode hard through Main Street in downtown St. Albans, hurling small bottles of whiskey-colored liquid at building after building. Where the bottles hit, explosions sounded and flames licked upward. But the sneers of satisfaction on the faces of the raiders quickly dissolved when the flames from their precious four-ounce bottles failed to take hold and ignite a blaze of any consequence.

❧

Lieutenant Bennett Young of the Confederate army was nothing if not tenacious. At age nineteen, after his capture by Union soldiers, he was shipped to a Chicago-area prison. From there, this die-hard son of the South escaped to Canada. While there, he hatched the notion of enacting a series of raids on northern U.S. towns in hopes of drawing troops to these soon-to-be hotbeds of crime, and thus away from the battlefields of the South, where his Rebel brethren were not faring so well.

As the northernmost land-based engagement of the American Civil War, the St. Albans Raid, as it has come to be known (though the perpetrators insisted on referring to it as an expedition), was nearly bloodless—although one local was accidentally shot and killed by a raider, and another was injured. The raid, organized by Confederate agent

George Sanders and led by Young, was largely a failure, as the raiders failed in their desire to instigate a border war between Great Britain and the United States. However, they did manage to steal horses from St. Albans liveries and made off with $200,000 from the three banks they robbed.

Fourteen of the men were captured in Canada. However, because the raid was considered an act of war, Canada, largely to maintain its neutrality, felt that it couldn't extradite the men to the United States. So the fourteen captured raiders were set free, after returning the $86,000 they stole. The six remaining men—and their own stolen loot—remained at large. Of these, William Travis made a most impressive escape. He disguised himself as a girl and wound his way south with his wad of ill-gotten cash, back into service for the Confederacy.

Denied amnesty until 1868 by President Andrew Johnson, Bennett Young ended up in Europe, attending universities in Ireland and Scotland. He returned to the United States a lawyer and set up practice in Louisville, Kentucky. He had a lengthy and impressive career, and along the way he engaged in many good works, among them the establishment of that city's first orphanage for blacks as well as a school for the blind. In 1911 he visited Montreal, and a delegation from St. Albans met with him there.

Something about the town of St. Albans appeals to seemingly misplaced raiders. In 1866, just two years after Lieutenant Bennett Young's odd raid, the Fenians, an Irish group nurturing a bold plan to seize Canada by brute force from Great Britain and transform it into an independent Irish free state, gathered in St. Albans before marching on Canada.

The Fenians, at 3,500 strong, were decidedly greater in number than the Confederates had been, if not in organization or dedication to their cause. After a handful of tussles, and having gotten no deeper than six miles into their proposed new homeland, the Fenians scattered and made their way southward. At the border their weapons were seized by armed U.S. troops. Those in charge were arrested, and the remainder were loaded onto trains and sent home to Boston.

27

AROOSTOOK LYNCH LAW
(1873)

In 1873 in the frozen reaches of northern Maine, when he steals a pair of boots, Big Jim Cullen never dreams he'll be the star of New England's only lynching.

∞

Deputy Sheriff Granville Hayden nodded to his deputized cohort, William Hubbard, as they stood to the side of the cabin's door. "Cullen!" Hayden shouted. He raised his fist to pound on the door again, his breath visible in quick plumes in the still, late-winter air, the night about them bright from the moon's reflection on the snow. The little cabin's door swung open, and light from the oil lamp's glow shone on the snow at their feet.

Hayden stepped back and regarded the man in the doorway. He saw that it was John Swanback, the German who owned the snug little camp. They tried to see past his slender frame into the cabin.

The deputy sheriff cleared his throat. "Jim Cullen, I know you're in there. We're here to arrest you for burglary and theft . . . of a certain pair of boots." The little man grunted and then shuffled aside to let them in. Warmth and light and the cloying odors of burned beans and drying wool socks assaulted the senses of the two travelers. They shook their heads and looked about the dim interior of the little cabin. Off to the right, in the corner, sat a younger man they both knew, Minot Bird, and dead ahead, leaned against the back wall, stood the man they had been tracking all day: Big Jim Cullen. And big he was—the bulk of the six-footer was thick like a tree. His wide shoulders were topped by a broad head crowned with a mane of red hair and rimmed with a thick, bushy beard.

They regarded each other for a moment, saying nothing. Hayden knew that he and Hubbard were too played out to make the return trip to Mapleton that night. They all appeared calm and resigned. Swanback offered them chairs and tin cups of bracing hot coffee. After an explanation of the impending arrest, the men all agreed to Hayden's plan of spending the night in the cabin, then making a trek of it back to town the following morning.

Hubbard noticed that Cullen seemed unusually resigned to the idea. Something told him he should be more careful. He knew that Cullen could be a handful, but he saw, too, that Big Jim seemed to accept the fact that he had been caught at a game he shouldn't have played.

❧

Grunts and a gurgling, gagging sound pulled John Swanback from sleep. He raised his eyes above the rim of the heavy wool blanket, and framed in the scant glow from the fireplace stood Big Jim Cullen over two prone forms on the cabin floor. Cullen's arm rose high and drove straight down. A hatchet chunked into something and then lodged there. Swanback sat up and saw that the two forms were the sheriff and Hubbard. In the low fire light, he also saw that Cullen and the two men were covered in gore.

Swanback scrambled to get out of his blankets and lunged for the door just as Cullen saw him and spun from his vicious task. As the little German whipped open the cabin door and darted out into the bright, cold night, he saw the now unrecognizable features of the two stricken men—and they were indeed dead, their heads hacked open and oozing out their last. Cullen didn't follow him.

When Swanback had bolted for the door, Minot Bird awoke from his sleep in the same bunk he had been sharing with the cabin owner. He had arrived with Cullen the day before, and now, in a flash of comprehension, he saw the sickening scene. He, too, bolted for the cabin door, but his way was barred by Cullen, who stood before him, swaying and leering, the hatchet gripped in his hand, his chest heaving.

"Where are you going?"

"Oh God, Jim, please, please don't kill me! Please!" Bird raised his praying hands together and nearly dropped to his knees, his voice tremulous with fear. "I been good to you, haven't I, Jim? Not saying you owe me, but. . . ."

Cullen scowled and pointed the dripping hatchet in Bird's face. "You say anything about this and there will be hell to follow, you got that, Minot?"

The young man nodded hard and fast and continued backing toward the half-closed door. Cullen lunged at him. Bird slipped through the opening and kept running. At the tree line, arms grabbed him and he screamed. A burly hand clamped over his mouth. "Hush yourself, man! We must get out of here—"

But the words died in his throat because both men saw Cullen emerge from the cabin, look about, then snatch firewood from the leaning shed, and head back into the cabin.

"We must make it to Mapleton before he catches us. I'd guess he won't be long," said Swanback.

"But we're in our stocking feet."

"No matter, boy. At least we got feet. Let's go!"

Inside the cabin Cullen built the fire until flames higher than his head licked up the chimney. Then he rummaged in the pockets of the dead men before dragging them into the fireplace. He stacked the men in the broad stone space and wedged the last of his armload of wood on, under, and between the bodies.

Outside the cabin door, he strapped on his borrowed snowshoes. As he strode away, he looked back at the cabin and half-smiled as flames lashed upward through the roofline and the cabin glowed with flickering light from within.

℘

The two men lurched into Mapleton just after dawn, their feet bloodied, ragged, and swollen from scrambling the eight miles over crusted snow. Within an hour the town was a mass of seething anger and shouted oaths. Ben Hughes, a Mapleton constable, organized a posse of thirty men, some armed with rifles, some with shotguns and pickaxes. And all thirsted for vengeance. They marched the mile or so out of town to the home Cullen shared with Rosella Twist and their toddler. When she answered the door, she swore to them that Cullen had gone the day before to visit his family in Canada.

"You're a liar, woman!" shouted one hothead as he pushed past her. "Out of our way."

When Constable Hughes told the woman what had happened, she broke down sobbing. "Where is he, Mrs. Twist?"

She pointed at a ring in the floorboards. The men surrounded the trapdoor and then jerked it open fast.

"We know you're down there, Cullen, slinking in the dark like a rat. Come out of there. Come out! Or we'll come down and drag you out. There's more of us than even you can handle!"

Soon a massive head of dirty, matted red hair emerged from the dank pit beneath the floorboards. As Hughes rushed to secure handcuffs on the man's wrist, the big brute lashed out with a vile oath and knocked two men to the floor. He bolted for the door, but Lew Griffin, a posse member with a rifle, jammed the barrel tip to Cullen's temple and said, "You keep 'er quiet, Cullen. Or I won't be afraid to do it." And the man was subdued, at least for a time.

The men gave the place a quick search, and just before they left, Hughes saw the toddler playing with something on the floor. He snatched it up and found it was a pocket knife. He held it up, and one of the men said, "By God, but don't that look like Hubbard's pen knife."

Hughes gritted his teeth and stared at Cullen hard. Then he slipped the dead deputy's knife in his pocket and prodded the prisoner out the door. Surrounded by the posse, Cullen could do nothing but walk toward town.

∽

"I tell you I want this brute behind bars in my jail tonight." Sheriff James Phair, of Presque Isle, rubbed the top of his head. "I know well enough that it's dark. But this is a matter that won't wait until morning. Now I only need a few of you to help with him. We'll take Dorsey's wagon. Parker and Barker will ride with the prisoner. We'll need rifles and a couple of lanterns."

Less than an hour later, on the dark, cold road from Mapleton to Presque Isle, Sheriff Phair saw random lights bobbing, as if riders on horseback were carrying lanterns. "Rein up," he said to Dorsey, driving the open wagon with two guards and Cullen in the back. Phair peered into the dark and saw what looked like a crowd of men advancing on them. "Trouble, boys." He cocked his Henry rifle and held it across his knees, both hands gripping the stock.

Before long, a crowd of what had to be nearly one hundred men, most on horseback, some on foot, came to a stop just a few yards from them. And to a man their faces were covered. Phair looked from man to man in the pale, flickering light. Hoods, feed sacks with eye holes snipped out, hats pulled low and Indian-type war paint slathered on faces—all were disguised. Though he knew why, still he asked, "What's this all about, gentlemen?"

"The murderer must die, sheriff." The voice was forced, deeper than a normal voice.

"That's against the law." Phair raised his rifle chest high, but weapons bristled outward from the costumed mass of men. Still, he held the gun up.

"I'll wager I know most of you. You're Presque Isle men. And to a man, I'd guess you'd be ashamed if I let you do this thing. I cannot abide this unlawfulness."

"Choice isn't yours, sheriff." Again the deep voice. "Now get Cullen down out of there."

A dozen masked, armed men approached the wagon, disarmed the guards, the driver, and the sheriff, and held them in a loose group beside the wagon. The rest ushered a bellowing Cullen to what the sheriff could now see was a tall, old tree with a stout branch stuck out like a rigid arm, a good twenty feet off the snow-crusted ground.

The noose hurtled up and over the branch, and then the end was tied off to the trunk. The masked men forced a kicking, shouting Cullen onto the back of a horse. Though he would soon die, Cullen snarled and bit at the hands of the man who jammed the loop about his neck. No moment of reflection was offered. As soon as the noose was ratcheted down tight, jutting like a bone beneath the man's left ear, the horse was whipped, and Big Jim Cullen swung.

Sheriff Phair fancied in later years that he had heard a sound like a carrot snapping. It carried high and clear above the rapid crunching sound of the frightened horse as it galloped off in the frozen night.

"Parker. Dr. Parker!"

One of Phair's two men stepped forward. "What?"

"We'll need you to check that he's dead, you being a doctor and all."

The doctor nodded, and they lowered Cullen's body to the ground. Parker felt the man's chest and detected a faint heartbeat. He knew that even if Cullen lived, he would be far less than a normal man, and no more than a root vegetable. As much as it pained him to say so, he told the men to hoist Cullen aloft for a while longer, that the job wasn't yet complete.

❧

But it didn't end there: When Big Jim Cullen's body was brought back to Presque Isle after the hanging, angry citizens filled the store where it was laid out for a public viewing. One man spit in Cullen's dead face, and it was reported that as they filed past, women stabbed at the corpse with hat pins.

W. T. Ashby, a witness to the scene, described Cullen thus: "He was still bound hand and foot with strong cords. His short, fat neck was stretched to twice its natural length, and his head was canted to one side, there was a big purple spot under one ear, his tongue was protruding from his mouth and his eyes were starting from his head and had the glassy stare of death."

After a one-hour inquest in which no party could be found to blame for the man's death, the coffin was nailed shut. On May 1, 1873, as the authorities ushered the body to the Fairmont Cemetery in Presque Isle, they were halted by an angry mob that threatened to exhume Cullen if the burial proceeded. They returned to town, and Cullen ended up back in the store.

From there, two dozen people accompanied the corpse to a spot close by the town dump, where a grave was dug, and he was dropped in without ceremony. Though the exact spot is not now known, the land is now privately owned.

Several versions of the story have been written over the years, and recently a line of thought has arisen positing that Cullen wasn't such an evil man, but that over the intervening 130-plus years since the grisly events, his reputation has been sullied and the tale embroidered. Some claim that he may indeed have been innocent of the crimes for which he was lynched. We may never know the truth, since all the players are long dead.

Big Jim Cullen's necktie party was New England's only official lynching, which by definition is a hanging by a mob for an alleged offense, with or without a legal trial. In a bizarre bit of coincidence, another man named Jim Cullen was lynched in 1907, in Charles City, Iowa, also for a double murder.

28

THE HARTFORD DISASTER
(1887)

On the frigid evening of February 5, 1887, the engineer of the night express from White River Junction, Vermont, running two hours late, tries to make up time. But it is winter, and track conditions are dicey, especially on bridges spanning frozen rivers far below.

∾

Iknow what I'm doing, for Pete's sake. Just pour on the coal, and I'll worry about the track conditions." Engineer Pierce glanced again at his pocket watch. A few more years of this, he thought to himself, and I can get out of this people-infested madness they call "civilization." He daydreamed of a small farm tucked somewhere in the foothills of the Green Mountains. There was a perfect spot out there for him, and he just knew it. Then the grinding noise and acrid smell of his job once again filled his senses, and he snorted at the thought of leaving life on the rails behind and knew it was just the blasted head cold talking.

"The bridge and pass are coming up. We need to back off the thing, let 'er edge down a bit. . . ."

Pierce turned on his subordinate and pointed a gloved hand at his nose. "I won't tell you again. We have a schedule to keep, and we're already nearly two hours behind. I have seventy-nine passengers back there, plus all manner of freight, U.S. mail, and payroll, and each and every person and piece of mail is on a schedule with other people depending on them." He paused and rubbed a begrimed jacket sleeve against the sooty right window.

Then he started talking again, as if to himself. "I didn't make this time delay, but I darn sure am the one who'll catch hang-fire if we're late. So I aim to correct as much of it as I'm able to. And we can't do that by slowing down at every little pissant bridge and curve on the route." He dragged a cuff under his dripping nose and said, "Now pile on that coal and give me something more from this old girl."

∾

The churning, rhythmic backdrop of Number 50's relentless rolling thunder served to keep Rafe Tillinghast and the other passengers lulled and, for most of them, asleep in the relative warmth of the swaying cars. Then, in his nodding half-sleep, Rafe saw the conductor race by, muttering an oath before he yanked on the bell. Within seconds, everyone in the car pitched forward, awakened by the scream of cold, unyielding metal slamming hard against cold, unyielding metal.

Rafe leaned out into the aisle, but the conductor had already left the car. What he didn't see, but the conductor did, was that the rear sleeper had slid off the rails. The hot steel was plowing a furrow in the frozen earth, and the trestle was next—a nightmare in progress.

As they approached a long, curving plain preceding the bridge, someone in the train pulled the bell at the same time that Pierce felt a jarring jolt and a drag that sent the train into a wobbling spasm, the telltale signs of something very wrong. He looked out back along the length of his train. What he saw made his jaw clench tight and his heart pound.

In that instant between realization and action, Pierce heard screams, real or imagined, from every one of the ninety-one lives aboard the train, himself included. Seventy-nine of them were passengers, some of whom he knew would never again see their loved ones. It's too cold to die, he thought, and we're too far from anywhere at all. He didn't even think there were houses nearby.

All this hit him at eyeblink speed. Then he shouted, more for his own benefit than his tender's: "Shut her down! Shut her down!" He grabbed the throttle, and the train squealed and screeched for what seemed like miles. But as it rounded the curve before the bridge, the sleeper slid farther sideways, jolting forward a few yards on the ties, before plunging off the trestle's edge and driving straight at the ice, forty-three feet below.

With professional speed born of long years manning engines, Pierce opened the throttle and rolled ahead in an attempt to pull the car to relative safety—anything but the black void it now hung out over. Deep in his mind he heard the passengers' raw shouts of terror. One moment they had been sleeping, and the next moment they were piling into one another, thrown about like dolls.

The train lurched forward, and instead of pulling the derailed cars along with it, the engine and the two cars following it separated from the last three cars—two coaches and the rear sleeper. Pierce barked an oath of fury and bolted down from the shuddering engine and into the freezing night. He was greeted by sounds he hoped to never hear—the grating, crushing, and grinding of metal and wood giving way. He exhaled as if gut-punched, and then the sounds became a crash and an explosion, one following on the heels of the other.

He reached the edge of the bridge, now becoming crowded with other passengers and his crew, just as flames the height of a house licked skyward, filling the scene before them with a horrid glow.

࿊

Scarcely a minute before, in the rearmost car, the passengers in the sleeper—the heat of blazing coal stoves protecting them from the 18-degrees-below-zero temperatures of that early morning—were jolted from the false safety of sleep. But even then it was too late. For their sleeper car pulled the two coaches preceding it off the rails, then off the trestle to hang for a second, no more. The cars' momentum pitched them out and upward before they buckled and drove downward with the speed of a battering ram toward the iced-over river, far below.

There were screams, but many more of the dazed people awoke in puzzlement as they slammed about in the dark, so quickly did the accident occur. The jolt killed some on impact, but many others were crushed as two more railcars, swinging and pitching, slammed down on the first.

As the cars dropped downward, the connection between the mail car and the smoking car snapped, preventing the two last cars from dragging sideways and adding to the pile-up on the frozen river.

The hot coal stoves touched off an inferno as the mineral sperm oil lamps spattered their fuel over everything in the cars—passengers' clothing, skin and hair, the drapery and thick upholstery of the seats, the varnished wood paneling of the walls and ceiling. Explosions blew the cars apart. Flames, sparks, blistering heat, and black smoke rose skyward in ever-increasing spires climbing high into the frigid black night. Soon, the wooden understructure of the bridge caught fire, and in minutes the entire thing collapsed on the wreckage below, as ragged steel fingers of track wagged and poked downward.

Engineer Pierce ordered his brakeman, Parker, to run ahead to the junction for help. Then Pierce turned his attention to directing the remaining crew before him. Four others besides himself—Thresher, Cole, Robbins, and Perkins—all slid, rolled, and climbed down the snow-crusted slope toward the conflagration on the frozen river. Time and again they worked to quell the flames enough at certain spots to free the trapped and screaming passengers. But as soon as they spotted someone, vicious walls of flame would drive them backward, blistering them and singeing their hair and charring their clothes and skin.

The remoteness of the location, except for a farmhouse a few hundred yards from the scene of the wreck, prevented help from arriving for what seemed a lifetime. And every minute was an eternity for the railroad men and other passengers who repeatedly drove themselves into the gruesome scene as they heard another trapped person screaming for help.

But no one there felt the stopped hands of time any more than did Engineer Pierce, as the crushing weight of guilt reminded him that every minute was an eternity he would relive in his mind for the rest of his days.

⟡

Among the ninety-one passengers and crew on board Train Number 50, twenty-eight people were killed, and more than three dozen were injured, most of whom spent their lives scarred and crippled. For using poor judgment and knowingly exceeding acceptable speeds, Engineer Pierce was convicted of manslaughter after a long governmental inquiry and lengthy trial. His employer, the Central Railroad, spent ample time and money defending itself in court, only to be found guilty of neglect and shoddy maintenance of its tracks. A steel railroad bridge replaced the old wooden structure.

New England is no stranger to train wrecks and other transport accidents. From coaches to ferries, trains to planes, the six New England states have seen their fair share of unfortunate crack-ups. On December 4, 1891, at 6:30 a.m., in East Thompson, Connecticut, four trains collided. Remarkably, considering they were passenger trains loaded with commuters, only three men were killed and four injured. Among the dead were a headless engineer, a mangled fireman, and a passenger who left little more than a wristwatch and charred, smoking bones. The wreck was blamed on miscommunication and fog.

In addition to trains, horse-drawn conveyances were the cause—or were at least involved in—a sizable number of incidents, horses being the most ubiquitous mode of transport well into the twentieth century, especially in rural regions of New England.

In Marlow, New Hampshire, in November 1885, a runaway team of horses rammed into William Abbott as he maneuvered his one-horse lumber dray. The jolt pitched him out of his seat and under his own wagon. His horse plodded onward and over him. Witnesses dragged him free. Other than extensive bruising and a broken jaw, he was fine.

And let's not forget automobiles. In the early-morning hours of August 12, 1908, J. Montgomery Sears, a wealthy young Bostonian, and a companion rocketed along a road unfamiliar to them just outside of Norwood, Rhode Island. They failed to follow the road and flew off a steep embankment, and the vehicle, a large cruising car, somersaulted into a field. Witnesses saw its tires flying off. Sears later died of his injuries. His passenger lived.

The skies of New England, too, were filled with all manner of transport as the decades rolled on, leading to various unfortunate incidents. In Rhode Island's Narragansett Bay, in August 1921, a pleasure boat was attacked by an unknown aircraft bearing the number "92." Witnesses saw what looked like a military airplane dive-bomb the little boat as its five occupants lounged on deck. As the plane neared, the mystery pilot raked the boat with machine-gun fire. The vessel was damaged and nearly didn't make it back to shore. Four of the boaters escaped injury, but one girl was shot in both legs.

29

NORTH WOODS FREEZE-UP
(1887)

Across northern New England, weeks of 40-below-zero temperatures force loggers to kill their horses, cut off frostbitten digits, and fight like caged rats.

⟳

Now look, by God." The boss, Reny Robbins, slapped a ratty-edged newspaper down on the end of the table. "We're all a little tense because we're caged up in this camp been near a week now, too cold to do much else but drink and grouse. But we can't drink 'cause there ain't no booze, and the grousin's getting hard to take. And since I'm the camp boss, I don't want to hear any more of it."

"Well, that's all well and good, boss," said Hank Jasper, his jaw thrust out. "But where's Tippy with the supplies and mail? He's living it up down there at the base camp, and we're freezing to death up here."

The boss sighed. "Jack McPheeter, Tippy to you, was a limber for half a dozen logging companies before half of you were out of short pants—and he's still in his prime. Tip was wise to stay put—travel that twenty-plus miles in such deep snow followed by a cold snap? Why any fool knows that would be too dangerous. Tip knows what's what in the woods. He'll be along."

Most of the men nodded, knowing the boss spoke the truth, but also wishing that Tippy had made it back by now. They had all been just about out of tobacco before the storm hit, and Cook had reduced them to two cups of watered-down coffee a day. He was nearly out of flour, and while there were still plenty of beans, the pork barrel was getting as low as their spirits.

With what snow they had before the storm, a good three or four feet on the flats, plus what the two-day storm had dumped, they had nearly eight feet of the hated white stuff. And then the blasted cold snap had crept in. Yes, sir, they were ready to see Tippy's smiling face.

Paulsen, a tall rail of a man, stood up from his bunk and rubbed his backside. "I'll go for wood, by gum. Need some fresh air anyway. Getting kind of crampy sitting here for so long."

Woodsmen playing cards in the bunkhouse. In the brutally cold winter of 1887–1888, loggers such as those in this Maine camp had to endure one another's company in close quarters indoors when big snows piled up and temperatures across northern New England dipped to 40 degrees below zero for weeks at a time. Teamsters caught out in the severe weather were forced to kill their horses, and many men lost fingers, toes, noses, and ears—or worse, their lives—to the bitter cold. *Courtesy Library of Congress*

Two other men went out with him to lend a hand, but the mood in the bunkhouse didn't shift much. The leak of fresh air that sneaked in only succeeded in reminding the men of the brutal cold and of how trapped they truly were.

Within a minute the door jumped and clunked on its strap hinges. "Let us in! Open the door!"

A half dozen men bolted for the door and flung it wide. For a moment they didn't know what they were looking at. It looked like Paulsen holding a bundle of rags.

"It's Tippy! He's in a bad way."

Oaths of surprise filled the long, low room as the men cleared a path to the fireplace. The boss barked orders: "Build up that fire, get some heat out of it! Cook, get—"

"I'm on it, boss."

Paulsen placed the impossibly small bundle on a mat of blankets the men laid down before the snapping fire.

The boss knelt before Tippy, his hands hovering in the air, not knowing what to do for the man. "Why, you was headed to Popple Stream, to the main camp," he said. "We thought you were there."

Tippy tried to drag himself even closer to the fire, but he still refused to pull his hands away from under his ragged sweater. "Never made it." His voice was almost a whisper.

"What happened, Tip? We saw you leave, you waved to us. You left in plenty of time to beat that storm." The boss's eyes grew wider. "Tip, oh my God, you had the Pearson boy with you. Where is he, Tip?" The boss knelt before him and pulled the shivering man to him. "Tip, what happened to Shaun Pearson? He left with you. I let him go for a few days. He was to see his mother. She's not well."

For a moment there was no sound as the boss's words hung in the air of the camp. Then a quiet popping noise came to them, followed by a breath, and they realized Tippy was crying. He drew in more breath, and louder sobs wracked him. At the same time, his little form unfolded on the floor before the fireplace, and he leaned back against the stone hearth. His left hand flopped free, then his right. They saw that his fingers had been wrapped in little more than rags and what looked like curls of birch bark peeled from a tree.

A round of gasps came from the men as they saw, in the flickering light of the burning logs, the blackened nubs of Tippy's fingers, drawn up into claws, misshapen and swollen from the cold. His face, too, was worse than they realized, now that his collar had slipped down. The one ear they could see fared no better than the man's hands, and his nose had also been sorely afflicted with frostbite, the worst case any of them had seen. They knew what they would find when they cut away the man's boots.

"Tip?" the boss whispered, looking the man up and down. Tippy lay still, save for the shivering, and tried pathetically to reach for the flames.

"Tip, what happened?"

"Sluiced."

The one word told them all they needed to hear. In a moment, he continued. "Halfway there—too far to turn back, too far to go ahead."

"And the Pearson boy?"

The damaged man's face quivered, then collapsed in on itself, and he shook his head. The men felt the blow to their core—young Pearson was a good lad, they were thinking. Keen to learn and helpful and a good young man to be around, too. But dead? Surely that's not what Tip meant. . . .

And then he spoke, even as Cook held a steaming cup of tea to his mouth, a grim look on the cook's face as his eyes flitted about Tippy's features.

"We was talkin', me and the boy." His voice hitched, but he kept on. "And the snow was really coming on hard, but it was quiet—you know how it gets? Quiet in the woods. . . ."

"Then what, Tip?"

Tippy nodded, swallowed more tea, and said, "Something spooked my boys. You know, my boys? Noble and Thor?"

"Sure we do, Tip. Sure. Best team of horses we've ever had here at camp."

The boss's comment brought comfort to the man, and his features softened. Then he said, "Sluiced, though. Got spooked, and the snow was so thick—I tried everything, but it was no good. I told the boy to jump, but even then it was too late. My team stumbled off the edge. It was that pass, you know the one, you come around that house-size boulder and then she drops off sheer for twenty feet. Oh God!" The memory jerked Tippy upright, and he howled a ragged cry that chilled the men to their core.

"I could barely see through the damnable snow." Tippy dropped forward to his knees and swayed there before the flames, talking out loud, not aware of the men gathered close about him. "But I found him after a spell. I heard the boy's coughing. Noble, too, he was hurt, something awful, I could tell by his moaning. The kid, though, his eyes weren't right. Looking dazed. But he gave me something to give to his girl. I wouldn't take it, made him hold on to it. I told him he was going to be just fine. I just needed to kindle a flame. By God, you think I could do that?"

His voice rose to a squeak, trembling in the still room. He looked up at each man with a defiant glint in his dark-rimmed eyes, his useless claw hands held before him.

"No, sir. Not a spark could I manage. And Noble, he was in a bad way. He kept trying to rise, to kick, but something was broken. Thor. . . ." Tippy's voice cracked again. "Thor didn't know a thing. Bless him. He hit hard enough that his head smacked a rock, and he . . . died."

They let him sob for a minute, for this was a beaten and broken man.

"He give me a little figurine he'd carved. Was of two people, said it was for his girl. They was to put it on their wedding cake. He was sneaking off to get married, you know." Tippy looked up at the boss, a smile almost visible on his cracked face, but then it faded. "Before his mother died, he wanted her to see his wedding day. He was a good boy, going to be back here next week, he was, just like he promised you, boss."

"Tip, where's your coat? Your mittens?"

The little wreck of a man looked at the boss like he had asked how to find the ground. "Why, I give 'em to the boy, didn't I? He said he was so cold, and his teeth rattled something fierce." His face crumpled again, and he said, "I couldn't kindle a spark to save him." He let his twisted hands rise and fall, helpless, to his lap. "I took the figurine at the end. He begged me so. . . . I took it and vowed to get it to his girl. Only I lost it somewhere in the snow."

"It's okay, Tip. We'll find it. We'll get it to her."

"I looked. Looked for two days. I made a promise. Dug in the snow and all. . . ." The broken man just sat there slumped, staring into the fire, close enough to burn up, but still not close enough. He would never be close enough to flame to get warm again.

✍

The saga of the unfortunate, wayward teamster is one of the more extreme examples of the dire predicaments that befell lumbermen in New England's vast forests in winter. And the winter of 1887 was indeed one of the coldest on record. Just as in other parts of the country, the Northeast experienced a string of unrivaled brutal winters from 1886 to 1888, the likes of which hadn't been seen for fifty years.

Snow in New England's North Woods topped eight feet deep before drifting, and the temperature dropped to more than 40 to 50 degrees below zero for weeks at a time. Men and horses still had to work in order to meet spring ice-out timber deadlines, and frequently they were too far from camp when severe cold crippled the horses. With no way to move them and, most important, no way to bring feed to them, men were sometimes forced to kill their teams rather than let them starve and freeze to death.

Logging had to be done in the North Woods in the winter, when surfaces were packed hard and frozen, and when rivers, lakes, ponds, and streams were passable. During other times of the year, the logging roads in the woods became little more than muddied ruts.

Foul weather would frequently shut down a logging camp for days at a stretch. And sometimes getting the men motivated after a longish rest proved a difficult task. A frigid Sunday in December 1909 at a logging camp on the Swift River in Conway, New Hampshire, had been preceded by three days lost to a blizzard. On this particular Sabbath, the outfit's boss demanded that the men work to make up for lost time. He gave them five minutes to get outside. After four minutes passed, none of the men had moved from around the woodstove. The boss jammed a lit stick of dynamite under the corner of the camp. The men departed with all possible speed, and the boss stamped out the fuse. Such tactics never failed to produce the desired results.

In the early years of the twentieth century, another logging camp on Mooselookmeguntic Lake, near Rangeley, Maine, contained five men bored with bad weather and low on supplies. A teamster showed up one evening and brought fresh goods and mail—as well as two prostitutes and a large supply of rum. Before long, fights over the women broke out. The glowing stove was knocked over several times, pistol shots rang out, and the one sober man in camp, after preventing the two fighting men from taking axes to each other, threw them both outside into the frigid night to either kill each other or cool off. They made peace in a remarkably short time.

30

THE GREAT WHITE HURRICANE
(1888)

In March, a nor'easter wallops the Northeast coast, dumping fifty inches of snow and whipping up fifty-foot drifts. City streets are plugged tight, and two hundred ships are grounded or wrecked. It is weeks before an accurate death count is reached.

༄

"Mama, where is Papa?"

Beulah Hammond turned to see her little boy, six-year-old Wilfred, staring at her, little puffs of his breath rising as he spoke. He stood shivering in the doorway of the apartment's one bedroom, his brown eyes seeming to stare straight through her. So like Raymond, she thought. She held out her arms, and he walked into them. "Why aren't you wearing your sweater, Willy?"

"People don't wear sweaters when they sleep, Mama."

"Well now, that's true. But special times make for special excuses. Remember last night when Papa told you how this was a special time, not just for us, but for the whole wide city of Boston?"

He nodded. She held him close and rubbed his bony little bird shoulders and back. "Now run and fetch your sweater, and I'll read you a story."

He pulled away and said, "But where's Papa?"

She sighed and said, "He had to go out to find us coal so we don't get too cold." She couldn't help herself and looked over at the coal scuttle before the small stove.

"Is that all the coal we have, Mama?"

"Yes, dearest. It's a long, cold storm."

"But you said spring was coming."

Beulah Hammond looked out the window. "I know, dearest. It will get warmer, and we'll be able to grow flowers in our window box again."

Willy looked out the window and down onto the street. As far as he could see, the whiteness of the snow covered every surface below. "But I don't see him."

His mother stared out the window at the thick white mess, no streetlamps on to light the coming dark. Ray had been gone most of the day. "Neither do I, honey. Neither do I."

✖

"There is no communication with Providence, captain."

The older man heard him, knowing already what the young officer's words confirmed. This storm not only was unexpected, but it might just be the last storm any of them would ever see.

Again the young man shouted. "Sir, I can't see a foot in front of my nose!"

"Do your best, man!" The captain wrestled with the helm but then shook his head. "There's nothing for it. We'll have to head back out of the bay, ride it out. Come about!"

Captain Carpentier's order passed down the ranks, and the great booms swung again, adding yet another challenge to his crew of frozen, ragged sailors, who had been fighting the storm for more than fifteen hours.

"Why don't he heave-to?" said a voice, muffled by the thick snow, a voice louder than it would have been had the weather not lent its exhausted edge an anonymity.

"Because we're in the lanes, for God's sake," yelled the captain. "And don't think I don't know your voice by now, Patton, you whining bastard! Now do your job!"

The only sounds for many minutes after the uncharacteristic bellowing outrage of the captain were the slap of sails, the whooshing of sheets pulled through block and tackle, and the grunts of men attending their tasks. No one dared speak—the captain had never shown such rage. To a man they would all agree he was fair, if not entirely talkative or jovial.

And to a man they knew he was right, and they sensed the fear in his voice. And to a man they hated this late-season storm. Snow in March certainly wasn't unheard of, but this storm was showing no letup at all.

And it was in this lull that the *Ruby B.* was rammed dead in the middle by a ship twice its size. There was no warning, no sound, no indication that anything other than the vicious storm was wrong. One second the captain was squinting into the driving snow; the next instant something little more than a shadow at the far outer edge of his sight intruded, slicing through the pelting white muck.

The Great Blizzard of March 12, 1888. In March 1888 a nor'easter called the Great White Hurricane walloped the Northeast coast, dumping fifty inches of snow, plugging city streets, whipping up eighty-mile-per-hour winds and fifty-foot drifts, wrecking two hundred ships, and causing the deaths of four hundred people. This Farmington, Connecticut, sidewalk shows the amount of snow the freak March storm dumped . . . on green grass and blooming flowers. *Courtesy National Oceanic and Atmospheric Administration/ Department of Commerce*

Then it breached their hull, and the cracking was louder and more violent than anything the men had ever heard. The sudden unexpectedness of it elicited screams from half of the twelve-man crew. The others were caught in the midst of the collision, crushed between the prow of the unseen ship and the splintering planking of the *Ruby B.*

Then screams and shouts, more than could have come from his small crew, erupted from all around him, and Captain Carpentier pitched forward, slamming into something hard and flat twenty feet higher than his ship's deck had been. As he slipped from the scarred wreckage of snapped timbers, the captain thought of his wife, Ruby, sitting in their little stone house, all alone in the dark, staring out the window at the sea, the damned sea.

‸

"I'm so sorry, Lucy. I . . . I never would have guessed we were in for such a storm. Or any storm. The weather's been so beautiful for weeks now. The first crocuses and tulips are up, for God's sake."

Clayton McCafferty and his wife, Lucy, had spent the day at his parents' farm fifteen miles down the coast in Saco, Maine, and had less than four miles to go until they were home, safe and sound. It was beginning to occur to them that they might not make it. The storm had come upon them with no warning and had dumped so much snow in such a short amount of time, filling the blowing, frigid air before them with nothing but white.

Between gusts, McCafferty couldn't see their horse's back, let alone the road. Soon the horse found it too difficult to drag their gig. McCafferty thrashed its back several times and succeeded in getting the horse to lurch forward a few yards more, but it was a fruitless endeavor.

The worst part was their lack of planning. It was the middle of March, and they had left home with little more than light clothes and one small lap blanket. And here was sweet Lucy, pregnant with their first child, and all he could offer her was a near-frozen horse—which had long since lain down and was now crusted with snow. Could it be that they were in for the same?

"I should go for help, Lucy. I'm sure we're near the Peabodys' farm. For all we know we're in their dooryard."

"No, Clayton! Don't leave me. I'm . . . so cold." She stuttered this through chattering teeth and pulled him closer with all her strength. They curled tight together, and he whispered in her ear of happy times, of warm summer sun, of their beautiful baby.

⚬⁀⚬

The Peabody brood had played on the forty-foot drift since the storm had passed nearly a week before. Now, as it melted, a foreleg of the dead horse was discovered, stiff and hoisted in the air as if beckoning someone. By the time the farmer and his wife dug out the horse's chest, they realized that the dead beast was harnessed to something.

Under a collapsed buggy canopy, they found a man, curled up like a baby, a blue glow just under the stark white skin of his face. It wasn't until they lifted his stiff form free that they found the small woman, who had been curled up tight under him. Their fingers were still locked together.

"My God, my God. . . ."

"She's pregnant, Lucian."

Then the farmwife staggered backward, her hand to her mouth.

"What is it?" asked her husband.

She pointed at the frozen couple. "It's . . . the McCaffertys."

"Oh, no." The big man looked close, saw that his wife was right, and broke down beside her. They hugged, not wanting to believe what they knew to be true, as their children peered around them at the dead people.

"We were right here," said Mr. Peabody. "My God, my God, how could they not know?"

✤

Crouch knocked the stiff leather boot one more time with the back of his spade, though he knew there was no way the boot belonged to anyone alive. The shovel rang as if he had struck a stone. "Got another one!"

"Yeah?" His friend, Amis, pushed through the waist-high pile, half as tall as the drift behind him. "What do you figure? Three, four days?"

"How should I know? Do I look like a doctor to you? I'm just collecting bodies for the city, same as you. Here, help me with him." The two men grabbed the boot with rag-wrapped hands and dragged the body out of the doorway.

"Hey, look at that. He's holding a ten-pound sack of coal like it was a baby or something."

"Probably just trying to stay warm."

Amis snorted. "You got to light coal to get any warmth out of it."

"That's not even funny. Now help me find his wallet. Then we go tell the boss so they can come get him."

"Says here he's a Mr. Raymond Hammond. You know him?"

Crouch shook his head. "Nah."

"Then why do you look so tore up about it?"

"He's dead, Amis."

"Yeah, so? We must've seen a hunnert of 'em today."

"Yeah, and doesn't it get to you? I mean, they all have families."

Amis nodded but said nothing. They both regarded the man for a moment. His eyes were open, and his lips were stretched tight over his teeth as if he had been making some great effort to escape the snow. But it hadn't worked, and in the end he had just settled for a cold doorway.

"Does it say where he lived?"

Amis squinted at the paper as a breeze ruffled it. "Can't be."

"What?" Crouch took the paper from Amis.

"Grosvenor Ave? But that's this street."

"Yeah, and he lives at 32½ Grosvenor. We're at 30 now."

Crouch stepped back, plowed through the snow pile, and looked up at the buildings. Amis was right. The man was nearly home, he thought. Crouch pushed back through the snow and said, "We can't put him with the rest. Not with him so close to home."

"What should we do with him?"

Crouch pulled in a lungful of cool air. He looked up, squinting an eye. The sun already had set to work on the eaves, and icicles were dripping. For all the snow that fell, the sun had quite a job to do. At this rate, the better part of it might be gone in a week, maybe more. But the boss had told him that the police said there were forty-, fifty-foot drifts in some parts of Boston.

"Crouch . . ."

"Huh?"

"I said, what do we do with him?"

"We bring him home. With his coal."

For once, Amis didn't argue.

∽

The storm that lambasted the Northeast from March 11 to March 14, 1888, was a nor'easter—so called because its winds drive in from the northeast. The region gets hit with them each year, but rarely do they pack such a wallop as that of the Great Blizzard of 1888. Also known as the Great White Hurricane, it is one of the most famous snowstorms in U.S. history. The brutal event caused large-scale destruction along the Northeast coast from the Chesapeake Bay through Maine and beyond.

Fifty inches of snow were dumped in Connecticut, Rhode Island, and Massachusetts, with slightly lesser amounts along New Hampshire's coast and into southern Maine. Fifty-foot snowdrifts were reported throughout the region, as were numerous accounts of drifts higher than three-story houses.

Because the storm was so unexpected, no one was prepared, especially after just emerging from a particularly long, cold winter. All over New England, flowers were blooming, fields were greening, and temperatures had crept into the 70s.

Shipping along the entire northern U.S. coastline seized in a frozen death grip. Two hundred ships were grounded or wrecked, and one hundred sailors lost their lives. Low temperatures—some spots hovered just above zero for days—and severe winds combined with the massive snowfall reduced visibility to dangerous levels. There were unofficial reports of eighty-mile-per-hour winds at various spots throughout New England, with an official wind speed of fifty-four miles per hour reported on Block Island, Rhode Island.

The total death toll for the storm reached four hundred; two hundred people died in New York City alone. Indeed, cities were particularly hard hit, including New York, Boston, Philadelphia, and Providence. In each city, power lines, which had been draped on poles lining busy streets, sagged and snapped. In addition, people were stranded for days on above-ground trains in cities all over the Northeast.

Following the storm, a number of afflicted cities enacted major reforms in the way power lines and trains were to be rebuilt. Boston took the lead and nine years later, in 1897, became home to the first underground subway system in the United States.

31

THE LAST VAMPIRE
(1892)

In an attempt to ward off vampiric spirits of the recently deceased, on March 19, 1892, a young Rhode Island girl's corpse is exhumed and dismembered, and the smoke of her burning organs is inhaled by family members.

✍

"I have seen this, I tell you, and what's more, heard of it, too, with the Tillinghast and the Rose families. They are the undead, and the only way to stop them from feeding on your Edwin is to—"

The farmer could listen no more. His sizable fist, hard like a rock and swung fast like a cannon shot, caught his friend high on the cheekbone and snapped the head sideways. This was a man George Brown had known his entire life, had grown up with, and had counted among his few true friends, but at this moment he felt as though he had never known him.

The assaulted man sat on the snow outside Brown's barn. He shook his head, trying to regain his wits. "What in the name of the good Lord did you do that for, George?" He stood and leaned against the rail fence, massaging his face and working his jaw.

"Do you know of what you speak? You are suggesting the unthinkable. The absurd!"

"George, I'm not asking you to believe it. I'm asking you to consider it if there is no other hope."

Brown held up a thick finger of warning in his friend's face. "I'm warning you. Never again bring up this idea of . . ."

The neighbor stood staring at Brown and shaking his head. Then he walked down the lane back to his neighboring farmstead, his breath fuming behind him in the waning daylight of the March day.

But as George Brown watched his neighbor walk away, he knew that there was at least a kernel of truth in what his friend had said. And his neighbor hadn't been the only one to bring it up. Other people, mostly the old ones, found a reason to visit him, and all hinted at the same thing. But to suggest that he dig up his daughters, his wife. . . .

Brown looked past the squat white farmhouse, past the edge of his fields and pasture, to the drab-gray arms of the denuded trees at the edge of the forest.

Not far away, his only son, Edwin, lay dying of the same wasting disease that first took his wife, Mary, eight years ago, and then six months later, his sweet daughter Mary Olive. And finally, just eight weeks ago, when it seemed they could endure no more, his darling daughter Mercy Lena died, too. She had become stricken and failed much quicker than the others. But now Edwin, his only son—a dear specimen of kindness and manhood—also lay dying. Eighteen months in the West, at Colorado Springs, had not helped nearly enough. And when he learned of his sister's decline and death, he had come back at once.

But this? To exhume the bodies of his wife, his daughters? As if that weren't enough, these fools suggested violating his loved ones' sacred rest by cutting them open, removing their very hearts and livers, and burning them, eating them! As if that would solve anything.

⁓

Dr. Harold Metcalf stood with one arm in the sleeve of his suitcoat, the other easing the coat onto his shoulders. "I cannot have heard you correctly, Mr. Brown."

The brawny farmer closed his eyes as if he were embarrassed and could not bear to face the piercing blue eyes of the young doctor. He swallowed once and said, "I know that it is an unusual request, Dr. Metcalf, but I am in a poor position, as you can see." He opened his eyes and looked again at the young man. "Do you understand? If I do nothing of the sort, then forever more my friends and neighbors, and more importantly, my family members, will wonder if we did enough."

The young doctor finished pulling on his coat. "And so will you, if we are to be honest here, Mr. Brown."

The farmer's shoulders sagged, and he nodded in agreement.

The young doctor regarded the broken man for some time. Finally, he said, "Then, against my better judgment, we will proceed . . . as we must."

∾

The first thing that George Brown noticed when the keeper opened the crypt was the coffin on the wooden rack, as if it were a loaf waiting to be slid from a baker's oven. It would be another month at least before the frozen New England ground could be breached with shovel and pick.

The coffin was larger than he had remembered from Mercy Lena's funeral nine weeks before.

Someone cleared his throat. Brown looked around him. "Mr. Brown," said the doctor in a low voice, "perhaps we should proceed?"

"Yes, of course." The two men followed the keeper into the crypt. The stone-lined walls did little to hold back the powerful smell of raw earth that hung in the still, cold air. And yet, there was something else in the air of the crypt, something he dared not think of. Brown felt certain that he would go to his own grave with that stink clinging to the inside of his own nostrils.

He reached out and touched the corner of the casket. It was smooth, the polished surface of a good coffin for a good girl. He felt himself tremble, and tears welled in his eyes. No matter, he thought. It is dark in here, and besides, she was my daughter.

The doctor nodded to the keeper, and the man began prying open the lid a little at a time as he made his way around the box. In two minutes he had finished and stood to one side, the crowbar poised beneath the rim.

Metcalf looked toward Brown, but the man had turned away, his broad arms tightly folded in front of him as if to defend himself from an oncoming evil. Beyond him a half dozen men stood silhouetted in the doorway, peering into the gloom of the crypt. Women and a few young people peered in between the men's shoulders.

The lid lifted with a squawk as the last of the nails pulled free. Though it was cold enough for the men to see their breath rising in the dim glow of the two oil lamps, it wasn't cold enough to quell the fetid stink of decay rising in a cloud from the casket. The doctor slipped out a hankie from his pocket and held it over his nose and mouth as he peered into the coffin.

The white gauze of the traditional shroud was stained across the girl's chest and had shifted from fully covering the girl's face. It had pulled to the side enough that when the keeper held an oil lamp close, the two men saw the grimace of the girl's face, the cheeks swollen and distending her mouth into a freakish leer. Her eyes were wide open, as if forced, their dark centers staring upward.

From behind, Metcalf heard a harsh intake of breath as Brown turned away from the scene, his hand covering his mouth. The man, he knew, would forever regret risking that peek at his daughter's corpse.

"The heart, doctor. You must remove the heart and the liver." It was a voice from outside. Dr. Metcalf heard the farmer's breath catch in his throat. How could the man endure this? thought the doctor.

Metcalf swallowed once and retrieved from his satchel a long glistening blade. He slit the bloodstained shroud and without pause proceeded on into the chest. With every harsh plunge of the scalpel, the doctor regretted accepting the task. He resented the rising murmurings and grunts of approval that seemed to be drawing closer. Did these people have no shame? Is it not bad enough that they as good as forced Brown into this undertaking? But he bit his cheek and proceeded.

The heart came out with relative ease, as he expected, because the body had been dead for little more than two months. It had dried somewhat, leaving the organ slightly shriveled, although it still held some blood. He sliced it free and held it up to inspect it in the light, his natural curiosity outweighing the reticence he had originally felt.

He repeated the procedure with the girl's liver, though it contained no blood.

Immediately from behind him he heard a crone's voice saying, "But the heart is bloody! Bloody I tell you. She's the vampire. . . ." The small crowd paused a moment but then pressed in, jostling one another, and soon all in attendance had peered in on the macabre scene in the wooden box.

Dr. Metcalf wanted to explain to them that this was as it should be, that the body was merely taking its time decomposing, especially given the cold temperatures, that of course there would still be a quantity of blood. But he knew anything he might say would fall on deaf ears. These people didn't want to hear cold logic; they were lost in their primitive minds, desperate and angry and clutching at the wispy smoke of superstition.

George Brown's cracking voice cut through the increasing murmur. "Now take them out to the stone and burn them. And there will be an end to it."

"The family must breathe in the vapors, I tell you." It was the old crone again. "Then you must save the ashes," she continued. "Mix them into a potion for the family members to drink of. You must!"

✍

Because of less-than-sanitary and crowded conditions, coupled with poor nutrition, tuberculosis often passed from one family member to another in nineteenth-century New England. Many people died of the disease, and shortly thereafter, other family members would often begin to show signs of it as well.

In centuries past, family members and the local community often believed that this ripple effect of symptoms was actually the manifestation of the deceased's coming back from death in vampiric form to bleed dry his or her relations. In such suspected cases, the most common recourse was to exhume the corpse, cut out the heart, burn the offending organ, and have family members inhale the sordid smoke. Sometimes the entire corpse was set alight in hopes of driving away the evil that had infested it. Sometimes the organs were ingested on the spot by the desperate, cursed family members.

What makes the tale of Mercy Brown so interesting is not that it is unique, but that it is merely the last such episode to have taken place (that we know of) in New England. Although George Brown did not seriously think that anything more than consumption had killed his loved ones, he gave in to powerful peer pressure and went along with the grisly deed. Those who had urged Brown on must have noted with great disappointment that his son died shortly thereafter of complications arising from advanced tuberculosis.

Such incidents were not unique, however. Each state in New England has a long history of exhuming, dismembering, and defiling the bodies of consumptives for the sake of preserving the lives of living relations. In one of the earliest documented cases of suspected vampirism in New England, in Vermont in 1793, Captain Isaac Burton's second wife, Hulda, became afflicted with consumption, as had his first wife, Rachel. He had the first wife's body exhumed and found that the corpse, three years in the ground, was bloated. Onlookers wrongly assumed that it had nourished itself by feeding off the good captain's new wife. Rachel's heart, lungs, and liver were removed and burned. Alas, poor Hulda died anyway.

32

. . . AND WITH AN AXE
(1892)

In Fall River, Massachusetts, on August 4, 1892, thirty-two-year-old Sunday school teacher Lizzie Borden opens her parents' heads with a hatchet—and is never convicted of the crime.

☙

"I'm sorry, Miss Borden," Eli Bence told the stern-faced woman for the third time. "I cannot sell you prussic acid without a prescription."

"But I told you I just want to clean my sealskin cape of the insects that have taken refuge on it." Lizzie Borden leaned over the counter, pounding a chunky hand on its surface in time with the words she spoke through gritted teeth.

"Ahem." Another clerk at Smith's Drug Store cleared his throat. Lizzie looked over at him and the male customer he was helping. She glared once more at Bence, shook her head, and left the store.

As the doorbell jangled, the clerk looked at the other two and said, "Prussic acid is poison. I can't sell that stuff to just anybody. Lord knows what they might do with it." The other two men agreed and looked out the front window, but Lizzie was gone.

☙

Andrew Borden, alone in his family's drawing room, sat down heavily on the velvet settee and grunted. "Oh, I'm tired." He leaned back with a sigh, grateful for a few minutes' respite from the already busy day and its requirements of him. He had just returned from making his rounds to his various business concerns, and he was not yet over the vile intestinal discomfort that his wife, Abby, was certain had been a poison placed in their food by nefarious hands the day before. Dr. Bowen had assured her, to no avail, that it had been a bad bit of food—the joint of meat, perhaps.

No matter, thought Andrew as he closed his eyes and leaned back for a quick nap. He relaxed, and his thoughts turned to the ever-present scowls

FRANK LESLIE'S
ILLUSTRATED
WEEKLY

Vol. LXXVI.—No. 1952.
Copyright, 1893, by Arkell Weekly Co.
All Rights Reserved.

NEW YORK, JUNE 29, 1893.

[PRICE, 10 CENTS.

The Borden murder trial, **Frank Leslie's Illustrated Weekly,** *June 29, 1893.*
Despite numerous bits of incriminating evidence—including the fact that she was caught
burning a soiled dress several days after the murders, that she was caught in a series of lies
pertaining to her whereabouts during the murders, that she had more motive than almost
anyone else, and that she was never asked to give testimony during her trial—Lizzie
Borden, a thirty-two-year-old Sunday school teacher from Fall River, Massachusetts, was
acquitted of the murder by hatchet of her parents on August 4, 1892. She went on to
share her father's sizable estate with her sister. *Courtesy Library of Congress*

of the townsfolk. That he was not a well-liked man in Fall River he knew and could live with. For he was a businessman and, if he said so himself, a good and just one. Chalk it up to the differences between those who have and those who have not. And thanks to his own work ethic, he had something to show for it. Why should anyone wish him ill because of it? And yet, even in his own home, there was an air of discord.

His daughters rarely spoke a civil word to him anymore and seemed to consider reprehensible all that he and Abby, his second wife, did. He knew that his girls were miffed that he chose to include Abby's family in his will. He also considered his girls lazy and spoiled. Little was expected of them, and their continued spinsterhood vexed him greatly. All this and more fluttered through his mind as he drifted off.

A light sleeper given to spells of prolonged wakefulness in the middle of the night, Andrew Borden's eyes snapped open at the exact moment that something hovered above him. It was, it seemed to him in his groggy state, the emotionless face of his eldest daughter, Lizzie, busy at some task. Such a bitter girl, he thought. But any further thoughts were robbed from him as a dark blur descended from above and became a hatchet that rammed into his skull.

It lifted, drove down again, and so repeated nine times more, each cleaving deeper, one blow slicing his nose from his face, another splitting in two his left eyeball as if it were a hard-boiled egg.

He would not have known that an hour and a half before, in the guest room directly above, his dear Abby had been laid low by the same person, using the same implement.

❧

Abby Borden had hummed to herself as she bent to tuck hospital corners on the sheets in the guest room. It was nice having John Morse visit. He was, after all, the girls' uncle. Oddly enough, the girls were out of town. That is, Emma was still in the country with friends. Lizzie had come back the night before, claiming she wanted to retrieve fishing lures before returning to Fairhaven to join her sister and friends. Abby secretly wished the girl had stayed away with her sister, at least for another day. The mood in the household was more jovial and relaxed without the girls. And Lizzie was always interfering and undermining her orders to Bridget, the Irish maid.

Before coming up to freshen the guest room, Abby had asked Bridget to wash windows at the front of the house. She had just plumped the pillows and smoothed the last of the coverlet when she heard something in the hallway, as if a breeze had lifted curtains or a dress had rustled as someone passed. She paused, her head half turned.

The first blow caved in the back of her skull, pasting hair into the shattered bone. Eighteen more blows succeeded in cleaving the woman's head nearly in half. One wayward stroke sliced deep into her neck at the base of her skull. She was left slumped forward over a chair as if inspecting something close to the floor, a thick rope of blood and hair connecting her to the sopping rug.

By the time the maid discovered Abby, her blood had drained from her drooped head and pooled in a thick black puddle that stained through the rug and seeped down between the floorboards. Her white dress was a soaked, unrecognizable clot about her shoulders.

∽

"I'm Sergeant Harrington, Miss Borden. I have to ask you your whereabouts this morning."

The officer, a dapper, trim man in a neat lightweight brown wool suit, held a notebook and a pencil poised above the paper. A uniformed officer stood nearby, his hands behind his back.

Lizzie pulled her handkerchief from her cuff and dabbed at her red eyes. "I honestly don't know what you think—" She paused. "You honestly don't think I . . . that I . . . ?"

"Miss Borden, all I'm trying to do is eliminate everything I don't need to think about, as it were, in order to proceed with this investigation. Now, where were you between nine and eleven o'clock this morning?"

"I went up in the loft of the barn to look for some fishing sinkers. I was to rejoin Emma and the others in the country."

Later, Harrington and the other officer investigated the barn loft, and the sergeant poked his head up into the stuffy space, motes drifting in the air. Other than a few broken bits of furniture, various crates, and old shipping trunks, it was empty. And thick dust covered everything—including the floor. It looked to him as if the floor hadn't been walked on in years. He asked the other officer to verify this. They exchanged glances and headed back to the house, where, on the dining room table, Dr. Dolan was busy performing autopsies on the two victims.

"Where is Miss Borden?" Harrington asked one of the many officers milling about. The uniformed man nodded toward the stairs and said, "Upstairs, sir." He leaned closer and said, "Deputy Marshal Fleet's grilling her."

Harrington looked up the stairs. Under his breath he said, "I almost feel sorry for her."

The young officer smiled, but he lost the grin when he saw Harrington's glare. Harrington mounted the stairs, and when the deputy marshal had finished, Harrington continued to question Lizzie Borden until 8:30 that evening.

∽

"This is preposterous," said Emma Borden. Murmurs of agreement rose from the crowd gathered at the gravesite.

"I understand your grief, Miss Borden, but I assure you it is necessary if we are to find your parents' murderer." Sergeant Harrington nodded to the officers, and the caskets were gently pushed back into the carriages.

"But to take their bodies at their burial?"

"A second autopsy has been ordered. I am sorry."

Lizzie stepped forward, dry-eyed and staring hard at the sergeant. "Did they not do all they needed two days ago?"

Harrington sighed and said, "I can only imagine how difficult this must be for you. I am very sorry."

Lizzie just stared at him, no sign of emotion showing on her face.

∽

"If I were you, I wouldn't let anybody see me do that, Lizzie." On August 7, three days after the murders, Alice Russell, the Bordens' neighbor, walked in on Lizzie ripping up a dress and poking the cloth into the flames in the kitchen stove.

"What? Oh, Alice. I didn't know you were there." She poked again at the last of the dress and clanked the lid down hard on the stovetop. "It's no matter. I stained the dress, ruined it, in fact, on some fresh baseboard paint." She faced her neighbor. "Why?" she stared at Russell as if daring the woman to say just one more thing.

∽

On August 11, day three of the four-day inquest, Judge Blaisdell of the Second District Court charged Lizzie Borden with the double murder. Alice Russell's testimony of finding Lizzie burning the dress convinced the judge that this was the proper course of action. On December 1, a Massachusetts grand jury heard testimony, including that of Miss Russell, and Lizzie was, oddly, charged with three counts of murder—one for each of her parents, and one for the pair.

Many strange points surround the case to this day. During the fourteen-day trial the following June, useful evidence—damning to Lizzie—was not admitted, such as the fact that she tried to purchase prussic acid (more commonly known as hydrogen cyanide, a lethal chemical) the day before the murders, the same day of the alleged family poisoning. The only time Lizzie ever testified was during the inquest, and that transcript was also not admitted as evidence.

Other evidence that should have made a difference in the outcome, but didn't, included Alice Russell's testimony regarding Lizzie's secretive burning of the dress, and the fact that Lizzie had apparently lied to Sergeant Harrington about rooting in the barn loft for fishing gear the morning of the murders.

It is also interesting to note that because fingerprinting was a new forensic technique at the time, the Fall River police regarded it with skepticism and didn't bother taking fingerprints from the hatchet believed to be the murder weapon, which was found in the basement.

Following the second autopsy, the victims' heads were separated from the bodies for further forensic study. The heads were boiled, and the soft tissue was removed and examined. Any further evidence gathered from this procedure was lost in the proceedings. Abby Borden's head was reunited with its skeleton, but Andrew Borden's head never was. His bones remain headless to this day.

If Lizzie Borden had a motive for murder, it was driven by anger and greed. She and her sister were outraged that their father was going to leave each of them just $25,000 on his death, while their stepmother got the bulk of the $500,000 estate. He had intended to set these wishes down on paper but never did.

Though she was the only official suspect of the double murder, Lizzie Borden was never convicted of the crime. Co-heiress with her sister, Emma, to her father's substantial fortune, she went on to live another thirty years. Lizzie died on June 1, 1927, of pneumonia. Emma, from whom she had been estranged for years, died nine days later from a fall.

33

LOBSTERMEN FISTICUFFS!
(1894)

In December 1894, escalating tensions cause Cape Porpoise, Maine, lobstermen to sink boats, threaten lives, and brawl in the streets. Instead of further rioting, the arrests, oddly enough, instigate conservation practices still in use today.

⤜

Russell Harmon didn't like the way the pier vibrated under his feet with each step. Together, he and his companion shuffled their way to the end of the pier. The stone they were carrying would more than do the job. They got the thing to within a couple of feet of the end of the pier and set it down with a thud, their breath rising in the cold night air.

"You don't have to put a hole in a boat to sink it," said Harmon, looking around him, though it was completely dark and the harbor had no lights. He dug his hands deeper into the pockets of his wool coat and shivered.

Austin Sinnett, his best friend, looked down at the boat. "You going soft on me?"

"No, it's not that, just that—"

"What, then?"

"Well, hell, Daniel Wagner is one of my father's best friends. I've known him since I was a kid."

"Me, too. But the man's a spy for the government. He's a traitor to lobstermen. Thinks he can get away with turning his fellows in because of those silly laws about lobster sizes. He's got to learn that nothing good will come of it. Best way I know is to sink his damn boat. Wish he was in it."

Harmon shook his head and turned away, walking back up the pier. Far behind him he heard a clunk, clunk, and then a splintering crash erupting into a splash. Howls of laughter followed, drifting up the wharf, as if chasing him. He smiled despite himself, smiled at the sheer glee his friend got out of everything in life, from a good day on the water to dropping a massive stone through the bottom of another fisherman's boat. The thought chilled him, and he walked faster.

∽

"That about do it, Daniel?" The man behind the counter at Pinkham's looked at Daniel Wagner, a man he had known most of his life, a man he considered a friend, and a man who wasn't afraid to call a situation like it was.

Wagner nodded.

"Heard you got your boat out, getting her fixed up, judging from the purchases you're making today." Both men glanced at the brass tacks and a tin of pine tar.

Wagner gave a half-smile but said nothing.

"You know, Dan," the store owner continued, "there's a pile of us think it's just plain wrong what they did to your boat. I heard you time and again talking about the lobster stocks, and I'll be honest, when I first heard you talking about how they'd disappear, I thought you were full of hot air. But I've seen fewer and fewer decent-size lobsters. Heck, any bigger than a pound, pound and a half, and people get excited. Rarely will we get a two-pounder in."

"That's all I've been trying to tell people. So many people are lobster-ing nowadays, and selling every single one they pull up. If we don't limit ourselves, keep some stock for breeding, there won't be one left within a few years, I'm convinced of it."

The clerk tallied the few items and said, "Well, I'm not the one needs convincing. It's the other lobster fishermen you got to worry about."

Wagner narrowed his eyes. "I guess I know who sunk my boat, all right. And I'll be waiting for him, give him something to think about."

"Just you be careful now. If it's who I think it is—and I know it is—he's a hothead. And he's half your age. And that's not the half of it." He leaned over the counter and lowered his voice. "Daniel, you know as well as I do that someone who's standing right here with us—and it isn't me—alerted the authorities that Sinnett was shipping short lobsters in a barrel out of the Kennebunk Depot."

Wagner returned the man's look for a moment. Then he scooped up his items and said, nodding, "See you later."

As he walked down the sidewalk, Wagner ran a hand across his bearded face, wondering not for the first time if he was wise to have opened this sack of snakes. But then again, he had never been one to back down from something that seemed just plain wrong to him, especially when it could be fixed with a little forethought and effort. Still, he was getting tired of

Dory fishermen hauling lobster pots off Cape Ann. New England lobstermen used rowing and sailing vessels well into the twentieth century. However, in the mid-nineteenth century, "smack" boats, vessels with a live well for transporting large numbers of lobsters greater distances, were introduced, thus increasing demand for lobsters significantly—so much so that by 1880 the average-size Maine lobster dropped from five pounds to less than half a pound. Lobstermen—and state governments—recognized the threat to their livelihood and enacted conservation practices still in use today. *Courtesy National Oceanic and Atmospheric Administration/Department of Commerce*

hearing the word "spy" being thrown at him in his own town whenever he walked down the street.

As if on cue, a too-familiar, taunting voice pulled him from his reverie.

"Hey, Wagner! You been studyin' law up to Saco?"

Austin Sinnett stood just a few feet from him, in front of the post office. Wagner stopped, tensing inside. The boy was indeed half his age and looked to be built of stout timber and wire. If I have to, thought Wagner, I'll throw my purchases in his face and see what happens then.

"What makes you say that, Sinnett?"

"You must know the law to get me turned in."

"Sinnett, I—" But Wagner never got the chance to finish his sentence, because the young man had set his feet and started swinging at him. By God, thought Wagner, Pap always said never to start a fight, but if someone does open up on you, then you better finish it. Wagner flung his few items at the young man's face, but Sinnett batted them away as if they were flies and swung hard at Wagner.

The first blow connected with the older man's cheek. He felt the hot sting, and something cracked. Wagner swung wide, his right fist glancing off the young man's tensed shoulder, but it was like slapping a charging bull.

Before he knew it, they were rolling on the ground, the crusted snow and cobbles digging into Wagner's back even through his wool coat.

"I've about had enough of you," Sinnett said as he landed another blow on Wagner's belly, "and your meddling with my livelihood!" Another blow rained down. "And I ain't the only one!"

Wagner felt himself begin to fade. What he thought were the muscles of a man still in decent condition were of little use against this young bull with so much pent-up anger. He felt Sinnett's breath against his face. The man hadn't cleaned his teeth in some time, of that Wagner was sure, as his breath was a fetid stink.

Wagner tried to turn his head away and hold off Sinnett at the same time, and he managed to secure a hard grip on the young rogue's throat. He might not have the strength of the vicious kid, but he did have strong hands—thickened and steel-like through fifty years of hard labor, of hauling in fishnets and lobster pots, of lugging boats, of plowing fields, of milking cows, of picking rocks to clear land. And it paid off.

The young man still swung, still landed solid, aching blows, but Wagner's throat grip had slowed him down. Any more conversation Sinnett might have had in mind had been reduced to a quiet match of straining muscles and huffing and panting as the two men reached a momentary stalemate. But Sinnett's younger strength was winning.

Wagner looked up into the reddening face and bulging eyes, the lank hair hanging down, the gritted teeth, and he felt no pity. He would have driven upward with a knee, but the young brute had his legs pinned. Wagner felt his arms weakening, shaking. He wasn't sure he would survive another round of blows.

And then the outside world rushed in, and he heard voices, the barking orders of men close by. He thought he heard a woman shouting, and he felt himself being dragged away. His eyesight came in pulsing waves of black clouds, and he felt as if he were being pelted with hot sand. One of the men helping him to his feet wore a long white smock—it was Darby from Pinkham's. He and another fellow helped him sit on a barrel. Someone else rubbed his shoulders. He felt as though he had been strapped to a bell buoy in a hurricane.

He looked up as loud shouts boomed out over the others, and there was Sinnett, still raging. Two men were dragging him backward, holding his brawny arms behind his back. Sinnett stared straight at Wagner, and his words reached him from across the street: "You wait, Wagner! I've not finished with you! You'll get yours!"

The only solace Wagner found in the situation was that Sinnett's throat was purple and bore the distinct impressions of Wagner's meaty hands.

∽

The troubles that visited the Cape Porpoise lobstering community that December 1894 were a long time in the making. If the lobstermen had considered the consequences of the unchecked exploitation of their resource, a fishery they all depended heavily on, they might have realized that Daniel Wagner had their long-term best interests at heart.

Austin Sinnett was arrested and fined $10 for assault and $50 for shipping short lobsters. Because of a timely tip, he had been caught in the process of shipping an unmarked barrel from Kennebunk Depot containing five hundred short lobsters. On appeal, Sinnett's assault charge was dropped, but the short lobster charge remained. In a subsequent trial, it was deemed illegal in the state of Maine to possess any lobster that measured less than 10½ inches. In addition, new wardens were hired to patrol the entire coast of the state, and slowly, over the coming decades, the bootlegging of short lobsters decreased dramatically as lobstermen realized they could gain bigger and better harvests over time.

In colonial New England, lobsters were so plentiful that farmers gathered them off beaches and in shallow water by hand for use as fertilizer. Lobster was considered a food fit only for prisoners, slaves, and servants. In Massachusetts, a law was enacted preventing servants from having to eat lobster more than three times a week.

By 1830, lobstering in Maine began to organize as an industry, with local groups informally attending to their own waters. The introduction of the "smack" boat, a vessel with a live well in the middle through which saltwater flowed, allowed shipment of live lobsters to southern markets such as Boston and New York, thus opening up an industry previously limited by the lobster's short shelf life. By the 1850s, because of overfishing, fifty-pound lobsters (approximately one hundred years old and four feet long), previously a rarity, now became unheard of, and it became increasingly rare for lobstermen to find once-common twenty- and thirty-pound lobsters in their traps.

In 1956, to protest reductions in per-pound prices paid to them dockside by dealers, 4,000 Maine lobstermen enacted a tie-up—refused to fish—and formed the Maine Lobsterman's Association in an effort to achieve equitable prices. The 5,000 non-member lobstermen were allegedly threatened with violence unless they joined, and the Justice Department stepped in, charging both the dockside dealers and the association with violation of antitrust laws.

Despite various advances in this and other such cases, New England's lobstermen, a fiercely territorial and perennially independent breed, are still largely at the mercy of dealer pricing, though in recent years some have begun to market their products directly to an always lobster-hungry public.

Currently, an estimated 6,000 lobstermen fish Maine's waters, hauling in 3 million traps containing roughly 70 million pounds of lobster meat—that's 80 percent of the North American lobster catch. Massachusetts comes in a distant second, bringing in roughly half that amount, followed by Rhode Island and Connecticut.

34

NORTH WOODS ICE-OUT
(1895)

After a long, cold winter in Vermont's North Woods, the first signs of spring thaw are evident—and that means ice-out and the beginning of the year's massive log drives. But a spongy lake, a load of logs, two horses, one teamster, and an unscrupulous clerk are a recipe for disaster.

❧

"By God, Rimmler, if you think I'm going to head out on that lake with my team, you've another thing coming. Why, it's nearly ice-out, so it is." The little Irishman waved his arms as if he were about to take flight and then turned on his heels and stroked Major's thick winter coat. "By God, by God. . . . I don't care what you say. Why, anyway, you're only the clerk." He continued to stroke the broad, steaming back of one of his team, his jaw muscles working hard, a sneer pulling his mouth down as if he were chewing on something distasteful.

Pete Rimmler, camp clerk, heard the stinging reminder and narrowed his eyes. "Now, Corrigan, we will keep the loads moving. If you don't drive that team out over the tote road, then I'll get someone else to drive them."

"Not my horses you won't."

"Need I remind you that they aren't your horses?" He'd be damned if he would let a lowly teamster give him guff. The clerk smiled and said, "Besides, the boss isn't here and I am. I'll get the work out of them one way or another."

Corrigan faced the man, his fists balled, the knuckles white. Then without another word, he turned back to the team, hitched them to the load, and followed the tote road out toward the lake. No one saw him leave.

"Easy does it, lads. Whoa, Colonel. Whoa, Major. You're in fine shape then, lads." Corrigan fought to keep his voice hale and light, but he hated lying to his boys, his team. For he knew deep in his heart that they sensed his deceit, but he had no choice. Rimmler would tell LeBeau, the boss of the woods, that Corrigan refused to haul a load, and they would fire him as teamster as sure as Sadie wore bloomers. And then where would his boys

Hauling logs with sled and team near Waterbury, Vermont. Teamsters in New England's North Woods often formed deep attachments with their horses, and though they worked them hard—one record dray-load contained 11½ cords of pulpwood hauled by a two-horse team in Lyman Brook, New Hampshire—teamsters often gave their lives for their horses, as evidenced in various true stories of teamsters diving through the ice to free their horses after they broke through a softening spring surface. More often than not, the man drowned with his team. *Courtesy Library of Congress*

be? He knew what sort of man the clerk was, knew he was not bluffing about sending them out with someone else. Corrigan couldn't have that.

At the edge of the lake, he squinted and surveyed the surrounding ice, the sun raising puddles on the flat gray-blue expanse before him. It was definitely warming up. The lake surface looked too punched up, sunken somehow, too warm for a load. "But," he sighed, "the sooner we get on with it, the sooner we'll be done." He snapped the reins lightly and clucked his tongue. The boys dug into the slushy surface with the ridged steel shoes on their plate-size hooves, and the load inched forward and then slid with increased ease.

They were well along the main tote road, marked by the grooves of previous loads of runners, and Corrigan was thinking it might all work out. He even considered working up a little whistling tune he knew the boys liked, when first Major and then Colonel slowed to a stop, balking with grumbling whinnies, shaking their heads and snorting, their breath rising in the warming air.

Their load and heavy harnesses prevented them from bolting, but Corrigan sensed that's what they wanted to do. And what's more, he felt the same way. He felt it as a quivering of nervous energy transmitted through the reins he held looped in his bare hands. "Right, lads. Let that weasel of a clerk Rimmler do what he will, we're going back. I'm sorry I pushed you into this."

Corrigan heard a deep sigh, loud and full like far-off thunder, rise up as if from beneath him. He heard the raw beginnings of a scream from Major, then the ice collapsed, and cold, black water closed over them all with the speed of a handclap.

Corrigan flailed to the surface, spluttering and gasping for breath. He had dropped the reins, and now the horses were not where he expected them to be—where he hoped they would be—fighting for air, heads jutting through the ice.

"Major! Colonel! My boys!" His body ached all over as the cold seeped to his core. Below him, just beneath the surface, the horses scrabbled and lunged, their eyes wide in terror, but already their big bodies were fading from sight, pulled downward by their load. Corrigan dove for them, thinking as he pushed himself downward that it couldn't be that deep here, it just couldn't be. And in the near-midnight water, he reached his two boys, the pair of big, beautiful bays. He clawed at their harnesses, the same ones he had fitted and unfitted a thousand times on their backs, below their barrels, across their broad chests. And, buckle after buckle, he worked to free them.

⁓

The camp's boss, LeBeau, and Dan Steward, the head teamster, paused along the tote road over the lake, near the camp. Their ice-scouting trip had taken them farther than they expected, and they had spent the night in the rough. As they followed the much-used route back along the lake, Steward nodded ahead of them at a large, water-filled depression on the iced surface, not far from the far shore. "Looks like ice-out's commencing."

The boss nodded but sped up his stride, squinting at the odd patch, a low groan building in his throat. As they drew closer, they saw what they feared most—wide runner marks and hoofprints ending at the edge of the slush-filled hole in the ice. Both men looked at each other and ran for the camp office, following deep-grooved sled marks all the way back.

∽

LeBeau, a tall, broad man as solid as any man from endless seasons of year-round log work, looked down at his clerk, the smirking Pete Rimmler, and with no warning lunged for him. It took Steward and an assistant cook standing nearby to pry the big man's hands from the throat of the rattled clerk.

"I told you not to send any more teams out on that tote road! It's closer every minute to ice-out! By God, you sent a man to his death, and his horses, too!"

"You didn't come back. I thought to get the loads moved out—"

The panting boss lunged again at the quivering clerk, but the men held him down. "I said to wait for me! Hell, I told you I was out with Steward here to check on the ice situation. I said to wait!"

∽

Later, the men fished around in the hole with gaffs and pikes rigged with extensions and found the wreck. They hitched two teams and managed to drag it out, and there was the little Irishman's body locked tight to the horses. He had managed to free all but one buckle. Unable to save Major and Colonel, he had slipped his arms under the remaining strappings of harness and held tight, ensuring he would not rise again to the surface without his lads.

The men had never seen the boss so angry or inconsolable. Over the long season, he had had plenty of opportunities to fire Corrigan but had instead finally placed him with a team, and with them, the little man had found his element and become indispensable to the entire camp.

"They was inseparable, by God," said an old limber named Grubby Dent, so bent and lame that he, too, was tailing out on his last winter in the woods. "Never saw beasts take to a man like old Major and Colonel took to our little Corrigan." His bottom lip quivered. He stuffed his pipe in his mouth and turned away as the grim-faced men took turns pitching in soil on the man and his two horses, all buried together, in a shoreside grave.

When they returned to camp, Rimmler the clerk was gone.

∽

Life in an old-time woods camp was anything but gentle and hospitable. Most logging took place in the winter, when surfaces were packed and frozen hard and when rivers, lakes, ponds, and streams were passable and thus often used as roadways. But a large amount of fair-weather work, such as building driving dams and camps for the next season, kept crews in the woods in the spring, summer, and fall.

The men had to deal with the maddening attacks of blood-gorging, stinging insects such as blackflies, mosquitoes, deerflies, and midges. They used the only methods available to them, including keeping their hair shaved bald in a wide arc about the ears and then slathering on a foul-smelling tincture of lard and tar. The results made an intolerable situation barely better. So infuriating were the insects that most men preferred to work in the woods in the winter, despite the bone-numbing cold and real danger of losing digits, ears, and noses to frostbite.

No matter the time of year, work conditions in the woods were only for the stout of will and numb of skin. Six-day weeks of fourteen-plus-hour days were considered accept-able. Logging camp mealtimes were somewhat monotonous affairs and often consisted of pork and beanhole baked beans (beans baked in an iron pot in a covered fire-pit in the ground), served thrice daily, and supplemented with molasses, gingerbread, and black tea—the stronger the better. Just after the turn of the twentieth century, when availability of goods and durability of storage were improved, canned food, meat, eggs, and dairy goods were widely introduced to the logger's diet, and rarely did he complain.

When a logging operation ran at full tilt, a packed camp could chew through an astonishing quantity of provisions in a short amount of time. Rough figures for a typical Maine lumber camp in the late nineteenth century estimate that for every million feet of logs cut, 1,000 bushels of oats, ten tons of hay, forty barrels of flour, and nine barrels of pork and beef were consumed.

In 1890, at the Quin and Mitchell camp at Wytopitlock, in Maine, four hundred pounds of beef, four bushels of dry beans, one hundred pounds of lard, and seven pounds of tea were used in a week's time by sixty men. At that time, wages were still low, though better than they had been during the widespread financial depression of the 1870s, when men worked in the woods for $5 a month. That paltry wage rose to $15 to $20 a month by the next decade.

✍

Teamsters were often faced with the vicious tasks of ferrying logs out onto frozen lake and river surfaces, or down impossibly steep mountainside runs with sledges laden with logs and only bridle chains (chains running crossways on a sledge's runners) to help slow down the deadly load.

Choppers often unwittingly dislodged a "widowmaker," a dead limb suspended in branches high above. If it struck the man, death was often the result, and that night in the "ram pasture" (bunkhouse), his silent fellows would pass the hat and offer up a week's pay for the widow of their dead comrade.

Despite these adversities, the majority of New England woodsmen in their dotage looked back on their years of logging labor as a formative time that helped prepare them for challenges later in life, such as marriage. One logger from Waterbury, Vermont, was heard to say, "There ain't nothin' meaner than a log, except a woman when she wants to be . . . and they're just as stubborn."

35

THE PORTLAND GALE
(1898)

On the night of November 26, 1898, the steamship Portland *is caught in an unexpected nor'easter that drags its 192 passengers and crew far out to sea soon after leaving Boston. The waves increase, the storm intensifies, the boilers grow cold, and the vessel bobs broadside to the waves.*

✑

The *Portland*'s captain, Hollis H. Blanchard, knew it was not the storm itself—the wind-driven sleet and snow—but the pounding of the incessant, giant swells that would get them in the end. He looked up from wrestling the wheel in time to see the arching might of another massive wave in a nighttime filled with monstrous waves. The foaming leviathan, so like a living being, dwarfed and pummeled the broadside of the top-heavy steamer. It had been happening more steadily since they had cast off at 7:00 p.m. It was now nearly 11:00 p.m., and the storm had grown into something more violent than anyone had expected, something that would have ruled out a voyage at all. Had they but known. . . .

And now it seemed the Atlantic was demanding payment for this insolence. Another swell rose, its green-black bulk a seemingly unbreachable wall. Within seconds, it broke over them. From the bridge, Captain Blanchard heard round after round of piercing, terror-filled screams that grew more frantic with each passing wave. He never felt so hollow or so frightened. And yet 191 people depended on him, not to mention all their families onshore, looking seaward and waiting, waiting out the storm, as the passengers on the *Portland* were doing.

Another swell advanced on them, more immense than any so far, and Captain Blanchard almost thanked the Lord that he couldn't see very far— almost. For there was no time to do much of anything but swallow his fear and brace his legs.

The knockdown slammed him against the wheelhouse ceiling, and he felt the warmth of blood on his head as pain pulsed from his right shoulder.

But there was no time for self-pity, for water now poured in the smashed windows of the wheelhouse.

More than two miles offshore, Blanchard fought with the *Portland*'s wheel and barked orders to his men, trusting that the rest of the crew could contain the raw panic of the passengers.

Onshore people headed home to Portland and points inland after a long Thanksgiving weekend in Boston, just as the storm, which seemed to come from nowhere, drove northward with unyielding menace along the northeastern seaboard. From the time the *Portland* cast off, at 7:07 p.m., they had dealt with foul weather, but it didn't seem to be anything the steamer couldn't maneuver in.

They had been in plenty of storms before that had whipped up a frenzy but had left the outside passage, their accustomed route, relatively unscathed. Such storms always felt, for a few moments, worse than they were. But the storm didn't slacken and had in fact increased in power. Within an hour of leaving Boston, Blanchard had known it was forming up as a doozy. And he knew they were in its teeth.

The churning currents and swells twice their height prevented him from turning back to Boston. The steamer's shallow hull wasn't built for travel in the rougher seas offshore, but by the time they had reached Thatcher's Island, just northeast of the city, the captain consulted with his top officers and navigation man and decided to head east toward open water. The shoals closer in would be far too treacherous to sail near. Their only real hope lay in riding out the storm offshore.

"If we can make it through the night, then surely the storm will have abated, if not passed altogether, and rescue will be imminent." The captain yelled to them as he held a firm grip on the wheel. "But we must keep the boilers fed so we can navigate! If we belly to the swells. . . ." The men nodded, not wanting to hear the rest of the dire sentence.

"But we'll run out of fuel—"

"I don't care what you use! Without power we stand no chance at all of keeping her headed into the waves! Strip the bulkheads, furniture, decking—anything that will burn, man! But do it now!" Even with this effort, there would be little hope.

⁓

For hours they worked to paddle offshore, but the current and wind conspired to push them southward, and they had been unable to make headway.

Between decks of an ocean steamer during a storm, **Frank Leslie's Illustrated Newspaper, *September 5, 1885*.** The nor'easter of November 26, 1898, sank 150 boats, killed four hundred people, and was named for the lost steamship *Portland,* on which 192 passengers and crew drowned. In order to keep the wooden, shallow-hulled, sidewheel steamers from swamping in large swells, crews had to keep the boilers fed. In another vicious gale off Boston in January 1886, the steamer *Katahdin* managed to stay afloat offshore by burning everything from furniture, decking, and bulkheads to all manner of cargo, including a shipment of hams. *Courtesy Library of Congress*

They were instead pushed south of Boston as if it were their intention. The storm labored against them, almost as if in single-minded opposition to their vague plan.

"Damn and blast!" Blanchard slammed a hand against the wheel. Between their violent rising and falling among the peaks and troughs of massive waves, he had seen the blinking lights of Boston, like far-off jewels in the night sky, so close and yet so far from reach.

Though his faith in the *Portland* never wavered—he had come to regard the nine-year-old craft as a gem of infinite power and capability, built by the impressive firm at Bath—no coastal, sidewheel steamer was built for off-shore work, no matter how impressive it had been in all manner of storms they had been through together.

Blanchard could now see beyond the swells, and that meant morning was dawning. Well deserved, he thought, after Lord knows how many hours—though it felt as if he had lived five lifetimes already. And though he gave little credence to the idea that with light comes salvation, at least it kindled a spark of hope in him. He wished the same for the passengers and crew.

Unceasing gusts whipped the driving snow into a fury as another swell dropped out from under them, followed by another that hammered down on them sooner than he thought possible. Then something cracked like a mighty tree being felled and shuddered the *Portland* to its very core. A side-wheel? The stacks? Blanchard had no way of knowing, but he knew deep down that the steamer was finished. His beloved *Portland* had fought its last fight, had given its all, and in the end had been defeated by the inevitable— its cradle, its foe.

"Captain!" The navigator's scream pulled Blanchard from his maudlin thoughts. It sounded as if the man had given over completely to the madness nibbling at them all.

Blanchard turned to see the man pointing to port, at the dim form of a ship, a schooner perhaps, listing badly but making straight for them with all possible haste. In the dim morning light, through the relentless snow, the ship seemed to be carved from smoke. He pulled hard on the whistle. The *Portland* gave up four brash, loud blasts, but it was no use. The ship bore down on them all the faster, carried the last length by a mammoth gray swell. Though smaller, the intruding schooner had been borne forward by the speed of an ocean eager to be done with this game.

The sea will always win, thought Captain Hollis H. Blanchard as the ships collided in a great shuddering crash. The *Portland* rolled, this time all the way over, and broke up even as it was pulled under by yet another mighty swell.

&

The man trudged along the Cape Cod beach, patrolling for signs of ships in trouble—or worse. Seven-thirty at night was later than he wanted to be out, but supper would wait. This storm had churned up a pile of mess, and he wanted to give this stretch one last look-see before calling it a day.

The long shift had taken its toll on the entire lifesaver crew. He took two more steps closer to the tide line, and a lifebelt washed up at his feet. Even before he lifted it from the sand, he saw the name *Portland* printed across it. Not a good sign. He yelled to other members of the crew, and within a quarter of an hour they found milk cans and other items bobbing in the surf.

Within a few hours, as the tide rolled in, larger hunks of wreckage came spinning toward shore, floating in the shallows—bulkheads, doors, and other bits of woodwork. This was proof that the *Portland* had not made it. And proof that those four desperate whistle blasts heard earlier that morning were from the steamer *Portland*. Even then, most of the lifesaver crew guessed they would never see the ship again—at least not whole.

⚘

Because the telegraph cables between Cape Cod and Boston had been ripped out by the storm, Europe received word about the wreck of the coastal steamer USS Portland before the anxious family members of its crew and passengers did. The news was telegraphed via transatlantic cable to France, then relayed to New York, and finally sent on to a waiting Boston.

Though the only passenger list was on board the Portland, it is believed that the number of passengers and crew totaled 192—of those, only 36 bodies washed ashore. The wristwatches of the victims had all stopped at roughly 9:15, presumably 9:15 a.m. It is assumed that the whistle blasts heard at 5:40 a.m. on November 27, 1898, perhaps indicated the captain's last-ditch cry for help.

Not until the summer of 2002 was the wreck of the Portland found, seven miles off Cape Cod. One-quarter mile away lay the wreck of the schooner Addie E. Snow. It is now believed that the two vessels collided, causing them both to founder.

The violent storm, the Portland Gale, which took its name from the lost steamer, killed four hundred people and crippled or sank 150 other seagoing vessels.

In the midst of a similar storm in February 1907, the steamer Larchmont was struck in the dead of night by the schooner Harry Knowlton off Block Island, Rhode Island. Hundreds perished in the frigid sea, and those who made it to lifeboats were ill-prepared for the harsh elements and consequently died of exposure in the subzero temperatures. One man killed himself, so pained was he by the cold.

36

KING OF THE RIVER HOGS
(1905)

A New Hampshire line-house full of drunken rivermen, a massive bouncer with arms like tree trunks, and one wiry little drive boss named Jigger Johnson. Guess who wins. . . .

✺

The little cookee slammed the platter of beef down on the plank table so hard that the cutlery jumped, interrupting a man in the midst of a long-winded tale. The talking man, a brute with a pocked face and a half week's worth of stubble, halted his story long enough to give the hairy eye to the new cookee, a short twelve-year-old cook's assistant. Then he resumed his tale.

The lad slammed down another platter and said, "No talking at chow time. If you don't know that, you do now."

The burly man was on his feet in an instant. He unleashed his anger by pitching the bench backward even as men in mid-bite struggled to keep from flipping over with it.

"Why, you back-talkin' pup! I'll teach you a lesson!" The man, whose height and girth far outmatched the boy's, reached out with a calloused hand to clout the youth as he turned back toward the kitchen. But the lad was prepared and turned to face his attacker.

The big man laid into the youth's boyish features with a meaty fist, but the boy didn't take it for long. He wormed his way upward with barely a grunt and clamped himself about the brawny logger, amidst bellowing shouts and cheers from the roomful of men. A few made motions to launch themselves into the brutal attack, but others who knew the new boy held them back. "He won't take kindly to your interference, Vern!"

The hungover, talkative logger growled and shouted oaths suited only for logging camps as the young man growled and clung to him, too close for the man to land solid punches. Then the big man howled in pure animal pain. The boy, young Albert Lewis Johnson, had clamped down with a full set of gleaming teeth hard on the big brute's ear.

By the time the men pried them apart, the two had wrecked half the room, overturning chairs, flattening others, and upending dishes. Blood flowed freely, and though the youngster took the raining blows like a full-grown man, the blood was not his. It came from the big man's mangled ear, now missing a chunk of flesh, which young Johnson spat out on the wood floor.

The brute who had attacked young Johnson was the loudmouth, blowhard, braggart Meilleur, who was doubly annoying when he was hungover. The men were forever trying to keep him quiet during meals, one of the general rules at all logging camps. Since the men had to eat in shifts, it was a long-standing belief held by management that chatting loggers wouldn't vacate the dining hall soon enough for the next shift. Everyone knew that the young cookee was in the right to tell Meilleur to shut his trap.

The other men were so impressed with the scrappy lad's showing that they took up a collection and bought the boy a fresh wool shirt to replace the one that had been shredded in the fight, plus a pound of B-L plug tobacco. Little did they know they were in on the birth of a genuine logging legend.

∽

"How in heck did that thing get in there?" said Lippy Newcomb. By then all of the men in camp had gathered around the dynamite shed at the rail line at the base of Gorham Hill in New Hampshire.

"What are you talking about?" said the cook, a robust man prone to stroking his drooping mustaches while he baked (consequently his whiskers were always thick with flour). He strode up, dried his beefy hands on his apron, pushed through the gaggle of men, and drove the toe of his boot into the cracked planking of the dynamite shed. The thrashing and hissing yowl that followed forced him backward, as if he had been pushed, into the gathered men.

"All right, all right, get out of the way, you young girls, and let a real man through." A short, wiry, barefoot man pushed through the crowd.

"You can't go in there, Jigger! That thing'll tear you limb from limb!"

Even as he spoke, Lippy knew that he had just said the absolutely wrong thing to Jigger Johnson, the camp boss. For if there was one thing the little man liked to hear, it was that he was forbidden to do something. Johnson regarded such claims as invitations, and this time was no exception.

Spring pulpwood drive in Maine. Rivermen were the toughest of the tough, the New England equivalent of the hardest-working, hardest-living cowboy on the trail drives. But the riverman's trail was a mighty, roiling springtime river, choked with logs that had to get downstream to market in a timely fashion. Sometimes his spiked boots slipped, and a riverman would end up unconscious, drowned, or ground to paste by the tons of long logs cascading through. When a riverman died, his spiked boots were hung from a branch on the bank near where he met his end. It's rumored that there are still the curled remnants of spiked leather boots in trees along New England's mightiest rivers. *Courtesy Library of Congress*

"'Can't' ain't in my way of thinkin'," said Jigger as he strode man-fully up to the door, cocked his head to one side, and then looked askance at the gathered men, all leaning forward, a few shaking their heads at him. "Look at you fools, gawpin' like fish. You think the CVL would hire men. . . ." The couple of dozen men looked about, folded their arms, but said nothing.

Then he smiled, winked, and whipped open the door just enough to slip in. Bang! He slammed the door shut behind him.

The scuffling, howling, and shrieking caused even the manliest in the bunch to step back with wide eyes.

"Someone ought to go in there, lend him a hand."

"You know better than that, Armand. Why, Jigger'd do worse to such a man than any wildcat could do."

Murmurs of assent circled through the crowd, though drowned out by fearsome shrieks. The door flew open and bounced back against the shed wall. For a few moments, nothing happened. Then from the dark of the shed out stepped Jigger Johnson carrying some sort of wildcat, sagging in death, by the scruff of the neck.

A shout went up through the crowd, felt crusher hats flew up in the air, and the men rushed forward to clap calloused hands on Jigger's shoulders. The sleeves of his wool shirt were slashed, and bleeding scratches stained his ratty thermal undershirt.

"Who's got a knife?" Jigger held up the dead cat and laughed.

⌒∾

Jigger Johnson made his way back upriver to where he had left his forty men at Beecher Falls, at the Vermont–New Hampshire–Canadian border. He had a lot on his mind these past few weeks, being the woods boss for the big Connecticut River drive this year.

He needed more men and had made good time in getting the drive this far, so he had gone on ahead a mile or so downstream to scare up a few more rivermen. He knew all the little settlements scattered along the length of the mighty river and knew he would be able, as in years past, to find plenty of good hands. He was, after all, a woods boss for the CVL, the Connecticut Valley Lumber Company, the largest in the Northeast.

This particular night the moon was playing hard-to-get with low, black clouds, and being early in the season—barely ice-out—it was still mighty snowy in the woods and along the riverbanks, and mighty cold come sundown. He stepped along lightly and felt no cold, though he was, as always, summer or winter, barefoot.

And he knew, though he had warned them not to, that his men might break from the river and head to the line-house, just up the road from where they were waiting for him. He quickened his pace. By God, if he could get rid of that booze pit, he would. At least for the time being. Sure, he liked a drink or three as much as any man, but the job at hand called for clear heads and fast feet—neither of which were likely from a bottle of rotgut hooch. Why, those men would be soured for days!

Sure enough, as Jigger crested the last rise, he heard none of the guffaws and banter of his men and saw no dancing flame from warming fires on the shore. They had up and vamoosed to the line-house. Even after all his threats.

He walked past the holding area, past the great mass of logs waiting in the dark, saw the handles of pikes and peaveys leaned here and there, abandoned by the thirsty rivermen, and scissored his wiry legs right on up to the blazing lamps and bawdy, hearty roars rolling out of the line-house.

Benson and MacCallan, standing just outside the half-open front door, never even saw the little man as he slipped up behind them and snatched the backs of their necks, ramming their heads together hard enough to dizzy them.

"Does this look like the river to you?" As he barked out the words, Jigger sent both men sprawling into the muddy front walk. "Get to work, by God, or I'll have your ears on a stick!"

"We was cold, Jigger. What's the harm?"

"Cold? Cold, is it? Why, I'll show you cold!" Jigger darted after them, but they slipped and slid their way down the lane back toward the river.

Without breaking stride, the little dynamo marched right through the door. The heavy odors of drying wool, tobacco smoke, and stale booze clouded about him. His muscles worked like coiled steel springs as he shoved men half again his size straight through the door. He growled and cursed at them the entire time, leaving them piling up outside and pushing one another in their haste to escape the wrath of their enraged woods boss.

As Jigger Johnson advanced into the crowd, he hurled oaths of revenge at their glowing red ears. Near the bar, he snatched up a sawed-off peavey handle favored by the bouncer when fists weren't enough. Thus armed, Jigger began swinging the lethal length of stick, scattering his men in all directions. They broke to either side of him like water around a midstream boulder, yelping and crying out in pain.

"You dere! Out now before I trow you out!"

Jigger turned to face the barrel-chested Canuck bouncer, LaPointe. In seconds, the brute's massive hands, like cured hams, had Jigger in a death grip. Before the little woods boss could twist free, he was slammed downward, and the big Canuck's spiked boots drove into him as if the man were in the midst of a dance and Jigger was the floor.

"Gaaah!" was all Jigger could say, though he managed to bite the trampling legs of the man, then jerk him upright.

The beefy bouncer pitched backward onto the glowing surface of the woodstove dominating the center of the room. Smoke and the sounds of sizzling meat and cries of pain filled the room. The man's screams were talked about for weeks afterward.

But Jigger didn't let up. The bouncer had nothing to grab to propel him off the stovetop, and the fiery little man, pocked and dripping blood from the spiked boot dance, managed to keep the bouncer's back and rump pinned to the stove. When he finally did let go, the big brute, though much wounded, launched up from the stove and swung blindly at the cheering mass of rivermen.

Jigger scrambled atop the bar and dove for the large kerosene reflector lamp. He swung outward on it, then ripped it from the ceiling and, in one swift jump, drove the entire apparatus down over the dazed bouncer's head. It lodged about LaPointe's neck, like a bizarre wreath of metal. The kerosene reservoir burst, soaking the bouncer, and then ignited.

Jigger snatched up the peavey handle and once again set to work on the bouncer. Jigger spewed a litany of choice epithets even as he chased the flaming bouncer outside, where a few men covered the screaming LaPointe with a blanket and rolled him on the ground.

Jigger's men limped back toward the river, rubbing their swollen heads, arms, and legs. They were speechless with awe at the sheer power and audacity of their little barefoot woods boss. It would be a long time, they knew, before they would allow themselves to be talked into crossing his orders again.

For a week afterward, Jigger Johnson dabbed a foul-smelling ointment on the puncture wounds that seemed to cover his entire body, except for his face. "Loggers smallpox," he called them, smiling and displaying them with pride.

⚬⚬

There were very few rivermen who did not bear the telltale pucker scars of another man's spiked boots. At the end of drives, rivermen were capable of great shows of brutish disregard, when entire New England river towns would be laid to waste in much the same manner that cowboys of the Wild West, on reaching the end of a long, grueling trail drive, would shoot, loot, drink, and carouse a town to its knees for days on end, until their money ran out.

For all their brawling ways, rivermen, who logged all winter, were caring, thoughtful, stouthearted men who were just as prone to great shows of respect and affection for their fellows as they were to acts of savage violence. On June 21, 1895, one much-liked young man, Charles A. Barber, a nineteen-year-old driver from Cherryfield, Maine, fell off a log and drowned while on a Connecticut River drive. His fellow drivers retrieved his lifeless body and covered him with a blanket some way off in the woods. When the boy's father showed up, he snatched the money and left his son's body where it lay. The rivermen buried the youth with all due care, erected a suitable headstone, and carved the lad's particulars on the grave themselves.

When a riverman died on the job, through drowning, crushing, pinning, or an ill-timed explosion, his spiked boots would be hung from a tree along the bank near where the man met his demise. Though the days of the long- and short-log river drives are gone, it is rumored that one may still find the curled husks of spiked boots on the branches of trees lining various waterways of the Northeast.

✧

Albert "Jigger" Johnson is widely known to have been one of the most respected, admired, and capable lumbermen of his day. As such, a certain level of mythmaking surrounds him. But several honest woodsmen who knew him verified the tales that are still repeated today. After surviving countless brawls, slashings with spiked boots, logjams, near drownings, ill-timed explosions, and more, Jigger ironically was killed in a car accident in 1935. Wanting to get back to his North Woods trapping cabin, he had hitched a ride in what he called, with a sneer, "a horseless carriage." The automobile spun on an icy patch and slammed into a telephone pole, just as Jigger opened the door to jump out.

37

THE HUMAN SHINGLE
(1907)

On January 29, 1907, a Berlin, Vermont, farmer takes advantage of a fair winter day to fix his barn roof. But his aging joints stiffen, the day grows cold and dark, and he freezes to the roof. His feeble shouts go unheard.

❧

George Salina sat in his comfy chair by the woodstove and looked over at his wife. She was in the midst of a nap. Lately, she had been making noise about getting more done about the place. He knew she was right, but she wasn't the one who had to go climbing ladders and fixing roofs.

He sighed and stretched and gave her one more look. She still didn't move. He grimaced and decided that there was nothing for it. Despite the fact that he would like nothing better than to keep on napping in the chair by the waning fire, warm January days like this didn't just happen without a reason.

Taking care to close the doors of the kitchen and woodshed, Salina walked out to the yard and eyed the blue sky. Much as he hated to admit it, it was the perfect day for a bit of repair on the barn roof.

He pulled on his wool coat, cap, and work gloves and lugged his wooden ladder from where it leaned along the side of the toolshed. It was only mid-day, so he still had a few hours before he had to start his afternoon chores. The cows would still be asleep, chewing their cud, or in a daze, munching hay.

He sighed again and jammed the end of the ladder hard into the pile of snow at the back roof of the barn. Then he trudged back into the tool-shed for his claw hammer and a tin of used nails. He scrabbled in the bucket and pulled out a handful that looked up to the task, and stuffed them into his overall pocket. Next he looped baling twine around his waist and double-looped it around and under the hammer head. As he walked back outside, the hammer bouncing on his hip made him feel a bit like an Old West gunfighter.

He scrambled up the backside of the roof, grabbing hold of the edge as he crabwalked sideways to the top. How many times had he come up here over the years? Enough to know that the view never disappointed. Straddling the peak, he paused and caught his breath. To the east lay New Hampshire and the White Mountains, and there was the Winooski River, most of it under ice and thick drifts of snow. But the sun today was playing hell with the white stuff. In another two months, they'd be on the good side of it for sure.

He scooted himself along the ridge, careful to not dislodge any of the aging shakes with a hard-placed boot heel. The last thing he needed was more leaks when the next thaw came. But he had a feeling he knew where the real culprit leak was located. He found it, nearly in the center of the roof. Beneath the ridge cap, just where the shingles met the overlapped ridge boards, a gaping hole had opened up big enough for him to insert a couple of fingers.

"Not quite big enough to toss a cat through, though." He chuckled softly at the thought of carrying a cat all the way up there—a man would never make it, especially not hauling one of his own half-wild mousers. He rearranged the shingles enough that the hole was covered and then looked for other holes. After making a few more repairs, he scooted back around to head down again.

He felt the sun on his face and smiled. "Good as a stove," he thought. "And a tad less work to fire up."

George Salina leaned back against the slope of the cedar-shingled roof, hooked his right arm over the peak, and lay back on the sun-warmed wood—just for a moment, he told himself. Some of it was still crusted with ice and snow, but as the sun's warmth saturated him, it felt better to him than even the old woodstove chock-full of rock maple on a bitter night.

"Yessir, it's these little pleasures we should take time for." He turned his face to the left and secured a boot heel on the side of a curled shingle.

✺

It was the cold that woke him. And a whole-body ache that settled over him like a blanket. When he opened his eyes and saw a darkening sky, he remembered where he was. "Fool." He tried to say it, but the word came out barely a whisper, for his face felt wooden, a tight mask that might crack should he move. Below he heard his cows bellowing. He worked to sit up, careful to keep his arms hooked over the ridge by his head. But his body wouldn't comply. He tried again, to no avail.

My God, he thought, I'm frozen to the roof. Then he thought that perhaps he could slip out of his coat and . . . no, that wouldn't work because he couldn't even move his arms, and they were both slightly above his head, locked into painful positions over the ridge. He exhaled and saw his breath plume upward in a cloud before him.

Salina had never been an excitable man, and he saw no reason to be. But as the minutes passed and his efforts to rise provided no results, he realized he needed to do something drastic. But what would that be? Even as he continued trying to yell—although his attempts to shout were barely hoarse whispers—he felt the cold close in. It was January 29, after all. Never had he felt so helpless.

From where he was, he could just make out one corner of the dooryard that someone would have to pass through in order to get to the barn. He heard a man's voice shouting. "Papa! Papa, where are you?"

It was his oldest boy, back from the woods for the day. Praise be, thought George. I'll soon be saved. But for the rest of my days, I will have to live down the fact that I fell asleep on the roof and froze fast to it. So be it, he thought, his teeth rattling together like pebbles in a can.

"Here I am! Up here . . . on the roof! Barn roof! Help!"

But there was no response. The air was still and clear and cold. It would be a very cold night, indeed. You could smell it on the air, a clean crispness that almost had its own taste. And worst of all, he knew it was deadly. It wouldn't surprise him if the temperature dipped well below zero.

Time and again his family members called—his eldest boy and the boy's wife, then his own wife and his youngest son. Someone must have fed the cows, for the only creature sound he now heard was the occasional bleat from a hungry calf.

If I could raise a boot high enough, they would surely hear it crashing back onto the roof. But try as he might, he could not loosen his boot from the roof. And like a fool, too, he thought as his body shivered as though he were in the grip of a terrible ague, he had worn only his thin work coat and wool hat and had taken off his leather work gloves to repair the shingles.

Surely the boys will venture around the back of the barn and see the ladder. They well might, he thought. They might, but too late. Maybe they will hear my bones rattling.

For what seemed like hours, he lay there, staring up at the black sky, clear and sparkling with the cold glint of all those stars. He heard his family shouting, his poor wife screaming his name over and over, and nothing he did could make them hear him.

It had been at least an hour since he had been able to muster anything more than a hoarse whisper. And when he had been able to shout, they hadn't heard him, so surely a whisper would bring no response. Even the back of his head was frozen in place—his hat and coat collar felt nailed together to the roof and held his head in place.

Still, he worked it back and forth as if disagreeing with something, but it got him nowhere except dizzy. He kept on with it, though, since it was the only thing he could move, except for his fingers and toes. After what seemed hours, as he stared at the stars, visible even when he closed his eyes, he knew they would be the last thing he would ever see.

⁓

On the night of January 29, 1907, the mercury dipped to 20 degrees below zero. Salina's family finally found him, though it was nearly midnight. Someone looked behind the barn and saw the fallen ladder in the snow. His son pried him off the ridge and lowered the stiff farmer down with ropes. A doctor was sent for, and as the parlor stove glowed cherry red, George was thoroughly examined and found to be near death from exposure to the bitter elements. His face, ears, and hands bore the telltale red patches and early swelling of frostbite. The prognosis was not good. But it is said that the old Yankee farmer surprised everyone by recovering sufficiently to resume his chores within a week. Thereafter his wife insisted on quizzing him every time he left the house.

New England winters can be brutal and deceiving, offering everything from thin ice to wide fluctuations in temperatures in a single twenty-four-hour period. During the day, temperatures often climb from below freezing to 40 degrees, only to drop down to well below zero again that night. And the cold season can "have teeth," as lifelong residents say, often beginning in October with road-plugging snowstorms and widespread power outages, then dumping a last parting shot of snow and blustery cold on much of the six-state region well into April and May. It's a rule of thumb in New England to not plant one's garden until after the first full moon in May—an old trope that has lasted in gardeners' minds for good reason, because killing frosts often creep up well into June.

On December 19, 1881, Allie Snow, six years old, and his brother, Freddie Snow, nine, were playing on a frozen factory pond in Ludlow, Vermont, when one boy fell through the ice. His brother went to his aid, but he also slipped under the ice and drowned.

In the early-morning hours on a cold December day in 1893, twenty-five-year-old James Conlon of Millers Falls, Massachusetts, was but a few yards from his home when, inebriated, he crawled into a hole in a pile of lumber, presumably to sleep it off. A little boy found Conlon the next morning, sitting upright, frozen stiff, and utterly dead.

And on November 19, 1920, a motorboat ferrying woodsmen across Maine's Chesuncook Lake caught fire. Many men jumped overboard into the icy water. Though seventeen loggers were rescued, sixteen others succumbed to the cold and, in their efforts to swim to shore, drowned.

38

MALAGA ISLAND
(1912)

The unwanted mixed-race population of Maine's Malaga Island is evicted—some are relocated to a school for the feeble-minded, and all traces of them are removed from the island. Even the bodies in the cemetery are exhumed.

∾

G overnor, we can't do that."
"We can and we will!" Maine Governor Frederick Plaisted closed his eyes and gritted his teeth. He would not argue this point one more time today. Wasn't he the governor, after all? He opened his eyes and spoke to George Pease in a measured, stern tone. "The state of Maine has complete governance over this island and has been subsidizing those people for years. It's time that changed. The deadline for evacuation of the entire island is set for July 1, 1912. Anybody left on the island will be forcibly removed. We've been more than fair, allowing them to take their very homes with them, such as they are, and giving them plenty of time to do so. And before I forget, here's the list of eight people I want relocated to the Maine School for the Feeble Minded."

"On what grounds?"

"On the grounds that they are unfit to mingle in normal society. Would that we could do it to the entire population of Malaga."

To this, Pease had no response.

"Now that we own the island, we can do what we feel is best, not only for the perpetually needy and impoverished residents of Malaga Island but also for the good of the state. Tourism is becoming an important part of our state's economy—and will be even more so in the years to come. There is no way people will want to tour Casco Bay if they see an island teeming with defectives and half-breeds." The governor set his spectacles on his nose and picked up a sheet of paper from the stack on his desk.

Pease understood that the meeting was done. He sighed as he walked down the hall that led from the governor's office. As the state's representative in this matter, Pease knew his work was just beginning.

✍

Even before Pease's boat maneuvered into the cleft on the rocky shore of Malaga, he knew something was different. Certainly he had hoped it would be, for that would mean his job would be easier. But by the time he wandered the well-worn lanes that previously led from house to house in the little village on Malaga Island, he was amazed—there were no houses to be seen.

"They actually did it," said Pease, marveling at the effort that must have gone into the task of removing an entire fifty-year-old settlement. He spent hours walking all over the island, and the only significant traces that remained of the settlement were the schoolhouse and the cemetery.

He made note of it all and duly reported back with his findings. He was not surprised at the governor's response.

"Not good enough, I'm afraid. I want all traces of those people removed from the island. Then we can sell it to the highest bidder and collect taxes on the resort hotel they'll build on it." He smiled and poured drinks for himself and Pease. "What do you say about that?"

Pease nodded but didn't smile.

"What's the matter now, Pease?"

"Well, sir, you said 'all traces.'"

"I did, indeed. I want the graves dug up and the remains relocated."

Pease paused, his drink in his hands. He had half expected to hear the absurd notion, but when he did, it was still a shock. "Why?"

"Because, Pease," said the governor, sounding as if he were explaining something complex to a child, "we don't want to give those unsavories any excuse to return to Malaga."

Pease sighed again. "Where?"

"I've secured room for them in the cemetery at the Maine School for the Feeble Minded."

✍

Bob Tripp gritted his teeth against the gale that rocked the patched, ragged shelter built on a crude scow. Lord knows it wasn't much, but it had been home to him and his wife, Laura, and their four children since they had been evicted, along with everyone else, from their home island of Malaga, two years before. He glanced back one last time at his sick wife and crying children before he closed the door tight behind him. He checked the scow's straining tethers, tied to trees on Bush Island, and then climbed down into the little rowboat to travel the three miles across the bay in the teeth of one of the worst winter storms to hit the southern coast of Maine in years.

He was headed for the doctor, and he prayed with all the power he could muster that he wouldn't be too late. It was the consumption, he knew. Laura had had bad patches before, but this time she just couldn't get a leg up and over it. His powerful muscles settled into the mechanical actions of rowing, but the buffeting winds, the lashing rain and snow, and the mighty chop of the bay's raw waters slowed the boat's progress. He couldn't let that happen; he had to get to the doctor. As he rowed, he reflected on their lives. A dazed anger and cold feeling filled him. Life on Malaga might have been hard, but it was theirs, and it was a damn sight better than these past two years had been. He knew in his heart his Laura wouldn't be near death right now if they hadn't had to leave their home.

In two years of trying, no one would let them settle on any local land. And his wasn't the only Malaga Island family treated that way. For all the good being his own free man was doing him, he might have been better off if they had put them all at the Maine School for the Feeble Minded.

⁂

Several hours and three miles later, after arguing with the doctor, Bob finally convinced the doctor to come back with him. They burst in on the most heartbreaking scene Bob knew he would ever see. His little Laura lay still, her skin so cold, her face a sunken mask of the woman she used to be. Her curled hands looked like those of an old crone.

And the children knew what had happened. They had been with her as she breathed her last, struggling the entire time. He should have been here, spending the last moments of their life together, but he hadn't been.

He and the doctor stood looking down at the scene of his Laura's death. It took all the strength of the two men just to pull the children from their mother's dead body. They clung to her like seaweed to a rock. Now without their mother, what chance did they have in life? What chance did he have without his Laura? What chance did any of them have with no place to call home?

⁂

New England has a long history of racial persecution, beginning with white European explorers such as George Weymouth, in 1605. In what is now Maine, Weymouth lured five friendly Patuxet Indians on board his vessel under false pretenses, set upon them, and shackled them in the hold before transporting them to Europe, where they were used as living representatives of the potential riches to be made in the slave trade in the New World. And a few years later, English slave trader Thomas Hunt regarded the region's native tribes as rich slave resources that he attempted to exploit. While not the first time Native Americans had been captured by those seeking to make money in the slave trade, this period marks the beginning of white European oppression of indigenous Americans. But Indians weren't the only oppressed race in New England.

At the beginning of the eighteenth century, there were approximately 1,000 African slaves in New England. Within fifty years the figure had reached 15,000 and continued to rise for the next hundred years as New England became the hub of the slave trade in the New World, cornering the market on supplying plantations in the South and the Caribbean with fresh slaves.

By 1750 Rhode Island had a slave population double that of its colonial neighbors Massachusetts and Connecticut. Between 1709 and 1807, merchants in Rhode Island sent 934 slaving expeditions to Africa, resulting in the capture of approximately 107,000 Africans sold into slavery. In the boom years following the American Revolution, this tiny state controlled up to 90 percent of the slave trade in the New World and beyond.

Some descendants of those slaves, who had long since intermarried with whites and other races, settled in pockets throughout New England, forming communities peopled with racial outcasts. These communities provided a level of comfort and safety for the residents in a world in which they were still very much persecuted for their skin color and racial origins. One such community was Maine's Malaga Island, settled during the Civil War. Despite their best efforts to live quiet lives, Malaga's residents were vilified in the press, which referred to them as degenerates and accused them of such heresies as using tobacco and tea.

The state of Maine, after mediating years of squabbling between the towns of Phippsburg and Harpswell—neither town wanted the forty-acre island off the mouth of the New Meadows River in Casco Bay, Maine, or its perpetually impoverished residents—set an eviction deadline of July 1, 1912, for Malaga Island's forty-five white, black, and mixed-race residents. Governor Frederick W. Plaisted, in particular, wanted Malaga's residents removed, as he considered them a blight on the face of the state of Maine. He committed eight people to the Maine School for the Feeble Minded.

In the space of a few short weeks, the little community on Malaga was no more than a memory, and its residents were scattered. To this day in the region there lingers a stigma attached to the memory of the mixed-race islanders. Two years after the eviction, Laura *and Robert Tripp became unfortunate statistics in one of the great shames in Maine's long history.*

As late as 1931, eugenics was practiced on members of the Abenaki tribe in Vermont, with the passage of a Vermont Senate bill called "An Act for Human Betterment Through Voluntary Sterilization." The program amounted to little more than state-sanctioned racism in which more than two hundred people of Abenaki lineage were sterilized. It arose from a University of Vermont–based campaign in the mid-1920s called the Eugenics Survey, which attempted to locate and isolate anyone with "bad," or non-white, blood.

39

LOGJAM FROM HELL
(1915)

Within days of commencing the Connecticut River's last great long-log drive, two men are dead. Later, 65 million board feet of raw timber cause widespread flooding in North Stratford, Vermont, that ruins homes, barns, bridges, streets, and railroad tracks. Then the lawsuits begin.

∽

The young man, George Anderson, scuttled out past the eastern edge of the wing jam at Perry Falls, eager to prove to the rest of the men that he was no softy, that he could hold his own on the river. By the time one of the men noticed him, he was already far out into the stream. Holding his peavey upstream, he walked along a log submerged a foot or more under the water, as the rushing current lapped up to his knees.

As he stepped on the log, scooting ever closer to the edge of the cluster of logs, the current caught his dangling peavey. As if he had been standing on a greased surface, he slipped right off the log. A handful of men scuttled out onto logs, shouting at him and motioning for him to keep his head up and grab hold of a log. But he was in the center of the stream, and the current forced him to swim what distance he could. The men felt a collective relief when a log bobbed by him.

"Grab the end, by God, the end of the log!" Pike, the drive boss, was shouting so hard that the men could see the veins on the tall man's neck and forehead throb with the effort. But it did no good. Anderson, in his panic, grabbed at the middle of the log and thrashed so hard that the log just kept spinning on the surface, rolling just out of reach.

"Stop wrestling that damn thing! Grab the end and keep your head up. The end!" Pike shouted as he scrambled, hopping from log to log out toward the thrashing driver. But the river was too wide, and the tangle of logs was far above Pike now, nowhere near the center of the stream where Anderson still clawed at the big spruce log, slapping at it in a blind panic.

By the time the current swung the log over to where Pike had positioned himself, Anderson was barely hanging on. At that very moment, the intense cold and churning water overcame the bedraggled youth. As Pike dropped down, putting himself in a precarious spot, Anderson slipped under the surface of the roiling brown water.

Pike lunged for him, soaking himself all over. He reached in the murky water, but the boy had slipped well beyond his reach. Then Anderson's hand popped up out of the water, once, as if waving farewell, and slipped from sight for the final time.

Vern Pike heard shouts, persistent shouts that rang in his ears, still beseeching the man to grab the end of the log, dammit, don't be a fool! Then he realized they were his own shouts. That was the second man they had lost at Perry Falls, on the Connecticut. And it was still early in the drive yet. How many more men would they lose, he wondered, as he slowly picked his way back toward the collection of men who had followed him out there in hopes of saving George Anderson.

Anderson had come from up in New Brunswick, just over the border at Houlton, Maine, Pike heard one man say. Already men raced down the bank and were strung out in a loose line, jumping like nimble goats from log to log in an effort find the man's body before he ended up too far downstream, battered and half-skinned by the frigid March temperatures, roiling currents, logs, rocks, gravel bottom, and hunks of ice clinging to everything in sight, their edges ragged like demon teeth.

∽

"Oh, good Lord, Mr. Pike. . . ."

The slack-mouth stare of the boy was enough to make Vern glance downstream. As soon as he saw it, he realized it was the biggest logjam he had ever seen in his forty-plus years of driving on the Connecticut. And it wasn't just logs, but great rafts of ice wedged in and around, above and beneath masses of logs that poked up, out, and every which way. Vern guessed that close to 35 million feet of logs were packed in one spot, with almost that many still to come downstream. And there was no holding them.

"This isn't good, boy. Not good at all. If we don't free up those logs, they'll commence to dam the river, as if great beavers were at work here. And if that happens, my God, this town can kiss itself good-bye."

"Surely it can't be all that bad," said Joe Barr, who was on his first drive. But even as he spoke, the cluster of logs seemed to take on a bulkier presence.

Landing and scaling logs, Aroostook Woods, Maine, 1903. Massive amounts of logs were transported by horse teams all winter long to landings such as this, where they were measured or "scaled." When ice-out came, the logs thundered down the landings into the rivers, and the log drive was on. As the logs from smaller feeder streams joined with those on the larger rivers, such as the Connecticut, four-hundred-mile drives lasted well into the summer months. Along the way, jams often backed up water that tore out bridges, roads, and railroad tracks and could be dislodged only with dynamite, such as the jam that occurred in North Stratford, Vermont, in 1915. *Courtesy Library of Congress*

Before long, most of the logs of the drive were piled up and waiting, rammed first behind vast chunks of ice that formed a bulwark across the river. Here, tens of millions of feet of logs, each twenty feet long, were crammed together. The buildup of logs flooded out the Grand Trunk railroad's tracks as the men watched, helpless to stop the destruction. The flood undermined the gravel track bed, causing miles of tracks to sink.

Within days the railroad's representatives descended on North Stratford, howled a blue streak, and set in motion all manner of lawsuits. And still the jam grew tighter with each log that pounded downstream into it. The waters rose until it seemed as if a lake of logs was all there ever had been or ever would be at that spot.

"God in heaven! Will this jam ever get undone? Good thing it's the last drive, because I don't think the CVL could afford another. As it is, half the town seems to be wiped out."

"There goes another one," said Pike, pausing in his labors at prying free logs for hours with seemingly little effect.

"Another what?" said the man beside him, without looking up. He bore down on the handle of his peavey until the hardwood curved and threatened to snap.

Pike looked at the man and then shifted his eyes back to the river. "Another house. Or maybe it's part of a barn. Farmers, all I know. Half of 'em spend most of their lives in their barns anyways, so it's not like it matters which it is. But I'll tell you, at this rate, this logjam will wipe out the entire town of North Stratford."

❧

Crews of hundreds of men worked day and night to dislodge the welded mess. And after days of picking and prying and trying to find the "keystone" log, all the while using dynamite, they had made little headway. And still the waters rose, wiping out roads, homes, and barns.

"Where's Dan Bosse?" Win, the driving boss, known far and wide as the Grinner, looked mighty close to scowling.

"I'm here, boss!" A thick fellow sprang to his feet and clapped his hands together. Though not particularly tall, Dan Bosse was all muscle and long on experience with logjams.

"Dan, we're mighty close. But I need someone to get this dynamite into a certain spot. We'll strap it to a long pole and really start to disrupt this mess."

"Well, sir, I'm your chicken!"

Bosse hurried over to the fire, around which sticks of dynamite sat propped, warming for use. He snatched up a couple of sticks and with a length of twine tied them to a long, thin pole one of the men had cut from the riverbank. From there he made his way to the shore, and without a break in stride, he scampered like a squirrel out onto the great jutting mass of logs.

He kept low, close to the water, and with little more fanfare than a grin back toward shore and his fellow rivermen, he lit the fuse and thrust the dynamite into the central crevice that the men had been working on—the most likely spot to instigate the breakup.

Bosse strode back toward shore, too casually for some of the men who didn't know him as well as others. He was greeted by hoots and jeers from the men who knew him too well.

Within seconds, a muffled *Thump!* greeted their waiting ears. As a few bits of wood came to a clunking, rattling rest nearby, groans of disappointment and mockery of Bosse's skills as a dynamiter filled the air.

"All right, all right. \ . . ." Bosse, now red-faced, snatched up a new, longer pole, fifteen feet this time, and repeated the procedure. But this time he worked the pole too long, angling it deep down into the knotted pile of logs, despite the shouts of warning from the men, his boss included. His only acknowledgment of them was a rapid headshake to denote that he had no intention of heading back to shore. The logs had vexed him for the last time.

The second explosion shifted the enormous, interlocking tangle of logs. The massive pile lifted in the center, blossoming skyward and pitching shards of wood as big as a man's leg outward for hundreds of feet. Ice and mud and logs pinwheeled in all directions, and for a moment smoke and water spray obscured the suddenly small-seeming form of Dan Bosse from view. Then the men on shore caught sight of him—lifted ten feet in the air and arching a bit backward.

When he came back down, he landed, nimble as a cat, on a log, his spiked boots digging in like claws. Downstream he rode, hands on his hips. Then with one hand, he snatched off his felt topper and gave his fellow rivermen a jaunty wave. A finger of his other hand dug in his ear as if to dispel an irksome ringing sound.

༄

Every spring from 1868 to 1915, massive long-log drives, known as the biggest annual event in the entire North Country, pulsed down the Connecticut River. The four-hundred-mile drives employed five hundred men and bisected the heart of New England, from

Canada through Vermont, New Hampshire, Massachusetts, and on to mills in southern New England where easy access to the sea was available down tidal rivers, either by rail or ship. But the spring of 1915 saw the last of the great long-log drives.

Short-log pulp drives continued on the Connecticut River for another fifteen years, and though drives on other Northeast rivers continued for decades after, the era of the great long-log drives was a thing of the past. The long-log drive was wiped out largely by more modern logging methods, better-built roads, and bigger machines far more efficient than a camp full of men might ever be.

In winter, in addition to being roadways, bodies of water were often used to a crew's advantage by piling the frozen surface with logs, in preparation for "ice-out"—the most exciting word a logger could hear at the end of a long, cold winter. It was immediately followed by the log drives down the Northeast's greatest rivers: the Androscoggin, the Connecticut, the Penobscot, the Machias, and others.

Death was a constant, unwanted dance partner for rivermen, who spent their days prying, rolling, and lifting slick, spinning logs in frigid, roiling water. Numerous accounts tell of entire rollways of logs passing over a riverhog who slipped while in its path—and when the tumult receded, his friends found little left of him to bury.

In 1876, at a stretch on the Connecticut River called Fifteen-Mile Falls, what has come to be known as the "Ross Year" occurred. The river that year reached its highest and lowest points in all the years of the drive, stranding the logs, up and down Fifteen-Mile Falls, high and dry by July. The drive boss, John Ross, couldn't beat nature, and the logs sat there until the spring of 1877, when normal spring flows lifted them and the drive resumed.

In 1930, when the New England Power Company excavated for a dam at a place called Mulliken's Pitch, at the end of Fifteen-Mile Falls, they found several old pork barrels buried there. Each contained the remains of a river driver who lost his life at that treacherous spot, his spiked boots still on his feet.

40

ROCKET RIDE
(1919)

Two young men climb aboard their own illegal slideboards to descend Mount Washington's Cog Railway tracks in mere minutes. But without brakes, their first and last trip is indeed quick—and painful.

❧

On that bright, cloud-free August day in 1919, two young men—Harry Clauson, at nineteen the younger of the two, and his friend, Jack Lonigan, twenty-one—strapped their homemade slideboards on their packs and wore smiles on their faces. It was a good day for a hike. And it was an even better day for an exhilarating ride down the tallest mountain in New England.

They hiked up Tuckerman's Ravine and waited for a break in the train traffic, the last for the day. They unstrapped their packs and slideboards—that's what the man in the bar had told Harry they were. He had been a worker on the cog railway for more than a decade and had told Harry about the thrill of riding down Mount Washington's Cog Rail line on nothing more than a narrow board built for the workers to use, whipping straight down that steel route in fifteen minutes on average, though one person made it in under three minutes. After a few more beers, he had described to Harry how to build them.

As they relaxed near the top, yards from the little belching cog railway engine that shuttled people up and down the mountainside, Harry said, "It's beautiful up here."

He spread his arms wide, and both men eyed the stunning scene that stretched all the way around them, taking in the entire Mount Washington range, the Whites, and the Green Mountains of Vermont, too. The day had been picture perfect—blue skies and a blazing sun with just enough breeze to cool their bare arms as they hiked.

"Are you ready for the ride of your life?"

"I'm game if you are."

"Unless you're yellow!"

Jacob's Ladder, Mount Washington Cog Railway, White Mountains, New Hampshire. The Mount Washington Cog Railway opened in 1869 to transport people up New England's highest peak, at 6,288 feet. On July 20, 1929, Old Peppersass, an original engine, was resurrected for a one-day-only ride, but a tooth snapped off its cog, and the relic plunged at breakneck speed 2,100 feet down the steep tracks, killing one person before finally vaulting from the tracks. Slideboards, or "Devil's shingles," were a popular method among railroad workers of zipping quickly down the mountain, usually in fifteen minutes, though one daring soul did the deed in less than three minutes. *Courtesy Library of Congress*

"Yellow, is it? I'll show you!"

"Hang on, hang on a minute. If we're going to take the fast track down, I see no reason why we can't smoke one more cigarette before we go."

Jack nodded. "Good idea, if I do say so." He flopped down on the grass beside Harry. "First, some water and a snack. I'm tuckered. Besides, we'll be down loads of time before the rest of them."

⌁

Harry Clauson clunked his board down onto the long, flat run of track near the summit. Not many people were around to tell them they shouldn't, and those who were up there were busy taking in the panoramic views, pointing and screening their eyes, trying to guess the names of far-off peaks. Harry shrugged his pack higher onto his shoulders. "You coming, or are you a yellow fellow?"

"Yellow, ha!" Jack laid his own board down on the track, but the slide-board's groove was a little sloppy on the center rail of the track.

"No matter," said Harry, watching his friend wiggle the board. "It'll straighten out as we get sliding."

The young men sat on the boards, about ten inches wide and three feet long, as if they were snow sleds. Harry said, "Here we go!" and pushed off with his hands. The long, flat stretch of track was slow going. Only as they neared the first slope of their descent did they pick up speed.

Within seconds the young men attained speeds that they hadn't imagined. And for those few seconds, they both howled and hooted in glee—this was indeed the best idea of the summer. The track leveled off a bit, and they kept right on hooting, with no intention of slowing down. Then the track plunged sharply, and their shouts of joy quickly changed to screams of terror. They found that braking as they had imagined it—with their boot heels—was impossible.

It was the smell of smoking wood that caused Harry to jam down almost reflexively with his feet not quite touching the track ties, despite the fact that he knew he was moving far too fast to slow down in such a manner. He gritted his teeth, all the while hearing his best friend yards behind him shouting and moaning unintelligibly. As Harry finally jammed down with his heels, the effect was immediate: His legs snapped instantly at the knees.

Harry had no time to utter a sound as his body pitched forward faster than his descent had been. He flew forty, fifty feet, his long, lean body arcing slowly as if he were performing an intricate dive. His slideboard departed the tracks on the opposite side and disappeared down the gaping maw of a sudden ravine.

Now his own moans, long and low, were interrupted as his head hit on the rocky, graveled slope that fell slowly away to either side of the tracks. Both his arms snapped, and his body kept on moving, pinwheeling at a freakish rate of speed, his broken limbs whipping akimbo. After a half dozen revolutions, his backpack, jacket, and shirt were all stripped from him and whipped away of their own accord. His body slammed to earth hundreds of feet from where he first tried to slow his descent.

Most of this had been witnessed by Jack, who was zooming hard on his trail just behind. "Oh God oh God oh God, Harry!" He had no time to make much of a decision. He just knew that if he stayed on his insufficient and ill-conceived sled he would die in a way too horrible to consider. He decided to bail off the rocketing death sled. And with a short scream, clipped shorter by the sudden and jarring impact he was soon to feel, Jack rolled himself off the slideboard.

The speed he and his friend had so eagerly craved was now his worst enemy. His body hit the left-hand rail and popped him up into the air. And at that spot on the mountain, the slope, a denuded and barbarous tangle of stumps and raw rock, was at its most unforgiving. Instead of coming away with a few broken ribs, a bandaged head, and a limp, Jack found himself airborne, screaming as he eventually descended, like a dropped stone, toward a mass of boulders and craggy rocks dozens of yards below. For one brief moment he looked down on the tops of tall spruce trees, their spires so very far down, but coming closer with each passing second. . . .

✍

The slideboards the two young men cobbled together had no braking mechanisms and quickly reached breakneck speeds. Their battered dead bodies were later found by a railway worker.

Cog railway workers invented slideboards (or "Devil's shingles," as they came to be known) before the cog railway opened on July 3, 1869, out of a desire to descend the mountain faster than if they waited to ride the train back down. The slideboards fit over the cog's central rail; measured approximately thirty-five inches long by ten inches wide; were made of wood, with iron fittings; and sported handles attached at the downhill end. They were also equipped with a braking mechanism. The average worker could descend the mountain in fifteen minutes, although one person is said to have made it down, alive, in the record time of two minutes and forty-five seconds, at times attaining speeds of 60 miles per hour. Use of the "Devil's shingles" was banned in 1906 after an employee died accidentally.

The Mount Washington Cog Railway, itself an unusual conveyance, uses a central rack into which a toothed gear, powered by the train engine, engages a tooth at a time to travel up and down the track. Initially built by local entrepreneur Sylvester Marsh to convey tourists who otherwise might not make the trip to the top of the mountain, the railway is still in operation today.

To date it has experienced only two significant accidents. The first took place on July 20, 1929, when the original cog railway engine, Old Peppersass, was restored. To mark its return to the mountain after being mothballed for decades, it was decided to let the engine make a final run up the tracks before being put on display. All went well going up, but on the descent a tooth snapped off its cog, and Old Peppersass plunged out of control down the tracks. All five passengers jumped free, though one died of his injuries. The engine rocketed 2,100 feet down the slope before jumping the tracks and wrecking splendidly before the dignitaries. Old Peppersass was eventually reassembled and is now on display at the train's base station.

On September 17, 1967, Engine Number 3 derailed a mile from the summit. The passenger car slid hundreds of feet, eventually coming to rest against a rock. Eight passengers were killed and seventy-two injured. Despite the sensational aspects of these wrecks, the railway has a long-standing record of safety and has transported more than 5 million people during nearly a century and a half of operation.

In addition to being the highest point in New England, at 6,288 feet, Mount Washington is also the official home of the world's worst weather—with the world wind-speed record of 231 miles per hour in 1934—and is the scene of a long history of unfortunate fatalities. Since 1849, 135 deaths have occurred on the mountain, most of them involving ill-prepared hikers, skiers, and climbers. The list of causes includes hypothermia, hikers lost in storms, drownings, falls from ice and rocks, burial by avalanche, and wrecks in trains, planes, automobiles, carriages, and slideboards.

Many such unfortunate events make the news, such as the carriage accident in July 1880, involving a party from Michigan descending in a six-horse mountain wagon. The driver, a man who had been on the job for ten years, was inebriated and took a corner too sharply. The wagon overturned, killing one woman and injuring five other people. The driver also received fatal injuries. This mishap holds the distinction of being the first accident with fatalities on the mountain's carriage road—a road which, oddly enough, is rated as one of the safest toll roads in the nation.

41

THE BOSTON MOLASSES DISASTER
(1919)

A massive storage tank bursts, and 2 million gallons of molasses pulse outward in a forty-foot-high wave. It's lunchtime, and people are out enjoying a warm winter day, if only for a few seconds more.

⤫

The first thing Duncan McCorcoran heard was a popping sound like rapid gunfire, but loud and close, from behind him. And within seconds an explosion the likes of which he hadn't heard since the Great War forced him to drop his hammer and nails and stiffen as if he were suddenly cold. He saw the whole thing. It was the big molasses tank, but as he watched it, it disappeared. Or rather it just came apart, collapsed, as he would tell it in later years.

But he would always pause in the telling. For in his mind even all those years later, he saw it as clear as if it were happening all over again. He saw the tank explode, the great steel lid bursting skyward, flying God knows where, and dark liquid rose into the air and outward from the fifty-eight-foot-high tank. Then it rained down with steel and rivets, pelting the surrounding area.

He had been helping the foreman at the freight yard, as he did every week on Wednesday, Friday, and Saturday. They rested a moment, leaning on wooden crates.

The boss nodded toward the tall tower and commented: "That ship there, she's from Puerto Rico. Fella told me that's the last shipment they can take for now. That tank's full up—two and a half million gallons of the stuff." He laughed and hefted another crate. "And that damn tower leaks like a sieve."

"Leaks?" Duncan asked.

"Yeah, look close sometime. Molasses runs right out of that thing." The boss smiled at him as he swung another crate onto the wagon. "Why do you think Purity Distilling painted it brown? Inspectors even told them it was dangerous." He slammed another crate on the previous one, corners lining up expertly, and said, "So their solution? Paint it brown."

"Out of sight, out of mind, eh?" Duncan shook his head.
"You got the picture."

❧

He found out later that they were rivets, but at the time they looked like far-off crows flying outward from the separating steel sides of the massive tank. The big brown tank was as much a part of the neighborhood as the harbor and the tugs plowing through the water.

As he watched the tank's great metal sides burst apart, forced by a living mass of black goo, nearby buildings were knocked down as if by a giant's breath. Beyond them, the steel understructure of the elevated rail line suddenly buckled and collapsed as if pressed from above by that same giant's massive hand. A tenement, where his friend Bill Duffy lived, buckled inward and collapsed, and a handful of other buildings nearby suffered the same fate.

A moment of shocked silence gripped the scene, a moment when nothing seemed to happen—but things were happening. The half-inch-thick sheets of steel of which the tank was constructed blasted outward as the contents consumed the structure. Screams echoed upward seconds before a forty-foot-high wall of thick, black liquid pulsed outward.

One great yawning mass of steel seemed to deliberate, taking its time deciding which way it would drop. And then it fell on the firehouse. A billiards table crushed one fireman to death, two others lay trapped in the rubble, and a fourth found himself launched out an upstairs window before landing in the sticky harbor below.

Even as he ran toward the scene to offer what help he could, Duncan heard screams and saw people running toward the mess. As they drew closer, what they saw almost made them stop. The great tank was now a leveled, twisted-steel mess, and struggling shapes became recognizable in the ooze. Duncan slowed as he approached the advancing river of molasses. Before him, it glistened, interrupted only by the pulsing of those things moving. Whether they were human or animal, he couldn't tell. But they were moving. A horse, crippled by the force of the blast, kicked and shuddered, trying to whinny in pain, though only bubbles and groans rose from its mouth. It looked as though all four of its legs were broken—the force of the blast must have bowled the beast over without warning. He wished he had a gun.

Duncan walked on, the molasses nearly knee deep but receding as it flowed outward. But soon the goop was little more than ankle high. He stubbed his foot against something in the black current. It looked like a doll and began to take on a more defined shape with the receding of the molasses. It was no doll. It was a girl, still small, years from being a teenager. He dropped to a knee, grabbed her, and drew her to him. She lay face down, and when he lifted, her body flopped like a worn doll. Thick black liquid flowed from her mouth and nose. He wiped the thick, sticky liquid from her face, but it just smeared. He shook her, but knew she was dead, and he prayed she had been killed by the blast, spared a slow death of drowning in this god-awful mess.

All about him people shouted, police sirens wailed, fireboat bells clanged in the harbor, and a horse-drawn fire wagon rattled and clanged, barreling down Commercial Street toward the scene. People rose from the molasses as if foul creatures rising from the sludge of a swamp.

Entire freight cars from the elevated line lay scattered and dumped, crushed by the impact of the blast, and the freight office, a long, low building, was mostly gone. Duncan was acquainted with three people who worked there. He wondered if some of them were the people lurching through the flattened, coated wreckage of the building. There was no way of knowing, so covered were they in molasses. He also remembered that the basement had a wide-open stairwell to the outdoors. He couldn't even see it. Being below ground level, he knew it had probably filled with molasses.

No matter where Duncan looked, over everything in sight lay the thick, black, dripping mess that disguised everything, changed everything about his neighborhood—as if nothing would ever be the same again.

∽

On January 15, 1919, a storage tank fifty-eight feet high and ninety feet across in Boston's North End burst, sending more than 2 million gallons of molasses pulsing outward at 35 miles per hour in a forty-foot-high wave. The wall of viscous liquid destroyed everything in its path for blocks in downtown Boston. It was lunchtime, and people were relaxed, enjoying a warm winter day as they nibbled their sandwiches, if only for a few seconds more.

United States Industrial Alcohol Company, Purity Distilling's parent company, claimed that a variety of contributing factors had caused the tragic events, among them an attack by anarchists and a rise in temperatures from the normally frigid winter temperatures to 43 degrees above zero on the morning of the event. What the company failed to mention was that Arthur Jell, overseer of the tank's construction a few years before the tragedy, neglected to fill the tank with water in order to check for leaks after it was built.

Once the company filled it with molasses, the tank leaked terribly. In an effort to conceal this problem, Purity painted the tank brown and allowed local residents to collect the molasses from the leaks for use in their homes.

The shockwave of the initial blast flattened buildings and hurled people great distances, as if the sweet/foul air were a giant's angry breath. Nearby blocks flooded to a depth of up to three feet, and buildings were knocked off their foundations.

Dogs, cats, horses, and people were among the injured and killed. They all struggled in the waist-high goop and were the worse for it, for they soon became even more stuck in it, and many drowned, exhausted. Twenty-one people died, and 150 were injured. It would be four days before rescuers stopped looking for bodies. Two of the dead were found on the last day of searching, but they were so unrecognizable that they remained unidentified at the time of their burial.

It took 87,000 hours of labor to scrub the residue off homes, businesses, cars, and streets. Fireboats blasted the affected areas with saltwater, and then the streets were coated with sand. For months after the explosion, molasses traveled all over the city of Boston on people's shoes, pants, and coats—even streetcar seats were covered with the sticky residue. The harbor retained a distinct brown hue from the spill for six months, well into summer.

After six years of litigation and hearings, and the testimony of 3,000 witnesses, the courts found the company liable and ordered it to pay from $500,000 to $1 million in settlements, totaling roughly $7,000 per victim. The company did so, under protest. The company did not, however, rebuild the tank.

Many buildings in Boston's North End still bear uneven, dark stains on their walls, and for decades following the disaster, especially on hot days, the North End carried the sweet aroma of molasses, a pungent reminder of a tragedy that is recalled every January in Boston.

42

RUM-RUNNING LOBSTERMEN
(1924)

One Maine island lobsterman doesn't take kindly to strangers nosing in his traps— which happen to hold bottles of illicit booze instead of crustaceans—but a shotgun blast to the offender's hull should solve his problem.

∞

W hat are you doing, Frenchy?"
The lobsterman stiffened at the sound of his name, dropped the trap back in the water with a splash, and then turned to see who had sneaked up on him. It was a little Chris-Craft with two coastguardsmen and Wilkins, that lazy mainland constable, and they weren't but twenty yards off. How in the heck had he let that happen? Frenchy swore at himself and vowed to give up before he got himself arrested . . . or worse.

One of the Coast Guard fellows wore a pair of binoculars around his neck. So they had seen him—but how much had they seen? And who's to say he wasn't doing something innocent? It's not like they were going to check his traps. Touch a man's traps and you best be prepared to swim, 'cause Frenchy had a 12-gauge shotgun in a cradle under the dash, and though she might not be the prettiest gun on Penobscot Bay, she'd make a right smart hole in that dandy little Chris-Craft.

Delmore "Frenchy" Tinker straightened up and stared at the slowly approaching boat, which looked as though it could run circles around his old *Charlene W.* Far beyond the boat, in the distance, he saw the long, low curve of his home island of Islesboro, and just to the south, North Haven and Vinalhaven, emerging in the gray glow of early morning, with sea smoke hanging thick and low. Must have hid in a cove, waiting, then followed me out, he thought. And without running lights. Brazen of them. But how did they know?

Wilkins shouted again. "I said, 'What are you doing?'"

"I heard you the first time, you big blowhard. And what I'm doing ain't none of your business!"

Wilkins continued as if he hadn't heard him. "We had reports of a lobsterman in this region placing orders for bottles of booze in his traps, then

Confiscated whiskey. Though a good deal of alcohol was manufactured within the United States, most of the booze sold during Prohibition made its way into the United States south from Canada and along the East Coast from ships anchored just outside the international marine boundary known as Rum Row, three miles from shore. The booze-laden ships waited for shore runners to ferry the hooch to the mainland. Frequently, lobstermen and other fishermen along the New England coast risked their livelihoods and necks for a chance to make in one evening's worth of running rum what might take months to earn while lobstering. *Courtesy Library of Congress*

pulling up full bottles twenty-four hours later. Doesn't sound like a bad deal, now does it, Tinker?"

Frenchy threw down the bait bag he was rigging and said, "All right, which one of you jackasses wants a lickin' first?" I may be an old island lobsterman, he thought, but there ain't no way these pups are going to accuse me of something illegal—even if they aren't wrong.

"Now, Mr. Tinker, there's no reason to get excited." The fellow with the binoculars held up his hands in front of him.

"Like hell there ain't! Do I look like a rumrunner? I got an old, broke-down boat, I'm an old, broke-down man barely meeting my needs with a few lobster traps, and you think I'm running rum? Instead of pickin' on folks like me, way I hear it you folks ought to be working a little harder on them bastards bringing in the booze from them foreign ships settin' offshore." Frenchy waved both arms behind him to indicate the general direction of Rum Row.

The boat drifted a little closer, the man at the throttle working it casually.

Mad as he was, Frenchy couldn't help but smile a little beneath his bushy gray-streaked beard. He let them drift on over until less than ten feet separated the two idling boats, each rocking with the light swells.

"That's far enough."

"Why, Frenchy," said Wilkins, "are you making a threat toward officers of the law?"

They drifted closer.

Frenchy bent low and unstrapped the sawed-off double-barrel 12-gauge from hooks tucked under the helm. "No," he said, pulling back both hammers. "I'm making a promise to a boat full of jackasses. Any closer and you'll swim home."

"I don't see any lobsters in your boat, Mr. Tinker," said the man with the binoculars.

Frenchy spat a stream of brown chew juice over the rail of the *Charlene*. It spattered the gleaming teak of the Coast Guard boat's hull. "That's why they call it fishing and not catching, city boy."

The two coastguardsmen smiled, but Wilkins just glared at him. Frenchy figured the other two might not be so bad. The Coast Guard boys were only doing their job, and for that he could forgive them. But Wilkins was after something more. There had been talk among the boys at the pier. Keep a sharp eye out for Constable Wilkins, they had been saying. And now here he was, thought Frenchy. I've got my two sharp eyes on him, and I don't think he likes it. Not one bit, no sir.

"We'll leave you to your traps, then, Mr. Tinker," said the man with the binoculars. He nodded at the throttle man, and they swung around. Wilkins looked from side to side, as if trying to take in the entire layout—of what?

Frenchy watched the stern of the sporty little craft recede, heading back toward shore. He shook his head. "Warning or not, Charlene, them boys bear watching, and none more so than Wilkins."

⚮

A few nights later, in the same spot in Penobscot Bay, just off Islesboro, Frenchy snapped his shotgun shut and said, "Wilkins, what did I tell you about trespassing on my water?"

"How'd you get out here . . . without me knowing?" Wilkins breathed fast and held his shaking hands up by his head.

Frenchy smiled and eased the cocked shotgun into the crook of his left arm. He plucked a lint-covered knob of plug chaw from his coverall's chest pocket. He inspected it in the narrow glare of the searchlight as if he were inspecting a bit of ore for traces of gold. Then he bit off a chunk and worked it in his jaws for a moment. "Wilkins, you ain't the only one can be sneaky, you know. Don't forget, I grew up on this piece of water. You're a mainlander. I'm surprised you'd come out here this far all alone. And at night, too. Pretty impressive."

"But . . . how'd you know I'd be out here?" Wilkins was getting bolder in his questioning, thought Frenchy. Might mean he's got something in mind. Keep a sharp eye, Frenchy, he told himself.

Still cradling the shotgun, he dragged the Chris-Craft over with his gaff hook until the boats clunked together. "Now, Wilkins, what say you pass those pretty things you stole from my traps on over here."

"I . . . I stole nothing. These are confiscated, and you are in serious trouble, Frenchy."

The lobsterman snorted and sent a stream of juice into the other boat. Wilkins watched it spatter but didn't move.

"Now!" barked Frenchy.

Wilkins passed three bulging, dripping burlap sacks over the rails and into the *Charlene*. He said, "Now see here, Frenchy. What if I was to make you an offer you couldn't refuse?"

"Aw, Wilkins, I ain't interested in anything you're selling." Frenchy settled the bags, the telltale clink of full bottles satisfying him. "I've heard too much about you. Me and the boys got our eye on you, Wilkins. Besides, I happen to know that boat you're in has been confiscated by the Coast Guard, and I'm not so sure you've got permission to use it to make your own booze runs. So if I was you, I'd make sure nothing bad happened to that pretty boat."

"I have no idea what you're talking about. This boat was loaned to me to catch lawbreakers." He stood taller, set his jaw, and lowered his hands. "Like you. . . ."

Ba-Boom! The buckshot from one of the two shotgun barrels splintered a head-size hole in the shiny speedboat's port side, just at the waterline. Wilkins's screams turned into hoarse shouts as Frenchy punched the throttle and circled the sagging teak craft. He ringed the boat once and yelled, "Better hit that throttle, Wilkins. . . . See you in church!"

As he tried to get his shaking hands to start the motor, the shouting lawman heard the lobsterman's laughter recede with the lights of the lobster boat as seawater bubbled up into the pretty Chris-Craft's new wound.

∽

For every local lawman who might have double-dipped by both arresting rumrunners and dealing in illicit liquor himself, there were scores of honest constables and sheriffs who did their best to keep the oftentimes lucrative local liquor trade in check, if not under control. Attracting the attention of higher-ups only resulted in closer day-to-day scrutiny and increased paperwork.

Prohibition was widely regarded as an unfortunate experiment in U.S. history that brought more harm than good to citizens, especially in rural communities along the Canadian border in New Hampshire, Vermont, and Maine. People who were otherwise solid, upright citizens and who would not have thought to break the law in "wet" times had now become outlaws merely to make ends meet.

During Prohibition, fishermen, like everyone else, had to find ways to supplement their meager income. One way for a lobsterman to do so was to turn to a bit of low-level rum-running. The lobsterman would place orders in notes in his traps and then retrieve the traps a day or two later. In them he found, in place of the notes, peculiar lobsters . . . in the shape of bottles of booze.

Lawmen often overlooked the occasional indiscretions of small-fry lawbreakers and instead focused on bigger fish. During Prohibition, as more and more lobstermen up and down the New England coast turned to the ever-lucrative pursuit of rum-running in a big way, they altered their boats and engines accordingly.

Lobster boats turned out to be ideally suited to the job. At a time when most Coast Guard cutters could reach top speeds of 8 knots, some lobstermen had their engines souped up enough to top out at 20 knots. Combined with hulls shaped for increased speeds, this new breed of lobster boat was a force to be reckoned with. Lobstermen from Brooklin, Maine, were known to wait for a thick, pea-soup fog to roll in and then make two or three runs a night offshore to Canadian boats laden with alcohol.

In July 1929 three Islesboro fishermen, in outer Penobscot Bay, pulled in a seventy-pound cod. When dressing it, they found a sealed full-size bottle of bootleg whiskey in its gut. Cod are notorious for swallowing anything within reach—and this bottle, no doubt, was pitched overboard by a rumrunner being pursued, perhaps even a rum-running lobsterman.

But running illegal goods, particularly booze, off the coast of Maine didn't begin with Prohibition. Way downeast, in Passamaquoddy Bay, between New Brunswick and Maine, the mouth of the St. Croix River at Lubec was a hotbed of smuggling activity—beginning roughly with the Flour War of 1809, running through the War of 1812, on through the Plaster War of 1820, and beyond. Pelts, timber, fish, alcohol, and a variety of other items made up the bulk of the goods smuggled back and forth across the border. At the time, trade with Canada was considered illegal and was punishable by severe prison terms, or worse. But the allure of tax-free trade, tidy profits, and the thrill of the chase far outweighed the dangers and kept locals occupied for years—proving, when Prohibition hit, that the more things change, the more they stay the same.

43

QUEEN OF THE BORDER RUMRUNNERS
(1925)

The brains of a border-hopping dynasty that ferries illicit hooch from Canada into north-
ern New England, Hilda Stone frequently drives the runs herself in her specially outfitted
roadster. But one night in Vermont, she is tailed by agents . . . and her smokescreen doesn't
work quite as planned.

∾

"Where in the hell are we, Henry?" The young woman took a last long drag on her cigarette and looked out her window at the black shapes of trees as they whipped by in the light of the nearly full moon. She downshifted and slowed a bit.

"What do you mean, Hilda?"

"I mean, we crossed the border, sure, but what town are we near?"

"Not sure. It's Vermont, though."

"Ha! How can you tell?"

" 'Cause I think I just saw a cow."

She laughed and flicked the cigarette butt out her window. Almost as if on cue, headlights appeared behind them, closing in. "Aw hell. . . ." She dropped it another gear and hit the gas. A siren from close by blared at them, and the glare of a spotlight filled the car. They both ducked instinctively.

"Tromp it, Hilda!"

"You don't have to tell me twice."

A sharp sound filled the air in the car, and before they could react, they each noticed that the back window had cracked and the front had a neat hole in the center. "This is my favorite car—I spent a fortune outfitting it!"

"Be thankful it's not your head!"

She said nothing but grunted once when the car behind drew closer, the headlights careening off trees all about them. The rattle of bottles became louder, but neither of them mentioned what they were both thinking: If we're caught, thought Hilda, not only will the booze get confiscated, but we'll be arrested and get a heavy fine—at best. Not to mention the fact that we would lose all that money and time. Maybe even the car. She gritted her teeth and hunched low over the wheel.

"You know where you're going, Hilda?"

"Not to jail."

"I meant the road. . . ."

"It's a road, isn't it? And it's headed south, isn't it?"

"Yeah."

"Then that's good enough for Hilda Stone. Should be enough for you, too, Henry Murdock."

The siren drew closer, and another shot pealed, grazing the paint on the big cruiser's rear panel. "Ha! They think they're going to shoot out our tires or gas tank."

"Will they?"

"Not with my modifications. They'll have to catch us first. Hang on to your wig, Henry!"

She pulled out a silver knob on the dash and hit the gas. For several seconds nothing seemed to happen. Then the car lurched forward, and the bottles rattled worse than ever.

Hilda loved all these back roads in Vermont, New Hampshire, and Maine and tried to memorize their locations, peppering them with landmarks in her head for the next time. Because there is always a next time with rum-running. You have to believe that, she told herself. Otherwise, you might as well give up and be somebody's secretary.

They blasted out of a ravine, and for a few minutes it looked as though they were alone on the road again. But the moment was fleeting.

"They're getting closer," said Henry, a nervous twitch to his speech.

"Then rummage on the floor there. You feel that little handle? Yank on it and dump that can of oil through it."

"What'll that do?"

"Less questions and more action, Henry! Do it now!"

The shaking young man did as he was told, and within seconds, smoke rose up into his face. He slammed the little hatch closed and looked out behind them. In the half-light of the moon-filled night, he watched as a great billowing cloud of black smoke seemed to hang in the air behind them. The pursuing cars slowed, as their headlights roved this way and that. Hilda shifted gears again, and the car roared ahead into the night. The headlights behind them receded somewhat but never fully disappeared.

Policeman with a wrecked car and cases of moonshine. In the four months between August and December 1925, Hilda Stone, "Queen of the Border Rumrunners," as she was known by U.S. Customs agents, was arrested four times. She was caught with a load of booze only once, but it was a doozy of a load: more than five hundred bottles. She was fined $500. She loved the thrill of the chase, and the fast cars of her fleet were outfitted with hidden compartments, license plates from various states, and all manner of devices, including smokescreens, to help drivers shake the law. *Courtesy Library of Congress*

"You're smiling, Hilda! How can you be smiling at a time like this?"

She looked at him, eyebrows raised. "How can you not be smiling, Henry?" She looked back to the road and said, "This is as good as it gets, kid. Life just doesn't get more exciting than this!" She pounded a hand on the steering wheel and told him to light her a cigarette.

He shook his head in amazement and lit the smoke. After she had taken a few drags, he said, "Your husband know you do this?"

She laughed. "Yep."

"And he doesn't mind?"

"He likes the money. And he likes me to be happy."

"And this makes you happy?"

"Couldn't be happier, Henry. I like the thrill of being chased by those customs boys. And you know, I think they like it, too. At least the ones who stick with it for a long time."

Henry didn't say anything.

"No offense, Henry, but I think you're better suited to working in the warehouse back down in Greenfield, Massachusetts, don't you think?"

The young man nodded and kept his eyes staring straight ahead into the dark night as they headed south. The forest grew thick on either side, and the road descended. Might be a nice ride in the daylight, she thought, but tonight it's nothing short of a hair-raising hell ride with a car filled to brimming with clanking bottles of illegal hooch.

She did her best to maintain her high rate of speed, despite the curving, twisting track. Even so, for Hilda it was more than just a white-knuckle race for freedom, even when she saw three sets of headlights in the rearview mirror and at least that many ahead of her.

"How many bottles did you say we're carrying, Henry?"

"Five hundred and sixty, give or take."

"Too many to jettison. Looks like we might be in for it."

"What do you mean?"

"Hoosegow, Henry. Unless this road widens a bit. I think I spy a road-block up ahead."

Hilda leaned the big, swaying car into the curves and told herself not to let those uniformed do-gooders get close enough, or they'll start cracking off more gunshots. And the last thing I need, she thought, is to plunge off the side of one of these damn Vermont mountain roads.

She barely slowed, even when she recognized the lights ahead for exactly what they were—a roadblock. They were expected. She took in the odds of escape, of going around the roadblock, and they were nonexistent. Couldn't go up the steep bank to the right, and to the left was a ravine. Behind, a handful of cars closed in. She slowed down.

∾

"Ma'am." The young Vermont deputy sheriff set down the cup of coffee beside her on the desktop and nodded toward Henry Murdock, sitting in the corner, a pinched look on his face, his arms folded across his chest. "He your husband?"

Hilda snorted. "Not hardly. He's not my type, if you know what I mean." She winked at the young officer and only then noticed the wedding band on his left hand. So much for tricks, she thought. But she swore he blushed.

"Where is your husband, ma'am?"

"Why . . . he's at our place in West Halifax. That's in Vermont. He operates a sawmill."

The young man seemed puzzled and just stared at her for a moment.

"It's the truth. And when I'm not, well, running the roads, I raise turkeys."

"You're kidding me." He started to smile.

"No, I swear it."

Then in walked one of the two customs agents. He eyed the young officer, who resumed his serious expression, and said, "Miss Stone, you'll be free to go in the morning."

"Didn't my bond go through?"

"Sure," he said, smiling. "But there's the little matter of a fine. And the judge won't be available until morning."

She nodded and shrugged. In another minute she was alone in a small, clean cell. Well, she thought, they got me. My car jam-packed with Canadian booze, the profits all gone. On top of that, the police had threatened to lock her up and forget about her for a while, threatened her with a strip search, threatened with this and with that. But she had been through these bluffs before.

Truth was, they had the booze and the car, and they knew she wasn't going to rat out the gang in Massachusetts. Still, she knew that one day the police just might make good on their threats. Lord help her when they did, because she knew it was a dangerous game that she might lose one day. But not for a while yet. . . .

She sat back on the bunk, leaned against the wall, and closed her eyes. As she recalled the events of the past few hours, she smiled. Now that, she told herself, was worth the trouble.

༄

Though most of the players at cross-border smuggling were men, a small but powerful number were women. And none were more powerful than Hilda Stone, considered by lawmen and lawbreakers alike as the most notorious female smuggler in northern New

England. Known by the U.S. Border Patrol as the "Queen of the Border Rumrunners," Stone reportedly ran an organization that included fast cars and a payroll of daring, hot-blooded employees who zipped her vehicles back and forth across the borders of three states—Maine, New Hampshire, and Vermont—ferrying illicit hooch into the waiting arms of her distribution network.

In a four-month period from late August 1925 through late December 1925, Hilda Stone was arrested four times for rum-running, although she was caught with booze only once. But it was a big haul of more than five hundred bottles. She was fined $500—and went right back to work.

Although she helped manage the gang, based in Greenfield, Massachusetts, Hilda also liked the thrill of the chase and made regular runs in her own specially outfitted auto. Like all the cars in her fleet, this one included a smoke-making device to help evade capture in case she was tailed by agents.

Through a hole in the floorboard of a souped-up, booze-laden touring car, the rum-runner would pour oil on the hot exhaust system. A smokescreen of great clouds of blue-black smoke would billow out behind, causing pursuing lawmen to pull over and burst from their cars, unable to see the road and coughing and fighting for breath.

Another diversion was the tactical use of bovines, especially effective and not wholly unexpected by law enforcement. Smugglers paid farmers handsomely to usher their cows across the road as soon as the smuggler's car, loaded with Canadian hooch, blazed on through. By the time the border patrol or liquor agents came upon the scene, their only mode of passage was clogged with cows strolling to the barn for milking.

When liquor was confiscated, lawmen often made a public show of smashing bottles and breaking kegs, often in public and with cameras in attendance, as a warning to would-be offenders that they would eventually be caught. But in Vermont, for example, it is estimated that only 5 to 10 percent of all confiscated booze ended up being dumped. The rest made its way to the hands of the public. Frequently confiscated liquor was sold by lawmen eager to supplement their own meager earnings, and often it was sold back to the very people from whom it had been seized.

One duo of Vermont customs officers, each day at lunchtime, took to visiting Canada, where they loaded the trunk of their official car with booze. Once they made it back to the United States, they sold the hooch for a tidy profit. They were eventually found out and lost their jobs.

44

KINGDOM DEATH RIDE
(1927)

A free afternoon and a fast car are all Winston Titus needs to make a bootlegging run from Canada through Vermont's Northeast Kingdom in July 1927. But the smiling teen doesn't count on two border agents—or their guns.

༄

He knew his mother would be sorely disappointed in him, but he also knew he could use the money. And the chance to make in a few hours more than he could make in four or five months working for his father on the farm was a temptation too great for Winston Titus.

"You guarantee they're going to pay me when I get to Barre?" Titus stood with one hand on the open door of his solid old cruiser. The car was rigged up to carry heavy loads, and the engine tinkered up enough to go like hell should the law come a-knocking.

The man in the suit, known to Titus only as Mr. Peters, wiped his hands on a white handkerchief and smiled. "Boy, you should know better than to ask for guarantees in this biz. You buys your ticket, you takes your chances."

Winston stared at the man a moment, long enough for the man to respond. "Your money will be there, don't you fret, kid. Now get going before that hooch turns into a pumpkin."

"Huh?"

The man shook his head and laughed. "Nothing, kid. Get gone."

༄

As he neared the border at North Troy, Winston sure wished his friend, Del Winkelman, was along for the ride. Del had asked Winston to postpone the run until he could come, and Winston almost had. They had always stuck together. But then Winston got to thinking and decided not to postpone after all. That way, he would get to keep all the money himself. He smiled and cruised on down the rutted road, careful to avoid any ruts that could disable the car, or worse, smash the precious cargo. He smiled and let out a

Remains of a borrowed Stutz touring car. The rum-running driver of this Stutz touring car was killed after hitting a tree at 70 miles per hour while being pursued by the law. Part of his load, fifty gallons of corn liquor, ended up destroyed, and the rest was confiscated. Such wrecks were not uncommon throughout northern New England, where twisting back roads led south from Canada—ideal for ferrying illicit hooch into a United States parched from the sobering effects of Prohibition. *Courtesy Library of Congress*

whoop at the thought that if this was all there was to it, he would be doing a lot more of this sort of thing.

He had slipped through the border at North Troy, on the old road—he had inspected it with Del, and it had seemed rough enough that no one would suspect a car to head through there, but not so rough that he couldn't make it. Then he would head to Jay, slip down through a few back roads, keep the speed under control, and make like nothing was out of the ordinary.

Then he saw the car, plain as day, waiting for him. Two men sat in the front, stern men with hard eyes boring straight into him as he neared. They watched him, and suddenly Winston knew exactly what they were. He knew, as sure as his mother's venison stew was the best meal he had ever tasted, that these two men were fixing to pull him over.

Everything seemed to Winston to slow down. He tried not to look at them. He kept his arm resting out his open window and one hand on the steering wheel, the breeze playing on his freshly shaved neck. He had had a haircut just hours before, and he was feeling fine. No reason to worry, Winston, old boy, he told himself. You're nearly nineteen, and you have a fortune in booze in your car, a car you bought at auction yourself just a few days ago.

Winston rolled slowly past the men. Their car, poised like a small, angry dog ready to bite as you walk by, shuddered to life and inched forward. One man—the passenger—leaned out and motioned to Winston to pull over.

"You buys your ticket, you takes your chances. . . ." The words of the Canuck smuggler echoed in his mind, and he thought of the haying he'd left his father to finish up alone. Winston tromped down hard on the accelerator. There was a pause, long enough for Winston to swallow against the rising clot of fear in his throat—his solid-bargain touring car was going to let him down when he needed it most. Then the car shot forward, and the feeling in his gut evaporated like a rain puddle on a hot summer day.

He looked back at the two men, and for an instant the looks on their faces said it all—pure shock. They thought I was going to pull over, he thought. He whooped out loud and leaned over the wheel.

He knew they wouldn't stand a chance against his big old cruiser. But he surely didn't want this sort of attention. Lot of miles between here and Barre. "You just have to shake 'em, Winston old buddy."

He stole another glance at the mirror. And dread rose in him again, a truly bad feeling. There they were, just a few hundred yards back. He down-shifted and took the corner onto North Hill Road too fast. A sudden noise erupted like his mother's chickens made when a rat crawled in after their eggs. It was tires squealing—his own, he realized—and he was tempted to slow down. But the two men were still there when he looked in the mirror.

This big old boat wasn't outrunning them after all. Of course, he knew now that they probably had dolled up their car for just such an occasion. No stopping now. He cranked it up, and even as he picked up speed heading downhill toward the little town of Westfield, he saw the car gain on him. He saw one of the men leaning out the window. He hit the gas harder and gritted his teeth, the phrase playing in his head like a Sunday choir song: "You buys your ticket. . . ."

A sound like far-off lightning erupted at the same time as he felt something punch him hard in his left shoulder. Hot pain flowered up the side of his head, and he saw the nose of his big car leave the road all on its own—it seemed there was nothing he could do about it—and drag itself up an embankment. At the top, just before it glanced off the trunks of two huge maples, another explosion of far-off sound slammed Winston's head forward into the steering wheel.

The car launched into the air, roaring high and loud, and landed on its roof, skidding for some feet. The passenger side wheels, having been sheared off when the car hit the trees, bounced past the car and down the road.

⁐

When State's Attorney Brownlee arrived, the officers had their hands full keeping locals from the sparsely populated road away from the wreck. He sat in his black car and took in the scene, sighing. It wasn't difficult to see what had happened. Tire tracks furrowed up the embankment toward two huge maples, each of which sported a large, nasty gash. The tree's pale flesh glared from beneath where the bark had been ripped away. From there the car had flown upward, tipped, and landed.

Ahead of him, smack in the middle of the road, lay the touring car, upside down. He saw a bloody arm, bent at an odd angle, poking from beneath the wreck. At least one dead. The road sparkled with glass and a sopping mess of gasoline, booze, and blood.

"I only meant to hit a tire, disable the engine, scare him a bit. I never meant to hit him, though. Oh God, Hines, he's dead," said Officer Faucher.

"You think?"

Faucher didn't look at his partner, Hines, but he didn't appreciate the man's sarcasm. Not at a time like this.

"Oh no, no, no, no," said Hines, looking closer at the driver.

"What?"

"I know this boy. He's a Titus. Good family. Farmers."

"Boy? How old is he, Hines?"

Hines turned a white face toward his partner and said, "He ain't hit twenty yet, that much I know."

"All this for booze," said Brownlee to himself as he walked up to the wreck and the waiting officers.

"What are we going to do?" The taller of the two nerved-up men spoke first.

Brownlee motioned them both over. "Anything I should know, fellas?"

"Like what?"

"Like, were any shots fired?"

"How'd you know?"

"Look, fellas, this isn't my first day on the beach. Tell me what I need to know."

"Two shots, that's what I fired," said the tall one.

Brownlee nodded and said, "Keep those locals occupied. I need to investigate. And don't mention that shots were fired. Ever. To anyone."

The men nodded. Brownlee hitched up his pants and crouched low, peering at the wreck. He thought he saw where the bullets had come from and pulled the side curtains—with the bullet holes—from the wreck. "Fat lot of good this will do," he said, knowing full well that the coroner's report would provide the most damning evidence of all.

∽

The Titus case gained local and national attention from a populace long convinced that Prohibition did far more harm than good. In 1927, seven years into Prohibition, that conviction was more widespread than ever. The two immigration officers, Faucher and Hines, gave chase because the boy did not comply with their demands to stop. At that point, they were convinced that he was transporting either alcohol or illegal aliens into Vermont. Either way, they couldn't lose. And they knew that few cars could match the speed of their own car.

But their shots, which they claimed were fired in an attempt to scare the driver enough to stop, instead killed him. One bullet went in just under the boy's left shoulder; the other entered the back of his head and came out his forehead. The coroner determined that either shot would have caused death.

Numerous stories abound of otherwise honest people meeting with misfortune during Prohibition. Boisterous but harmless young Rene Malloy of Norton Mills, Vermont, and his brother, Philip, were known to cross the border and smuggle back carloads of booze from just over the line, in Hereford, Quebec. But on the night of November 11, 1930, something went wrong, and Albert St. Pierre ended up shooting both boys that night. St. Pierre, a convicted felon, was known as the "Al Capone of the North Country" for his wide control of the illicit liquor trade along the New England states' border with Canada.

Rene was killed, and his brother, though injured, fled on foot and traveled ten miles home. Though St. Pierre turned himself in for the shooting, he received no leniency. He was hanged for the crime in Quebec in May 1932.

45

Black Duck's Big Night
(1929)

On December 29, 1929, packed with full bottles from an English freighter off Rhode Island's Narragansett Bay, the notorious Black Duck *is raked with machine-gun fire from a Coast Guard cutter. Soon, the deck is covered with blood, booze, and glass.*

❦

"So," said Charles Travers, skipper of the *Black Duck,* "you're the new fella. . . ."

The Coast Guard officer, a boatswain named Alexander Cornell, narrowed his eyes and scanned the smaller boat berthed next to the cutter. "Yes, that's right."

"Welcome to Narragansett Bay." Travers smiled and spread his arms wide, an oily rag clutched in one hand.

As Cornell turned back to his task, he said, "Best watch yourself, else someone might fire into that pretty boat of yours one day."

"Is that a threat, Cornell?"

The Coast Guard officer gritted his teeth and said nothing.

"Oh, I've heard about you, don't worry." Travers kept his smile pasted on, though he seethed inside at the man's audacity. He had heard from a couple of sources that Cornell was trigger-happy and had opened fire with a machine gun on a shore runner in Jamestown in July. Dangerous man, thought Travers, as he went back belowdecks to work on his engines. But not fast enough for the *Black Duck.*

Charles Travers took pride in his sleek craft, *Black Duck,* in its ability to outmaneuver—so far—anything the feds or the Coast Guard could send its way. With its twin 300-horsepower World War I airplane engines, it was the fleetest shore runner on the upper East Coast, of that he was confident. But Travers knew it was a game of chance, and the slightest turn of events could slant the odds against him. Still, as his grandmother used to say, "In for a penny, in for a pound." And he was well and truly in for a pound, and a whole lot more. And he loved every minute of it.

Oceangoing rumrunner caught by U.S. Coast Guard. During Prohibition, from 1920 to 1933, the U.S. Coast Guard had its hands full along the New England coastline chasing bootleggers who made shore runs from the fleet of suppliers anchored in Rum Row, well offshore in international waters. The Coast Guard was allowed to use machine guns only after offering "fair warning," but sometimes the warnings were ignored. Many smugglers' crafts bore the telltale pockmarks of bullets. Those less fortunate caught fire, sank, or were found drifting, their crews dead or injured. As Prohibition wore on, the Coast Guard rechristened former rum-running vessels, most of which were outfitted with souped-up engines, and used them to overtake the lawbreakers at their own game.
Courtesy Library of Congress

⟳

"Perfect night for a run, Charlie," said Johnny Goulart, Travers's brother.

Travers nodded in the dark at the comment. He knew they were closing in on the bell buoy known as The Dumpling that marked the entrance to the harbor. He could hear its slight clang increase as they purred ahead in the thick fog. "Yep, fog's up and dark as a snake's belly. Just as well—with four hundred sacks of the tasty stuff in the hold, we need to make it in without any—"

Sudden light, raw and brighter than midday, filled the *Black Duck*'s pilothouse. "Damn!" But Travers's oath was lost, drowned out by a bullhorn ordering them to stop. A Coast Guard cutter!

Then with no more warning, the slapping pops of machine-gun fire slammed into the pilothouse. Travers heard shouts and screams from his three-man crew and knew their luck had run out. He lunged for the rail and jumped overboard, hanging in the water. Only then did he feel the stinging in his left hand. Had he been shot? What about the others? He didn't dare call out. A few more shots were fired. As the searchlight traveled slowly down the length of the boat, Charlie swung himself quickly back into the cockpit and jerked the boat hard to port, gunning the powerful engines as he nosed toward the mouth of the harbor. The *Duck* responded as he hoped it should—nothing mechanical had been damaged, then. He knew he could put distance between him and the sluggish cutter. Then he could take stock of their damage.

"Hank? Pete?" No responses reached him. He almost hated to shout the last, his brother's name. "Johnny?"

He thought he heard something. He cut the engine, and as the boat rolled forward with the swells from its wake, he dropped to his knees, squinting into the dark. His left arm hung limp and throbbed to beat the band. He had definitely taken a hit.

"Johnny?"

"Charlie . . . uhnn . . ."

"Hang in there, Johnny. We'll get you to the doctor."

Travers got no response, but he felt the slow rise and fall of his brother's chest. Fighting back the urge to scream and gritting his teeth against his own pain, Travers checked for the other two and found them dead. We never should have crowded in the pilothouse, he thought. But who knew we would be fired on? And with no warning. . . .

He went back to his brother, who was still breathing. That was something, at least. Charlie scrabbled for the radio. "This is *Black Duck*. I have a man all shot up, but still alive. We're coming in."

The crackle of static filled the air, and then the reply came: "Negative, *Black Duck*. Stay where you are. We'll tell you when you can come in."

Travers recognized Cornell's voice and fought the urge to tell him a few choice words.

⌇

Charles Travers sat down, his back to the pilothouse wall, and cradled his dying brother's head in his lap as he talked to him. He tried to give him water, a little booze, but it just burbled up. He kept trying the radio as the minutes ticked by. Finally he stood, revved the motors, and said, "To hell with it." He ran back in toward The Dumpling, where the Coast Guard cutter lay in wait like a twitchy cat.

Travers gritted his teeth and steered with his good arm. Within minutes he pulled up alongside the cutter, read the name, "CG-290," and knew for certain it was Cornell who had done this. And it didn't matter anymore. Because his brother and the other two men were all dead. And for the first time in his life, a part of him wished he was, too.

∽

A righteous furor arose over the events of that dark December night in 1929, a decade into Prohibition. For years, many people had perceived the crew of the Black Duck *as Robin Hood–type characters flouting the law and risking their necks in a game of chance that might, at the worst, land them in prison.*

But after the shootings and the capture of the Black Duck, *the public demanded proof that the Coast Guard had offered "fair warning" before opening fire on the smuggling vessel. Some claimed that the officers had used unnecessary force. Public reaction was swift and surprisingly forceful, from threats made against the Coast Guard skipper and his family, to charges of murder, to public riots in Boston against the Coast Guard.*

Within weeks of the incident, a grand jury acquitted the skipper and crew of CG-290 of all charges. It was determined that "fair warning" had been given, although the skipper of the Black Duck *denied this.*

To date, no one has figured out who tipped off the Coast Guard that they should lie in wait and pump twenty-one rounds into the wheelhouse of the swift little vessel now regarded as more heroic than criminal. But the Black Duck *ended up decidedly on the side of the law—with a new paint job, it was reborn as Coast Guard vessel 808.*

Prohibition was not the first anti-alcohol scheme of its kind to hit New England. Portland, Maine, was home to the "Father of Temperance," Mayor Neal S. Dow. In 1851 he had helped put into effect a law that prevented the manufacture and sale of alcohol in Maine, save for medicinal and mechanical purposes. But his prohibitive plans didn't work out quite the way he intended. In Portland, on June 2, 1855, 3,000 people rioted in the streets protesting their mayor's abuse of this unpopular law.

Mayor Dow tripped himself up in his own net when he illegally maintained a sizable supply of alcohol within city limits. Though he intended it for sale for medicinal and mechanical purposes, per the law, a massive crowd grew highly agitated at Dow's perceived hypocrisy and flagrant use of double standards. As the mob swelled and its fury increased, Dow called on the militia for assistance. The militia fired into the crowd, killing one man and wounding seven others. Later, ironically, Dow was prosecuted for improperly acquiring the alcohol in question. Though he was acquitted, the trial helped in the repeal of the law the following year. There was dancing—and drinking—in the streets for several nights following the official repeal.

Less than twenty years later, in October 1870, Boston customs officials uncovered a $250,000 booze-smuggling ring that ended up implicating a handful of prominent Beantown merchants who had used the schooner D. H. Hodgkins *to smuggle whiskey, rum, gin, and brandy into the city. The four primary players were eventually arrested.*

A half century later, on October 11, 1921, the skipper of the Coast Guard cutter Acushnet *grew suspicious of the movements of the British schooner* S. B. Young, *which had ventured close to shore at Nantucket, Massachusetts. He had also been informed that the schooner was laden with 1,300 cases of whiskey. The cutter gave chase and caught the schooner fifteen miles offshore. When quizzed, the* Young's *master swore that he was bound for Nassau. The cutter let the ship proceed but followed it for some time because the Coast Guard skipper was convinced that the schooner planned to sell its wares to shore runners from Nantucket—many of whom no doubt lamented the departure of the British schooner and her valuable cargo.*

46

THE SEA FOX
(1932)

Cape Cod Captain Zora's new boat is overloaded with his biggest haul of hooch yet—but a Coast Guard cutter is closing in. Losing the vessel will wipe him out, but it sure beats going to jail—or worse. Zora reaches for the gasoline and matches just as the machine guns open fire on him.

✎

Captain Manuel Zora, Manny to his friends, and "Sea Fox" to anyone really in the know, let out a calming breath in the full dark of the late July evening. He puttered out to Rum Row in the *Mary Ellen*, nearly a dozen miles off the Cape. A few years before, it had been just a six-mile round-trip; now it was an all-night affair. But it was still worth it.

They had fished for a few hours and had the catch in the hold. On top of that, Jack and Jimmy, his crew, had arranged the false floor for the booze. If there was much more than what it could hold, he would stack it on deck, Coast Guard be damned. He wanted to be able to ditch it quickly if need be. But he hoped it wouldn't come to that. It hadn't yet. Was it luck, or something more?

The quiet thrum of the engine, the gentle swells, and the warm air set him to musing on the long, floating road that led him from a childhood on the sea in his native Portugal to life as a sometimes fisherman, all-the-time smuggler. All his kin were seagoing folks, and more so than that, they were seagoing rogues. He came from a long line of smugglers, so he liked to think that gave him an edge when confronted with the threat of the Coast Guard, the local police, or even the odd Rum Row captain or crew who thought they could hoodwink him, maybe because his lingo was a little different from the boat captains born and bred on Cape Cod. Ha! He shifted the matchstick to the other side of his mouth and whistled a jaunty tune.

Soon, the iron freighter was in sight. This was his first big load as an independent operator, and despite his urge to remain calm, Manny's gut tightened the closer they pulled to the hulking hull of the British ship.

A rumrunner afire, 1923. With big risks come opportunities for big rewards—or big losses. In much the same manner as the crew of the rumrunner *Linwood,* pictured here in flames, smugglers commonly set fire to and scuttled their vessels in the hope that any incriminating evidence would be destroyed if it appeared that capture by a pursuing patrol boat might be imminent. Such evidence—usually hundreds of cases of illegal booze—was purchased by the captains of the smuggling vessels from foreign freighters anchored just offshore in Rum Row. But the shore runners—who nightly ran a gauntlet of Coast Guard patrols, hijackers, and nautically inclined gangsters, all prowling the New England coast—took most of the risk. *Courtesy U.S. Coast Guard*

He had cobbled together orders from a couple of hotels, plus a sub-stantial order from a local big-timer named Papa Pereera, as cheap a man as was ever born. But at this point in the game, all of the cash outlay was Manny's, and that $2,500 in wadded bills seemed a mighty hefty load to lug in his front trouser pocket.

He needn't have worried, he told himself as they settled the rest of the booze on deck. The boat was loaded to the gills. It should be—the transac-tion relieved him of the cash in his pocket but helped fill *Mary Ellen*'s hold with seventy-five cases of Scotch, twenty-five cases each of bourbon and cognac, and twenty cases of beer, always a sure seller.

The *Mary Ellen*, with Manny at the helm, puttered its way back toward shore, without running lights, and all was as it should be—calm and quiet, good on such a foggy, sea-smoke-filled night, for his visibility was hampered to within a few dozen yards.

"Manny! Cut the engine—I hear something."

Manny did as Jack bid him, for Jack's hearing was spot-on, like a dog's. They drifted slowly forward, their forward momentum generated by the swells of their wake. Manny had kept his lights off. And there it was, from somewhere out there. Starboard? Port? Who knew? But it was definitely the thrum of a motor—was it a Coast Guard patrol boat?

"Where the devil is she?" said Manny. Without knowing for sure, he could have just as easily run smack into the boat as run away from it.

"I think she's starboard." Jimmy leaned out into the fog, shaking his head. "Or not." He turned back to his captain. "Manny, we got to dump this booze. It's no sense risking it!"

Manny frowned, about to say "no way," when just off the starboard nose, the cutter emerged.

"Dump it all!" Manny shouted.

His crew members obeyed, elbows, grunts, and curses flying. But it was soon apparent that it wouldn't matter—the cutter, if that's what it was, was coming in too fast, its spotlight smack on them now, blinding them as they reached for the sacks and crates. But before they could dump the load, bullets flew across the surface of the sea, eating up the space between the two boats.

Within seconds the bullets slammed into the boat and ruptured the booze stacked on deck. The *Mary Ellen* was so loaded that she moved sluggishly at best—they stood little chance of zigzagging their way out of it.

❦

"We're cooked, Manny. Time to give up."

"Ha!" said Manny. "They may have ruined this run, but they'll never get me, and they'll never have my boat! Now, I'm going to head for the beach. You fellas dump what gas you can from the cans down below in the bilge. Spill them down there and up here, topsides. All over the deck and load. Now go!"

As the men darted below, Manny kept low, praying no bullets found him. They continued to chew up the railing, the decking, the booze—the air was filled with shredded wood, hunks of glass, and spraying alcohol.

"All set, Manny!" The men crouched low, breathing hard, worry and excitement warring on their faces. These are real men, thought Manny. They know what it's all about!

"Good, now when I head her back out to sea, you guys jump, and far! Otherwise the props will chew you up, and if they don't, the Coast Guard cutter will! I'll jump last, just after I touch off a few matches!"

⚬

The dark of the night concealed the three men's dives overboard. Sucking in breath and working his arms to keep afloat, Manny prayed they made it off the boat and out of harm's way. He watched the blazing *Mary Ellen* head for open water. The cutter not far behind, still plying his boat with bullets.

He wondered, What did the Coast Guard hope to gain by doing that? But he didn't wait to see. He crawled for the beach, soaked but pleased that he had a fighting chance to keep out of jail. He knew that if he was caught, he would face at least ten years, perhaps more since he was known to the law. As he dragged himself onto the beach, he wondered if maybe he was ready for Prohibition to end.

Then he thought of all that money still to be made, just because people wanted something they were told they couldn't have. It would always be that way. Soon, he heard shouts from his men and lay back on the sand, finally relieved. I don't want to stop now, he thought with a smile. It's in my blood. But on the other hand, if I keep this up, I may not have any blood left. . . .

⚬

Manuel Zora, self-styled as Cape Cod's most notorious rumrunner, was one of many men whose fishing operations, legitimate in all respects, were but a cover for the real source of their incomes—rum-running. Zora, aka the Sea Fox, blew through a handful of boats in his years ferrying illicit hooch from Rum Row to shore and then selling it to various "respectable establishments."

After he set fire to the Mary Ellen *on that July night in 1932, he and his three crew members paid a local man $100 to drive them to Boston and keep mum about it. There they bought new clothes, and over breakfast, Manny Zora decided to call it a day on rum-running. He saw the writing on the wall—Prohibition would soon be repealed, and the chance for big money would be gone. He still had his smaller, older fishing vessel and a couple of hundred dollars in his pocket, and he wasn't in jail—or dead. He was one of the lucky ones.*

Hundreds of fishermen-turned-rumrunners weren't so fortunate—they met their ends increasingly through interference by organized crime in the form of enforcers who seeped up the coastline from Boston and New York. If caught with booze, the small-fry runner could expect to have his load stolen and to receive rough treatment at best, and a bullet in the head more than likely.

Bootleggers operated bottling plants on board ships in Rum Row. They used counterfeit labels, bottles, caps, and faked revenue stamps for their illicit whiskey. And the most important part of the product, the liquid inside, was often no more legitimate than its packaging. This alcohol was "stretched" in cutting plants, either on ship or on land, often in tenement slums. Creosote was used to color this raw, near-poisonous alcohol, and glycerine was added for viscosity. What these things did to a person's stomach—and brain—were often too tragic to relate.

Cutting plants also diluted decent whiskey with inferior alcohol fermented with food waste (peelings, eggshells, rotten fruits, curdled dairy goods, and worse) before selling it as the undiluted, top-shelf brand.

It is estimated that during Prohibition poorly made alcohol led to the poisoning deaths of 50,000 people in the United States. And those who didn't die frequently ended up blind, crippled, or insane. In August 1932, in one of many such cases, a man in South Troy, Vermont, bought a bottle of bad alcohol—likely made with deadly rubbing alcohol—and lost his mind. He killed his wife and their four-year-old son with blasts from a shotgun and then killed himself with a .22-caliber revolver.

Nationwide, sales of vanilla extract increased dramatically during Prohibition, as the flavoring had a high alcohol content, and for a time, grocery stores couldn't keep enough of the stuff in stock. Apparently men who before 1920 never gave a thought to baking suddenly developed a keen interest in the craft, because they began buying vanilla extract by the case. Federal revenue agents eventually got wind of the fad and enforced laws that helped curtail the sale of the flavoring.

47

Brady Gang Slain!

(1937)

A lust for more firepower brings the infamous Brady Gang to a Bangor, Maine, sporting goods store, but their request for a tommy gun draws the FBI. On the morning of October 12, 1937, bloody history is made.

$\mathscr{S}$

From behind the counter of Dakin's Sporting Goods, Louis Clark shouted across the store to Everett Hurd, owner of the shop. "Get a load of the fellas comin' in." He nodded toward the front door of the shop. "You evah?"

"Takes all types."

The two strangers, dressed alike in long wool overcoats and creased fedoras, walked into the sports shop on Central Street in Bangor, Maine. They stood for a moment just inside the door, taking in the large space filled with all manner of outdoor and recreational equipment.

Hunting bows hung overhead; boots, hats, and wool jackets filled racks throughout the store; and fishing rods jutted along one wall. And there, thought one of the strangers, just beyond the hick in the plaid shirt, stood a pretty little rack of shotguns and rifles, all lined up like soldiers at attention.

"A beautiful sight, am I right?" Clarence Shaffer nudged James Dalhover and nodded toward the guns.

Dalhover slid the toothpick to the other side of his mouth. "They'll do, all right. Let's see what else they got." They made their way, with the deliberate casualness of people with other things in mind, over to the counter where the clerk stood.

"What can I help you gentlemen with today?"

"We're looking to do a little hunting. It's that season, right?"

"Um, yes. Depends what you're hunting, though. What you have in mind?"

"Whatever. We'll take two of those Colt .45s and extra clips. Ammo, too."

The other one piped up. "Any other sporting stores around? You know, that sell guns?"

Clark wanted to say, "Look buddy, you don't like our selection, hit the bricks." But he didn't. It was obvious to him these fellows weren't interested in hunting, and they certainly weren't local folk. Instead he just said, "Well, there's Rice and Miller, just up Broad Street."

The man nodded and kept looking at the display case.

In a few minutes, they were gone, and Clark was glad of it. "I tell you, Mr. Hurd, there's something suspicious about them. Who hunts with a .45-caliber pistol?"

"Not just that, how about all those extra clips, the rifle—and they ordered another .45?"

"That's what I'm saying."

The two men were silent for a few minutes, and then the clerk said, "What if they were just eyeballin' the place? What if they're after our fire-arms and want to come back and rob us?"

Everett Hurd shook his head and said, "Might be a stretch, but the man on the radio said Al Brady and his gang were tracked to New England." He shrugged, went back to his office, and called Bangor Police Chief Thomas Crowley.

✒

Louis Clark was startled that he hadn't heard the door, and now he found himself staring at three tough men lined up at the glass counter before him. The two of them eyeballing the pistol case were the ones he had seen before. The third, in the center, was a man of medium height with a long nose, prominent chin, and piercing, wide eyes. And he was star-ing straight at Clark. The clerk felt more frightened than he had two or three weeks before, back at the end of September, when the other two had been in.

Good God, he thought, they found out we called the police on them. His throat felt dry, and he wondered, as he had on their first visit, just what these fellows had hidden under those wool overcoats.

"Hello there," said Louis Clark. "Those .45s work out for you?"

The man nodded, kept staring, and then finally spoke. "Yep, just fine. In fact, we'll need another." Then he smiled. "And we're also wondering if you got any Thompsons in stock."

"Thompsons? As in submachine guns?"

"Yeah, those."

"Nah." Clark swallowed and laughed. "Not a lot of call for those 'round these parts."

The man didn't smile. "Can you get them?"

Clark lost his smile and nodded quickly. "Oh, yes. We can order most anything, yep."

"How long?"

"That'd take . . . oh, a couple of weeks."

The man leaned on the counter, looking past the clerk at the wall calendar, and pointed. "If we come back on the eleventh or twelfth?"

"It'd be in by then."

"Good. Now about that .45. . . ."

∽

On Columbus Day, the morning started out nippier than usual, but by the time Everett Hurd opened Dakin's, the sidewalk was filling with people heading to their offices and shops, and the sky showed blue and full of promising sunlight.

"You don't think they rabbited, do you?" Louis Clark asked as he rearranged the knife display on the counter. Despite himself, he found his hands shaking.

"Too early to tell yet, Mr. Clark." Special Agent Walter Walsh smiled. "He told you they were coming back on the eleventh or twelfth. If they show, it'll be worth the wait, believe me. They're officially public enemy number one."

"I know, you told me." Clark gave a half-smile and shook his head.

"Sorry, pal. Didn't mean to make you nervous."

"Ha—too late for that, Agent Walsh."

"Shhh!" Another agent hushed them from a blind spot near the side of the store. "There's the Buick now. Yep, Ohio plates and all, cruising by . . . and looks like three, no, four men inside. They're looking . . . and driving on by."

"Giving us the once-over. They'll be back," said Agent Walsh. "Okay, boys, look lively. This is it." He nodded to Clark and Everett Hurd. "You good?"

"I'm fine. No worries here."

"Excellent."

But the car drove by the storefront two more times and then pulled over, just up the street from the shop.

Clark watched as two men got out of the car and walked to the store. One of them, the taller of the two—Clark recognized him from previous visits as one of the men who did the most talking—came into the store. The other man stood by the door, his hands thrust into his coat pockets, and he stared up and down the street.

The taller man approached the counter. Louis Clark cleared his throat. "Good morning, sir. I believe you're here to pick up your special order?"

"That's it, Jack. I'm in a hurry, though."

"No, you're not. You're under arrest. Surrender now." Special Agent Walsh stepped out from behind a partition where he had been posing as a clerk. He had two pistols drawn and trained on James Dalhover and strode forward, even as the bandit reached for his own gun. Dalhover growled and spun on him, but the agent was quicker and clubbed the man into submission. As Walsh handcuffed Dalhover, the man on the sidewalk saw the scuffle taking place inside and drew his pistol. Agent Walsh burst through the front door, a second too late to avoid taking a bullet in the shoulder.

That was all the signal the fifteen FBI special agents and fifteen Maine and Indiana state troopers—arranged up and down Central Street on rooftops, in windows, and at street level—needed. They opened fire, and as the gangster scrambled out into the street, squeezing off random shots, they gunned him down. His body flopped onto the paved street, sprawled across the trolley tracks, jumping with each bullet pumped into him.

At the same instant, G-men rushed the Buick, slamming open the doors. With guns drawn, they shouted, "Federal officers! Get out of the car with your hands up! Now!"

Al Brady, who was in the backseat, and the driver moved to comply. "Don't shoot! Don't shoot!" shouted Brady as he slowly edged toward the open door. And as he bent low to exit the car, he pulled out a .38-caliber revolver and managed to squeeze off four shots at the nearest agents while he bolted for the street.

Brady didn't make it but a few feet before a fusillade of lead cut him down. The driver attempted the same, and he, too, was dropped in his tracks as he bolted up the street. The pistol that Brady was clutching as he exhaled his last was the one he had taken from the body of Indiana State Trooper Paul Minneman, whom the Brady Gang had killed five months before.

Gangster Al Brady (foreground) and Clarence Lee Shaffer Jr. On the morning of October 12, 1937, fifteen G-men and fifteen Maine and Indiana state troopers fired forty-five shots—forty-three of which met their marks—at members of the Brady Gang as they tried to shoot their way to freedom on Bangor, Maine's normally placid Central Street. Al Brady and his cohorts, topping the FBI's most-wanted list, thought that because it was hunting season in Maine, the tommy guns they ordered through a local sporting goods store would go unnoticed. Instead it drew the feds. Bangor Daily News *File Photo*

On the day of the shootout, fifteen G-men and fifteen state police—from Maine and Indiana—were assembled up and down Central Street. Officers were perched in hiding on all sides, from windows and rooftop vantage points to doorways and storefronts lining the downtown scene. Lawmen fired forty-five shots, and forty-three hit their marks in the bodies of the three gangsters trapped outside.

The vicious fusillade cut down the three kill-crazy gangsters, ending lives that had no regard for any other than their own. The fourth gangster, Rhuel James Dalhover, who had gone inside Dakin's Sporting Goods to retrieve the ordered Thompson submachine gun, was brought to the basement of Bangor City Hall, a block away. From there he was trans-ported back to Indiana, where he was tried and convicted of the murder of Indiana State Trooper Paul Minneman. On November 18, 1938, he was executed in the electric chair.

Although the bodies of the two gang members who were gunned down in the street with their leader, Al Brady, were retrieved by family members, Brady himself had no living relatives, and so no one came forward to claim his corpse. He was buried in Bangor's Mt. Hope Cemetery in an unmarked grave.

In October 2007, to mark the seventieth anniversary of Maine's bloodiest shootout, Brady's grave was topped with a stone, and a religious ceremony was performed. Afterward, the shootout was reenacted in downtown Bangor, on the very spot where the Brady Gang met its end.

⁓

In the months leading up to their grisly end, the Brady Gang committed between 150 and 200 holdups and other robberies, leading FBI officials to put the Brady Gang on its "public criminals number one" list. One of the gang reportedly made the claim that they intended to "make Dillinger look like a piker." That they nearly did, as evidenced by the smoking trail of brazen crimes and violence they left behind.

The FBI found the gang's stash of weapons, which included thirty-five guns—pistols, machine guns, rifles, shotguns—plus ample ammunition, tear-gas grenades, and more. And yet this hadn't been enough for the gang.

After years of armed robberies, car thefts, and brutal murders, after failed plans to raid a police station for weapons in Ohio, and after talk of looting the exhibits at the FBI's museum in Washington, D.C. (not aware that the arms displayed had been rendered unusable), the Brady Gang's hunger for more and better weaponry drove them to New England in the fall of 1937.

The gang briefly considered Bridgeport, Connecticut, but then they made their way north. They figured that since it was hunting season, the hicks in Maine would cough up arms with few questions, though it's doubtful that the savvy men working at Dakin's Sporting Goods would have done so, even if the gang had not acted like big-city gangsters and ordered a tommy gun, among other pieces not normally associated with deer hunting.

Special Agent Walter Walsh was still alive in 2010, at 103 years old, despite being wounded in the shoulder at the Bangor takedown of the Brady Gang. Only one of Brady's last four shots had any effect—it blazed through an agent's coat and shirt and bore a hole through the agent's leather pistol holster before exiting without further damage. That agent then managed to squeeze off several rounds that met their target in the form of Al Brady.

48

HURRICANE OF THE CENTURY
(1938)

Within hours, on September 21, 1938, this savage lash of weather whips the coastal communities of New England's rugged coast. In Rhode Island, a manned lighthouse disappears, a school bus never unloads its kids, and an entire summer community is washed out to sea.

❦

Walter Eberle kissed his wife, Agnes, on the forehead and said, "Keep yourself and the children safe, and I'll be home before you know it." He looked over his wife's head at his six children and winked. "Take care of your mother now, you hear?" Like little birds they all nodded and said, "Yes, Daddy." He winked once more, kissed his wife again, and left.

She did her best to hide her fears from him and the children. She knew it would sound so silly. After all, he was a navy veteran with twenty years of service, and a master diver, to boot. But sometimes, especially when a storm crept up the coast, she couldn't help feeling she might never see him again.

This isn't helping anyone, she thought. She breathed deeply and, smiling, turned around to face the kids. "So, who wants to make cookies?"

❦

Walter Eberle arrived at the Whale Rock Lighthouse in time for his shift, relieving the light keeper, Dan Sullivan. As he watched Dan descend the stairs, he heard the older man's last words echo in the still air of the top story of the lighthouse: "Keep your wits about you, Walt. It's fixing to be a big blow out there." He stopped then on the steel stairs and said, "But you'll be fine. Good night, Walt."

"G'night, Dan."

And now he was alone. The wind had increased until it was a constant, harsh companion, like loud radio static, punctuated with hard, pummeling gusts that vibrated the very glass of the lighthouse. In the sweeping glare of the beam, what Eberle saw jellied his insides—the fleeting light of the beam revealed air so thick with pelting rain and slashing sea spume that it was almost impossible to make out the massive walls of water that moved straight up the West Passage of Narragansett Bay toward him, sitting like a duck on Whale Rock, the sole person on the smallest island in the entire bay.

The closest land, Conanicut Island, was nowhere to be seen, so thick was the night. Each subsequent wave seemed to crash higher and harder, and his light was only four stories high—tall enough, he would have thought, for any storm. Until tonight. For seawater pummeled the little lighthouse—up and over the light, around it, encircling it, hugging it like a giant, many-armed monster.

Something fluttered on the roof, thrumming like a wire under extreme tension, and then the sound stopped. Whatever it was is long gone now, he thought. Thick green foam slammed the windows, parted, and ran down, looking more like rice pudding than the nurturing element that he had been in or on for twenty years—half his life. But something about this storm, unlike so many others he had been through, chilled him to his marrow.

He turned back from facing inland and looked seaward. And what he saw in the light's beam was the last thing he would ever see, as the harshest of all nights forced its way in.

No longer did the ocean embrace the little Whale Rock lighthouse. Now it was a lover spurned, a furious thing that would bear no further resistance. With one mammoth, slamming wave, far higher than the lighthouse's seventy-three feet, the ocean snatched the entire structure free of the nub of rock on which it was anchored and ripped it away with the man inside, forty-year-old Walter Eberle, father of six and husband of one.

"Agnes," said Dan Sullivan through the phone lines very early the next morning, "the light is gone."

 confo

Joseph Matoes Sr. drove hard toward the Thomas H. Clark Elementary School, but the children had already left for home in the school bus. He turned around, and as he neared Mackerel Point, on the water, the swells raced in, increasing in intensity, and with no warning, his car and another one nearby were pulled from the road and into the water. Managing to free himself, Matoes swam toward shore. But the other car, containing a mother and son, did not fare as well, and they were drowned.

Whale Rock Lighthouse. In Rhode Island, on September 21, 1938, Narragansett Bay's Whale Rock Lighthouse was completely destroyed by the savage fury of the Hurricane of 1938. Assistant keeper Walter Eberle was inside the tower when it was consumed and swept away by the sea. His body was never found. His was but one of six hundred deaths in New England caused by the storm. The majority of these deaths occurred in Rhode Island, including motorists trapped in their cars when thirteen-foot flood tides rolled into downtown Providence. In Massachusetts, a 186-mile-per-hour wind was clocked. *Courtesy U.S. Coast Guard*

Within minutes the school bus rolled toward him, not seeming to slow. Matoes stood in the road, the frothing green water swirling about him. He waved his arms and motioned for the bus driver, Norman Caswell, to turn back.

"No! No, turn back! What are you doing? You fool!"

The bus kept to its course. And as he watched, as if conjured out of the violent air itself, a massive wave peeled the bus from the road.

Dead ahead Norman Caswell saw what looked like Joe Matoes Sr., standing in the road, waving his arms, motioning him to stop. Why on God's green earth would he stop here? He had to barrel through and get the kids to safety as soon as he was able. He guessed that Matoes wanted to pull his four kids from the bus. That's half of the lives I've been entrusted with, thought Caswell. But there's no way I'm stopping here, exposed like this to the sea!

He downshifted, keeping firm to his plan, hard-pressed to find a better alternative to landing the kids at a safe spot. Then the bus was slammed—hard—by a wall of water that would leave the bus, seconds later, well off the road. The water surged and swelled all about it.

Caswell looked back at the eight frightened, crying faces staring at him. If we don't get out of here, we will be drowned like rats, he thought.

"We can't stay in here, kids! We have to get out of the bus. Form a human chain—grab each other's arms tight, and don't let go!"

Caswell pushed open the doors, and he and Clayton Chellis, the largest of the eight children, took the ends, with the seven smaller children between them. But as they slipped out of the bus, a wave, bigger than the one that had pulled the bus off the road, curled over the little group and dropped right down on them.

It ripped the children from one another. Two little girls slammed forward into the bus and scrambled on top, screaming for help. Matoes saw them gripping tight to the roof of the bus—they were two of his four children! And then a wave washed over them, and they were gone.

Caswell went under once, was thrust upward, and was pulled back down again. When he finally rose to the surface, he saw only the Chellis boy swimming, looking for the children, for his sister, thought Caswell, because the Chellis family had two kids. Where were they all? He shouted, but the wind sliced sheets off the violent seawater and pummeled everything with bitter, piercing spray. There were no other children to be seen. Nowhere. Then another wave washed over him. The next thing he knew, something dragged him ashore, nudging and kicking him in the ribs.

"Please let me die. I lost a whole bunch of kids in the school bus. Everything's gone. Please don't move me. Let me die."

But Joseph Matoes Sr. did not let Caswell die. Grim-faced, he hauled him to safety, to his own home, revived him, and gave him dry clothes. And later, when they went back to the causeway, they stared at the shattered hulk of the bus, each man in his own hell.

Mr. and Mrs. Carl Chellis, the Beavertail Lighthouse keeper and his wife, showed up looking for their children.

"I got your boy," spluttered Caswell. "But your daughter . . . is dead, gone."

In his anger, Chellis snatched up rocks and smashed out every remaining window of the leaning, swamped school bus. His daughter, little Marion, was indeed among the missing.

⁂

Over the following days, the bodies of the children were found, except for Dotty, the youngest Matoes child. Joseph Matoes Sr. had learned from the bus driver, Caswell, that his son, Joseph Jr., could have saved himself but drowned trying to save his younger sister. The family spotted what might have been her body four or five days after the storm. They noticed something red and white floating out to sea and guessed it was a lobster buoy. Only later did they realize that their youngest, Dotty, had been wearing a white blouse and a red skirt.

Clayton Chellis recalled that before they left the bus, as he held tight to his little sister's hand, Marion said to him, "Clayton, don't let the water get in your eyes." Though he was the only child on the bus to survive the storm, Clayton Chellis nearly drowned in an ice-skating accident a few years later, as a teenager. Seven years after the hurricane, while serving in the Pacific in World War II, he did drown.

Norman Caswell, the ill-fated bus driver, died shortly after the hurricane. Those who knew him said his death was caused by the shock and grief of the children's deaths. The body of Whale Rock Lighthouse's second keeper, Walter Eberle, was never found. However, in recent years, remains of the little lighthouse were located at the bottom of the bay. A plaque dedicated to Eberle is now in place at the Beavertail Lighthouse Museum, in Jamestown, Rhode Island.

The hurricane killed eight hundred people, six hundred of them in New England. Rhode Island fared the worst of all the New England states, suffering most of the storm's deaths—one hundred in the town of Westerly alone. Narragansett Bay was especially hard hit. As the storm moved in, the bay's funnel shape compounded the intensity of the surging water, already unusually high because of the autumnal equinox and full moon, driving it to sixteen feet above annual high-tide levels. Such structures as the Whale Rock Lighthouse found themselves dwarfed by massive waves and for the most part were unable to withstand the crushing, relentless power of the storm.

Hundreds of coastal homes in Rhode Island were swept out to sea, many with their inhabitants still inside. The state's capital, Providence, experienced thirteen-foot flood waters in the downtown area, trapping and drowning motorists in their cars. Napatree Point, a jut of land off Little Narragansett Bay and home to dozens of families, was completely wiped out, with nary a trace of the forty residences once the storm abated. In nearby Watch Hill, Rhode Island, the famous Watch Hill Carousel was buried under tons of sand. It was exhumed and continues to run today. Built in 1876, it is the oldest flying-horse carousel in the United States.

Tracked for eleven days, the killer storm had veered at the last minute and headed north, straight for Long Island, New York. The storm measured approximately five hundred miles wide, and the eye of the storm was fifty miles across. South winds from the storm were clocked at the Blue Hill Observatory in Milton, Massachusetts, at 186 miles per hour, and a five-minute sustained wind of 121 miles per hour left just one wind meter standing, most impressive considering they remain the second-highest winds ever recorded on earth. So powerful was the storm that California seismographs recorded its impact.

✌

In addition to the Hurricane of 1938, two others help form the trio of storms that meteorologists and historians refer to as the most devastating blows to hit New England in the last four centuries. The Great Colonial Hurricane of 1635 slammed into the Jamestown region, bringing with it estimated 140-mile-per-hour winds.

The Great September Gale of 1815 reached a similar intensity—135-mile-per-hour winds and massive storm surges and flooding. This storm was all the more devastating because of the increase in population in the intervening 180 years.

49

DOWNEAST NAZIS

(1944)

A German U-boat creeps twelve miles up Frenchman's Bay to sleepy Bar Harbor, Maine. Two Nazi spies slip ashore, lugging suitcases and trying not to look out of place—Operation Magpie is off to a promising start.

⁓

S chweinhund!" William Colepaugh had timed his step wrong, and his leather dress shoe filled with the Atlantic's frigid water.

"Shut your mouth! And remember, only English from now on."

The man with the sopping foot narrowed his eyes at his mission partner, the German Erich Gimpel, but said nothing. He would bide his time.

They watched the two uniformed U-boat sailors shove off in the rubber raft that would carry them back to the submarine, the Nazi vessel U-1230, that had been their home for the two months it took to travel the 4,000 miles from the Fatherland across the Atlantic to Canada. From there they had made their way down the coast of Maine, then twelve miles up Frenchman's Bay, and now the submarine lay partly exposed on this frigid night of November 29, 1944. She lurked there, just a few hundred yards off the bleak, coastal backwater known on the map as Bar Harbor, Maine.

The two men slipped, slid, and groped their way up a half-treed gravel bank, high above the constant wash of the frigid surf. The moon was bright and high, but a fog hovered close to the land and swirled about their feet as they lugged their heavy suitcases, clunking them against their legs, and walked westward.

"I wish it wasn't so cold," said Colepaugh. They trudged along the side of the gravel road, sometimes slipping in the sopping slush and runny snow. "My foot is frozen. These clothes are not appropriate for this weather. They should have known this."

Gimpel stopped, set down his own suitcase, and regarded him for a moment. "I am surprised you have not yet died of exposure to the elements." He raised his arms and then let them drop to his sides. He had said this louder than he wanted to, but he was angry. It seemed that Colepaugh had done nothing but complain since they landed. Typical American, he thought. I trained him for four months, and he's still lazy.

A schussing sound caused them to look up the road behind them. Soon headlights bobbed with the ruts in the road. It was a vehicle.

"We should hide. . . ."

"A perfect way to attract attention to ourselves. No, we should try to get a ride with them. Dummkopf." This last word Gimpel said under his breath as he bent to retrieve his suitcase. But he was sure Colepaugh heard him.

The car was a fairly recent Chevrolet. It puttered up to them and made no attempt to slow. As it passed, they saw the faint outline of a woman staring at them. Then the head turned forward, and the car sped ahead. The night was once again dark and cold and wet. They resumed walking. Within a few minutes, another car roared up behind them, faster and bolder than the first. Its bright headlights were almost upon them before they could tell what sort of vehicle it was. Then it, too, rolled by.

After a half hour of walking, lugging their heavy suitcases, a third vehicle came along and slowed down. They raised their hands to their eyes to cut the glare as the vehicle pulled up.

And then they saw that it was a late-model taxicab. They smiled at each other as the driver rolled down his window and leaned an elbow out.

"You boys are lucky as all get-out, I tell you. I don't make it out here all that often, but I just brought someone back from Ellsworth. Where you headed?"

"Our car slid off the road. We need to get to Boston," said Colepaugh.

"Well, first thing's first. Let's get them portmanteaus in the trunk of this rig." He made to get out, but Gimpel said, "No, thank you."

The driver pulled the door shut and eyed the two men. "Suit yourself. Climb in, and we'll get a move on."

The two men smiled and sighed quietly as they sat in the warm car's backseat.

After they geared up and rounded a few corners, the windshield wipers slapping and smearing the wet snow, the driver said, "I can get you to the train station up to Bangor, and then you can take the train south. How'd that suit you?"

"That sounds ideal."

The driver eyed them in the rearview mirror and nodded.

The men made it to Bangor and rode the train to Portland, arriving in the small hours of the morning. They stopped for breakfast in a diner, and for the first time since they walked ashore in Hancock, Maine, hours before, Gimpel felt his usual confidence flag, just a bit.

"Hey, Mack, I asked what kind of toast you want with your ham and eggs. Not a big decision—wheat, white, rye, muffin, raisin."

Trying to smile, Gimpel blurted out, "Wheat, please."

The short-order cook gave him a quick look, nodded, and turned back to the grill.

"What's the matter with you?" Colepaugh said under his breath.

"Bread is bread. I've never had the choice of five before."

Colepaugh nodded and smiled as the waitress filled their coffee cups.

Later, on the train, when he was assured that they would not be overheard, Colepaugh leaned over to Gimpel and said, "It's nearly seven. We'll be in Boston soon. I think we should hot-foot it to New York, get set up there."

"No," said Gimpel. "We'll stick with our plan and rest in Boston. Then tomorrow we'll move on to New York." Gimpel stared at his traveling companion until the man looked away. "Without plans, we have nothing."

Colepaugh leaned back and looked out the window, even though it was still dark. "Yeah, you're right. I'm just anxious."

That afternoon in Boston, as Gimpel shopped for a new necktie, the clerk fingered the sleeve of his trenchcoat admiringly. "Say, that's not American styling."

Gimpel, again, was taken aback. First the bread and now this, he thought. Such minor things to shake my confidence so. "Actually, I bought it in Spain."

The clerk nodded and smiled. Innocent enough, thought Gimpel, and yet I will not risk wearing this coat again. Such a little thing. . . .

⁂

Indeed it was more than a little thing that ground Operation Magpie to a halt. It was a string of occurrences that conspired to bring it to an end. Two days after their arrival in New York City, the U-boat in which Colepaugh and Gimpel had traveled to Maine sank the Canadian freighter Cornwallis, *killing all but five of its forty-nine-man crew. The vessel was nearing the end of its trip, from Barbados to St. John, New Brunswick, carrying nothing more threatening than sugar and molasses.*

FBI agents grew concerned that an enemy submarine so near the U.S. coast might have landed spies on the Maine coast. And soon enough, agents found the two people who, a week or more before, had driven past the two spies, struggling with their suitcases and wearing big-city clothes. Both local residents—Mary Forni, twenty-nine years old, and Harvard Hodgkins, seventeen, son of the town of Hancock's deputy sheriff and a Boy Scout—filled in the agents as best they could.

As helpful as their information was, it was actually American–turned–Nazi spy William Colepaugh who caused Operation Magpie to fizzle and broke wide open the FBI's scant case. On December 21, 1944, Colepaugh absconded with both suitcases, containing $60,000 and ninety-nine small diamonds, the bulk of the money the pair expected to live on for two years while spying on the Manhattan Project, the top-secret U.S. nuclear weapons development operation.

Leaving Gimpel high and dry might have been Colepaugh's plan from the start. When preparing for the mission, he had gone to great lengths to convince his Nazi higher-ups that they would need roughly $15,000 each per year to survive in the United States, at a time when the average American household required approximately $2,250 per year to get by. The diamonds had been supplied for use should the ample cash supply run out.

While on the lam from Gimpel, Colepaugh met up with an old American friend and convinced him that he was indeed a spy for the Germans. The friend called the FBI, and the FBI, in turn, arrested Colepaugh, who spilled the beans about everything. By December 30 an FBI manhunt, focused on Manhattan, captured Erich Gimpel.

By February 1945 the pair of spies were tried, convicted, and sentenced to death by hanging. But President Franklin Delano Roosevelt died in April, and all federal executions were postponed for four weeks in honor of the mourning period. During that time, the war ended, and President Truman commuted their sentences to life in prison.

Colepaugh served a seventeen-year prison term and then settled in the Philadelphia region, where he ran his own business. He was active in the Boy Scouts and Rotary. He died in 2005. Erich Gimpel served a ten-year sentence in Leavenworth and Alcatraz. He returned to West Germany in 1955 and eventually settled in South America. He wrote the book Spy for Germany, *which was published in 1957 in Great Britain. It was finally published in the United States in 2003 as* Agent 146. *He died in 1996, at age ninety-eight.*

⚭

The New England coast has a long history of submarine activity, beginning in 1775, with the invention of the Turtle, *a one-man submarine created by Connecticut patriot David Bushnell for the purpose of affixing explosives to enemy ships moored in harbors. In theory, the wooden acorn-shaped vessel was a sound idea, and Bushnell had tested it extensively in the Connecticut River. It was used on September 7, 1776, on the flagship of British Admiral Howe's fleet, the HMS* Eagle, *off Governor's Island, south of*

Manhattan. Alas, a turn in tides and the operator's lack of familiarity with the sensitive craft may have contributed to the mission's failure.

On July 21, 1918, the German sub U-156 attacked and sank a tugboat, the Perth Amboy, *and its four barges off Orleans, Massachusetts, before shelling the town itself. This marks the only time during World War I that enemy shells landed on U.S. soil.*

On May 5, 1945, the German sub U-853 sank the U.S. coal carrier Black Point *just off Newport, Rhode Island. The U.S. Navy responded immediately and layered the region with depth charges. Oil slicks and debris were spotted in the region the next day, and the navy was satisfied that the submarine and its crew were destroyed. The wreck has since been located, and the intact hull, with hatches open, is a popular dive site. It is located in 130 feet of water off Block Island, Rhode Island.*

50

Maine Coast Trap Wars

(1949)

Deadly force comes into play as island lobstermen squabble over territory. Trap lines are cut, threats are made, gas tanks are filled with rotted fish—and then the shooting begins.

⨍

"Here he comes. And he don't look none too pleased." Mort Jenkins Jr. nodded toward the dirt road leading toward the wharf. His brother, Pal, sent a stream of chaw juice sluicing toward the paint can on the floor of the fish shack.

Pal peeked through the window and said, "Your eyes need fixing?"

"Why?" said Mort. He looked again, just to be sure. "That's Timmy, all right."

"Yeah, it's him. But he's carrying his 30.30!"

Mort groaned and stood up, not sure what to do next. The only exit was also the entrance to the fish shack used by him and his brothers and cousins, of which Timmy St. Peters was one. The little shanty was crammed full with old ropes, traps in various stages of repair, and ragged hunks of netting hanging from nails pounded in all over the walls.

He didn't have long to think about his exit plan, for within seconds, Timmy burst in on them. From his long-faced look it appeared that he had spent the entire ten-minute walk down to the harbor from his house chewing on something that had him cranked tighter than the seal on a jar of his mother's homemade mincemeat.

"By God, boys, what in the name of Sam Hill are you thinkin'?" yelled Timmy.

Mort and Pal both jumped back, despite their efforts to look a bit tough as Timmy stormed in. Though he was no more imposing a character than any of them, for they had all grown up together on the island, when one of them had a rifle in his mitts, he was the one with the floor. And just now, that man was Timmy.

Mort sucked in a slow breath and let it out again. "Just what are you on about, Tim?"

"I guess I don't have to tell you that my brother's traps have been cut. Nineteen of 'em to date. Knowing you, Jenkins, there's a couple hundred more dragging the bottom out there in the bay."

Timmy stared at them, wide-eyed, as if he had asked each of them in turn to answer a trick question. Neither of the brothers said anything to him. Then Mort held up his hand, flicked a finger at Timmy, and said, "You ain't got no right to come in here and tell me all that—you think we did that? Why would we do that?"

Mort saw that he had rattled Tim by taking the upper hand, so he pushed it a bit more and stepped toward his rifle-toting cousin, his finger still pointing out in front of him. "You think we cut them traps? Huh? Come out and say it, I dare you, you sap!"

Gun or no, Mort Jenkins felt a knot of anger rise up in him. By God, he thought, I'll not take this from him or any man. He balled his right hand and swung hard, landing a solid smack to Tim's forty-nine-year-old jaw. His cousin reeled backward, slamming against the doorframe. "You chose the wrong chicken to pull that stunt with, Jenkins!"

Tim stepped backward and raised the rifle to his shoulder. Mort pulled back, but Pal whipped an open hand forward in front of his brother and shouted, "No, Tim! No! This ain't the way!"

"Hell it ain't!" Tim's face was a mask of hate and rage, and his hard face shook with anger; one side of it was already swelling where his cousin had clouted him. His left ear buzzed from the blow. "Baah!" he barked. Whipping the rifle downward, he pulled the trigger, cutting a hole in the shack's wood floor inches from Mort's shaking boots.

The cracking sound filled the close shack and barely covered the tight little screams the two Jenkins brothers emitted.

"You ever touch me again and there's going to be more of the same, only next time I won't pull my shot!" Timmy St. Peters lowered the rifle and stepped forward. "You keep that in mind before you haul off and cuff me one." The enraged lobsterman turned and stalked back the way he had come.

As the sound of his boots crunching gravel receded, Pal said, "There any truth to what he's saying?"

Mort looked at his younger brother as if Pal had just asked him to speak Chinese. "Of course there is. I know for a fact it was just an accident. I think old man Willey got too close to one of their buoys."

"So why's he all riled up then?"

Lobster boats, Stonington, Maine. Feuds among lobstermen go back for as long as people have been fishing. Trap wars are most often territorial disputes arising from real or imagined slights, resulting in a one-upmanship game of trap-line cutting. Often such antics get out of hand: Docks are burned; boats are filled with trash, or worse, sunk; and guns are drawn. Not only do cut traps damage a lobsterman's livelihood, but they also end up floating free on the bottom; they are ghost traps or death traps because lobsters work their way in and can't get out again. It is estimated that there are millions of ghost traps in Maine waters alone. Approximately 200,000 traps—up to 10 percent of the 2 million traps set in Maine waters each year—are lost to the bottom. *Photograph by Jennifer Smith-Mayo*

"Well, since Tim and Charlie as good as accused me of cutting that one trap line, I figured if I'm gonna be blamed, might as well be for somethin' rather than nothin'."

"So . . . ?"

"So," Mort said, "I up and cut about eighteen more of his brother's lines."

The brothers were silent for a moment, and then Mort said, "Got a problem with that?"

"Nah, I'd a done the same thing myself."

They both stared absently up the empty wharf lane, while a vein on Mort's temple pulsed with each new thought that occurred to him.

∽

Within minutes of puttering out of the mouth of the little harbor, Timmy St. Peters heard the throaty roar of a lobster boat closing in fast from behind. He turned, and sure enough, there were Mort and Pal bearing down fast on him. Tim had no time to slip away, no time to evade them at all.

Foot by foot they plowed closer. They must be wide open, he thought as he gunned his engine, but still they gained on him. He pointed his own boat, *Ruthella P.*, toward open water and scrabbled for his rifle, but there was no time. At the last possible moment, their boat sliced to port and lashed him with a wall of spray. He had not even made it inside his little pilothouse before the water drenched him through. Their receding laughter and jeers galled him more than the soaking. He pulled out the rifle and vowed to use it with a Jenkins in his sights should they even think of puttering within range of him again.

∽

"What's the matter with this thing? I spent all Sunday workin' on it, and it ran fine then. . . ." Mort Jenkins slammed a hand down on the cowling of his boat's engine.

"Problem?"

Mort looked up at the dock and saw his brother staring down at him.

"Yeah, there's a problem all right. Can't make her turn over. Come on down and help me, will you?"

Pal clunked down the dock and then dropped into the back of the boat he worked with his brother. He folded his arms and looked around. Then his eyes settled on something.

"What are you doing?" Mort poked his head from the engine compartment. "Trouble's in here, last time I looked."

"I don't think so."

"What do you mean?"

"I mean, brother, look at the fish grease around the fuel pipe."

Mort bent close, eyed the silver cap, and then snatched it off and sniffed. Sure enough, fish stink mixed with fuel vapors. "Timmy."

"Timmy."

Mort's mouth stretched wide over his teeth, and a vein on his temple throbbed. Pal let loose a stream of chaw juice and said, "I'm going to the house. Fetch the other rifle."

⧆

A couple of days later, Tim headed out to tend the last of his traps in the channel before calling it a day. As his boat rolled with the swell—No Man's Island off his port side, home back behind him—a dozen gulls swooped close enough, they hoped, to get a free lunch of bait fish. He thought he heard another motor. He scanned the surrounding water, and sure enough, there was a boat. It was too far off to tell whose it was, but if he had to make a guess, he would say it was Mort and Pal's.

"They ain't got no traps out here," Tim said out loud, with one hand on a lobster trap and the other shielding the sun from his eyes. He finished setting the trap and then dropped it over the side of the boat before pitching the ratty end of his cigarette into the water. He looked up again, and the boat had puttered closer. It looked more like the Jenkins brothers with each passing foot.

Tim was sorely tempted to pull out the rifle and drive right at the jackass, Mort. I should let him have it once and for all, he thought. Any man who will cut another man's traps and then act like he don't deserve a bit of rough treatment for it, why he ain't a man at all. Instead, Tim took a deep breath and turned back to the wheelhouse. He was tired, and he had just four more traps to check, then he could head in.

A second later, Tim's glass windshield cracked before his eyes, and then he heard the telltale report of a rifle, the delay caused by distance. Another shot pocked the rail by his right hip, furrowing and splintering the wood. He dropped to the floor, swearing and afraid, all at once.

"I get my hands on him, and that's all she wrote. I shoulda shot him when I had the chance."

He waited a few minutes and then raised his head up above the rail, higher and higher. He saw nothing—no boat in sight. He breathed easier and stood again, still looking for the offending vessel. As he finished hauling his last few traps, Tim St. Peters continued to swivel his head but saw no sign of the boat.

As he puttered home, he wondered if he should have even started this madness more than a week before, by shooting the floor of the fish shack. "Or it could have been the bait fish in the fuel pipe," he said aloud, then smiled. Too late now, he thought. But one thing he knew for certain: The next shot's got to be for keeps.

❧

As it turned out, the men involved were called to court in Rockland, where the judge ordered each of them to post a hefty bond in an effort to stop their feuding. It worked . . . for a time.

Matinicus, Maine's most remote year-round occupied island at twenty miles out to sea, is no stranger to tense situations. The island was first inhabited, in 1750, by one Ebenezer Hall, a squatter who set to farming, burning the land for hay crops, and instigating trouble with the Penobscot Indians, who used the island to hunt. They wrote twice to authorities in Boston, asking for assistance. Receiving no replies, the fed-up Indians scalped and killed Hall in 1757.

Though no one has been scalped on Matinicus for quite some time, it is an insular place with a reputation for frontier justice, which the fifty or so year-round residents don't do much to downplay. Most problems usually arise because the island lobstermen want to protect the rich fishing grounds surrounding their island. Should someone find himself a newcomer in a tight lobstering community, and without close family ties to the region, which can help soften the transition period, more often than not the newcomer's buoys will be swiped, threatening notes may be placed in his traps, and then his trap lines may be cut, or traps may be damaged or mangled beyond repair. One man, prevented from fishing on Matinicus some years ago, showed an interesting bit of ingenuity by releasing raccoons on the island—the pests aren't native to the island and caused quite a mess.

Such squabbles, known as trap wars, have been around as long as lobstering has been a source of income. An elaborate system of lobster "gangs," each based in its own home port, exists up and down the New England working waterfront. Maine is home, by far, to the largest percentage of them. Maine's trap wars are among the more notable in the news, primarily because Maine has more coastline, more lobsters, and more lobster fishermen than the other New England states.

One of the largest trap wars came to a head in mid-August 1949 when the state of Maine called for an end to the violence raging up and down the coast. This widespread trap war had reached near-epic proportions, with more than 2,000 trap lines cut. The entire warden staff of the state's Sea and Shore Fisheries Department had been ordered to work overtime. The disputes were eventually settled, though not before boats were filled with garbage, wardens were shot at, docks were burned, and boats were sunk.

Trap wars are hardly a thing of the past. In the summer of 2009, a handful of hotheaded lobstermen from Matinicus made international news when one lobsterman shot another in the neck with a .22-caliber pistol because of a territorial dispute. A couple of weeks later, on the mainland at Owls Head, two lobster boats were sunk and another nearly so in a dispute over fishing territory.

Apparently, the more things change, at least where Maine lobstermen are concerned, the more they stay the same. Case in point: One old-time lobsterman, when asked why he refused to upgrade to a fiberglass boat, claimed that his old wooden boat would be better able to stop a bullet.

ART AND PHOTO CREDITS

Page 3: Mayflower approaching land, Johnson. Library of Congress, LC-USZ62-3046.

Page 8: Dungeon Rock, Lynn, Massachusetts. Library of Congress, LC-DIG-pga-02100.

Page 20: *Take Care of Yourself.* Illustration by Roy F. Heinrich, 1939. National Life Insurance Company.

Page 25: *The Witch No. 2.* George Walker. Library of Congress, LC-DIG-pga-02985.

Page 36: Boon Island Light Tower, Boon Island, York County, Maine. Library of Congress, HABS ME,16-BOONI,1–1.

Page 45: *A Buccaneer.* Illustration by Alfred Rudolph Waud. Library of Congress, LC-DIG-ppmsca-21120.

Page 56: *Do Women Need Life Insurance?* Illustration by Roy F. Heinrich, 1942. National Life Insurance Company.

Page 67: Hauling guns by ox teams from Fort Ticonderoga for the siege of Boston, 1775. National Archives (111-SC-100815).

Page 74: Colonel Benedict Arnold. Library of Congress, LC-USZC4-12377.

Page 100: Alexander Crowell, Barnard, Vermont, 1881. Library of Congress, LC-USZ62-98286.

Page 124: Crawford Notch from Willey Station, White Mountains. Library of Congress, LC-D4-11747.

Page 129: The wonderful fish. Illustration by Charles A. Barry. Library of Congress, LC-USZ62-127763.

Page 154: Woodsmen playing cards in the bunkhouse, Maine. Library of Congress, LC-USW3-030238-C.

Page 161: The Great Blizzard of March 12, 1888, Farmington, Connecticut. National Oceanic and Atmospheric Administration/ Department of Commerce.

Page 172: The Borden murder trial. *Frank Leslie's Illustrated Weekly,* June 29, 1893. Illustration by B. West Clinedinst. Library of Congress, LC-USZ62-123237.

Page 179: Hauling lobster pots off Cape Ann, Massachusetts. From a photograph by T. W. Smillie. National Oceanic and Atmospheric Administration/Department of Commerce.

Page 184: Hauling logs near Waterbury, Vermont. Library of Congress, LC-USF34-053624-D.

Page 191: Between decks. *Frank Leslie's Illustrated Newspaper,* September 5, 1885. Library of Congress, LC-USZ62-122654.

Page 196: Spring pulpwood drive, Mooselookmeguntic Lake, Maine. Library of Congress, LC-USW3-030649-E.

Page 213: Landing and scaling logs, Aroostook County, Maine. Library of Congress, LC-USZC2-6213.

Page 218: Jacob's Ladder, Mount Washington Cog Railway, White Mountains, New Hampshire. Library of Congress, LC-D4-11834.

Page 227: Confiscated whiskey. Library of Congress, LC-USZ62-96026.

Page 234: Policeman with a wrecked car and cases of moonshine. Library of Congress, LC-USZ62-96757.

Page 239: Remains of a bootlegger's Stutz touring car. Library of Congress, LC-USZ62-96152.

Page 244: Oceangoing rumrunner caught by U.S. Coast Guard. Library of Congress, LC-USZ62-42087.

Page 249: The rumrunner *Linwood* afire, 1923. U.S. Coast Guard. Photo No. 5-4-23N.

Page 257: Brady Gang, Central Street, Bangor, Maine, October 12, 1937. *Bangor (Maine) Daily News* File Photo.

Page 261: Whale Rock Lighthouse. U.S. Coast Guard.

Page 272: Lobster boats, Stonington, Maine. Photograph by Jennifer Smith-Mayo.

BIBLIOGRAPHY

Acheson, James M. *Capturing the Commons: Devising Institutions to Manage the Maine Lobster Industry.* Lebanon, NH: University Press of New England, 2003.

———. *The Lobster Gangs of Maine.* Hanover, NH: University Press of New England, 1988.

Allen, Everett S. *The Black Ships: Rumrunners of Prohibition.* New York: Little, Brown, 1979.

Balkan, Evan. *Shipwrecked! Deadly Adventures and Disasters at Sea.* Birmingham, AL: Menasha Ridge, 2008.

Barker, Capt. F. C. *Lake and Forest as I Have Known Them.* Boston, MA: Lothrop, Lee & Shepard, 1903.

Bell, Michael E. *Food for the Dead: On the Trail of New England's Vampires.* New York: Carroll & Graf, 2001.

Bellamy, John Stark, II. *Vintage Vermont Villainies: True Tales of Murder and Mystery from the 19th and 20th Centuries.* Woodstock, VT: Countryman Press, 2007.

Bellesiles, Michael A. *Revolutionary Outlaws: Ethan Allen and the Struggle for Independence on the Early American Frontier.* Charlottesville: University Press of Virginia, 1993.

Blanton, DeAnne, and Lauren M. Cook. *They Fought Like Demons: Women Soldiers in the American Civil War.* Baton Rouge: Louisiana State University Press, 2002.

Boylan, Brian Richard. *Benedict Arnold: The Dark Eagle.* New York: W. W. Norton, 1973.

Buker, George E. *The Penobscot Expedition: Commodore Saltonstall and the Massachusetts Conspiracy of 1779.* Annapolis, MD: Naval Institute Press, 2002.

Butler, Joyce. *Wildfire Loose: The Week Maine Burned.* Camden, ME: Down East Books, 1997.

Campbell, Susan, and Bruce Gellerman. *The Big Book of New England Curiosities: From Orange, CT, to Blue Hill, ME, a Guide to the Quirkiest, Oddest, and Most Unbelievable Stuff You'll See.* Guilford, CT: Globe Pequot Press, 2009.

Carse, Robert. *Rum Row.* Mystic, CT: Flat Hammock Press, 2007.

Chenoweth, James. *Oddity Odyssey: A Journey Through New England's Colorful Past.* New York: Henry Holt, 1996.

Citro, Joseph A. *Green Mountains, Dark Tales.* Lebanon, NH: University Press of New England, 2001.

———. *Passing Strange: True Tales of New England Hauntings and Horrors.* New York: Mariner Books, 1997.

Clark, Charles E. *The Meetinghouse Tragedy.* Hanover, NH: University Press of New England, 1998.

Clifford, Barry. *Expedition Whydah: The Story of the World's First Excavation of a Pirate Treasure Ship and the Man Who Found Her.* New York: HarperCollins, 1999.

Cole, John N. *Maine Trivia.* Nashville, TN: Rutledge Hill Press, 1998.

Coolidge, Philip T. *History of the Maine Woods.* Bangor, ME: Furbush-Roberts Printing, 1966.

Corbett, Scott. *The Sea Fox: The Adventures of Cape Cod's Most Colorful Rumrunner.* New York: Thomas Y. Crowell, 1956.

Cordingly, David. *Women Sailors and Sailors' Women.* New York: Random House, 2001.

Corson, Trevor. *The Secret Life of Lobsters: How Fishermen and Scientists Are Unraveling the Mysteries of Our Favorite Crustacean.* New York: HarperCollins, 2004.

Cottle, Samuel S. *In Danger at Sea: Adventures of a New England Fishing Family.* Camden, ME: Down East Books, 2007.

Cowan, Mary Morton. *Timberrr!: A History of Logging in New England.* Brookfield, CT: Millbrook Press, 2003.

Cronon, William. *Changes in the Land: Indians, Colonists and the Ecology of New England*. New York: Hill and Wang/Farrar, Straus & Giroux, 1983.

Druett, John. *She Captains: Heroines and Hellions of the Sea*. New York: Simon & Schuster, 2000.

Eaton, Louis Woodbury. *Pork, Molasses and Timber: Stories of Bygone Days in the Logging Camps of Maine*. New York: Exposition Press, 1954.

Eckstorm, Fannie Hardy. *Penobscot Man*. Fannie Hardy Eckstorm, 1931.

Emerson, Marie, ed. *St. Croix Cuisine*. Calais, ME: Calais Press Printing, 2004.

Feintuch, Burt, and David H. Watters, eds. *The Encyclopedia of New England*. New Haven, CT: Yale University Press, 2005.

Fennelly, Catherine, ed. *Architecture in Early New England*. Sturbridge, MA: Old Sturbridge Village, 1967.

Fleming, Thomas. *Liberty! The American Revolution*. New York: Viking/Penguin, 1997.

Formisano, Ron. *The Great Lobster War*. Amherst: University of Massachusetts Press, 1997.

Freedman, Lew. *The Way We Were New England: Nostalgic Images of America's Northeast*. Guilford, CT: Globe Pequot Press, 2009.

Garland, Joseph E. *Eastern Point: A Nautical, Rustical, and Social Chronicle of Gloucester's Outer Shield and Inner Sanctum, 1606–1950*. Peterborough, NH: Noone House, 1971.

Greenlaw, Linda. *The Lobster Chronicles: Life on a Very Small Island*. New York: Hyperion, 2002.

Hall, Richard. *Patriots in Disguise: Women Warriors of the Civil War*. New York: Paragon House, 1993.

Hansen, Harry, ed. *New England Legends and Folklore*. New York: Hastings House, 1967.

Hempstead, Alfred Geer. *The Penobscot Boom and the Development of the West Branch of the Penobscot River of Log Driving, 1825–1931.* Alfred Geer Hempstead, 1975.

Higginson, Thomas Wentworth. *Travelers and Outlaws: Episodes in American History.* New York: Lee and Shepard, 1889.

Hill, Ralph Nading. *Yankee Kingdom: Vermont and New Hampshire.* New York: Harper & Bros., 1960.

Holbrook, Stewart. *Holy Old Mackinaw: A Natural History of the American Lumberjack.* Sausalito, CA: Comstock Editions, 1956.

Holbrook, Stewart H. *Yankee Loggers: A Recollection of Woodsmen, Cooks, and River Drivers.* New York: International Paper Company, 1961.

Howe, Nicholas. *Not Without Peril: 150 Years of Misadventure on the Presidential Range of New Hampshire.* Boston: AMC Books, 2001.

Hunt, C. W. *Whisky and Ice: The Saga of Ben Kerr, Canada's Most Daring Rumrunner.* Toronto, Ontario: Dundurn Press, 1995.

Johnson, Claudia Durst. *Daily Life in Colonial New England.* Westport, CT: Greenwood Press, 2002.

Jones, Eric. *New Hampshire Curiosities: Quirky Characters, Roadside Oddities and Other Offbeat Stuff.* Guilford, CT: Globe Pequot Press, 2006.

Jordan, Charles J. *Tales Told in the Shadows of the White Mountains.* Lebanon, NH: University Press of New England, 2003.

Kramer, Barbara. *Images of America: Belfast and Searsport.* Dover, NH: Arcadia Publishing, 1997.

Lemke, Karen. *Down East Detective: True Stories of the Maine State Police.* Augusta, ME: Blue Heron/Lance Tapley, 1987.

Lemke, William. *The Wild, Wild East: Unusual Tales of Maine History.* Camden, ME: Yankee Books, 1990.

Lippincott, Bertram. *Indians, Privateers, and High Society: A Rhode Island Sampler.* New York: J. B. Lippincott, 1961.

Lisle, Janet Taylor. *Black Duck.* New York: Philomel/Penguin, 2006.

McCain, Diana Ross. *Mysteries and Legends of New England: True Stories of the Unsolved and Unexplained.* Guilford, CT: Globe Pequot Press, 2009.

McDevitt, Neale, ed. *Eyewitness Travel Guides New England.* New York: Dorling Kindersley Publishing, 2001.

Moray, Alastair. *The Diary of a Rum-Runner.* London: P. Allen, 1929.

Morison, Samuel Eliot. *The Maritime History of Massachusetts, 1783–1860.* Boston: Northeastern University Press, 1979.

Mosher, Howard Frank. *Disappearances: A Novel.* New York: Mariner Books, 2006.

Murphy, Martha Watson. *A New England Fish Tale: Seafood Recipes and Observations of a Way of Life from a Fisherman's Wife.* New York: Henry Holt, 1997.

Murray, Stuart. *Eyewitness Books: American Revolution.* New York: Dorling Kindersley Publishing, 2002.

Nowland, Alden. *Campobello: The Outer Island.* Toronto, Ontario: Clarke, Irwin, 1975.

Oliver, Sandra L. *Saltwater Foodways: New Englanders and Their Food, at Sea and Ashore, in the Nineteenth Century.* Mystic, CT: Mystic Seaport Museum, 1995.

Oppel, Frank, ed. *Tales of the New England Coast.* Secaucus, NJ: Castle Books, 1985.

Pettengill, Samuel B. *The Yankee Pioneers: A Saga of Courage.* Rutland, VT: Charles E. Tuttle, 1971.

Philbrook, Kate, and Rob Rosenthal. *Malaga Island: A Story Best Left Untold.* [Photo and radio documentary; www.malagaislandmaine.org.] WMPG FM and Salt Institute for Documentary Studies, 2008.

Philips, David E. *Legendary Connecticut: Traditional Tales from the Nutmeg State.* Willimantic, CT: Curbstone Press, 1992.

Pike, Robert E. *Spiked Boots: Tales of Logging in New England.* Woodstock, VT: Countryman Press, 2008.

———. *Tall Trees, Tough Men: A Vivid, Anecdotal History of Logging and Log-Driving in New England.* New York: W. W. Norton, 1999.

Puleo, Stephen. *Dark Tide: The Great Boston Molasses Flood of 1919.* Boston: Beacon Press, 2003.

Quinn, William P. *Shipwrecks around New England: A Chronology of Marine Accidents and Disasters from Grand Manan to Sandy Hook.* Orleans, MA: Lower Cape Publishing, 1979.

Rapaport, Diane. *The Naked Quaker: True Crimes and Controversies from the Courts of Colonial New England.* Beverly, MA: Commonwealth Editions, 2007.

Rogak, Lisa. *Stones and Bones of New England: A Guide to Unusual, Historic, and Otherwise Notable Cemeteries.* Guilford, CT: Globe Pequot Press, 2004.

Rolde, Neil/WCBB. *So You Think You Know Maine.* Gardiner, ME: Harpswell Press, 1984.

Rondina, Christopher. *Vampires of New England.* Cape Cod, MA: On Cape Publications, 2008.

Russell, Howard S. *A Long, Deep Furrow: Three Centuries of Farming in New England.* Hanover, NH: University Press of New England, 1982.

Schlosser, S. E. *Spooky New England: Tales of Hauntings, Strange Happenings, and Other Local Lore.* Guilford, CT: Globe Pequot Press, 2003.

Seavey, Wendell. *Working the Sea: Misadventures, Ghost Stories, and Life Lessons from a Maine Lobsterfisherman.* Berkeley, CA: North Atlantic Books, 2005.

Sherr, Lynn, and Jurate Kazickas. *Susan B. Anthony Slept Here: A Guide to American Women's Landmarks.* New York: Times Books/Random House, 1994.

Silverstein, Stu, and Richard Searls. *Dead River Rough Cut: A Woods Movie* [DVD]. Stu Silverstein and Richard Searls, 2002.

Simons, D. Brenton. *Witches, Rakes, and Rogues: True Stories of Scam, Scandal, Murder, and Mayhem in Boston, 1630–1775.* Beverly, MA: Commonwealth Editions, 2005.

Sloane, Eric. *Diary of an Early American Boy: Noah Blake, 1805*. New York: Ballantine Books, 1965.

Smith, David C. *A History of Lumbering in Maine, 1861–1960*. Orono: University of Maine Press, 1972.

Smith, Joshua M. *Borderland Smuggling: Patriots, Loyalists, and Illicit Trade in the Northeast, 1783–1820*. Gainesville: University Press of Florida, 2006.

Smithsonian Guide to Historic America: Northern New England. New York: Stewart, Tabori & Chang, 1989.

Smithsonian Guide to Historic America: Southern New England. New York: Stewart, Tabori & Chang, 1989.

Snow, Edward Rowe. *Tales of Terror and Tragedy*. New York: Dodd, Mead, 1980.

St. Antoine, Sara, ed. *Stories from Where We Live: The North Atlantic Coast*. Minneapolis, MN: Milkweed Editions, 2000.

Stanley, Jo, ed. *Bold in Her Breeches: Women Pirates Across the Ages*. New York: HarperCollins, 1995.

Starbuck, David R., ed. *Historical New Hampshire*, vol. 49, no. 4, Winter 1994. Concord: New Hampshire Historical Society, 1994.

Stark, Suzanne J. *Female Tars: Women Aboard Ship in the Age of Sail*. Annapolis, MD: Naval Institute Press, 1996.

Stevens, Peter F. *Notorious and Notable New Englanders*. Camden, ME: Down East Books, 1997.

Teller, Walter M., ed. *Twelve Works of Naïve Genius*. New York: Harcourt Brace Jovanovich, 1972.

Thorndike, Virginia L. *Maine Lobsterboats: Builders and Lobstermen Speak of Their Craft*. Camden, ME: Down East Books, 1998.

Titler, Dale M. *Unnatural Resources: True Stories of American Treasure*. Englewood Cliffs, NJ: Prentice-Hall, 1973.

Tougias, Michael J. *Fatal Forecast: An Incredible True Tale of Disaster and Survival at Sea*. New York: Scribner, 2007.

Van Winkle, Ted. *Fred Boynton, Lobsterman, New Harbor, Maine.* Camden, ME: International Marine Publishing, 1975.

Vaughan, Alden T. *New England Encounters: Indians and Euroamericans, ca. 1600–1850.* Lebanon, NH: University Press of New England, 1999.

———. *New England Frontier: Puritans and Indians, 1620–1675.* Norman: University of Oklahoma Press, 1995.

Vietze, Andrew. *Insider's Guide to the Maine Coast,* 2nd ed. Guilford, CT: Globe Pequot Press, 2007.

Warren, Rusty. *Days in the Life of a Fisherman's Wife.* Rockland, ME: Island Institute, 2000.

Waugh, Charles G. *Lighthouse Horrors: Tales of Adventure, Suspense, and the Supernatural.* Camden, ME: Down East Books, 1993.

Weir, William. *Written with Lead: America's Most Famous and Notorious Gunfights from the Revolutionary War to Today.* New York: Cooper Square Press, 2003.

Wells, Robert W. *Daylight in the Swamp! Lumberjacking in the Late 19th Century.* Garden City, NY: Doubleday, 1978.

Welner, Stacy L. *Tragedy in Casco Bay.* Harpswell, ME: Anchor Publishing, 2006.

Wheeler, Scott. *Rumrunners and Revenuers: Prohibition in Vermont.* Shelburne, VT: New England Press, 2002.

Wilbur, C. Keith, M.D. *New England Indians: An Informed and Fascinating Account of the 18 Major Tribes That Lived in Pre-Colonial New England,* 2nd. ed. Guilford, CT: Globe Pequot Press, 1996.

Williams, Mark S. *F/V Black Sheep.* Gloucester, MA: Silver Perch Press, 2006.

Willoughby, Malcolm F. *Rum War at Sea.* Amsterdam, Netherlands: Fredonia Books, 2001.

Wilson, Donald A. *Images of America: Logging and Lumbering in Maine.* Charleston, SC: Arcadia Publishing, 2001.

Winslow, Dena Lynn, Ph.D. *They Lynched Jim Cullen: New England's Only Lynching.* Presque Isle, ME: Sleepy Hollow Publishing, 2000.

Wood, Pamela, ed. *The Salt Book*. New York: Anchor Books, 1977.

———. *Salt 2*. New York: Anchor Books, 1980.

Woodard, Colin. *The Lobster Coast: Rebels, Rusticators, and the Struggle for a Forgotten Frontier*. New York: Viking/Penguin, 2004.

Young, Alfred F. *Masquerade: The Life and Times of Deborah Sampson, Continental Soldier*. New York: Alfred A. Knopf, 2004.

INDEX

A

Abbott, William, 151
Abenaki (First Nations people)
   American Indian tribe, xix
   attack on Boscawen settlement, 29–30
   Candelmas Massacre (1692), 18–22
   Skinner's Cave legend, 110
   taking white captives, 31–33
   use of eugenics toward, 210
Acadia National Park (Maine), xix
Adams, John Quincy, 43
Addie E. Snow (sailing ship), 193
Agent 146 (Gimpel), 268
alcohol. *See* Prohibition era
Alden, John (pilgrim, father), 5
Alden, John (son), 22
Alderman, John, 17
Allen, David, 122, 126
Allen, Ethan, 59
Allen, Ira, 59
Allerton, Bartholomew, 1
Allerton, Isaac (pilgrim), 1–2, 5
Allerton, Mary (daughter), 5
Allerton, Mary (mother), 1–2
Allerton, Remember, 1
American Civil War, St. Albens Raid,
   137–41
American Revolution
   Ann Story and the Green Mountain
     Boys, 54–59
   Army service of Deborah Samson,
     79–84
   Arnold raid on Quebec City, 22
   Battle of Bunker Hill, 65
   Battle of Ridgefield, 73–78
   capture of *HMS Margaretta*, 65
   enduring life as returning soldier, 93–94
   Penobscot Expedition of 1779, 65
   siege of Boston, 66–72
   siege of Quebec City, 78

   use of *Turtle* (submarine), 268–69
"An Act for Human Betterment Through
   Voluntary Sterilization," 210
Anderson, George (logger), 211–12
Androscoggin River, 216
Arnold, Benedict, 22, 73–75, 77–78
Aroostook Woods (Maine), 213
Ashby, W. T., 146–47
Ashton, Philip (pirate captive), 48–49

B

Baker, Remember, 59
Bangor, Maine, 253–58
Bar Harbor, Maine, 265
Barber, Charles A. (logger), 200
Barnard, Vermont, 100–101
Barr, Jack (logger), 212
Barton River Valley (Vermont), 111–15
Barton Village, Vermont, 114
Battle of Bunker Hill, 65
Battle of Ridgefield (Conn.), 73–78
Beavertail Lighthouse Museum (Rhode
   Island), 263
Bellamy, Samuel "Black Sam" (pirate
   captain), 40–43
Bence, Eli, 171
Bender, Margaret, 88
Bennington, Vermont, 99
Berlin, Vermont, 201
Biggs, Maynard, 137–38
Bird, Minot, 142–44
Bissunda (sailing ship), 86
Black Duck on Rum Row, 243–47
Black Point (coal ship), 269
Black Snake smuggling affair, 102–6
Blackbeard the pirate (Edward Teach), 45
Blanchard, Hollis H. (ship captain), 189–93
Blanchard, Nathaniel (ship captain),
   130–32
Blaney, Joseph (shark food), 128–32

blizzards. *See* weather

Block Island, Rhode Island, 165, 193, 269

Blue Hill Observatory (Mass.), 264

Boon Island lighthouse, 34–39

bootlegging. *See* Prohibition era

Borden, Andrew and Abby, 171–76

Borden, Emma, 173–76

Borden, Lizzie (ax murderer), 171–76

Boscawen, New Hampshire, 29–30, 33

Bosse, Dan (dynamiter), 214–15

Boston, Mass.

    bootlegging operations, 247

    British occupation of, 66

    Great Blizzard of 1888, 165

    molasses disaster of 1919, 222–25

Brady, Al (gangster), 254–58

Bridgeport, Connecticut, 258

Brinkman, Ralph, 24

British Army, 13–17. *See also* American
    Revolution

Brookfield, Vermont, 95–98

Brooklin, Maine, 230

Brown, Edwin, 167, 170

Brown, George, 166–70

Brown, Mary, 170

Brown, Mary Olive, 170

Brown, Mercy Lena (vampire), 167–70

"A Buccaneer" (Waud), 45

Bull, Dixie (pirate captain), 45

Bunker, Jack (colonist), 60–65

Burlington, Vermont, 104

Burton, Hulda, 170

Burton, Rachel, 170

Bushnell, David, 268

Butterworth, Mary (criminal), 89

Buzzard's Bay, Massachusetts, 132

C

Cambridge, Mass., 71–72

Canada

    Confederate raid on Vermont, 137–41

    Fenians (Irish) seizure of, 141

    forced march of captives to, 21–22,
        31–33

    fugitive slaves escaping to, 105

    Old Sow Whirlpool, 135

    siege of Quebec City, 78

    smuggling operations from, 107–10, 231

    smuggling operations to, 102–6

    See also Prohibition era

Candelmas Massacre (1692), 18–22

cannibalism, 36–37

Canonchet (Narragansett chief), 13

Cape Ann, Massachusetts, 179

Cape Cod, Mass., 5

Cape Porpoise, Maine, 177–81

Captain Pedro (pirate captain), 88–89

Carver, John (pilgrim), 1–2

Casco Bay (Maine), 209

Castine, Maine, 65

Caswell, Norman (bus driver), 261–63

Catamount Tavern (Bennington, Vt.), 99

CGC *Acushnet* (Coast Guard cutter), 247

Chaffee, Cecil (drowning victim), 135

Chamberlain, Spencer, 112, 115

Charlene W. (lobster boat), 226

Charles City, Iowa, 147

Charlton (customs officer), 107–9

Chellis, Carl (Mr. and Mrs.), 262–63

Chellis, Clayton, 262–63

Chellis, Marion, 263

Cherryfield, Maine, 200

Chesuncook Lake (Maine), 205

Civil War, St. Albens Raid, 137–41

Clark, Louis, 253–56

Clauson, Harry (slideboarder), 217–20

Clifford, Barry (ocean explorer), 43

Cole, Eunice "Goody" (convicted witch), 27

Colebrook, New Hampshire, 117

Colepaugh, William (German spy), 265–68

Conanicut Island (Rhode Island), 260

Conlon, James, 204–5

Connecticut

    Battle of Ridgefield, 73–78

    slave population, 209

Connecticut River, 197–200, 211–16

Connecticut Valley Lumber Company
    (CVL), 197, 214

Conway, New Hampshire, 157

Corey, Giles (accused witch), 23–27

Corey, Mary (accused witch), 23, 25, 27

Cornell, Alexander (Coast Guard), 243–46

Cornwallis (Canadian freighter), 267

Corwin, George (sheriff), 23–28

Crawford Notch (New Hampshire), 122–26

Crowell, Alexander, 100–101

Crowley, Thomas (police chief), 254

cruel and unusual punishment

    dismemberment and
        disembowelment, 17

    eaten by sharks, 128–32

    enduring life in wilderness, 90–94

    massacre of Indian women and
        children, 14–16

    scalpings, 19–20, 32–33

    sterilization of Native Americans, 210

    torture and brutality of "Ned" Low,
        44–49

    treatment of mixed-race populations,
        206–10

    for witchcraft, 25–27

Cullen, "Big Jim," 142–47

Cullen, Jim, 147

D

D. H. Hodgkins (sailing ship), 247

Dalhover, Rhuel James (gangster), 253–58

Davis, Thomas (sailor), 43

Dean, Cyrus B. (smuggler), 104

deaths

    Candelmas Massacre (1692), 18–22

    collapse of Wilton meeting house, 50–53

    eaten by sharks, 128–32

    enduring hardship of frontier life, 90–94

    freezing during winter, 201–5

    Great Blizzard of 1888, 159–65

    Great Earthquake of 1658, 7–12

    Great Swamp Fight of 1675, 13–17

    gunning down Brady Gang, 256–58

    at the hand of pirates, 44–49

    by hanging, 88–89, 146–47

    hatchet murder by "Big Jim" Cullen,
        142–44

    hatchet murders by Lizzie Borden,
        171–76

    Hurricane of the Century, 259–64

    Indian attacks on whites, 29–33

    from landslides, 122–27

Mount Washington Cog Railway,
    217–21

North Woods logging, 153–58, 183–86,
    199–200, 216

Old Sow Whirlpool drownings, 133–36

poisoned bootleg whiskey, 252

rumrunners & bootleggers, 238–42,
    244–46

Salem witch trials, 23–28

shipwrecks, 34–43

sinking of *USS Portland*, 193

starvation and disease, 1–6

traffic accidents, 151–52

train wrecks, 148–51

from tuberculosis, 166–70, 207–8

Dent, Grubby (logger), 186

Devil's Shingles (slideboards), 217–20

Dibble, Nehemia, 77

Dillinger, John (gangster), 258

"Do Women Need Life Insurance?"
    (Heinrich), 56

Dow, Neal S. "Father of Temperance,"
    246–47

Drake, Ellis, 102–3

Duffy, Bill, 223

Dungeon Rock, 9–12

Duston, Hannah (Indian captive), 28–33

Duston, Martha, 28–29

Duston, Thomas, 28, 33

E

East Thompson, Connecticut, 151

Eastport, Maine, 129, 132, 133

Eberle, Agnes, 259–60

Eberle, Walter (lighthouse keeper), 259–
    60, 263

Embargo Act of 1807, 102–6, 107

Emerson, Elizabeth (murderer), 33

Empire Knight (British freighter), 39

English, Phillip (accused witch), 27–28

eugenics, practice of, 210

F

Fall River, Mass., 89, 171–76

Farmington, Connecticut, 161

Farrington, Daniel, 102–3

Fasles (Jesuit Fr.), 22
Federal Bureau of Investigation (FBI)
    capture of German spies, 267–68
    "Most Wanted" list, 257–58
Felton, Horace, 111
Fenians (Irish) seizure of Canada, 141
Fifteen-Mile Falls, 216
Finback (sailing ship), 130–32
Flour War of 1809, 231
Flucker (Mr. and Mrs.), 72
Forni, Mary, 268
Fort Crown Point, 59
Fort George, 68
Fort Saint-Jean, 59
Fort Ticonderoga
    capture of, 59
    hauling cannon to Boston, 66–71
    retreat from Quebec City, 78
Frenchman's Bay (Maine), 265
Fundy Star II (fishing boat), 136

G

Gannett, Benjamin, 84
Garnette, Dicky (sailor), 87
Gilman, Solomon, 99
Gimpel, Erich (German spy), 265–68
Glover Day (Vermont), 115
Goat Island (Rhode Island), 48
Goulart, Johnny (rumrunner), 244–46
Grafton, Vermont, 94
Granby, Vermont, 121
Graves, Clarence, 95–96
Graves, Emma, 95
Graves, Esther (frontier woman), 95–98
Great Blizzard of 1888 (Great White
    Hurricane), 159–65
Great Blizzard of 1978, 36, 39
Great Colonial Hurricane of 1635, 264
Great Earthquake of 1658, 9–12
Great September Gale of 1815, 264
Great Swamp Fight (Rhode Island, 1675),
    xvii
Green Mountain Boys, 57–59
Green Mountains (Vermont), xviii, 105
Greenfield, Mass., 237
Griffin, Lew, 145

H

Hallet, Maria "Goody," 40, 43
Hamlin, Emma, 55
Hamlin, Esther (Indian captive), 55
Hammond, Beulah and Raymond, 159–60,
    163–64
Hammond, Wilfred, 159
Hammond, William (shipwrecked sailor),
    34–38
Hancock, John, 84
Hancock, Maine, 267
Harlow, Jim, 10–11
Harlow, Lucas, 7
Harmon, Russell (lobsterman), 177
Harpswell, Maine, 209
Harry Knowlton (sailing ship), 193
Hartford, Vermont, 148
Haverhill, Mass., 33
Hayden, Granville (sheriff), 142–44
Heinrich, Roy F. (artist), 20, 56
Hereford, Quebec, 242
HMS Beagle (British ship), 268–69
HMS Greyhound, 48
HMS Margaretta, 65
Hodgkins, Harvard, 268
Hooke, John (pilgrim), 1
Howe, William (British general), 71–72
Hubbard, William (deputy sheriff), 142–44
Hubbell, Hallie, 90–93
Hubbell, Hortense, 93
Hubbell, Seth, 90–94
Hughes, Ben (constable), 144–45
Hunt, Thomas (slave trader), 209
Hurd, Everett, 253–56
Hurricane of the Century (1938), 259–64

I

Isle of Shoals (Mass.), 85–87
Islesboro, Maine, 226
Izard, Lawrence (customs officer), 105–6

J

Jacob's Ladder (Mount Washington), 218
Jamestown, Rhode Island, 263
Jasper, Hank (lumberjack), 153
Jefferson, Thomas, 102, 104

Jenkins, Pal and Mort, Jr. (lobstermen), 270–75
Jenny, Ezekial (Tory sympathizer), 56–58
Johnson, Albert Lewis "Jigger" (logging legend), 194–200
Johnson, Andrew (president), 141
Julian, John "Julian, the Indian" (pirate), 40–43

K

Keeler Tavern (Ridgefield, Conn.), 77
Kidd, William "Captain" (pirate captain), 89
King Philip. *See* Metacomet
King Philip's War, 16–17
Knox, Henry, 66–72
Knox, John, 68
Knox, Lucy Flucker, 72

L

Lake Champlain, 105–6
Lake Memphremagog (Vermont), 107–10, 114–15
Lancey, Elizabeth, 50–51, 53
Lancey, George, 50–51, 53
Lavigne, Armand (customs officer), 105–6
LeBeau (lumber camp boss), 185–86
Lennardson, Samuel (Indian captive), 31–33
Leverett, John, 18, 22
Linwood (rumrunner), 249
lobstering/lobster industry
    protecting future of, 177–82
    rum running by lobstermen, 226–31
    trap wars and feuds, 270–76
logging/lumberjacking
    hanging boots in trees, 199–200
    hauling logs at ice-out, 183–86
    last great long-log drive, 211–16
    legend of Jigger Johnson, 194–200
    Logger's smallpox, 199
    logging camp operations, 187
    New England reputation for, xx
    North Woods winter, 153–58
    teamster duties, 187–88
Long Island, New York, 264

Long Pond (Vermont), 111–15
Longfellow Mountains (Maine), xviii
long-log drives, 215–16
Lonigan, Jack (slideboarder), 217–20
Low, Edward "Ned" (pirate captain), 44–49
Lubec, Maine, 231
Ludlow, Vermont, 204
lynching of "Big Jim" Cullen, 142–47
Lynn, Mass., 7–9
Lynn Woods (Dungeon Rock), 11–12

M

Machias, Maine, 65
Machias River, 216
Mackerel Point (Rhode Island), 260
MacMawe, Rafe (shipwrecked sailor), 34–38
Macomber, Jason, 19, 21
Madison, Maine, 22
Madockawando (Penobscot warrior), 18
Maine
    Acadia National Park, xix
    Arnold expedition to Quebec, 78
    Boon Island lighthouse, 34–39
    Chesuncook Lake, 205
    downeast coastline, 64–65
    lobster industry, 177–82, 270–76
    Longfellow Mountains, xviii
    Malaga Island, 206–10
    Old Sow Whirlpool, 133–36
    sharks in water of, 129, 132
    Spring pulp wood drive, 196
    wild animals of, 99
Maine Lobsterman's Association, 182
Maine School for the Feeble Minded, 206–10
Maliseet (First Nations people), 22
Malloy, Rene and Philip, 242
Manhattan Project (weapons program), 268
Mapleton, Maine, 142–45
Marble, Edwin, 11–12
Marble, Hiram, 11–12
Marlow, New Hampshire, 151
Marsh, Asa, 103
Marsh, Sylvester, 220
Marshfield, Vermont, 99

Mary Anne (pirate ship), 40
Mary Ellen (rumrummer), 248–51
Massachusetts
  hanging of pirate Rachel Wells, 88
  Hannah Duston scalps her captors,
    29–33
  lobster industry, 182
  Salem witch trials, 23–28
  slave population, 209
Massachusetts Bay, shark attack, 128–32
Matinicus Island (Maine), 275–76
Matoes, Joseph, Sr., 260–63
Mayflower , arrival in New England, 1–5
McCafferty, Clayton and Lucy, 162–63
McCorcoran, Duncan, 222–24
McPheeter, Jack "Tippy" (teamster),
    153–57
Metacomet (aka King Philip, Wampanoag
    chief), 13–17
Metcalf, Harold (Dr.), 167–69
Miery Swamp (Rhode Island), 17
Mi'kmaq (First Nations people), 22
Miller Falls, Mass., 204
Milton, Mass., 264
Minneman, Paul (police officer), 256–57
Mitchell, James Roland (drowning victim),
    135–36
Mohegan (First Nations people), xix, 13–17
Montgomery, Richard (Revolutionary
    officer), 78
Mooselookmeguntic Lake (Maine), 158
Morse, John, 173
Moulton, Jeremiah, 18–22
Mount Mansfield (Vermont), 127
Mount Tambora (Indonesia), 116, 120
Mount Washington Cog Railway, 217–21
Mount Washington (New Hampshire),
    xviii–xix
Mulliken's Pitch, 216
Mullins, Priscilla (pilgrim), 4, 5
Murdock, Henry (rumrunner), 233–36

N

Napatree Point (Narragansett Bay), 263
Narragansett (First Nations people), xix,
    13–17

Narragansett Bay (Rhode Island)
  aircraft attack on boat, 152
  Black Duck affair, 243–46
  Whale Rock Lighthouse, 259–61
Native Americans
  assistance to Pilgrims, xix, 5
  bounty on Indian scalps, 32–33
  Candelmas Massacre (1692), 18–22
  Great Swamp Massacre, 13–17
  treatment by Pilgrims, 6
  use of eugenics toward, 210
  white enslavement of, 5–6, 17, 43, 209
  See also individual tribes
Neff, Mary (Indian captive), 28–33
New Albion, naming of, xix
New England
  arrival of *Mayflower*, 1–5
  freezing to death during winter, 201–5
  frozen summer of 1816, 116–21
  geographical definition, xviii–xix
  Great Blizzard of 1888, 159–65
  lobster industry, 182
  lobster trap wars and feuds, 275–76
  long-log drives, 215–16
  Native American tribes, xix
  North Woods logging, 157–58, 183–88
  origins of name, xix
  racial persecution, 209–10
  regional reputation, xvii–xviii, 264
  Rum Row, 227, 244, 248–49, 251–52
  slave trade, 209
  smuggling operations, 102–6
  See also individual states
New England Power Company, 216
New Hampshire
  Crawford Notch, 122–26
  Mount Washington, xviii–xix
  White Mountains, xviii
New York City, 165
Newcomb, Lippy (logger), 195
Newport, Rhode Island, 48, 269
Newport, Vermont, 110
Nickerson, David, 122, 126
No Man's Island (Maine), 274
nor'easters. *See* weather
Norridgewock (First Nations people), 22

North Haven, Maine, 226
North Stratford, Vermont, 211–16
North Woods. *See* logging/lumberjacking
Northeast Kingdom (Vermont), 115
Norton Mills, Vermont, 242
Norwood, Abner & Robert (drowning victims), 133–36
Norwood, Rhode Island, 152
Nottingham Galley, shipwreck of, 34–39

O

"Ocean Born Mary," 89
Old Peppersass (cog railway engine), 218, 220–21
Old Sow Whirlpool (Maine), 133–36
Operation Magpie, 265–68
Orleans, Mass., 269
Ormsby, Jonathan, 103
Owl's Head Mountain House (Vermont), 110

P

Papineau, Oliver, 127
Park, Rebecca, 94
Park, Thomas, Jr., 94
Passamaquoddy (First Nations people), xix, 22
Passamaquoddy Bay (Maine), 133, 231
Passamaquoddy Tidal Power Project, 136
Patterson, John (Revolutionary general), 82–83
Patuxet (First Nations people), 209
Patuxet (Wampanoag village), 5
Pearl Harbor, Japanese attack on, 65
Pearson, Shaun (lumberjack), 155–57
Pease, George, 206–7
Penobscot (First Nations people), xix, 22
Penobscot Expedition of 1779, 65
Penobscot River, 216
Pequot (First Nations people), 13–17
Pereera, Papa (bootlegger), 249
Perkins (ship captain), 35–37
Perry Falls (Vermont), 211
Perth Amboy (tugboat), 269
Phair, James (sheriff), 145–46
Philadelphia, Pennsylvania, 165

Phinney, Barnabas (Dr.), 83
Phippsburg, Maine, 209
Phips, William (governor of Mass.), 28
Pike, Vern (log drive boss), 211–15
Pilgrims
    arrival of *Mayflower*, 1–5
    deaths from starvation and disease, 1–2, 4–5
    survival with Indian assistance, xix, 5–6
    Thanksgiving celebration, 5
pirates/pirating
    arrival at Lynn, Mass., 7–9
    brutality of Captain "Ned" Low, 44–49
    burial of Thomas Veal at Dungeon Rock, 9–12
    Captain Pedro and "Ocean Born Mary," 88–89
    mistress of Captain Kidd, 89
    New England reputation for, xx–xxi
    She-Pirate Rachel Wells, 85–88
    wreck of *Whydah*, 40–43
Plaisted, Frederick (governor), 206–7, 209
Plaster War of 1820, 231
Plymouth Plantation, 5
Portland, Maine, 246
The Poverty Year (1816), 120
Presque Isle, Maine, 145–47
Prohibition era
    Black Duck on Rum Row, 243–47
    chasing border bootleggers, 238–42
    rumrunning by fishermen, 248–52
    rumrunning by lobstermen, 226–31
    rumrunning by women, 232–37
    Skinner's Cave (Vermont), 110
    Smuggler's Notch (Vermont), 105
Providence, Rhode Island, 165, 263
Provincetown, Mass., 43
Purity Distilling (Boston), 222–25

Q

Quebec City, Benedict Arnold raid, 22
Quickstep (sailing ship), 133–36
Quillens, Louise, 117–20
Quillens, Norbert, 116–20
Quincy, John, 43

R

racism/racial discrimination, 206–10
Rangeley, Maine, 158
Ranger (pirate ship), 48
Redfield, Josiah, 116
Revere, Paul, 84
Revolutionary War. *See* American
    Revolution
Reynolds, Hannah Ann. *See* Story, Ann
Rhode Island
    Beavertail Lighthouse Museum, 263
    Block Island, 165, 193, 269
    Great Swamp Fight (1675), xvii
    Miery Swamp, 17
    Narragansett Bay, 152, 243–46
    slave population, 209
    Whale Rock Lighthouse, 259–61, 263
Richford, Vermont, 121
Ridgefield, Connecticut, 73–78
Rimmler, Pete, 183, 186
rivermen/river drives. *See* logging/
    lumberjacking
Robbins, Reny (lumberjack), 153–57
Rockland, Maine, 275
Roosevelt, Franklin D., 5, 268
Rose, Elmer, 137–38
Ross, John (log drive boss), 216
Rum Row, 227, 244, 248–49, 251–52
rumrunning. *See* Prohibition era
Russell, Alice, 175–76
Rutland County (Vermont), 101

S

S. B. Young (sailing ship), 247
Saco, Maine, 162
Saco River Valley (New Hampshire),
    126–27
Salem witch trials
    accusation and punishment, 23–28
    accusation of John Alden, 22
    killing suspects, 89
Salina, George (farmer), 201–4
Salisbury, New Hampshire, 58
Samson, Deborah (aka Robert Shurtleff),
    79–84
Sander, George (Confederate agent), 141

Sears, Montgomery, 152
Shaffer, Clarence Lee, Jr. (gangster),
    253–57
Sharon, Mass., 84
shipwrecks
    Boon Island legacy of, 34–39
    Great Blizzard of 1888, 159–61, 164
    New England reputation for, xx–xxi
    sinking of *USS Portland*, 189–93
    wreck of *Whydah*, 40–43
short-log pulp drives, 215–16
Silliman, Gold S. (Revolutionary
    general), 77
Sinnett, Austin, 177–81
Skinner, Uriah (smuggler), 107–10
Skinner's Cave (Vermont), 107–10
slavery/slave trade
    capturing Indians for, 5–6, 209
    fugitives escaping to Canada, 105
    Indians sold into, 17, 43
    New England as hub of, 209
Smith, John (Captain), xix
Smuggler's Notch (Vermont), 105
smuggling. *See* Canada; Prohibition era
Snow, Allie and Freddie, 204
South Kingstown, Rhode Island, 16
Spring pulp wood drive. *See* logging/
    lumberjacking
Spy for Germany (Gimpel), 268
Squanto (Tisquantum), 5–6
St. Albens Raid (1864), 137–41
St. Croix River, 231
St. Peters, Timmy (lobsterman), 270–75
St. Pierre, Albert "Al Capone of the North
    Country," 242
Steward, Dan (logging camp teamster),
    185–86
Stone, Hilda "Queen of the Border
    Rumrunners," 232–37
Stonington, Maine, 272
Story, Amos, 54
Story, Anne "Mother of the Green
    Mountain Boys," 54–59
Story, Solomon, 54–59
Sullivan, Dan (lighthouse keeper), 259–60
Swanback, John, 142–44

T

"Take Care of Yourself" (Heinrich), 20
Tamano (Narragansett warrior), 14
Tarrytown, New York, 83
Taylor, Zachary, 5
Teach, Edward (aka Blackbeard), 45
Tefft, Joshua, 17
Thanksgiving celebration, Pilgrim (1621), 5
Thatcher's Island (Mass.), 190
Tillinghast, Rafe, 149
Timms (British naval commander), 64
Tinker, Delmore "Frenchy" (lobsterman),
    226–30
Titus, Winston (bootlegger), 238–42
Train Number 50 to Hartford, wreck of,
    148–51
Travers, Charles (rumrunner), 243–47
Travis, William (Confederate raider), 141
Tripp, Bob and Laura, 207–8
Troy, Joseph, Jr., 132
Truman, Harry S., 268
Turtle (submarine), 268–69
Twist, Rosella, 144
Twitchell, Mary, 61
Twitchell, Rufus (colonist), 60–64
Tyron, William (British general), 76–77

U

U-1230 (German submarine), 265
U-156 (German submarine), 269
U-853 (German submarine), 269
United States Industrial Alcohol Company,
    224–25
University of Vermont Eugenics
    Survey, 210
USS Larchmont (steamship), 193
USS Portland Gale (steamship), 193
USS Portland (steamship), 189–93
Uxbridge, Mass., 79

V

vampires, lingering myths of, 166–70
Veal, Thomas (pirate), 9–12
Vermont
    Ann Story and the Green Mountain
        Boys, 57–59
    bear attacks and wild animals, 98–101
    eastern timber rattlesnakes, 101
    enduring life in wilderness, 90–94
    Esther Graves and the bear, 95–98
    flooding Barton River Valley, 111–15
    Green Mountains, xviii
    North Woods logging, 183–88
    Northeast Kingdom, 115
    Skinner's Cave, 107–10
    Smuggler's Notch, 105
    St. Albens Raid, 137–41
    use of eugenics toward Indians, 210
Vinalhaven, Maine, 226

W

Wagner, Daniel (lobsterman), 177–81
Wall, George (pirate), 85–87
Wall, Rachel (female pirate), 85–88
Wallace, James, 89
Wallace, Mary "Ocean Born Mary," 89
Walsh, Walter (FBI agent), 255–58
Wampanoag (First Nations people), xix, 5
Wamsutta (Wampanoag chief), 13
War of 1812, 231
Warner, John (Dr.), 99
Warner, Seth, 59
Warwick, Mass., 99
Washington, George, 66–72
Watch Hill, Rhode Island, 264
Waterbury, Vermont, 184, 188
Waud, Alfred Rudolph, 45
weather
    Crawford Notch landslide, 122–26
    Great Blizzard of 1888, 159–65
    Great Blizzard of 1978, 36, 39
    Great Colonial Hurricane of 1635, 264
    Great September Gale of 1815, 264
    Hurricane of the Century, 259–64
    Mount Washington, 221
    New England reputation for, xx–xxi
    nor'easter grounding *Whydah*, 40–43
    nor'easter sinking *USS Portland*, 189–93
    North Woods ice-out, 183–88
    North Woods winter, 153–58
    "The Year There Was No Summer,"
        116–21

West Halifax, Vermont, 236

Westerly, Rhode Island, 263

Wetamoo (Narragansett woman), 13–17

Weymouth, George (explorer), 209

Whale Rock Lighthouse (Rhode Island), 259–61, 263

Whetherby, Jedediah, 10–11

Whetherby, Jory, 7

whiskey. *See* Prohibition era

White, Peregrine, 4, 5

White, Resolved, 4

White, Susanna (pilgrim), 2, 4

White, William (pilgrim), 4

White Mountains (New Hampshire)

    Crawford Notch landslide (1826), 122–26

    frontier settlement, xviii

    Mount Washington Cog Railway, 217–21

White River Junction, Vermont, 148

Whitingham, Vermont, 94

Whydah (pirate ship), 40–43

Whydah Pirate Museum, 43

wild animals and bears

    Esther Graves and bear attack, 95–98

    legend of Jigger Johnson, 195–97

    panthers and catamounts, 99–101

    rattlesnakes, 101

    shark attacks, 128–32

Willey, Polly, 122–26

Willey, Samuel, Jr., 122–26

Williams, Paul (pirate captain), 40

Williams, William (lighthouse keeper), 39

Wilton, New Hampshire, 50–53

Winkler, Abe, 51–53

Winkler, Prudence, 51

Winkler, Samuel, 51

Winooski River (Vermont), 102–6

Winslow, Edward (pilgrim), 4

Winter, John, 99

Wiscasset, Maine, 61

witchcraft. *See* Salem witch trials

Wolcott, Vermont, 90–94

women, stories of

    Ann Story and the Green Mountain Boys, 54–59

    Army service of Deborah Samson, 79–84

    counterfeiter Mary Butterworth, 89

    enduring life in the wilderness, 94

    Esther Graves and the bear, 95–98

    mistress of Captain Kidd, 89

    "Ocean Born Mary," 88–89

    pirate Rachel Wells, 85–88

    "Queen of the Rumrunners," 232–37

Wooster, David (Revolutionary general), 76–77

World War I, 269

World War II, 265–69

Wright, Simeon, 53

Wytopitlock, Maine, 187

Y

"Yankee," origins of name, xix

"The Year There Was No Summer" (1816), 116–21

York, Maine, 18–22

Young, Bennett (Confederate raider), 139–41

Z

Zora, Manuel "Sea Fox" (rumrunner), 248–52

About the Author

Matthew P. Mayo is the author of fiction and nonfiction books, including the novels *Winters' War, Wrong Town,* and *Hot Lead, Cold Heart,* and the recent best-selling nonfiction work, *Cowboys, Mountain Men, and Grizzly Bears: Fifty of the Grittiest Moments in the History of the Wild West.* Raised in Rhode Island and on a farm in Vermont, Mayo is a member of Western Writers of America, Western Fictioneers, Maine Historical Society, and Historic New England. He and his wife, documentary photographer Jennifer Smith-Mayo, live on the coast of Maine and explore New England year-round. Visit him on the Web at matthewmayo.com.